THE
EDGE *of*
BELONGING

THE

EDGE *of*

BELONGING

AMANDA COX

Revell

a division of Baker Publishing Group
Grand Rapids, Michigan

Published by Revell
a division of Baker Publishing Group
PO Box 6287, Grand Rapids, MI 49516-6287
www.revellbooks.com

Printed in the United States of America

Library of Congress Cataloging-in-Publication Data
Names: Cox, Amanda, 1984– author.
Title: The edge of belonging / Amanda Cox.
Description: Grand Rapids, Michigan : Revell, a division of Baker Publishing Group, [2020]
Identifiers: LCCN 2020005248 | ISBN 9780800737405 (paperback) | ISBN 9780800739188 (hardcover)
Subjects: LCSH: Adoption—Fiction
Classification: LCC PS3603.O88948 E34 2020 | DDC 813/.6—dc23
LC record available at https://lccn.loc.gov/2020005248

Most Scripture used in this book, whether quoted or paraphrased by the characters, is taken from the *Holy Bible*, New Living Translation, copyright © 1996, 2004, 2007, 2013, 2015 by Tyndale House Foundation. Used by permission of Tyndale House Publishers, Inc., Carol Stream, Illinois 60188. All rights reserved.

Some Scripture used in this book, whether quoted or paraphrased by the characters, is taken from the New King James Version®. Copyright © 1982 by Thomas Nelson. Used by permission. All rights reserved.

20   21   22   23   24   25   26   7   6   5   4   3   2   1

For Mom and Dad.
Thanks for not getting too mad all the times I stayed up
reading way past my bedtime.

And for Lily.
When I started writing this story, I wrote simply
from a love for family and a heart for adoption.
I had no idea that before this book made it into print,
adoption would transform my own family
in such a twirly, sunshiny, smiley way.
Aunt Manda loves you.
Forever and always.

• CHAPTER •

ONE

People considered him homeless because he didn't have an address of his own, but Harvey James would've been homeless even if he owned the turreted mansion off State Route 460. To have a home, you'd have to feel as though you belonged. The edge of the highway was the closest he'd ever been.

Unending blasts of headlights and rushes of wind from passing cars on the bypass glanced off the brush he scoured for bits of other people's lives. Things not missed. Some flung out of car windows in anger. Others, accidental losses from poorly secured luggage racks. He brushed his humidity-damp mop back from his eyes, detaching the sprigs plastered to his forehead.

Straining to decipher shapes out of step with the wild tangle of weeds, Harvey walked the line—the boundary between what the state groomed to maintain the road's scenic status and the places left untouched and feral. He raised the flashlight he'd found last week. The beam cut through the descending darkness.

A suitcase lay on its side, scarred by road rash. He knelt and fumbled with the zipper. He groaned. More Hawaiian-print shirts and swim trunks. It'd be nice if someone lost normal clothes for a change.

He grabbed the stack of shirts and three miniature bottles of hotel shampoo and crammed them into his bag.

A break in the swift-moving traffic swathed the shoulder in an eerie silence. An odd sound reached his ears—soft but jarring in its inconsistency with the road noise. Mewling. An abandoned kitten?

Harvey's heart dropped three inches in his chest. In all his scavenging, nothing horrified him more than living things discarded.

He'd tried to keep an abandoned dog once. Poor old fella. Deaf and half blind he'd suspected. The dog didn't last long. Highways were places for rush and madness. Not living things.

With a lingering sigh, he turned back toward his camp. It was an ugly truth, but the creature would be better off if he let nature take its course instead of nursing an animal along, only delaying the inevitable.

Three cars raced past, each vying to overtake the other. They torpedoed the silence with the harsh roar of their re-moved mufflers, sending a jolt down his spine.

As the sound trailed away, Harvey's ears retained a ring. He massaged the hinge of his jaw to rub out the sound. The tiny cry sounded in the stillness. This time stronger, angry. Harvey froze.

Human.

Making a slow turn, Harvey raised his flashlight to scour the brush in search of the source.

Traffic resumed, and the rushes of wind threw sound. He opened his mouth to call out, to let the little thing know he was coming, but the ridiculousness of the impulse resealed his lips.

The flashlight in his trembling hand sent a jittering stream of light along the scrub. He walked on, straining his ears.

Finally, another break in traffic. In the silent interlude, the cry sounded, coming from deeper in the brush than he'd originally thought.

There. A trail tramped down where someone had gone before him. He slapped away the limbs hanging across his path, sweeping the flashlight from side to side. The pounding of his heart mirrored the urgency of the feeble wail.

Harvey stopped midstep. Five feet ahead, a bunch of fabric squirmed on the ground. He sucked in his breath and crept forward.

He knelt, and the undergrowth pricked his knees. A funny smell hung in the air, both sweet and sharp. Harvey laid the flashlight on the ground, aiming the light, then reached for a corner of the fabric to uncover this foreign being whose squall had receded to feeble grunts and whimpers.

He recoiled. The tiny thing with squinched-tight eyes was covered in drying blood and a white cheesy substance. Taking the corner of the fabric, he wiped the baby's face, crouching close as he inspected for injury. The baby stilled at his touch and gave a languid blink. Their gazes locked for a fleeting moment.

Everything faded. No sound of road noise. No buzz of mosquitos by his ear. A tiny fist raised. He brushed the baby's palm, and it wound its pink fingers around Harvey's thumb.

Warmth exploded in his chest, then traveled all the way through him. He swept the bundle into his arms and with a spare shirt rubbed until the child's perfect pink skin was cleared of blood. An injury-free baby girl. Naked. Wrapped in a man's flannel shirt.

Harvey stood and turned a slow circle, babe pressed close. Where had she come from? Who left her behind?

He undid the top two buttons of his large shirt and tucked the baby inside to share his heat. Would the wild pounding of his heart hurt her ears?

She had a full head of dark, downy hair. Now dried, it stood up in fuzzy curls that tickled his chest. He stroked her cheek, and she jerked her head toward his touch, searching. Faint grunts. She bobbed her open mouth against his skin. "Sorry, little one. I don't have anything for you. Let's get back to camp, and we'll figure something out." He had boxes of things stored for the day he found a use for them, but none contained bottles and infant formula.

Baby girl, finally convinced food wasn't available, ceased her fretting, nuzzled, and fell asleep, lulled by the sway of his long stride. Harvey pressed his lips in a line.

Should he pack her in a basket and deposit her on the doorstep of a nice suburban home? A hospital? A shudder ran through him, and she squirmed against the movement. No. He wouldn't leave her. He'd spent his own childhood tossed about at the whims of others, and he didn't want that life for this little one, who was no more than a few hours old and had already been abandoned.

Back at camp, a clearing in the middle of a circle of towering pines, he entered the lean-to he'd built over the past few years from lost lumber, cinder blocks, and a tarp and settled the baby on the pallet so he could dig through his supplies.

His supply bins were overflowing with boxes and boxes of noodles in Styrofoam cups. After cleaning up an over-turned eighteen-wheeler last spring, a road crew had left hundreds of cups of noodles behind as trash. He'd be eating lost noodles for years.

Harvey might be labeled homeless, but he didn't beg. In thirty years of walking this earth, he'd never asked anything from anyone. Didn't need to. People abandoned and lost enough for him to live on, but since newborns couldn't eat noodles or the fish he caught from the creek, it was time to deviate from his well-oiled life plan.

He couldn't wait for a diaper bag to fall off a luggage rack.

TWO

PRESENT DAY

The atmosphere in her office shifted—that almost imperceptible awareness of another's presence. Ivy closed a file and lifted her head. A pair of chocolate-brown eyes set in smooth tan skin peered around the corner of the doorway. Emmet Rawlings, the darling of the fourth grade.

Those expressive eyes normally danced and laughed and spoke a thousand stories. But today there was only one message in those deep, soulful pools. Something broken and jagged. An expression that should never be on a nine-year-old's face.

As much fun as it was to put on antibullying and character-building assemblies with her troupe of bright, silly puppets, these one-on-one moments with students were why she'd chosen to become a school counselor in the first place. But the pain in Emmet's eyes made the ink on her diploma seem too fresh. As though it would smudge if touched.

"Hi, Emmet."

The child lingered in the doorway, a scroll of paper gripped in his trembling hand and a hall pass in the other.

"Mrs. Lee sent you?"

A single nod.

"Come on in."

He slouched into the small office and curled into the chair across from her desk, wrapping his arms around his knees. Tiny in that adult-sized chair.

"What's going on, kiddo? You don't seem yourself today."

Emmet buried his head in his knees. His hand tightened on the paper.

Fair enough. Not the smartest way to open the conversation. She bit her lip. Maybe it would be better to call in Marilyn. The seasoned counselor would surely handle this with more finesse than Ivy had thus far.

She studied the scroll wadded in his hand. "Do you have a note from Mrs. Lee?"

He shook his head, slid the hall pass onto her desk, and buried his head back in his knees.

"Do you want to talk?"

Another head shake.

Ivy stifled a sigh. Counseling 101. First, never open a session with closed-ended questions, not if you want to get someone talking. Second, nine-year-old boys almost never volunteer to talk about what's bothering them.

Ivy massaged her forehead. She was putting too much pressure on herself. She wasn't the school nurse who handed out cartoon character Band-Aids for scraped knees. There might be nothing Ivy could do to ease Emmet's pain. But she could be present with him and offer an understanding heart. Love.

"You know, I'm having kind of a long day myself. What do you say we take a break for just a few minutes? I've got a whole wall of cool stuff over there." She pointed to the other side of her office. "Puzzles, games, a few toys, books. And those bean bags are *way* better than the stiff old chair you're sitting in."

Emmet eyed the tall corner bookshelf of promised fun.

"Pick out a game or something for us to do. I don't know about you, but I could use some laughs."

He stood, still stoic, scanned the shelves, and chose a tiny plastic toilet. One hand still clutched his paper. He turned, a spark of mischief and a question in his eyes.

Ivy mock groaned. "That one? No, come on, Emmet. Any game but that one." It was a pretty gross game—a toy toilet that sprayed water on you if you rolled the wrong number on the plastic toilet paper roll. When she purchased it, her fiancé, Seth, had treated her to a verbal dissertation on the dumbing down of American children. But she hadn't bought the silly game to spur the kids on in their academic pursuits.

Emmet cracked a smile.

"All right, you're on. Pull up a bean bag." Ivy filled the plastic toilet with water from the sink behind her desk. "You go first, kiddo."

He spun the plastic toilet paper roll. "A one," he whispered. His lip disappeared between his teeth and he pressed the lever. The toy emitted a flushing sound. He flashed her a tentative grin. "Your turn."

Ivy spun the roll. She groaned. "A four? I'm doomed."

Emmet snickered.

Wincing, Ivy flushed once, twice, three times. Emmet

leaned away from her, giggling. She winced. This was it. But on the fourth flush, she was still in the clear.

"Your go, Emmet. You're gonna get soaked."

He spun the roll. "A one!" He punched his hand in the air.

"It's going to get you," she wheedled.

He pressed the flusher. Still no spray. He full-on cackled. "Ms. Ivy, better keep your mouth shut."

Ivy moaned and groaned, hamming up dismay for all her pathetic acting skills were worth. She rolled a three. Flush one, flush two. Spray. Right up her nose. She choked, nose burning.

Emmet rolled on the floor laughing. Between gasping breaths, he said, "Okay, new game now."

"Uh-uh. No way. It's payback time."

They played three more rounds, both of them getting sprayed. Emmet's mischievous cackles sent a jolt of joy through her, but his crumpled scroll never left his clutch.

Ivy returned the game to the shelf and occupied the bean bag across from Emmet, where he poked through her basket of puppets. "Hey, what's that in your hand?"

His gaze dropped to the multicolored rug.

"Mind if I take a look?"

He shrugged but held out the crumpled page.

Ivy unfurled the paper and smoothed it across her knee. An ache twisted in her chest as she studied the assignment, at the care he'd put into his family tree.

Detailed shading added depth and texture to the trunk and branches. His name painstakingly written on the appropriate line. The spaces where his parents' names belonged had been written and erased so many times, he'd worn clear through the page.

She ran her fingers over the blank spaces, barely breathing. "Can I tell you a secret, Emmet? Something I've never told anyone."

He raised his head.

"It is my professional opinion that family tree assignments are the single worst idea on the face of the planet."

A ghost of a smile twitched at the corners of his mouth.

"Can I tell you something else?"

He nodded and swiped at his cheeks with a loud sniffle.

"I'm adopted."

He straightened, his dark eyes searching hers.

"It's hard to know the right way to fill the spaces, isn't it? I don't know who my birth parents are. I wish I did. What about you? What's your beef with family trees?"

Emmet took a heavy breath. "Don't know my bio dad. I get a few letters from my bio mom. I have good parents, the ones who foster me. They love me. I love them. Been with 'em a long, long time. No matter how I tried to make this stupid tree, it felt like I was doin' it wrong."

Didn't she know that feeling. Ivy hadn't realized as a third grader that everyone in her small town knew she was adopted. Brassy Britney Hall called her out in front of the whole class during Ivy's family tree presentation. Said Ivy cheated. That her adoptive parents weren't her *real* family. That none of the people she'd written down were even related. Funny how a simple memory could leave her heart so raw and exposed even after all this time.

Ivy cleared the tightness in her throat. "Family trees can be tricky things, and that's okay. Yours is pretty special and deserves a little more time and care. How about I send a note to your teacher to let you take this home. Then you and your foster parents can make your tree together. I have a feeling that with all of you working together, you can come up with a tree that you're satisfied with."

She checked the schedule. "You have ten more minutes until recess. I'll write that note to your teacher, and you can read or build with LEGOs while I work. If you're up for it, you can rejoin your class on the playground." That transition would come a little easier than having to walk back into a quiet classroom in the face of curious stares.

Emmet offered a small smile and nodded.

A few minutes later, Ivy stood in the doorway watching Emmet rejoin his class on their way outside. The familiar jaunt back in his step. A warm bubble blossomed in her middle, replacing the ache. *This. This is why I do this job.*

Cheryl, the secretary, poked her head out of the main office. "Hey, girl. What kind of magic did you work on Emmet? He went in a storm cloud and came out like he was walking on sunshine."

Ivy shrugged. "Sometimes a person just needs to know that they're not alone in this world. That someone else understands things that hurt."

"You're good with these kids. I hope you know that. They eat up those zany puppet shows. And I've seen others come out of that office like Emmet did. With a little hope and light in their face that wasn't there before."

Ivy ducked her head. "Oh, stop it. Why are you buttering me up? Need someone to fill in for car duty?"

Cheryl propped her hands on her hips, one corner of her mouth twitching. "Excuse me? When have I ever been guilty of such a thing?"

Ivy laughed. What Cheryl didn't butter up, she sugar-coated.

"All I want to know is if you're coming over for girls' night."

Ivy twisted her engagement ring around her finger. "I don't—"

"Girl, don't you dare put me off with some vague answer again. You said last week you would think about it."

"It's not that I don't want to be there. It's just Seth told me yesterday about this charity event. Key players in his firm are attending and—"

Cheryl pursed her lips. "Uh-huh. We've hardly seen hide nor hair of you since Mr. Fancy Pants put that ring on your finger."

Ivy sighed, a feeble attempt at shoving away the weight settling on her chest. "I know, I know. Seth's under tons of pressure from his dad to show he's worthy to take over the firm. His dad's giving him all these hoops to jump through." She shrugged. "Seth needs me there."

Cheryl raised a well-sculpted eyebrow. "Next time, then? I know you'd have more fun with us than at some stuffy shindig."

"I'll be there," she said, knowing the promise was empty. Between the pressure from Seth and her friends, it was no contest. Her friends might be annoyed, but they wouldn't hold it against her.

● ● ●

After the dismissal bell rang, Ivy tucked away her files and trekked across the sunbaked parking lot. She checked her phone as she sank into the leather seat of her car. The new-car smell, intensified by the trapped sunshine, wrinkled her nose.

Six missed calls from Mom. Ivy leaned her head against the headrest and closed her eyes. Last time Mom had blown up her phone like this, she'd wanted help transferring her contacts from her flip phone to her new smartphone. Who knew what it would be this time.

Her thumb hovered over the call back button, but then Ivy placed the phone on the center console. Whatever it was, it could wait. She needed those few minutes on the drive to unwind. To somehow transition from the counselor who sat on the floor playing a toilet game with a child to the role of imposter socialite who failed at small talk and sometimes forgot which fork she was supposed to use.

As she drove, she eyed the highway signs. What would happen if she took an exit ramp and drove until her car ran out of gas? Straight out of all the expectations pressing in. From her mom and dad who constantly tried to draw her back into their fold. From her fiancé who was intent on helping her discover *his* definition of the best version of herself—insisting she could overcome her small-town roots. Whatever that meant.

Instead, Ivy pulled into her designated parking spot at the gated community. Seth had secured the apartment for her after their engagement. It was a gorgeous place.

Still, she missed her quirky starving artist friends with tie-dyed curtains and her elderly neighbors who sat around gabbing in lawn chairs on the weed-infested green space.

Despite her protests that she was comfortable in her old apartment, Seth had insisted it wouldn't look right for his future wife to be living on *that* side of town. There was never a soul out and about in her new picture-perfect neighbor-hood where even the blades of grass stood at attention.

Ivy exited her car and mentally prepared to trade her midi skirt, blouse, and flats for the black, sequined sheath dress and heels Seth's mother had sent over the day before. She'd slip out of one life and into another, like changing skins.

THREE

SEPTEMBER 8, 1994

After a twenty-minute hike from his camp, with the tiny babe tucked close, Harvey reached the corner of Nolensville and 41. He knelt behind a stand of bushes, hidden from the cars lined up at the stop sign to make their turn. Harvey settled the swaddled baby beneath the greenery.

He glanced over his shoulder at the yellow backlit shine of the bargain store. One hour until closing. Swallowing the bitter lump of pride rising in his throat, he scrawled his message on a scrap of cardboard under the light of a streetlamp. Harvey inhaled and steadied. He could do this. For her sake.

Forcing himself to make eye contact with the drivers, he held the sign in front of his chest. They averted their gaze. Blinker lights flashed in tempo with his pounding heart. Car after car filed past.

One lady gave him the number for a drug addiction hotline.

A man offered to bring him a meal from a fast-food joint.

"No, thank you, sir. But if you could spare some change—"

The man's eyes narrowed, his face hardening—then came the whir of the automatic window rolling tight.

Harvey's knees shook, bearing the weight of every judgmental glare, longing for the ground to open, or for the chance to explain. Infant formula and diapers. An abandoned baby. Beautiful. Delicate. Hungry. Deserving. His heart burned in his chest.

But if he voiced those things, the powers that be would swoop in, and the system would swallow this baby whole.

A woman with a car phone to her ear pulled forward and rolled down the window. She pressed a dollar into his hand, eyes trained forward. Into the phone, she said, "I helped a homeless man. It makes my heart feel so good."

Harvey, he wanted to say. His name was Harvey, and someone was depending on him for the first time in his life.

He trained his eyes on the baby. The bundle in the bushes, still and silent. How soon did a baby need to eat after it was born? Sweat beaded and rolled down his face.

This would never work. Standing on this street corner, he was nothing but a beggar scamming for drug money. He clenched his hands until the cardboard collapsed in half.

Turning to face the bargain store, he placed a hand over the solitary dollar in his pocket. One by one the fluorescent lights flicked off until the store was dark. Darker still was the feeling growing in Harvey's middle.

Tossing the cardboard scrap aside, he knelt and scooped the child into his arms, so fragile in his giant hands. He tucked her back inside his shirt, her downy skin against his. Warm. The delicate rise and fall of her back, a mystery. This new person, all potential. Blissfully unaware of her circumstances. Her eyelids twitched and her mouth stretched as though her dreams were sweet.

Harvey closed his eyes. "I'm so sorry. So, so sorry. I thought I could find a way . . ." His chin quivered, cutting away the words. He squeezed his eyes tight against the pain and gasped a breath that faltered in his chest.

How had this tiny person slipped through his ironclad defense so quickly?

Now alone at the empty intersection, he clung to the child under the glow of the streetlamp.

Harvey chose a road with a few houses ahead. Maybe there was one with toys in the yard. They would know what she needed.

He passed house after house, most of them dark. His feet wouldn't stop.

A name. If he left her with a name, she would always have something from him. Harvey searched for inspiration in the darkness. A massive oak stood on the corner of the road he walked. English ivy wrapped around the tree, the foliage so dense the bark was hidden.

"Ivy. Ivy Rose. How do you like the sound of that?"

The baby grunted and squeaked in her sleep like a newborn pup.

"If you must know, I'm naming you Ivy for the way you've wrapped yourself around me quicker than I could blink, squeezing this heart of mine to life. And Rose is for . . . for someone I wanted to help, but I failed her. I won't fail you. I'll be stronger for you."

He brushed his lips across the fuzzy head resting under his chin, inhaling her scent, locking it in his memory. "You are loved, Ivy Rose. You are wanted."

Harvey turned onto the next street. Fog descended as the cool night air married with the humidity of the day. He peered through the wisp, hunting the moon.

God, if you're up there . . . I don't know you. But somehow, I know you know this child. Help me find the person who is supposed to take care of her . . . Amen?

Did God receive simple prayers like that?

A steepled building crept into view as he rounded the bend, a white apparition in the fog. One light glowed in the front, and there was another at the rear.

He walked around to the back. The light illuminated a hanging sign that read THE PANTRY. Cradling Ivy with one arm, he used his other hand to cut the glare on the glass, detecting the outline of baby clothes, diapers, bottles, and formula within.

Harvey's heart pounded in his chest as he reached for the handle, his breath lodged in his throat. He released the doorknob like it branded him. This wasn't who he was. But Ivy needed him.

Taking three steps back, he spotted a hedge of chokeberry bushes. He slipped the baby from beneath his shirt and again stowed her under sheltering limbs.

Harvey swallowed to still the slithering sensation in his stomach. He'd never taken anything before. He would grab only what was absolutely necessary and then find another way to provide for her. After talking to God for the first time in his life, this church appeared. So that meant something—right?

He turned the knob and slipped through the door, cringing when the creak of the rusty hinges shattered the still night. Harvey froze and held his breath, listening for any signs of movement within. He left the door open behind him, letting moonlight spill in. Scavenger bag at the ready, he inhaled an odd scent—dank basement melded with baby powder.

He grabbed diapers and wipes. Then he went to the formula, scanning each label in case there was a special kind for new babies. A bottle. A book on baby care. He stood by the door in the silver light of the moon, thumbing pages. His heart hammered loud enough to alert the police in the next county.

Clothes, of course. He chose a purple footed pajama from the rack and held the outfit up, gauging it for Ivy's size. Tiny as it was, the pajama still seemed too big.

As he stuffed it in the bag, fluorescent light flooded the room from overhead. Harvey's heart jumped to his throat and stopped beating.

"Hey! Sss-stop . . . thief?"

Harvey held up his arms in front of his face, squinting for the source of the uneven voice that accused from the shadowed stairs. He backed toward the door.

"Hey. I mean it. Stop."

Harvey's feet rooted to the spot.

• CHAPTER •

FOUR

PRESENT DAY

Ivy stared out the window at the headlights on the other side of the highway. Seth's voice droned on beside her, the background noise to her thoughts. He'd been on a call since he picked her up. Something big must be going down. Usually there were flowers and compliments on her dress. Tonight he hadn't bothered to get out of the car, hardly glancing in her direction.

She shifted toward him in the seat when he finished the call. "Everything okay?"

"Of course. Why?"

"You seem distracted."

"Just work stuff. Nothing you need to concern yourself with."

She placed a hand on his knee. "If it's a part of your life, it's a part of mine."

His gaze flicked downward. "What are you wearing? That's not the dress Mother sent over."

She tugged her dress-length sweater back over the exposed yellow fabric of her dress. She'd thought he would like it. It was bright and fun, the cut of the fabric elegant. At least she thought so.

"I'll get the shop on the phone right now. Mistakes like that are completely unacceptable." He straightened his white tuxedo tie and grabbed his phone from his lap.

"They didn't send the wrong dress, I—"

He huffed and smacked the phone back down on the console. "Closed. Of course they are. That is the last time I purchase from—"

"Seth."

"I am so embarrassed this happened. That dress is . . ." He sucked air through his teeth and shook his head.

"They didn't make a mistake." Heat pricked behind her eyes. "I was just in the mood to wear something with a little color. Something fun."

He locked his focus on the road. "Darling, we talked about this."

Like Alice in Wonderland drinking a potion, she shrank as she swallowed his tone. Soft and firm, as though he spoke to a wayward child.

"You'll stick out like a sore thumb. This is a black-and-white function. You'll be the only one in color."

Ivy blinked rapidly and clenched her hand. Her nails bit into her palm. The taillights ahead became blurred red orbs. "I . . . I didn't realize . . ."

"The invitation I sent over said as much. I'm trying to help you find your place, but you refuse to follow simple instructions. I don't understand you."

Ivy winced at the tightening in her chest. "I'm sorry."

Her phone rang inside her purse. Desperate for any escape from this discussion on her endless string of faux pas, she answered without looking at the ID.

"Where are you? I thought you'd be here by now." Concern tinged the rich timbre of her childhood friend's voice. A voice she hadn't heard in months.

She flipped through her mental calendar. Had she forgotten a birthday? Some celebration? "Reese? What are you talking about?"

The line went quiet for a moment. "Ivy, sweetheart, have you spoken to your mom or dad?" His solemn tone sent her stomach churning.

"I missed some calls from Mom, but I've been so rushed I haven't called her back yet." Her voice cracked. "What . . . what's going on?"

Ivy glanced up. The car felt like it had lifted off the asphalt as they darted in and out of traffic. Seth's jaw was set. The speedometer's needle crept higher. Her heart rate climbed. "Seth, please. Slow down."

"Ivy, are you still there? You're with someone?" Reese's voice jerked her attention back to the call.

"Yes, I—"

"Good, good. Listen, you need to come home. Your grandma's not doing well. The doctors are trying to make her comfortable, but that's all they can do at this point. She's lucid, telling everybody who will listen that ninety-four is a good long run, and she's ready to see Jesus. But she's asking for you."

An ache swelled in her middle and tightened her throat. "How long does she have?"

Reese sighed. "They're not sure. But I would hurry. She's a fighter, but she's tired."

"Of course. I just need to run home and change and I'm there."

"I was worried when I got to the hospital and you weren't there. It wasn't like you. Be safe, okay?"

The tenderness of his tone was almost her undoing. She choked out a reply and hung up the phone.

Seth glared out the windshield. "I can't believe you took a call from him while you're with me. I don't care how many times you say the two of you are just friends, I don't like it."

Ivy blinked back tears. "Can you please take me home?"

Seth shook his head. "We don't have time for you to change. You're going to have to go in what you're wearing."

Ivy pressed her fingertips to the corners of her eyes. "Not to change. I need to get to Triune. My grandmother's dying."

His head tipped sideways. "Oh, that's unfortunate." Still darting the car in and out of traffic, he picked up his phone and began scrolling through his emails.

Ivy sniffled and clenched her jaw, willing the tears filling her eyes to recede. Mile markers passed and she strained her eyes for the next exit sign, their opportunity to turn around. But Seth didn't change lanes as the exit loomed. "Aren't you going to take the exit?"

"We are only five minutes away from the gala. Let's just go for a little while, show our faces, and then we can leave."

Is he serious? "I . . . I'm not exactly up for hobnobbing with strangers. I'd really rather not."

"Honey, I know you're hurting, but being seen at this event is a really big deal."

"My family needs me." Could he not understand that?

"They're grown adults. They can manage without you for a little longer."

"I need to tell her goodbye."

Seth patted Ivy's leg. "And you will. After we stop at the gala. Your family has had you drive back three different times to say goodbye to her over the last year. I'm sure this is just another one of those times. And if the worst happens and she passes before you get there, you know that woman has to know how much she means to you."

Ivy sucked in a breath. "Seth, that's my family you're talking about. The people who raised me." She twisted the ring on her finger, around and around, trying to soothe the unusual tightness. Her hands must have swelled. "You don't understand. My uncle, he—"

"You're right. I don't understand. I know you all are close, but it's strange how your family acts like you have to be at the center of everything. You've got to cut those apron strings sometime. Those ties will strangle us if you don't."

Ivy bit her lip and swallowed, the lump in her throat thick and heavy. "Mom has already been on edge lately, going on about how you're trying to isolate me from them. She . . . she thinks the engagement was a mistake. If they find out I went to a party when I knew Grandma was dying . . ."

Seth's hands tightened on the steering wheel. Again, the needle on the speedometer crept upward. Ivy braced herself with the grab handle.

"These are the people you're desperate to go see?" He

zipped in and out of traffic, cutting across three lanes to take the exit.

She clamped her eyes shut, pressing down nausea. "Seth, please."

"You'd think instead of hating me, they'd show a little appreciation. I saved you from the dead-end waitressing job you'd gotten yourself stuck in. Opened the door to a prestigious private school even though you had zero experience. Not just anybody could have pulled that off. Don't they get that I'll take care of you?"

Ivy's jaw went slack. Sure, he'd boasted on several occasions that he'd helped make her job happen, but never had he been so outright demeaning. Had he? "Come with me, Seth. Let them get to know you better." *Prove them wrong.*

He shook his head. "Can't. I'm working on a major case." Seth pulled into the lot of the enormous country club and up to the valet.

It seemed so easy for him to spew words like "cut ties." How would he feel if she said those same words to him, about his family? At least her mother wasn't trying to dress him and give him uninvited etiquette lessons.

Of course, Seth Aaron Walker III, Mr. Blood Is Thicker Than Water, didn't understand her family. A family in which not a single pair of them was biologically connected. But she'd expected a little more understanding. Compassion. These were the people who'd raised her. Shaped her. Did he like that girl at all, or just the one he thought he could make her into?

Seth stood from the car as the attendant opened her door. She trailed after him, three steps behind no matter how fast she tried to walk in the high-heeled shoes that pinched her toes.

The doorman opened the tall door leading into the vast open room. Bright and shining, overflowing with elaborate decor and tuxedoed waiters balancing shimmering trays of champagne. Seth marched through the door without looking back. He found a group of his associates and melded into the room.

"Miss, may I take your sweater?"

Ivy jolted at the address and wrapped her outerwear tighter around her as though it could shield her from more than the evening chill. "No, thank you."

She walked the perimeter of the room, surveying this world that did not belong to her. Wearing beige would've been better than sunflower yellow. At least then she could have blended in with the walls.

Ivy closed her eyes for a moment, shutting out her surroundings. She was eight years old again, sitting side by side with her grandmother on her porch swing. Belly full of homemade chocolate chip cookies and milk.

Grandma had brushed crumbs from Ivy's cheek with her wrinkled thumb, smiling down at her. *Ivy, do you have any idea how much joy you bring to the world just by being you?*

Ivy blinked away the memory and cleared the tightness in her throat.

Minutes turned into an hour and still Seth mingled. She shot him pointed looks and he averted his eyes, refusing to acknowledge her presence in the room.

This wasn't where she belonged. Especially not when a sleepy town in Tennessee called her name—where her family huddled around the hospital bed of a woman who'd spent her lifetime pouring out all the love she had to give.

She glanced at Seth, whose back was to her. He was deep in conversation, so Ivy found a quiet corner, pulled out her phone, and scheduled an Uber. Her pulse thrummed wildly as she exited the ballroom. When had her relationship started feeling like a hostage situation?

FIVE

SEPTEMBER 8, 1994

Harvey blinked at the floor, the sudden light searing his eyes. Sweat dripped down his spine. He tuned his ears for the baby nestled in the bushes as he edged closer to the door. The symphony of cicadas and bullfrogs, muted before, now seemed a raucous commotion. "Sir, I'm sorry. The door was unlocked. I—"

"Think you're entitled to anything behind unlocked doors?"

"No." Harvey lowered his hands by inches and stole a glance to the darkened stairway.

The man appeared from the shadows as his polished black dress shoes left the bottom step. Dressed in a trim-cut suit with his tie loosened, top button undone, and red-rimmed eyes, he looked more like a melancholic city lawyer. Not the blustery country pastor fed on biscuits and fried chicken Harvey had envisioned haunting the place.

His gaze roved over Harvey, wide-eyed at first, but then

relaxing. "This is a pantry for single mothers. Hardworking members of this church made these donations. Explain yourself."

"I—" The words lodged in his throat. He dredged up the image of what this man saw in him. Hair overlong, face stubbled. Ill-fitting clothes. Sandals with his toes hanging over the edge. Bulging bag across his shoulder full of stolen charity. He inhaled and released the air, and with it came a lie so smooth he stunned himself. "I didn't know what else to do. My sister just had a baby. Her boyfriend left her, and I . . . I . . . The baby needs food. And then when the door was unlocked . . ." He lifted the bag from his shoulder, holding it out as an offering. "Please. I'll leave this here. You'll never see me again. Just don't . . . She needs me . . ."

But the man had already grabbed a phone from the dock on the wall. He ran his hand through his dark hair, taking it from tidy to disheveled in seconds. Harvey's eyes darted to the open door behind him. How far could he get with Ivy before the police caught up? A lightning bolt raced from his brain to his feet. His breath caught.

"Hey, Miri. I'm sorry. I know I told you I'd be home earlier and it's—" He flicked a glance at the gold watch on his wrist.

The pastor's weary tone rooted Harvey in place.

"Oh, wow, later than I thought. Well, I know I said—"

The man's head dropped forward, and he massaged the bridge of his nose.

"Okay, I'll make it up to you, I promise. You know how it is, trying to adjust—"

Silence stretched to the corners of the room. Harvey's pulse throbbed in his ears.

"Yes, dear. Anyway, I called to tell you I've had a delay.

There's been a . . . uh . . . a man came to get help. I'll try to hurry your way. I love—"

The man held the phone in front of his face, wincing when the disconnecting beep cut off his sentiment.

Harvey took two steps back.

"Wait."

Ragged breaths heaved Harvey's shoulders.

"Don't go. I really do want to help."

Harvey stared at the ground. "She needs me. She doesn't have anyone else."

The man tapped his index finger against his lips. "You wouldn't happen to know anything about landscaping or maintenance work, would you? I happen to have a position open here at the church." A crooked smile softened the man's face.

"A job?" Harvey started shaking. From relief? Or was it because every chirp and squeak in the night might be Ivy about to wail? Or an opossum in the woods? His pulse upticked again. Surely an opossum wouldn't bother a baby though.

"The pay isn't great, but it'll give you something steady. The church has an assistance program for single mothers too, if your sister is interested."

"Oh." Harvey shook his head. There should be blue lights flashing outside the door by now. Instead, this man was offering him a job. The thief asked to be the groundskeeper. At a church.

The pastor's shoulders slumped a fraction. "So it's a no, then?"

"No, sir. I'll take it. I just didn't expect . . ."

"I'm Pastor Thomas Lashley, by the way." He stepped forward, hand out.

Harvey stared at the outstretched hand a beat, then remembered what was expected. He clasped the man's perfectly manicured hand but kept his eyes lowered while the pastor pumped his arm. "Harvey, sir. Harvey James."

The pastor stilled the handshake. "Say, you look familiar. Have we—"

Harvey slipped his grease-stained palm away, slick with sweat, and shoved it into his pocket. "Uh, no, sir. I don't think so." He backed toward the door, eyes trained on the concrete floor. As he stepped across the threshold, pushing the creaking door wide, Ivy cried out.

"Harvey?"

Dread twisted in his gut. He'd been so close.

"Can you be here at nine?"

Harvey released a shuddered breath. "I'll be here."

"Oil that old door first thing, if you don't mind. It's been driving me crazy."

"Yes, sir."

Harvey closed the door behind him. Through the glass, he watched the pastor trudge back up the stairs like he had lead in his shoes. Harvey let out another long, rattled sigh and then raced to the chokeberry bushes.

● ● ●

Miriam Lashley sat cross-legged in the middle of the second-floor room. Empty. And so was the room. She swallowed, ashamed of the way she'd spoken to Thomas.

But when he called, he'd caught her sitting in the middle of this room again—the room he'd begged her to fill with an office, a hobby, a library, anything but the useless space it was. Guilt and shame, pain and sorrow—emotions that lingered and wouldn't leave her—twisted her inside until her words came out harsh and cold, exposing the emptiness she couldn't seem to shake. But no words could explain that though the space appeared vacant, it was already full. Full of disappointment for what should have been.

Miriam stood and smoothed the red curls that had gone frizzy in the Tennessee humidity away from her face. Even her hair missed life in California. Walking to the open door, she turned and her gaze lingered on the braided rug in the center of the hardwood floor. Thom had called half an hour ago. He'd be home any minute. She turned away and closed the door behind her.

Each hundred-year-old step creaked underfoot as she made her way downstairs to the kitchen. She popped his plate in the microwave and stared at her modern decor out of sync with the beadboard backsplash.

Miriam released a weary sigh. Why did she worry so much about cooking his meal to perfection, knowing he'd linger at the church late into the night while his food congealed on the plate? She wiped a smudge from her mother's recipe box—filled with step-by-step instructions and dependable outcomes.

"Miri." Thomas's smooth voice broke through the silence.

She spun around, heart skittering in her chest.

A sad smile stretched one side of his face. "I didn't mean to startle you."

She flicked a glance over him. "You look like you've been mugged."

His eyes widened. He smoothed the hair standing wild on his head, then removed the loosened tie and draped it over the dining room chair.

It was no wonder the church grew at such a rapid rate back in California. When he was put together, he fit the part. Voice, warm and soothing. Handsome. Young but not too young—appealing to the upper-middle-class businessmen and their pretty wives who were building companies and growing families. He spoke with a conviction that even made Miriam believe they'd be all right the first time he'd said it. But they weren't. She tore her gaze away and went for the dinner waiting in the microwave.

He sat with his elbows propped on the table, face resting in his hands. "Whew. It's been a day, Miri."

Full of sitting in rocking chairs with the elderly? She bit her lip and slid the steaming plate in front of him. Truthfully, she hadn't a clue of what pastoring the small-town church entailed. Hadn't been in the frame of mind to care anything about this new life her husband had chosen for them.

She lifted her gaze from the congregant-donated farm table—the only item in the old house that looked like it belonged. When they'd opened their moving van on arrival, it was immediately apparent the massive glass-top table hadn't survived their tire blowing out two miles from their exit. She still couldn't shake the image of the man who came out of nowhere to help Thomas in the pouring rain.

Thomas stared at her, a questioning look in his eyes. What was the last thing he'd said? Something about his day . . . "What happened?"

"I finally hired a groundskeeper."

Her eyes widened. "The board approved?"

A snort slipped out as Thomas reined in a laugh. "We'll see. I told them when they hired me, I would need help in that department unless they want to change the name from Triune First to The Wilderness Wanderings."

"Who is it?"

"A man I met this evening. He's . . . eccentric. But he was needy, and so was I. I took a chance."

"Don't you think you should have cleared it first?"

He shrugged. "Figured I'd just play it by ear. A lot of people who come to the church for help want a handout, nothing more." Thomas reached for her hand, his expression tender.

Miriam willed herself not to pull away.

"How was today?"

She attempted a smile. "Better than some."

He squeezed her hand. "I love you. It'll get better. With the church. With us. You'll see. Let's give it time."

Weighed by his incessant optimism, she sank into the spindle-back chair. Was he trying to convince her, or himself?

• CHAPTER •

SIX

Present Day

Ivy blinked and scrubbed her grainy eyes. The never-ending white lines flicked past the glow of her headlights. She was almost there. Almost home. She pressed the accelerator harder, inching the speedometer needle higher.

When the Uber driver dropped her off at the apartment three hours ago, Ivy hurriedly packed a few essentials and hoped her thoughts of Seth and their future together would keep until she returned.

A foolish hope. As evidenced by Seth's forty-two missed calls and twenty text messages. At least that was the tally the last time she'd turned her phone on to check for news about Grandma.

Ivy took the exit and pulled into the hospital garage. She hurried for the entrance, hands slick with cold sweat.

She pulled up short at the sight of Reese standing just outside the entrance. His hands were shoved in his pockets, head bowed.

"Reese?"

He lifted his chin; his eyes were red-rimmed. He shook his head. "I'm so sorry."

Ivy wrapped her arms around her middle. "I tried."

"I know."

She swallowed convulsively. "When?"

"Just a little while ago." He stepped forward and pulled her into a hug. She refused to let herself relax into his embrace. She couldn't fall apart, not yet.

"Mom and Dad?"

"They're inside."

Ivy stepped out of Reese's embrace. "Uncle Vee?"

He pointed to a walking path. "He headed that direction. Over by that stand of trees. I came out here to check on him. He said he needed air."

The lump in her throat swelled. There would never be enough ways to thank Reese for holding the place she should've filled. "Will you tell Mom and Dad I'm here?" Her voice cracked over the words.

"Of course."

Leaving Reese behind, Ivy ventured down the dimly lit trail. Peering through the dark, she spotted her uncle hunched on a park bench beneath the trees. Mom's and Dad's hearts might be breaking inside those hospital walls, but they had each other.

"Uncle Vee?"

He lifted his bowed head, his expression vacant. His hands trembled in his lap. "She's gone." His face crumpled and he took a heaving breath.

Her chin trembled and the tears she fought so hard to keep at bay welled in her eyes. "I . . . I . . ." But there were no words. None enough to apologize for not being there. Or to express the ache of losing someone who'd shaped so much of their lives.

"Sh-she was asking for you. Trying to hold on for you, but—" He gasped for air.

Ivy sat and opened her arms. Though he dwarfed her with his large frame, he sank into her embrace, shoulders shaking in silent sobs. How could a heart shatter while being held together all at the same time?

• • •

The morning after the funeral, Ivy pulled out of Grandma's gravelly driveway, leaving her family huddled on the porch and a cloud of dust in her wake. They weren't ready for her to leave any more than she was ready to go.

All morning Mom had hung close to Ivy's side, hinting that she and Dad were staying one more day before returning to their home in Kentucky. Uncle Vee checked and rechecked the tire pressure and fluid levels in her car.

And Reese—Reese spoke truth too hard to hear. Which was why she had to get back home before she lost her nerve.

Standing in Grandma's living room, as calm and carefree as could be, he'd said, "Ivy, I think there's something wrong with your phone."

Her phone had been buzzing every fifteen minutes like clockwork no matter how many times she'd replied with promises to talk with Seth as soon as she returned.

Reese leaned against the arm of the couch. "Is Seth on his way?"

"He's not coming."

He gestured to the phone, once again vibrating against the

countertop. "I know it's not my place, but what he's doing, it's not normal."

Oddly enough, the thing that had hit the hardest was Reese's assertion that it wasn't his place to speak. As her best friend, it should've been exactly his place. But somewhere along the way, Ivy had cut him out of the ugly parts of her life.

When she'd moved out from under her parents' roof six years ago to attend her dream school on a full-ride scholarship, she'd felt so brave. Adventurous. Landing a job had been the next step. An expected easy feat. She'd been the top of her class, after all. But her bravado dissolved when her diploma became little more than wall art in her apartment. No one wanted to hire a counselor with no experience. She'd had to return to serving tables.

Until Seth.

As much as she loved her new job and enjoyed all the things Seth credited himself for, at least back then she hadn't spent so much energy trying to keep him happy.

Miles passed, and Ivy rehearsed the words she'd say. Anticipating the arguments Seth would throw her way. All the ways he'd shift blame.

Three hours later, road weary and heartsore, she parked in front of Seth's townhouse and cut off the engine. She took a deep breath. This was it. The first step in reclaiming her life.

Ivy pressed his doorbell. She clenched her fists to stop the trembling that had started the second she exited the car.

Seth pulled the door open and widened his eyes in feigned shock. "Oh, look who finally decided to show up. I suppose you expect me to drop everything now that you're finally in the mood to talk."

He stepped aside with a bow. "Please, do come in." She shivered as she passed him. Had he always been this condescending? He closed the door behind him and clicked off the basketball game blaring on his television.

Ivy crossed to the opposite side of his living room.

Seth paced slowly, his hands clasped behind his back. "Do you have any idea of the stir you caused when you ditched me at the gala? You've never embarrassed me more than you did that night. I'm starting to wonder if you'll ever understand what it takes to be part of my life."

Ivy crossed her arms over her chest, armor for her heart. "That's just it. I don't think I want a life with you."

His posture stiffened, and he narrowed his eyes. "You don't know what you're saying. Don't be rash." Seth reached for his water glass on the side table and took a long drink.

Ivy twisted the ring from her finger and set it with a clunk on his coffee table. Her pulse pounded in her ears.

The glass he held slipped a fraction, sloshing water onto his hand. He fumbled it back onto the table and methodically wiped his hand on his trousers. The vein on his forehead appeared.

He reached her in two strides and towered over her slight frame. She backstepped, bumping into the couch behind her. Seth placed his hands on her shoulders. The touch was gentle, but it blocked her escape.

"Let's sit down and talk this out." His voice was calm, tender. Though his words sounded like honey, he'd use them to cut her to the quick if given the chance.

"There's nothing to discuss. I don't want to marry you, Seth." A bead of sweat dripped down her back, and her knees shook from the adrenaline coursing through her.

"Here you go again. Driven by emotion. I know losing your grandmother has put you in a weird place, but that's no reason to throw our future away."

"My family and I were grieving, trying to process her loss, and you were blowing up my phone begging me to leave so that we could talk about our relationship."

"You left the gala without a word to me and then would barely respond to my calls. I was worried about you."

You weren't worried about me, you were worried about losing control of me. She took a slow, steady breath. "If you were concerned, you would've showed up. Supported me while I grieved."

He rolled his eyes. "Don't guilt trip me. I was stuck here prepping for a big case. I told you that." He scrubbed a hand over his face. "We can work this out if you'll calm down and be rational."

She pressed her trembling lips tight and lifted her chin to meet his gaze. "I don't want to work this out."

"How can you say that? Do you have no conscience? No shame about the embarrassment you'll inflict on my family? When you accepted my proposal, you made a commitment."

She nodded at the ring resting on his table. "I gave the ring back."

He jerked his head backward like she'd slapped him. "That's what commitment means to you? That when you run into a rough patch, you simply back out? No harm, no foul? I knew once you were around those people again, they'd poison you against me."

Do not let him twist this. Ivy repeated the mantra over and over inside her head, drowning out his voice. "That's not what this is about. And *those people* are my family."

His fists tightened at his sides. "Gorgeous women were falling at my feet, their rich daddies pushing them in my direction, and yet I chose you. I stood up to *my family*, even though they didn't approve."

Chose me? Targeted me is more like it. She attempted to step around him. He blocked her with his body.

"I want to leave. Now. Let me pass." Fear raced through her veins, fear she would not let win.

One corner of his mouth curled upward. "If you walk away, I'll tell everyone *I* ended it. I'll let them in on the little secret about how emotionally unstable you are and how I couldn't risk someone like you ruining my family's name. That will do wonders for your counseling career, don't you think?"

He was bluffing. Surely he was bluffing.

"Are you really going to throw away all the good I've done for you because I made one mistake?" Seth tilted his head. "See, there, I can admit it. I should've taken you home instead of dragging you to that gala. Can't we move past this?"

How many times had she heard those exact words when they disagreed? She'd thought herself so magnanimous, always choosing compromise over conflict. She was an idiot. "It's not just this one thing. And the fact that you can't see that and the fact that I am just now realizing it is proof that we shouldn't be together."

"Don't think for one second I'm going to let you dump me and then skip off into the sunset living the life I built for you. I can make sure it *all* disappears. Are you ready to give up that nice apartment I put you in? The car? The clothing allowance?"

"*Nothing* is worth losing myself more than I already have."

His eyes lit as though he'd struck gold. "What about those kids you help at that job I made happen?"

Her stomach roiled. She took a breath, attempting to calm her throbbing pulse and the rising acid burning her throat. "Move out of my way."

He stepped back and she edged around him. Ivy took two steps before his voice followed her, quiet and icy calm.

"How are you going to get home, Ivy? In the car you drove over here? The one in my name? I'll report it stolen. Blue lights will light up the sky behind you before you make it five minutes down the road."

Ivy pulled the keys from her pocket and smacked them down on the glass table next to the ring. "I'll find my own way then."

He darted forward and grasped her wrist as she straightened her posture.

Ivy bit back a cry of pain at his grip.

His teeth were clenched. A flush crept up his neck. Dr. Jekyll transformed into full-blown Hyde. "You can't do this to me."

She put her body weight to full use, attempting to wrench free. He released her. She stumbled backward and twisted, trying to catch herself. When she fell, the apple of her cheek struck the corner of the coffee table. The world exploded. Her hands flew to her face and a groan rose from her chest.

Seth stood over her, shaking his head. He dropped the keys into her lap. "Go home and cool off. Come back when you're ready to have an adult conversation instead of flailing about like a toddler."

Ivy stood and staggered out the door, hurrying to the car, covering the injured side of her face with her hand. She should leave the car and all ties to that man, but this was the fastest way out of there.

By the time she reached her apartment, her cheek was so swollen she couldn't open one eye and tears leaked from the other.

SEVEN

SEPTEMBER 9, 1994

From the living room came an insistent wailing, an unending caterwauling. Harvey was in foster home number ten, and the foster parents had just brought home their newborn baby. He crept around the corner and watched, awestruck by the way the woman gazed at the child with consuming adoration, even though the odd-looking thing scrunched its red face and let out furious demands to be satisfied.

No one had ever looked at him like that. Weight too heavy for his skinny eleven-year-old frame slipped over his shoulders. This tiny person had eclipsed his existence; surely he'd be shuttled to another foster placement, or perhaps another children's home soon. No one really wanted preteen boys.

Harvey blinked awake, shoving the dreamed memory away. A ray of light sneaked through the lean-to. His brain told his body to move, but he'd become one with the ground.

He inched up with a groan, wincing at the earsplitting cries of the tiny person next to him.

Ivy lay beside him, fists clenched against her red face, mouth wide in midcry. He brushed her cheek with the back of his knuckle, and her crying ceased as she jerked her head toward his touch, mouth gaping. He couldn't resist a smile, despite his sleep-weighted eyelids. "Well, little bird. Hungry again, are we?"

He scuffled about, mixing the formula with the water he boiled last night. Whew. Babies weren't much for sleep, but eating on the other hand . . .

Harvey fumbled her into his arms. Such a tiny, fragile thing. He brushed the rubbery tip of the bottle against her lips. Perfect and pink, they flared and latched as her tongue curled around the bottle's nipple. She sucked noisily with satisfied grunts between gulps.

"Easy there. Slow down. There's plenty, little piggy."

He held her close, inhaling her scent. Delicate, sweet, and something more, a quality he couldn't name.

Her initial hunger satisfied, her swallows took on a regular rhythm. She stared up at Harvey, her expression entirely open—not questioning or trying to make sense of him. Blissful acceptance.

Propping the upturned bottle under his chin, he stroked the top of her head. He could sit all day, just looking at her. He didn't know his heart could feel like this—aching but full.

What kind of person could leave this child to die, forgotten in the scrub brush?

Her diapered bottom rumbled against his hand. "Nice, Ivy." He scrunched his nose. While he'd clumsily managed a few wet diapers in the twelve hours she'd been his, this was a first. She paused her suckling, and her lips stretched, pleased with herself. Her eyes fluttered closed as she continued her breakfast.

Harvey squirmed. He could let her finish the bottle and then change her. But maybe he was supposed to do it immediately. The baby book, just out of reach, probably had the answer.

Disgusting. She couldn't be left sitting in a dirty diaper. He wriggled the bottle, trying to break her suction. Ivy clamped her pink gums in a vice grip. Her eyes flashed open.

Whoa. Never mind. Diaper change after breakfast.

Harvey focused on her warm featherweight in his arms. Ivy's swallows slowed, punctuated by brief pauses. Her bottom lip quivered against the nipple.

Her pauses lengthened until formula dribbled out of one corner of her mouth. The bottle slipped from between her lips as he pulled it away.

Harvey's voice was soft and low as he crooned, "Oh, Ivy. You weren't supposed to fall asleep. How am I going to change you?" Laying her on the bed, he tugged the purple blanket away from her bottom a fraction at a time—a man disarming a bomb. Her lashes fluttered but stayed closed.

He had those elbow-length kitchen gloves in the supply bin. Harvey shook his head. She was tiny. How bad could it be?

His fingers fumbled as he pulled both diaper tabs loose at the same time. Ivy twitched. He froze.

Harvey inched open the diaper. Ivy's entire body tensed, and she let out a piercing wail. Her scrawny legs scrunched and kicked. He jerked his hand back, and his heart went to his throat.

Ivy's bottom—and now her legs—were smeared with an inky tarlike slime.

He'd chosen the wrong formula or something. Nothing like that should ever come out of a human being.

Harvey reached for the baby care book. His fingers turned to sausages trying to turn pages that stuck together in the humidity.

Ivy kicked, arched, and flailed—streaking her hands, her hair, the blanket.

Harvey let out a breath in a whoosh when he landed on the desired page. Meconium. It was normal. She was okay.

But she was mad. And disgusting. He pulled two handfuls of baby wipes from the plastic box and scrubbed. It smeared.

Finally, he abandoned his lost cause and stoked the fire to warm a little bathwater. She cried harder, gasping and coughing. Harvey's chest tightened. She was going to choke herself.

He grimaced at the filthy writhing thing on the soiled blanket, sighed, then scooped her to his chest. In a second nature born overnight, Harvey crooned, bouncing at the knees.

She stilled and stared up at him, her rosebud mouth in a perfect pout, meconium smeared across her cheek.

Then Harvey's arm grew warm. Very warm. And wet. She blinked at him. "It's a good thing you're cute, kid."

An hour later he had her bathed, dressed, and settled. He sat down on the mattress beside her. As he peered out at the new day, with the twitter of birds lulling his tattered nerves, Harvey's eyelids lowered, wavered, but then shot wide.

The time.

Harvey didn't live by a clock, and if he did, it would have exactly four segments. Eating, fishing, scavenging, and dark.

It had to be at least nine already. He'd be fired before his first day started.

Better to be a no-show than face the pastor's disappointment.

Harvey held up the formula tin, already lighter. Although, the guy was crazy enough to give him a job in the first place, so maybe he was crazy enough to give him another chance.

At the supply bins, Harvey pulled out the bolt of gray knit cotton. He rolled out about three yards and snipped a straight line. Grasping the middle of the train of fabric, he placed it against his chest, remembering.

The foster mother had cradled her newborn baby to her chest and wrapped the fabric. Eleven-year-old Harvey would watch, entranced, memorizing the pattern in which she crossed and wound the fabric into a labyrinth from which the tiny babe couldn't wriggle free. No matter how her baby fussed against her chest, he was protected and bound tight until he ceased his fretting and settled to sleep.

How he'd longed to be that woman's son. But Harvey had always been more like a kite at the end of a string, buffeted and jerked in the middle of a gale until the thin line snapped.

Ivy Rose now rested, perfectly wrapped to his chest with her mouth parted in sleep. He planted a kiss on the top of her head. She was no kite on a string. They were bound. Together.

Pulling on his largest shirt, yellow with palm trees and waves, he buttoned her beneath. The loose fit allowed the air to flow freely. Her tiny curled form gave him a Santa Claus paunch on a tall scarecrow frame.

Before leaving camp, Harvey pulled a utility knife from his pocket and made a notch in a thick cedar beside his lean-to.

If by some miracle he made it back at the end of the day with Ivy still wrapped to his chest, he'd put another notch next to the first and add one every day he succeeded in keeping her safe. He loaded his bag with diapers and formula and hiked toward town.

• CHAPTER •

EIGHT

PRESENT DAY

Ivy stood in front of her mirror, wincing at the discoloration below her eye. The swelling had mostly receded. A thick layer of concealer might be enough to disguise it. She couldn't afford to take a sick day. Not after the time she'd just taken off for Grandma's funeral and Seth's threats hanging over her head.

More than that, her kids with special needs depended on her to be their testing accommodator for their end-of-year tests today. She couldn't let them down when they needed her familiar presence the most. If she could just get through the next couple of days, she'd return the car Seth had bought for her and find a new place to live. Cut all ties.

Makeup on, she checked her reflection. She straightened a few wayward brown strands and tilted her chin in different angles, catching the light. Maybe no one would notice the bluish tinge coming through.

Ivy grabbed her purse and headed for her car. Seated, she

pressed the start button. Nothing, not even the familiar beep signaling her car coming to life. She pushed the button again, making sure her foot rested heavy on the brake.

Still nothing.

Had she left the key inside her apartment? She riffled through her purse, searching for the key fob. Maybe the remote's battery was the problem. She grabbed it, held it against the start button, and pressed.

No response.

Ivy swallowed hard and dug her phone from her purse. Better call Cheryl and let her know she wasn't going to make it in time for car duty.

Ivy stared at the phone screen. No service? She took a shaky breath. Seth wouldn't disconnect her phone. She paid for her half of the bill, not him.

She jogged back inside and dialed Cheryl on her landline.

"Hey, girl."

"Cheryl?" She swallowed. "I'm having car trouble this morning. Stupid me, I think I left a light on or something and killed the battery. I'm going to be late."

"I'll give you a ride. I'm just down the street from you. I'll be outside in two minutes."

When she arrived, Ivy plopped down in her car. "You're a lifesaver."

But Cheryl didn't respond. Or put the car in drive.

Ivy looked at her friend.

"What happened to you?"

Ivy's hand went to her cheek. "N-nothing. I fell."

Cheryl glanced from Ivy's cheek to her bare left hand and back. "Don't lie to me."

"I'm not lying. I fell. Promise. Let's go before I make us late."

Once they parked at the school, Cheryl held out her hand. "Andrew isn't working at the shop today. I told him about your car trouble on my way to pick you up. He offered to stop by your place and check the battery. He just needs to be able to get into it."

Ivy handed Cheryl her keys. "What did you bribe your husband with to get him to spend his day off working on another car?"

She shrugged. "It's not a big deal. He's happy to help."

"Thanks. Seriously. I owe you both big-time."

Cheryl winked. "I think our long overdue girls' night might make up for it."

● ● ●

Throughout the day, Ivy did everything in her power to give her kids the attention they deserved. But thoughts and fears intruded without permission, stealing her breath and quickening her pulse.

He'd disabled her phone. What was next? Would all her possessions be on the curb when she returned home at the end of the day? Seth had paid the rent. Not her.

Ivy spent her lunch break staring at files on her desk. Reading and rereading without comprehending a word.

Cheryl slipped into Ivy's office. She closed the door behind her and then glanced out the glass frame. "I tried to text you."

Heat crept up Ivy's neck and flooded her face. "My phone isn't working."

Cheryl flattened her lips in a line and then spoke in a

hissed whisper. "Andrew looked at your car. The battery wasn't dead. Somebody pulled the fuse to your starter."

Ivy wrapped her arms around her tightening stomach. Air squeezed in and out of her lungs. "I . . . I'll talk to security. See if they can go back on the cameras and find out who did this."

Cheryl crossed the room and sank to her knees next to Ivy's chair. "You and I both know who tampered with your car." She brushed a strand of hair off Ivy's bruised cheek. "The same person who did this."

Ivy shook her head, choking on her own breath. "He didn't hit me. I fell."

Cheryl placed her hand on Ivy's knee. "Fine. But let me ask you this, did this happen in his presence?"

Ivy looked away but nodded.

"At any time did he use his size and strength to his advantage against you? Did he stop you from leaving? Did he touch you without your consent?"

Ivy stared at her lap.

"That's all I needed to know. Andrew and I will go over and pack up as many of your things as we can before the end of the school day. You can stay with us until this gets sorted out. Please."

• ● •

"Thanks again for opening your home to me."

Cheryl passed Ivy a cup of coffee over the kitchen island with a smile. "You know you don't have to say that every morning, right?"

Maybe not, but after two weeks of living with them, it was all she had to offer beyond carefully cleaning up behind herself and making sure all her belongings remained tucked away in their guest room. Ensuring her presence didn't spill over into their lives any more than necessary.

"I've been looking at apartments. There's a vacancy at my old place. I liked it there. I never should've let Seth talk me into moving."

"Are you going to take it?"

"Maybe." She'd spent most of her savings on a replacement car. The dinged beige sedan wasn't much to look at, but it was reliable. And it was hers.

The next logical step was a new place to live.

"Take your time. It's nice having someone to carpool with. Otherwise I resort to talking to myself." Cheryl glanced at her watch and sighed. "We better get a move on. Last day of classes. Those kids will be off the rails."

Ivy shouldered her bag. "I'm ready if you are." How would she survive the next few months not doing the one thing that made her feel useful?

"Oh!" Cheryl turned and grabbed a stack of envelopes from the bill sorter on her wall. "Andrew picked up your mail on his way home from work last night. You were so quiet in your room, he was afraid you were asleep."

On the way to the car, Ivy flipped through the assortment of junk mail and bills. The next to last item was a lavender envelope with no return address. Ivy ran her finger beneath its seal and pulled out the single sheet of notebook paper.

She blinked. Grandma's script filled the page—the swooping, slanting letters only the older generations seemed to possess.

"Whatcha got there?"

Ivy swallowed. "I don't understand. It's from my grand-mother."

"Oh. Wow."

Ivy's chin trembled and the words on the page blurred, regret gutting her all over again. If only there was a way to trade this piece of paper for the comfort of Grandma's arms.

Dear Ivy,

My sweet girl, first and foremost, I hope you know how dearly loved you are. I had hoped to speak to you before I went home to be with Jesus. Many months ago, I decided to write this letter in case we never had the chance to have this chat.

There are things I never told you. Sometimes I kept silent because I lacked wisdom to know how to speak difficult truths. I always questioned if it was my place, or if it was the wrong timing. As much as I wrestled with myself on this, I knew I couldn't leave this world without giving you answers to the questions that have plagued your mind since you were a little girl.

These secrets I've kept for many years. It's your choice whether you open this door to where you came from, as it should have been all along. In my home, I've left something for you that explains everything.

If you do choose to go back to explore your past, I ask you to be the one to go through my possessions and ensure my estate is handled with care. I think you'll find the process to be rather enlightening. Don't worry, you won't face this task alone. I've arranged for ample assistance.

No matter what you decide, always know that you

were fearfully and wonderfully made. And God does not make junk.

Always,
Grandma

• ● •

Ivy sat in her office, toying with the edge of Grandma's letter, trying to make sense of her words.

A soft knock sounded. Principal Watkins stood in her doorway. He offered her a tight smile. "Ivy, may I have a word?"

She stowed the letter and straightened. "Of course."

He closed the door behind him and sat in the chair opposite her desk. He sighed. "I have some unfortunate news. I've been putting this off, trying everything I can to fix it." He rubbed the space between his eyebrows. "A few days ago, we lost one of our major donors to the school."

Ivy pressed her fingertips over her mouth to mask her trembling bottom lip.

"Unfortunately, we're having to make some cuts. I can't tell you how much this pains me to tell you this, but we don't have the budget for two counselors next year, and Marilyn has seniority. Please understand this is no reflection on your abilities."

She attempted to inhale a solid breath, but she'd forgotten how in the midst of piecing together his words. "Yes, sir. I understand."

Ivy folded her hands in her lap, fighting for professionalism, stuffing down what she really wanted to do. To yell and cry, to rip things from the shelves.

Principal Watkins stood. "Again, I'm so sorry to be the bearer of such bad news. Truly, I wish you all the best. And if something changes, you're the first person I'll call. I wanted to give you as much heads-up as possible so that you can secure a new position before next school year. I'll write any recommendation letter you need." He offered her a sympathetic smile. "You're a wonderful young lady and you've been such a fantastic part of our team."

She nodded her thanks, her words wedged and jumbled in her mind. He graciously exited the room. Ivy propped her elbows on her desk and buried her face in her hands, pressing the heels of her palms against her eyes. She would not cry. Could not. If she started, she might not ever stop.

She lifted her head at the faint squeak of her office door. Cheryl crossed the room and wrapped her in a hug.

Ivy took a slow breath. "You heard?"

She nodded against the top of Ivy's head.

"Was it him? Did he do this?"

Cheryl sat back on her heels, crouched by Ivy's desk. "You didn't hear it from me. I'm not supposed to know these details in the first place, but I saw a fax come through from a certain law office."

So Seth wasn't bluffing. He really had made her job at the school happen—and with the stroke of a pen, he'd ended it.

• CHAPTER •

NINE

SEPTEMBER 9, 1994

The churchyard was still and quiet. Harvey swallowed, struggling against the lump of dread in his throat. That pastor had been willing to give him a chance, and he was late for his first day.

A breath lodged in his ribs as he took the first step on the tall stack of stairs leading to the arched front door—its vibrant red paint peeled, revealing hints of brown beneath.

Sleeping Ivy expelled a whisper-soft sigh, steeling his resolve. He mounted the stairs and pulled the handle on the towering doors.

Harvey's sandaled feet echoed on the floor of the foyer. He inhaled the faint scent of wood polish and old carpet. Soon his footsteps became muffled by the red runner that lined the center aisle of the sanctuary.

The ceiling, vaulted with intricate trim work draped in cobwebs, was high enough he didn't feel caged. The tall stained-glass windows every few feet spilled colored light across the length of the building. It made sense why people came here in search of peace.

He ran his hand over the corner of the back pew, the finish worn away in that place as if every congregant had touched the same spot coming and going.

Someone cleared their throat and snuffed into a tissue, the sound echoing in the empty expanse. The pastor sat in the front row, facing the pulpit. Harvey took halting steps forward, touching the corner of each of the twenty pews on his right, as if the repetition would anchor him to the place.

His employment was likely ending before it ever started. If the job was still his, he faced the next impossible task— hiding a sleeping baby bound to his middle.

The pastor straightened and turned in his seat. "Harvey. You're here. I didn't hear you come in. I was lost in prayer or thought. Maybe somewhere in between." With a sheepish expression on his face, he swiped quickly at his cheek and stood.

Harvey's heart thumped. He'd wake the baby with the racket going on inside of him.

Pastor Thomas checked his gold watch as Harvey approached.

"I'm sorry, sir. I walked the floor with my sister's baby all night. I didn't mean to oversleep." He winced. Coming to church was making a liar out of him.

"Harvey, you're five minutes early."

"Oh." He wanted to melt into a puddle on the floor, all the dread dissolving in a moment. He willed his knees to solidify.

The pastor lowered his head as he rubbed the back of his neck. "Do you own a watch?"

Harvey swallowed. Humiliation sure had a bitter taste. "I . . . I did, but . . ."

Thomas unhinged the clasp at his wrist and wiggled his arm until the watch slipped into his palm. He stretched the watch toward Harvey. "Here. It's yours."

Harvey stepped back and stared at his shoes with his chest heaving. "No, sir. No, that's not—"

"Take it. I don't need it. I have a box full of them at home."

Harvey froze.

Thomas stepped forward, took Harvey by the forearm, and pressed the watch in his palm. Harvey closed his fingers around the weighty timepiece—the smooth sweep of the second hand kept time of the awkward silence.

Stepping back, Thomas cleared his throat. "For today, I guess walk around the grounds and get your bearings. You'll know what needs to be done better than I would. Just stop by my office before you leave today, okay?" He nodded a dismissal and headed for the door to the left of the platform.

Taking measured steps out of the church, Harvey fought to get oxygen through the band squeezing his chest. When the outside air hit his face, he wrapped his arms around the baby snuggled to his middle and fled for the side of the church—the hidden side lined by the woods. Backing against the building, his knees wobbled beneath him. In one hand he clenched the watch, in the other he gripped his hair.

What did that pastor possibly think he could get out of Harvey? Giving him a job without checking him out first. The high-end watch. Harvey heaved shuddering breaths.

Ivy squeaked. He slid to the ground to sit and laid his cheek on her head.

• ● •

Pearl Howard scuffed into the kitchen in her pink bunny slippers to refill her coffee cup. Today's choice was the yellow one with pansies—the cup she always chose when she woke with the impression it was going to be a good day.

Catching her reflection in the window, she retied her bright Chinese kimono, then patted her brittle blue-gray hair. She kissed her fingertips and pressed them onto the silver-framed photograph of her son resting in her kitchen windowsill, so handsome in his military uniform. And then she did the same to the picture of her husband who stood in front of the church in his classic navy suit and red tie.

She peered out the window at the black sedan in the parking lot. Was the young pastor from California already at the church? Bless his heart.

Her husband, the shepherd of that flock for forty years, was a tough act to follow, especially in this tight-knit community. Pastor Thomas had a good heart, but he was trying too hard.

Pearl's eyes widened. A tall man with shaggy hair hurried from the entrance of the church, hands clutched around his middle like he had a bundle of groceries tucked under his shirt. Then he darted around the other side. She blinked.

This could end up being an interesting day, after all. Pearl leaned close to the glass, as if staring hard enough would make the man come back. She wiped away the moisture fogging the slick surface.

The stranger reappeared a few minutes later and paced around the churchyard like he was lost, talking to himself it seemed. He was awfully jittery. Then he picked up the tree limbs littered around the huge churchyard until he established a substantial pile.

What in the world . . . ?

She slipped out the door and sat on her front porch swing with her mug clutched in her hands. From here she had a clear view of the man and his exploits.

It was a blessing the church had voted for her to retain the parsonage after Elliot passed away. Though cancer ripped through her husband's body for two years, he'd persisted in being in the pulpit every Sunday even if he had to preach from a wheelchair, voice failing. Until they'd lost their only son. After Marshall was gone, Elliot lost his verve. A month later, Pearl was alone.

She sighed. Seeing that church every day was a gift and a trial in equal measure. She gulped the last of her tepid coffee, and then slipped out of her bunny slippers and into the garden shoes waiting by the door.

The mystery man had disappeared into the church's toolshed and appeared moments later wrestling the rusty push mower.

She headed to the garden, pulling on her gloves as she went, stealing glimpses of the wild-haired young man who now fiddled with the unresponsive old mower. It was high time someone paid attention to the grass, but he seemed an odd choice for church groundskeeper. Pastor Thomas must be getting desperate. She had a growing suspicion he'd had a full staff at his last church. Triune First was traditionally a one-man operation.

Pearl perched on a three-legged stool between the rows of vegetables, weeding and keeping an eye on this newcomer. He'd strewn tools on the grass and stared at them as though trying to decide which to pick up first. Then for no apparent reason, he jumped up and hurried back around the side of the church facing the woods. The same place he'd gone before.

Hands on her hips, she stared at the place where he'd knelt moments ago.

Ten minutes later he returned and resumed work like nothing had happened. Shortly after, his face twisted in disgust, and then he ran behind the church again.

After a while, he was back, shoulders hunched, fidgeting with his shirt, glancing around, on guard. As he turned in her direction, she stooped behind her cornstalks.

She shook her head. Drugs, probably. Something wasn't right, anyway.

There was nothing dearer to her heart than helping troubled young people, but having a drug addict employed at the church was too big of a risk. As much as she didn't want to be another voice questioning the pastor's leadership, she'd have to speak to Pastor Thomas about this.

When the sun inched higher, shy of noon, she pulled off her gloves, left them on the stool, and headed into the house. Before she spoke to Pastor Thomas, maybe she ought to check things out for herself.

The man had yawned his way through the past two hours. A cuppa joe might be just the thing to break the ice. She picked a navy and green plaid mug and filled it to the brim. He looked like a plaid kind of chap.

Lost in tinkering with the motor, the man didn't lift his head at her approach. He sang softly. A lullaby? *Definitely* drugs. She cleared her throat.

His wrench jumped from his hand and clattered against

the rusted motor. He jerked straight and then crossed his arms over his middle. Eyes wide and chest heaving.

"I'm Pearl. Sorry to have startled you. I just wanted to offer you a cup of coffee and say hello." She studied his dark-circled eyes. They were the color of rich, turned earth. Clear and lucid. "You seemed like you could use it." She held out the coffee and nodded. "Here. This is for you."

He stared at the cup, and then reached with unsteady hands streaked with black grease. The man's gaze reminded her of the hummingbirds that visited her feeder every afternoon. Flitting here and there but never lighting on a particular perch. His mouth moved but there was no sound. It was several long moments before anything intelligible emerged. "Harvey. Working for Pastor Thomas. My first day." He shifted his feet.

Pearl offered a gentle smile and stepped back to make him more at ease. "Nice to meet you, Harvey. I live right over there if you need anything. You can leave the mug on the porch when you're finished."

He gave a tight nod.

Her heart twisted. It wasn't drugs, but something wasn't right.

TEN

PRESENT DAY

The tension in Ivy's stomach unfurled a fraction as her car inched past the weathered clapboard church. Gnarled oaks and maples concealed the quaint cottage at the end of the driveway.

Though Ivy had moved from Triune, Tennessee, when she was fourteen, no place felt as much like home as that tidy white cottage. It should be remembered the way it was the summers before. With Grandma coming out to greet her, carrying a tray laden with a pitcher of fresh-squeezed lemonade and a tin of butter cookies. Not still and quiet like an open casket.

Like fireflies flickering in the night whenever she'd spend summers at Grandma's, Ivy had gotten glimpses of the childhood version of herself—strong, fearless, and confident she could take on the world. Could whatever waited inside the house help her find that girl again?

Rounding the final curve, she offered a muttered prayer

that the heartache of this particular trip wouldn't mar the magic of perfect childhood memories.

Ivy parked in front of the garage and unfolded from her car. The tidy flower beds were abloom with irises. Bird feeders were filled. The vegetable garden's neat rows weeded and thriving. The scent of freshly mown grass wafted through the air. Despite her heavy heart, she smiled at her uncle's handiwork.

Her mouth parched, tasting the phantom tart of Grandma's lemonade. Ivy closed her eyes, begging to catch the sound of her tinkling laughter just one more time.

She took a steadying breath and headed down the walk. A shadow shifted on the porch and someone stood from the porch swing. Ivy squinted against the glare of sunlight coming over the peak of the rooftop. *Reese?*

All her lingering apprehension dissolved and something lighter filled its place.

From their first day of kindergarten, her stomach churning with nerves, he'd always been there for her. While all the other kids snickered and wrinkled their noses when she got sick all over the front of her white eyelet blouse, Reese went to his cubby and lent her his Batman T-shirt. She'd claimed him as her best friend from that day forward. At least until she'd let Seth's jealousy come between them.

"Ivy?" He stepped from beneath the shadow of the porch with his thumbs hitched in the pockets of his well-worn jeans. Classic Reese. Put together, fit, at ease in his own skin.

Ivy swiped her tangled hair back from her face, regretting all the time spent on the highway with her windows down. She lifted her hand. "Hey, Reese."

He walked to her and pulled her into a quick half hug.

"I came over to give your uncle a hand in the garden this morning. You just missed him."

"You've been keeping an eye on him?"

He shrugged, a hint of a smile tugging one corner of his mouth. "Promised, didn't I?"

"Thanks."

"Anything you need. What brings you back so soon?"

Ivy pulled the letter from her purse. "This."

Reese scanned the letter and let out a low whistle. "Wow. What do you think that's all about?"

"The first three months of my life are a complete mystery to me. Maybe Grandma knew more than she let on."

Reese stepped toward the house. "Well, let's go. I can help with the house. Maybe we'll find some answers along the way."

She glanced across the churchyard to his old truck parked behind the church. Ivy reached into her purse for the house key. "I can handle it."

Something softened in his eyes, causing her heart to do a funny flip. A sensation she did her best to ignore. But he made it difficult, taking her hand right then.

Her smaller hand fit in his warm, calloused palm like a puzzle piece.

"Sure you can, Rosie-girl. But what kind of friend would I be to let you dig through that house of memories all by yourself? Besides, I got a letter with instructions of my own."

Rosie-girl. Only he could get away with that awful nickname. "*You're* the help she was referring to in my letter?"

He nodded.

Ivy opened her mouth, but with nothing to fill the space, clamped it shut. She wriggled her fingers free from his gentle grip, refusing to let him become the security blanket she craved.

"Your grandma was a force to be reckoned with in life, and I'm not going against her wishes in death. Even if she isn't here to swat me with her newspaper the way she threatened to every time I picked all the strawberries out of her garden."

Ivy choked on a laugh. Swallowed by the memory of the two of them, charged guilty by their juice-stained cheeks, giggling at Grandma's feigned scolding.

Grandma would've let the two of them get away with murder, but not before she lectured first. Ivy inserted the key in the front door and let it swing wide.

"All right. Just know you're free to back out any time."

One by one, Ivy opened the living room windows, releasing the cloying air. Light streamed in, illuminating the dust fairies their footfalls roused from the carpet.

Reese flicked a switch. Incandescent lamps brightened the time capsule of a home. In Ivy's lifetime, Grandma never redecorated. Not once. Other than a fresh coat of paint on her wood-paneled walls every so many years.

Ivy peered around the room, eyes hungry for any signs of whatever Grandma had left for her. "I'm guessing there's a list somewhere in here, a way to sort all her trinkets and odds and ends."

Reese chuckled, the sound low and warm. "There's plenty of those to go around."

On every flat surface, a myriad of figurines rested on crocheted doilies. Ivy's childhood playthings. On Grandma's living room floor, Ivy had acted out entire plays with ceramic kittens and Victorian ladies.

Reese clattered about, plugging in box fans to stir the stifling air. Their rackety thrum hindered conversation, which was fine by Ivy. Reese was sure to have questions. About the absence of her ring. How long she planned to stay. Answers Ivy wasn't ready to give.

She found a task list posted on the refrigerator and passed it to Reese. She left him studying the paper and continued searching. Wandering past the end tables and the upright piano, fingertips brushing familiar photo frames as she passed.

She entered the bedroom she occupied whenever she came to visit during the summers after her family moved to Kentucky. She traced the sunflowers on the comforter, colors of joy and warmth. How strange to think she'd never stay in this room after this trip.

Now that the house was vacant, would the church convert the place into a day care? Or more Sunday school classrooms? Ivy stood and sighed, shoving the thought away. An envelope on the dresser caught her attention.

"Hey, Ivy?" Reese appeared at her side. "Did you find anything yet?"

She picked up the envelope, fumbling the seal with her trembling fingers.

He stepped closer. The waft of his breath ruffled the tendrils that had slipped from Ivy's ponytail. Gooseflesh rose on her arm and a flutter released in her middle. Ivy stepped away, seeking a buffer between them. Reese crossed the room and sat on the edge of the bed.

She peeled open the envelope and removed the slip of paper and a tiny skeleton key.

My dear child,
    I wonder, sometimes, if you'll ever truly realize

what you mean to us all. Our little vine, pulling us all together. Before you, we were just broken individuals looking for love.

Broken people make choices, choices that might make little sense from your standpoint. Please look upon each of us with grace. Though we were misguided at times, our desire was to love you in the best way possible. The enclosed key goes to an antique cabinet in my room. On the third shelf, you'll find a journal. Something I began in your early days so that we could all look back and remember. But things took an unexpected turn, and I found myself unable to share this with you until now.

I attempted to be as raw and honest as possible. Some accounts are my own, while others are from the perspectives of those who shared their part in your story with me. I'm sorry. For the things you will learn that will hurt. For the ways we fell short. The ways I, most of all, let you down.

With all the love in my heart,
Grandma

Ivy sucked in a breath, lifted the key from the dresser, and rushed down the hall.

"Ivy?" Reese called after her.

In Grandma's room, Ivy faced the antique barrister bookcase and pressed her hands to the glass, peering inside at various figurines. A thin layer of dust covered the empty third shelf. One polished rectangle in the center, roughly the size of a book, only a ghost of what once rested there.

A wave kicked up in the pit of her stomach. Rolled and crashed. Bitterness burned the back of her throat.

Reese's solid presence appeared at her side. "What's wrong?"

Ivy listed, bumping into Reese's chest. She sank into the embrace when his arms folded around her. His T-shirt smelled of fresh cut timber—an earthy smell that grounded her. The ache to be held that had throbbed inside her since that awful night at Seth's apartment quieted.

No matter how welcome his comfort, Ivy promised herself she wouldn't lean on Reese. And she would stop. As soon as she could feel her feet again.

Ivy slowed her breathing and extricated herself from his arms. She sank onto the bench at the foot of the bed. She shook her head. "The journal Grandma left me, it's gone."

Reese studied the bookcase, opening each cabinet, shuffling items aside. Then he examined the glass door to the third shelf.

He turned to her, brows raised. "The wood around the lock is chipped."

• CHAPTER •

ELEVEN

SEPTEMBER 9, 1994

Harvey was a fool for showing up—for getting involved with these people. The pastor's offer was too perfect, too nice.

A pink curtain moved from within the white house across the way. The little blue-haired old lady who had been traipsing through her vegetable garden in a flowery bathrobe earlier in the morning was now back inside, always watching.

The borrowed mug sat on the ground, begging to be returned. He'd tinker with the rattletrap mower a few more minutes, waiting until she wasn't staring out the window at him. With a bit of luck, he'd be able to slip over and leave the cup on the porch before she caught him.

Then it should be about time for Ivy to wake and eat again. A living, breathing alarm clock—sleeping, eating, and then sleeping again. Babies didn't do that forever, he knew that much. When this sleep-all-the-time phase ended, they would be back to square one.

Harvey shook his head. One notch on the tree at a time.

His only goal today was to make that one notch become two. But with the blue-haired Neighborhood Watch on the case, the jig would be up before his first day ended. He stowed the tools and dragged the mower back to its dusty corner in the shed. Maybe he could get the rust heap running tomorrow. He'd go prune the hedges next so at least it would appear he'd accomplished something.

Harvey crept up the walk, mug in hand, scoping out the windows. All clear. He reached to set the mug on the porch rail.

The front door opened while he slipped his fingers from the handle. He started and the cup fell onto her concrete porch, shattering into pieces. The sound ricocheted inside his head, seeming far louder than the crash warranted. Harvey froze, hunched over the shards.

Pearl balanced a tray laden with sandwiches. "Oh dear."

Ivy arched and squirmed against his chest. His knees trembled when he quick-stepped backwards. "I'm sorry, I'll replace it. I'm sorry. So sorry." He turned on his heel and bolted as quickly as he dared without jarring Ivy. Her delayed startle-reflex cry was—he hoped—masked by his fake coughing and the distance he put between himself and Pearl. Heat spilled over him. He'd left that elderly woman to clean up his mess.

She called out from her porch, "Oh, stay. Harvey, it's all right. Come back. Please."

●　●　●

Pearl stared as Harvey strode down the road, hunched and coughing. The crashing mug must have triggered his reaction. Pearl cringed against a memory—the worst Fourth of July in her life, huddled in a closet trying to convince her son, fresh from the war zone, that he was safe. Stepping over the ceramic pieces, she walked to the church with the lunch tray.

At the door of Pastor Thomas's study, she balanced the tray one-handed and tapped on the door. "Hello, I've come with a peace offering."

"Pearl?" Thomas opened the door. "Peace offering? What have you done now?" He gave a teasing wink. "Whatever it is, I forgive you. I'm starved."

She set the tray on his desk. Inhaling the scent of books and leather, an image played in her mind as tangible as the desk itself—Elliot poring over his Bible for the Sunday sermon.

"It appears I've run off your new groundskeeper."

Thomas sank into his desk chair. "What?"

"I—well, I'm not sure what happened, actually. But I startled him, and he left."

"Left?" Thomas stood and faced the window overlooking the green space between the church and Pearl's home.

"So, he *is* the new groundskeeper?"

Thomas turned and studied the rug beneath his feet, rubbing his hand through his dark hair. "In a manner of speaking. That is to say . . . not officially."

Pearl propped a hand on her hip and arched her brows. "I had a feeling this wasn't a board-approved hire."

"There was something about him. I can't explain it. I was *compelled* to offer him a job." Thomas walked back to his chair, motioning for Pearl to take the seat across from his desk. "You know the board doesn't trust my judgment, *whippersnapper* that I am. And even if they did, Harvey doesn't exactly fit the image of a prime candidate for the church staff. I couldn't turn him away . . ."

"And how exactly are you going to pay him?" Pearl eased into the chair and leaned in.

A mischievous glint lit his eyes. "I was going to save up my lunch money since you're so kind to feed me every day."

She smiled through the ache in her heart. "It's a forty-year-old habit, bringing lunch to the pastor's office. I'm a bit set in my ways."

"How are you doing? Truly?" He reached over and squeezed her wrinkled hand, his expression gentle and open.

She blinked and sniffled, pressing the emotion back down to the reservoir that faithfully held until someone asked that dreaded question. "I'm hanging in there. The Lord is with me, Pastor Thomas. He's near to the brokenhearted."

"That he is."

She nodded. He was. He really, really was. Didn't mean it didn't hurt though.

"Hello? Thom?" The cautious call pulled Pearl's gaze to the doorway. Miriam poked her head into the office, her hair a glorious cascade of red curls.

Pearl turned back to Thomas. Light filled his expression as he stood and crossed the room to kiss his wife's cheek. "Miriam, I wasn't expecting you today."

Pearl's heart squeezed. His adoration was so precious.

Miriam must turn heads everywhere she went with her flaming hair and that statuesque build of hers. She was what people call big-boned, but she had a breezy way of moving, like a runway model. It was her eyes, though, that pulled at Pearl's heart. Pale blueish-green, they were the saddest seascape she'd ever seen. Pearl didn't know Miriam's story, but she felt it in her presence. And it felt a lot like hers. Swirling loss that left her adrift.

"Come, sit. Join Pearl and me for lunch if you can spare the time."

"I have a few minutes." Miriam turned to her. "Hi, Pearl. How are you this afternoon?"

"Good, good. It's been interesting at least."

Miriam sat beside Pearl. "Oh?"

She handed Miriam a ham sandwich. "I accidentally ran off your husband's new hire."

"He showed?"

Thomas chuckled. "He did. Then this intimidating woman scared him away."

Pearl cut her gaze playfully in Thomas's direction. "Oh, hush. I was just keeping an eye on him. Mercy, he's an odd character."

"He certainly is nervous, the way he stares at the floor and disappears as soon as the conversation lulls." Thomas clicked the end of his pen against his desk. "So what do you say, Guardian of Triune First, did I make a mistake?"

Pearl lifted her shoulders, ignoring the ache settling in her joints. "I wanted to talk to you about that. He darted off every so often, talking to himself the whole time. At first I thought some addiction was the cause, but after meeting him, I think he may have an anxiety disorder."

Thomas leaned against the back of his desk chair. "What more can I do to help him?"

Pearl tapped her lips with a fingertip. "I can't figure him out. His odd manner. His clothes. The gigantic shirt he wore reminded me of those tent-like maternity shirts I wore back in the day."

Miriam stood abruptly, turned away from Pearl, her voice tight. "It's probably time I get out of here. I'm meeting a young woman that's been coming to the Pantry. What time—" She glanced at the still clock on the wall. The battery hadn't been replaced since Elliot passed.

Miriam's attention went to Thomas's wrist. "Did you forget your watch?"

He choked. "Something like that."

With her eyes narrowed, Miriam sidestepped toward the door. "Okay . . . I'll see you this evening."

The exchange was stiff, stilted—a full conversation underneath the few words. Swallowing a lump in her throat, Pearl traced her hand across the edge of what was once her husband's desk. What she would give to have that back—a language with another person only the two of them understood. Glances, posture, and tone.

Miriam offered a crooked smile before she slipped from the room. "Thank you for lunch, Pearl. Keep an eye on him. Don't let his bleeding heart get him into too much trouble."

"Will do," Pearl called out the door, her voice light. "Though I hope you'll make a habit of stopping by. We'd fare better if it was two against one."

A soft chuckle punctuated with the click of heels on hardwood floated back to her.

Miriam had abandoned her sandwich, one corner nibbled. Thomas, across from her, picked at the crust of his own uneaten lunch, eyes cast downward. The heartache in the room was palpable.

Thomas leaned forward in the chair, elbows propped on his knees. "What do you say? Will you help me figure out a way to help Harvey?"

Pearl managed an impish wink. "I'll be your accomplice. I just hope he comes back."

She'd promised Elliot she would keep an eye out for the people of Triune First, and something was off about this whole situation.

• CHAPTER •

TWELVE

PRESENT DAY

In the living room, Ivy tackled the film of dust on a vase with a vigor that threatened to rub a hole in the sturdy amber-colored glass.

"Maybe the cabinet lock was always damaged." Reese handed her some old newspaper.

She wrapped the vase and boxed it. "Mom and Dad never would give me straight answers whenever I asked about my adoption. What if they took it?"

Something flickered in Reese's expression. His mouth twitched like he was resisting the urge to speak.

"What?"

Reese opened his mouth and pulled in a breath, concern creasing his forehead. He sat on the couch, elbows propped on his knees. "Whatever your grandmother knew, I think they'd want you to know it too. It's not like you were born back when adoptions were kept secret."

"You don't know how tense they used to get whenever I asked about my life before they adopted me."

"Ivy, your parents are the most upstanding people I've ever met."

He thought she was losing her mind. Maybe she was.

"It's more than just this missing journal. It's the bits and pieces that never added up." Ivy tucked another newsprint-wrapped vase in the box and paced.

"Like?"

"Remember the story we overheard back when we were kids?"

Every Sunday Reese and Ivy would crawl under the pews after service with her Crayola Big Box while they waited for Mom and Dad to finish talking with lingering parishioners so they could have lunch and take Reese home. She'd write stories in robin's egg blue crayon and he'd illustrate.

One week Mrs. May had stood in the aisle chatting with her favorite gossip partner, Mrs. Coulter. "That Ivy is something."

Ivy's writing hand stilled, leaving her fearless heroine dangling above a toothy alligator, fate unknown. What was her latest indictment? Had she forgotten a page of her story on the front pew—the one where she wrote Mr. Coulter as a maniacal villain? Left the light on in one of the classrooms?

"It's hard to believe she's the same sickly baby left on a doorstep all those years ago."

An odd hum thrummed in Ivy's ears as her stomach clenched.

Mrs. Coulter had chimed in, voice hushed. "I still can't believe a mother could leave her wee babe without a by-your-leave."

Ivy paced around the oval coffee table and then sat for but a moment before repeating the circuit. "People don't actually abandon babies on doorsteps. That stuff is reserved for movie drama. It reeks of fake cover story—what if my parents invented it to keep people from asking questions because something was off about my adoption. And they made sure I never found out the truth."

"But you've seen your adoption paperwork. It confirmed everything."

"It called me a foundling. But what if that's just what they *told* the authorities?"

"So, what, Ivy? Your parents were kidnappers?" He crossed his arms over his chest. "Just talk to them."

The same thing always came out of his mouth whenever she questioned where she came from. He hadn't changed a bit from the day they'd overheard the gossip.

Sitting across from her at the pizza parlor after church that day, Reese had spent the entire meal nudging her pristine white stockings under the table with his ratty hand-me-down Nikes, clearing his throat in a pointed way.

She picked the grease-slicked pepperonis off her pizza, avoiding his begging gaze. As a kid, Reese was always straightforward. The proverbial bull in a china shop, he plowed ahead while Ivy tiptoed around corners to avoid breakage. Even at eight, she was burdened by an awareness of the delicate nature of things. Feelings. Hopes. Dreams. Families.

For reasons unknown, Ivy had been too much for her birth mother. She never again wanted to be too difficult. Or ungrateful. Or any of the hundred reasons her childhood imagination invented for being left behind.

Reese ran his hand through his hair. "If your grandma knew something all this time, I don't understand why she never said anything until now."

Ivy sank into the old wingback and traced her fingers over the raised brocade. "I don't know, but sometimes when Grandma looked at me, sadness flickered in her eyes. As though she wanted to say something. Especially when I got older."

Reese stood and continued packing the box with the glassware Grandma had bequeathed to Mrs. Benson, the retired secretary at the police department. "I still don't think your parents would have taken something Grandma wanted you to have."

Ivy stood from the chair and paced, tapping her finger against her chin. "What if Mrs. Benson knows something? Or one of the other people on her list. Maybe they remember something about the past. Something bad enough that someone wants it to stay buried." Ivy walked across the room and flicked off the living room lights.

"Ivy . . ."

"You coming?"

• ● •

It was a mystery why Grandma thought Mrs. Benson needed more glassware. Depression-era moon and star glass graced almost every flat surface in the woman's home, including a curio-cabinetful in the corner. The afternoon sun spilled through her windows and glinted off the rainbow of colors. A hint of cinnamon and allspice floated in the air.

"Come in. Come in." The short, plump lady motioned Reese and Ivy in with the vigor of one who hadn't had a houseguest in years. "I've got an apple pie cooling, if y'all want to stop in for a spell."

Perfect. Dessert and company would be just the thing to get the woman talking.

"Pearl was the sweetest thing. She and Mother were such dear friends. So kind of her to have set something aside for me." A wistful smile stretched Mrs. Benson's age-lined face.

Ivy set the box on the cushion of the worn microfiber couch. "Her collection of moon and star glassware." She sent Mrs. Benson a wink. "For some reason, she thought you might want this."

Mrs. Benson slid the lid from the cardboard filing box and removed the packing paper. "Oh my. Some of these were part of my mother's collection at one time. She'd gifted them to your grandma. So sweet of Pearl to remember." She flashed them a watery smile. "Would the two of you like some pie?"

Reese crossed his arms over his chest. "Ivy, don't you think we ought to—"

Ivy cut off the rest of his excuse with the heel of her sandal on his toe. "We'd love a slice."

Mrs. Benson tottered to the kitchen with Reese and Ivy in her wake.

"I actually had a question for you about something Grandma left for me."

Mrs. Benson glanced over her shoulder. "I'll help if I can. Let me get us all situated and we can chat."

Reese and Ivy sat in the vinyl seats at her Formica dining table. Mrs. Benson hummed softly as she sliced her pie. Ivy wiped her palms on her thighs. Reese shot her a look she couldn't decipher. Probably considering having her committed.

Or he was annoyed because he actually had somewhere important to be besides assisting her unlikely interrogation.

Mrs. Benson slid two Corelle saucers their way, the same butterfly gold print on the rims as Ivy's grandmother's. "This was my mom's recipe. What I would give to make one more apple pie with her."

Ivy averted her gaze and blinked back the moisture that welled in her eyes without warning.

Mrs. Benson settled into a vacant chair. "Now what was it you wanted to ask me about? One of her antiques? I do love discovering origins of things from days gone by. There's this show on television where people bring in old stuff to find its value. I'm an absolute addict."

"It's about my adoption."

Mrs. Benson's fork stilled. "Your adoption? What does that have to do with your grandmother?"

Ivy leaned in. "She told me she left me a journal, but it's missing. I think it's about my adoption. Do you remember Grandma coming to you about anything unusual when you worked at the police department? Any specifics about my adoption? Something someone would want kept hidden?"

Compassion—or perhaps pity—softened Mrs. Benson's look of concentration. She reached across the table and squeezed Ivy's hand. "No, honey. Your arrival in Triune sure shook the town up though. I'll never forget the stir that caused."

"My parents, they told the police I arrived on their doorstep?"

Mrs. Benson shifted in her seat and picked at her acrylic nails. "Yes, dear. Not much more was ever discovered. But if you've got questions, you ought to talk to them, sweetie."

Mrs. Benson picked up her fork and rolled the stem between her fingers, eyes focused beyond Ivy. "Hold on, now. There was this one time your grandma called, asking questions about a young woman. A potential missing person. I only remember because it was such an odd conversation. That was a while before you showed up though, so I doubt it was connected. More likely she'd been watching too many *Unsolved Mystery* shows. I figured a story got ahold of her, and she wanted to do something to help. She was like that, you know, always searching for a way to help the hurting."

• CHAPTER •

THIRTEEN

SEPTEMBER 12, 1994

On Monday Harvey stood at the end of Pearl's sidewalk. The morning sun filtered through the trees, splotching the yard with oak leaf shadows.

He straightened his shoulders, ensured his large shirt didn't cling to Ivy's sleeping form, and trudged down the cracked concrete path. All he had to do was ring the doorbell, apologize, and then hand her the replacement mug. Like a normal person.

His sandaled feet echoed too loud on the concrete porch. The cord of muscles down the length of his spine tightened. He reached toward the doorbell, index finger out. An inch from the glowing button, he froze. Harvey curled his finger into a fist, squeezing his hand so tight his knuckles whitened.

Breathe in. *Normal person.* Breathe out. He jabbed the button. A tinny song burst through the interior of the house, faintly muffled by the door.

Nope. He couldn't do this. Harvey placed the mug on the weathered yellow table and made a quick retreat.

"Harvey?"

So much for his attempted doorbell dash. Turning slowly, his pulse throbbed in his ears. "Uh . . ."

A smile lit Pearl's face. "Good morning. I'm so glad you stopped by. I wanted to apologize for what happened Friday."

The back of his neck heated. She didn't have anything to apologize for. Without his consent, his feet traveled back down the walk to the old woman in her threadbare pink bunny slippers. One was missing a black button eye.

"No . . . I . . . I'm . . . I brought you a cup." *I'm sorry.* He closed his eyes for a beat. Why didn't his words ever come out right?

She picked up the mug, white with a black bear and the words THE GREAT SMOKY MOUNTAINS in curling script. A hairline crack ran the length of the handle. Pearl pressed a hand to her chest. "Oh, Harvey. You didn't have to replace it. I wish you hadn't troubled yourself. It was just a mug."

Harvey swallowed hard. "I didn't mean to"—he gestured to the place the ceramic had shattered—"leave the mess. I—"

Pearl held up a hand, tenderness in her eyes. "Please. You don't have to explain. I barge around here, flinging open doors and pouncing on unsuspecting visitors." She held the coffee cup toward him. "You don't have to do this. I have plenty."

Idiot. She didn't want a stupid cracked mug, not when he'd broken one in perfect condition. Heat spread from his neck to the tips of his ears, then radiated off the top of his head.

If only he could vanish into thin air. But he and his humiliation remained a fixed presence on Pearl's front porch.

Pearl tilted her head, then she pulled the mug to her chest, stepping toward him. "On second thought, I'll hang on to this if you truly don't mind. When you come by, this can be yours. I always like to pick a favorite mug to match my mood. This one I'll keep and think of you."

His heart pounded as the porch ceiling closed down on him. The space between them narrowed as she took another step.

It was just a coffee cup. Admittedly, the best of his hodge-podge dish collection, but it was only his pathetic attempt at making amends. Not some sort of representation of him.

She reached for his shoulder, and he went rigid. Instead of touching him, she lowered her outstretched arm to her side and stepped back, her eyes searching his face. Pearl lifted the cup. "How about a cup of coffee? I made a fresh pot."

She reentered her house before he had the chance to answer. Great. This wasn't supposed to be the start of a morning tradition.

Harvey tugged his collar away from his chest and stole a peek at sleeping Ivy. It was so much easier over the weekend when it was just the two of them. Tucked away where he didn't have to worry about anyone finding out about her.

Wait. Was that why Pearl was being so nice? She suspected something and was drawing him closer to discover why he had Ivy. Then she'd turn him in for having a baby that didn't belong to him. He went from burning with embarrassment to ice cold.

Pearl appeared, this time gently opening the door. She stepped to him, full coffee cup outstretched. There was such warmth in her expression that Harvey swallowed his dark thought and reached to receive the mug.

"Would you like to stay for breakfast? I have country ham and eggs frying."

Harvey edged backward though the scent wafting from the front door made his mouth water. "I . . ."

"We could eat out here if you're more comfortable."

A loud and rude noise came from Ivy's diaper area. Harvey gulped and cringed as the place she rested warmed.

"Are you all right?" Pearl's forehead creased.

There was no way she hadn't heard. "Excuse me. My . . . my stomach. Another time." Teeth clenched, he turned and walked away, the scalding coffee sloshing over the rim as he hurried around the side of the church. He walked over the crest into the gully, his normal hideaway to feed and change Ivy.

Without quick work the diaper wouldn't hold. He set the cup on the ground and threw out her blanket in a cleared spot in the undergrowth. "Ivy Rose, I'm beginning to think you've been sent for the sole purpose of stripping me of every ounce of my pride." At least he was getting faster at changing her.

She gurgled and stared up at him while he replaced her diaper. Her eyes held a depth he could swim in.

"So, little wise one, what's going to become of the two of us?"

• ● •

Pearl watched for Harvey from her kitchen window while she washed her breakfast dish. Hopefully he was feeling better. What a shame his anxiety was so bad it affected his digestion.

Her mind flashed to the pain on his face when she'd tried to give the mug back. Rejected. The impulse to hug him in that moment had been strong enough to send tears to her eyes. Pastor Thomas was right. There was something compelling about the man.

Harvey had a way about him that reminded her of her boy, Marshall, the time he wandered off at the county fair. She saw her child before he noticed her. He spun in a slow circle with a lost look in his eyes, scanning faces for the one he belonged to.

But Harvey wasn't a little boy. He was a tall, strange, rough-around-the-edges man.

She bowed her head.

Lord, give me wisdom. I thought I knew how to help Marshall after he got back from combat. But I didn't understand. I missed things I should have seen. And the cost . . . Oh, Lord, forgive me. Help me know how to help Harvey. Help me lead him to your peace.

The sound of the rusty wheelbarrow screeched through her open window. It was loaded down with stray limbs and weeds from the flower beds. Harvey's stooped-shoulder stride reminded her of a cowed dog with its tail tucked. As though he tried to make himself smaller than he was. His toes were going to get injured in those sandals he wore.

She turned from the sink and went to the room she only entered once a month to dust. It looked the same as the day of Marshall's funeral. All his memorabilia, uniforms, and clothes neatly arranged. The tattered teddy bear he'd had since childhood sat propped in the corner chair.

Marshall had moved in with them after his second deployment, a rescue mission in Somalia, so he could heal.

As it turned out, some war injuries couldn't be seen. She hadn't understood the depth of Marshall's wounds until it was too late.

Blinking back tears, she dug in the closet, pulling out a box she'd shoved to the back. A Christmas gift her son never had the chance to open.

Pearl held the boots in front of her. They seemed the right size. But would Harvey accept them?

FOURTEEN

PRESENT DAY

After leaving Mrs. Benson's, Ivy slumped against the passenger seat of Reese's truck, the wind gone out of her like a deflated balloon.

Reese closed the truck door on his side. At the heavy metallic clank, Ivy jerked her head in his direction.

"Sorry. Old Bessie lacks refinement, but I can't bear to part with her."

Ivy was with him the day he bought the truck off an old farmer. He'd worked two summers to earn it. Reese had driven around, narrow teenage chest puffed out, proud as could be of that ugly orange and white truck. He'd likely drive the thing until it wouldn't run anymore. Old Bessie gave Reese his first taste of freedom from the family who had too many kids and not enough love or resources to go around.

Ivy shrugged. "I'm just a little frazzled." She pulled the faded gray seat belt across her chest as the engine cranked.

The summer they were sixteen the two of them rode all over the county every day of Ivy's monthlong stay. Ivy didn't think a thing about it until Lilah Hudson cornered her after youth group and told her to stay away from Reese. That it wasn't fair for Ivy to swoop in and steal one of the few guys worth dating in that town.

She'd laughed off Lilah's jealousy at first. Ivy and Reese had never been more than friends. But the truth was, Lilah's words woke something sleeping—how hard Ivy had fallen for Reese without even knowing. From that day on, Ivy checked her heart at the door to protect their friendship. She'd never quite forgiven Lilah Hudson for stealing the automatic ease she'd felt in Reese's presence.

"Hey, Earth to Ivy."

Ivy shook herself. She'd been staring out the windshield unseeing, the idling truck a distant rumble.

"Whatcha thinking about?"

Warmth bloomed in her cheeks. "Nothing."

A curtain slid back into place within the house. Reese's low chuckle filled the truck cab. "I think somebody was keeping an eye on us." He elbowed her and gave her a wry grin. "You do know that this whole town had big plans for us back in the day. We were their greatest disappointment."

She forced a laugh. Maybe if she skipped over the last thing he said, it would go away. Her battered heart might spill out words she'd regret. "There's always somebody watching in this little town. Somebody has to know what happened to the journal. Or about the secrets Grandma kept."

He covered her hand with his. "We'll figure it out. I still think it was a misunderstanding. Surely someone took it by mistake, or your grandma moved it and forgot. Seriously, call your parents. Or your uncle. No one was closer to your grandma than him."

She slipped her hand away and tucked it under her thigh. "Maybe." But even the thought of exhuming those long-buried conversations squeezed air from her lungs.

When eight-year-old Ivy had finally gotten the nerve to ask about the gossip she'd overheard, her parents had glanced between each other, eyes filled with worry. Their pauses and expressions spoke a thousand things Ivy couldn't decipher.

Suffocating under the weight of the discomfort she'd brought to the room, Ivy had shut down the conversation almost as soon as she started it.

Ivy pulled her phone from her bag, running her fingers over the smooth rim.

Reese put the truck in gear and pulled out of Mrs. Benson's gravel drive. "Just consider it, okay? What if the answer to all this mystery surrounding your adoption is you finding the courage to ask?"

As he drove on, she stared at the wild daylilies growing along the ditches. Blurred orange beacons among all the green.

It sounded simple. But Reese didn't understand.

Tiptoeing, Ivy had spent her entire life trying not to step on any fragile feelings. Her parents chose her. She wanted to be the perfect choice. For them. She winced. For Seth.

And he had chipped away at her heart bit by bit, taking pieces so small she didn't notice at first. By the time the ache registered, she believed the lie—the person he wanted her to be was better than the person she was.

Ivy didn't know who she was anymore. She had been reaching and striving to be who she imagined everyone expected her to be, like a caterpillar gone into a cocoon. Not to transform—to hide.

Was it possible to resurrect the little girl who ran around her grandma's yard chasing fireflies until even they went to bed? If only she could go back in time—return to that cozy world, perpetually sheltered by her mismatched family.

The truck slowed as Reese pulled into a parking lot.

By the time she registered the clank of Reese's door shutting, he was standing outside hers. Why had they stopped at Carla's Cafe? Her door swung open with a groan.

Ivy pushed off her seat to hop out, but her seat belt was still attached and yanked her back.

A snort slipped from Reese, and she cut him a glare.

"Seriously, Ivy. Are you okay?" To his credit, he gave a valiant effort at remaining somber.

Something about the expression on his face, the juxtaposition of genuine concern and irrepressible mirth, swept her in a wave of laughter that left her gasping. She braced her hands on her knees, shoulders shaking.

He reached through the space between her arms and stomach. Ivy gasped at his nearness. "Reese, what are you—" Her laughter-doused words were cut off by a yelp as he unhooked the seat belt and leaned her over his broad shoulder like a sack of potatoes. "Put me down." Blood rushed to her head.

His frame shook with laughter. "No, woman. I'm gonna get some of Carla's miracle-working chocolate cake in you before you break down on me."

"I'm fine."

"Sure, you're fine. I've been with you for a few hours and you've gone weak-kneed, accused your parents of illegal activity, stared out the window like I wasn't there, and then you tried to jump out of my truck with your seat belt on." He let out a snort with the last sentence.

It occurred to her that a crowd could be witnessing her, rear end skyward, being marched into Carla's Cafe. "Seriously, put me down." Dangling, she watched his work boots stride on the asphalt.

"Nope."

"Put me—" Her words were cut off as Reese's toe caught on a pothole. Ivy shrieked.

Using a leftover skill set from his football days, knowing how to navigate a fall, he ended up on his back with Ivy across his chest like he'd been about to carry her across a threshold. Ivy scrambled off him. Reese sat up. A funny groan came out of him, the involuntary sound a person makes when they've had their wind knocked out.

Ivy knelt. A flutter danced in her chest when his hazel eyes flashed open, and he gained a solid breath.

Heat radiated from the sunbaked asphalt. A bead of sweat rolled down the bridge of her nose. "You okay, Number 28?"

A corner of his mouth curled when she used his old nickname. "Yep." He winced as he stood. "You all right?"

"Now that you've felt the weight of me, you know I definitely don't need any chocolate cake to wash down my apple pie."

The half-smile dropped from his face. "Don't do that."

She shrugged. "Do what?"

His eyes searched hers. "You're not that girl." He held out his hand and pulled her to stand.

He had no idea who she was. Sure, he'd met other versions of her—from before Seth. When she didn't have to constantly count calories to ensure the formfitting cocktail dresses selected for her always fit. Was it normal to segment one's life like that—before a person comes into your life and after they're gone from it?

"Let's go inside. It's hotter than blue blazes out here." Reese didn't let go of her hand for the first stride toward the glass door, so she slid her sweaty hand from his and stuffed it into her back pocket, giving it somewhere to go that made sense.

FIFTEEN

SEPTEMBER 18, 1994

Sunday morning, Miriam lay in bed, thick drapes drawn tight. One thin sunbeam insisted on peeking through, spilling light in the darkness. She blew into a tissue, wadded it, and added it to the pile on her nightstand. Thomas's disappointment that morning burned in her mind. But she hadn't been able to bring herself to put on the mask and smile through church today.

She groaned and sat up, fluffy comforter pulled up under her chin. It was too hard, playing the part of dutiful pastor's wife, smiling and praying for others. How could she beseech God for burdens to be lifted from others when her own had kept her secluded in her home for the past three days?

Most of the time she could pull it off. Nice clothes, fresh makeup, and a pasted smile. She pushed her red curls gone rogue back from her face.

Other days were too dark. Too heavy.

Miriam dragged herself out of bed and stepped out of the

darkened bedroom, blinking in the bright morning light. Her footfall was leaden as she walked down the stairs.

A blueberry bagel with cream cheese and a vase with a single wildflower waited on the kitchen table. There was a note.

Hey sweetheart,

   Eat something, okay? Coffee is on the warmer in the kitchen. I love you, and I'm praying for you this morning. I'll come home later this afternoon, after service. A walk together, maybe? It almost feels like fall this morning. Our first true fall in the eastern US. I can't wait for the colors.

                    Always yours,
                    Thomas

His graciousness made everything harder. She could picture his hopeful expression, optimistic she was turning a corner, so sure she was learning to let go of the past to start living in the present. It'd be better if he yelled—showered her with righteous anger. It would give her something to fight other than herself. She nibbled at the bagel and then went for the coffee.

Thomas meant well by trying to nudge her out of her funk, but he didn't understand. The desire wasn't the same for him. What if he'd been told he couldn't pastor, his lifelong dream? Would it be so easy then?

She dumped the half-eaten bagel in the trash and poured her sipped coffee in the sink. Maybe a movie was the distraction she needed to get her head in a better place.

The comfort of her bed called as she trudged back up the stairs. Grabbing her bedroom's doorknob, a magnet-like impulse pulled her attention to the room at the end of the hall. The forlorn space where she kept the things Thomas couldn't know about, hidden among other miscellaneous items that hadn't found their place in the new home. The non-necessities.

The door was cracked and light from the east-facing window spilled out a sunbeam where the dust particles of the old house danced. Calling her.

She let go of the knob and turned. She shouldn't go in there, not if she planned on being in a good place when Thomas returned. The purposeless room pulled harder than reason.

That room was her reality.

Miriam unstacked three boxes and opened the one on the bottom. With trembling hands she lifted out the white cube tied with a mint green ribbon.

She returned to the rug and tugged the crumpled ribbon she had tied and retied a hundred times. She lifted the knit baby hat, creamy yellow, made of the softest yarn she'd ever touched. Pressing it to her face, Miriam savored all the hope she'd felt once upon a time. She placed it on the rug and pulled out the matching booties.

With each piece laid out on the rug, about the length her baby might have been from head to toe, she stared at the empty space between, unable to complete the mental image. She shook her head and then swiped the booties and hat into a tiny pile.

Miriam had promised Thomas she wouldn't buy baby things. Wouldn't make things harder on herself. For years she kept that promise, but the hat and booties in the boutique window had caught her attention on the way back from an afternoon appointment.

Everything had looked positive that time around. She'd prayed and felt like the Lord had told her she'd have a child, and this was their last embryo. So she'd purchased the set, every day imagining bringing home her baby from the hospital in the yellow hat and booties. Every day for one week, and then she found out the procedure hadn't taken after all. She'd never told Thomas about the box.

She crammed the baby things back inside, tied the ribbon, and pushed the package aside. It was stupid, the way she hung on to them. She was never going to have children, and the hopefulness attached to the box needed to go. The gift belonged at the Pantry. The baby things should go where they'd have purpose.

That could be her first step to freedom. But if she released this symbol of her dream, would she come apart at the seams?

Miriam knew all the right verses in Scripture. She'd memorized the verse about peace that passes all understanding, but all she felt was the weight of depression. She knew how the Lord worked together all things for the good of those who loved him, but she felt forsaken.

She pressed her palms to her eyes. It was time to let go of the baby things. She'd take them tomorrow. Maybe if she went through the right motions long enough, she'd break free. Miriam tucked the box into the folds of an extra quilt and walked to the bathroom.

The reflection stared back with red-rimmed eyes and dull skin. Hair mussed. Nothing makeup and hair product wouldn't hide. Miriam splashed cool water on her face and began putting on her makeup. When she was finished, she practiced smiling in the mirror until she thought it might pass for genuine.

The front door creaked open. Thomas. She slipped into her closet to dress. Miriam paused for a few breaths and then walked down the stairs. He sat folded, with his elbows propped on his knees, staring at the floor between his feet.

Miriam fixed her smile in place. "Hey, sweetheart. How was service?"

He jumped up and stood with a peppy smile of his own. "Miri. How are you?"

"Better. How about we take that walk."

"Sounds perfect."

Had he spent as much time practicing his smile as she had? Were either of them convinced?

●　●　●

Monday afternoon, Miriam got out of the car at the church. A man fumbled pansies from their plastic planters and mashed them into tiny holes in the sidewalk flower beds with his large hands. He must be Thomas's new hire. She checked to make sure her husband wasn't near and carried the box into the single mothers' pantry. The box was strangely heavy for such paltry contents.

Inside, she placed it on the shelf. Rearranged it. Turned it catty-corner and then straight. Unsatisfied, she moved it to the other side of the room on a higher shelf.

She sat and shuffled through her files, checking off the names of the program members. The church hoped in the future they'd have more classes and assistance to offer. Structuring all that had somehow landed on her. She tapped her pen on the desk. Ashley, the teen mother she had met with, mentioned wanting to learn how to cook simple healthy meals. There might be more with the same need. Cooking, with its predictable ingredients, steps, and outcomes, was the sort of thing she could handle. Maybe she'd have someone to pass her mother's recipes to after all.

Miriam glanced up from her work. The box stared back. The thought of one of the young women taking it home for their own child ought to make her heart swell, but it stiffened her spine.

The hat and booties were supposed to be for *her* baby. She heaved a breath, went to pick up the box, covered it in the trash, and headed for her car before she could change her mind.

She could have sworn she heard a baby cry as she closed the car door. Did she still have the number for her therapist back in California? Auditory hallucinations had to be a sure sign she was in desperate need for a phone session.

• • •

The next morning, Thomas stood in the bedroom doorway in jeans and a polo, coffee in hand. "Come on, Miri. Let's have a nice day together. I took the day off."

Miriam rolled away from him and tightened her grip on the blanket pulled up to her chin. "I didn't ask you to." *I can't be what you want. Not today.*

Footsteps approached and then the edge of the mattress compressed with his weight.

"Throw on your sweats. Let's find a hole-in-the-wall diner for breakfast and then take a drive."

She turned toward him. "Sweats? Are you out of your mind?"

His lips stretched into his poster-worthy smile. "I counted on that getting a response."

"I'm not in the mood. Please. I just want to be alone." Alone with the ache of leaving the precious emblem of her baby dreams sitting in the trash. To relive the feeling of walking away. It was pathetic, her wallowing, but there was nothing else left to cling to.

Thomas rested his hand on her blanketed shoulder. "I'm worried about you. I thought things were getting better. But you've been acting so strange since yesterday."

Miriam shrugged away from his touch. "I went on a walk with you on Sunday."

"Yes. Twenty minutes out of the house two days ago. If you won't go out, at least talk to me."

The plea in his voice, and his dogged pursuit, crashed against the crumbling walls around her heart. Her eyes teared as she sat up. "You wouldn't understand."

He set his coffee on the side table and took her in his arms, tucking her head under his chin. The beating of his heart was solid and steady. His voice muffled in her hair as he said, "You might be right, but at least give me the chance. Let me in."

"It's not pretty."

"I didn't ask for pretty, Miriam. I'm asking for real."

Her chin quivered, and her words came out a blubbered mess. "Why are you so nice? You should lose your patience. Get angry."

"I'm not so great." He kissed the top of her head. "The way I figure it, we all fall apart sometime or another. What

I'm doing is selfish, really. I'm taking care of you so when I go off the deep end, you'll be there to catch me."

She pulled back to look into his eyes, tears trickling down her cheeks.

He winked.

"You're terrible." Her voice came out as a whisper.

He sobered. "Us not being able to have children? It's troubling you again, isn't it?"

As if it had ever stopped. With a shuddered sniffle, she retreated into the cocoon of his arms.

"Miri . . ." He said it in that knowing tone of his.

She shook her head against his chest. But he spoke anyway.

"Childbirth isn't the only way to grow our family."

"Stop. I've heard your adoption speech. I get that fostering and adopting are beautiful things. But I've dreamed of motherhood since I was a little girl, and it wasn't by raising another person's child." She sat up, edging away.

He placed a hand on her shoulder. "Life doesn't always go—"

"Thomas. I get it. You ought to know. Your scheme to fix your wife failed. You left your dream job for her, and your new job is sucking the life out of you. And then your wife went off the deep end anyway." Miriam turned her head away and stared out the window. The quivering of her chin bent the stubborn set of her mouth downward.

He placed a thumb to her turned cheek, pulling her back to him. "Honey, we aren't talking about me right now. We're talking about you. If we're going to move forward, it's important we ease our clutch on our own plans in order to see what wonderful things God has for our future."

Grief welled in her throat, thick and hot. "I just can't. I

can't foster a child. I'd look at them every day knowing they were plan B in my life." She sucked back the sobs spilling out between her words. "It wouldn't be fair . . ." The last of it rolled out, lost in a mournful sound.

"Oh, Miri." Thomas pulled her back against his chest and rubbed slow circles on her back. "I'm here for you. I'll walk with you as long as it takes. I know you can't see it yet, but I have faith God is somehow going to heal what feels impossible. I don't know how or when, but please, I just need you to be honest with me."

She nodded against his chest.

"And, since you brought it up, yes, the church work is not going as well as I'd hoped, but let me be clear. I don't care if this congregation ever accepts me or if you ever decide you want to foster or adopt a child as much as I would like to. I don't care about the church we left behind in California. All that matters to me is that you and I are together, and that we give this mess to Jesus. Even if it isn't pretty right now. Are you hearing me?"

"Yes," she whispered.

"Can we please go for a drive? Even a short one. I promise you don't have to say a word. Just come with me."

• CHAPTER •

SIXTEEN

PRESENT DAY

Reese parked in front of Grandma's house as the setting sun painted the sky pink.

Ivy hurried out of the vehicle to avoid a repeat performance of the seat belt debacle. She retrieved her duffel bag from the back seat of her raggedy sedan.

"You're going to be all right? Staying here alone?"

She scuffed the bottom of her sandal against the gravel and fixed a smile on her face. "Of course. It's not like I believe in ghosts. Although being haunted by Grandma could actually be pretty entertaining."

He chuckled and followed her to the porch. His laugh held a warmth she'd like to wrap herself in. Ivy paused in front of the door, shifting her weight between her feet. She didn't want to be alone. Not in this house. Not anywhere. She wanted somebody to put their arms around her and tell her everything was going to be okay. *No.* The fact was, everything didn't have to be okay. She just wanted to know if *she* could be okay again.

"Uh, Reese?"

His head jerked up from where he'd been studying the cracks in the sidewalk.

"Do you . . . do you want to come in?"

He took a step forward, then stopped. "It's probably better if I didn't." He spoke in a low tone she almost didn't catch.

Her face heated. She'd already taken up so much of his time. The guy had a life beyond checking up on her uncle and escorting her around town digging up information from her past. "Sorry. I took up your whole day, didn't I?"

"It's not a problem. If you need anything, I'm just a phone call away."

The first firefly of the night winked underneath the old oak tree in the churchyard.

"Hey, Reese?"

"Yeah?" He rubbed his index finger over his thumbnail. An old nervous habit.

"I'm sorry I haven't been myself. That I . . . that I let us grow apart this past year. I just . . ."

He backed toward the edge of the porch. His mouth curved upward, but the look in his eyes made her heart heavy. "Don't worry about it. I'll see you tomorrow morning? Is nine okay?"

"Yeah, sure. Nine."

The truck cranked to life and rambled down the gravel drive in a cloud of dust.

Ivy reached in her purse for the house key. Her hand landed on gum wrappers, a few loose dollars, her car key.

Everything but the key to the front door.

Only me.

When Ivy closed her eyes, she saw the key, clear as day, next to the porcelain lady with a basket full of flowers in the crook of her arm.

She checked all Grandma's old hiding spaces—under the ceramic frog who perched in the flower beds and inside the hollow log next to the shed.

Defeated, Ivy sank onto the porch swing and ran her finger around the cool metallic rim of her phone, resisting the itch to call Reese. There was nothing he could do. Besides, after Seth, she was done being someone's charity case. She shouldn't let someone have that kind of hold over her again.

There was one last place she hadn't checked. The church office maintained a drawer with spare keys to all the outbuildings, including Grandma's house. At least it used to. The door to the church basement used to have a trick to it. She could get in if they hadn't replaced the lock.

Ivy hiked across the wide churchyard, darkness quickly falling. She never would've imagined that at twenty-four, she'd be back in Triune traipsing about in the near darkness to break into her old church.

Crickets and bullfrogs cried out their alarm. The wind whipped the leaves and the retreating sun cast dancing shadows across the grass. Ivy shivered. An eerie sensation spiderwaltzed up her spine. She jogged over to the basement door and jiggled the knob.

Headlight beams bounced down the drive. Ivy froze.

Reese's orange truck rolled into view.

Unable to hide her harebrained plan, she walked to the driveway.

He pulled to a stop with the window down. "Ivy, I spotted your key on the floor of the passenger side. Must have fallen out of your purse." His brows arched to impossible heights. "What are you doing all the way over here?"

Her face flamed. "I was going to see if I could still pick the lock on the church basement. Or . . . or get in through the defunct crawl space hatch to see if there was still a spare key inside."

"This was your solution, instead of just calling me?" An edge in his tone betrayed a hurt deeper than the present circumstance.

Ivy shrugged. "I thought the key was inside. There was no use bothering you over it."

He shook his head. "Except I might have helped. Like being able to tell you *I* had the key. I tried to call—"

"My purse is on the porch."

He squinted, peering through the windshield. "Is that where it's been all the times I tried to call over the past year?"

Her lips parted.

Reese massaged his forehead. "Sorry. None of my business." He held his hand out the window, the key resting in his palm.

Ivy reached for the offered key. When she grasped it, his larger hand closed over hers. Ivy's pulse took off like she'd been shot out of a rocket. She yanked her hand free, startled. Her stomach rebelled.

He tilted his head. "What's up with you?"

"I guess I'm a little jumpy, being out here alone in the dark."

"It's more than that. It's the way you . . ." He released a heavy sigh. "At least let me give you a ride down the drive."

She didn't want to say yes, but her knees were gelatin. Ivy longed to borrow his strength. To have someone sort through the mess inside her head.

Reese would. He'd hold her. Even find Seth and throttle him if she asked him to. But that was the problem with Reese. He was too good and too nice. And he couldn't fix her, no matter how much he might want to.

Inside the house, her thoughts roamed in a disorganized jumble of past, present, and future. She pulled her phone from her purse. It wasn't that late. Mom and Dad would be awake. Reese was right. She should get up the nerve and call.

Her knee bounced up and down.

The phone vibrated in her hand. The notification sucked the oxygen from her chest.

> I gave you a year and a half of my life. The least you could do is have an adult conversation with me. Instead, you skipped town and changed your number. If I want you, you're not that difficult to find. Save us some time and call me.

Heart pounding, Ivy dialed Cheryl's number.

"Hey, Ivy. You settling in all right?"

"How did Seth get my number?"

Cheryl groaned. "He contacted you?"

"Just now."

"Did you have him down as your emergency contact at the school? If you didn't change it, somebody probably gave it to him. You and I both know he can concoct whatever story he needs to get what he wants."

"I didn't even think about changing my emergency info."

"Whatever you do, don't call him."

Would he really track her here? Was there any chance she could call him and he'd really let her go? That the nightmare could really be over?

She ended the call with Cheryl and dialed, her fingers flying over the digits etched in her memory. The phone thrummed in her ear. Her throbbing pulse slowed.

"Hey, sweetheart."

Ivy released the breath she held. Somehow the sound of his voice always calmed her, clearing her racing thoughts no matter what she faced. Ivy relaxed into the sofa. "Hey, Uncle Vee. I didn't wake you, did I?"

"Nope. Just finished unpacking and now I'm kicked back reading that Robert Frost anthology you bought me. What are you up to?"

"I'm in town taking care of some things for Grandma. Would you like to come over and have dinner tomorrow? Like old times?"

He'd lived in Grandma's house for as long as she'd known him. Always so devoted to making sure she was cared for. Ivy wasn't the only one whose world had been turned upside down over the past several weeks.

Grandma always said that when the world was shaky you should stick close to the people you love. Advice Ivy had ignored for far too long.

SEVENTEEN

September 20, 1994

Harvey walked along Church Street humming a tune, the slight chill in the air hinting at fall's approach. A smile snuck up on him. He'd carved the twelfth tally mark into the tree last night. Twelve days he'd succeeded in keeping Ivy safe.

As odd as it was, he was getting the hang of the little arrangement. The pastor kept to himself, so if Ivy happened to fuss, no one was around to take notice other than the elderly lady. And as long as she did her watching from inside the house, he didn't worry about her hearing Ivy's rare cry. Of course, it would be easier if the woman stopped trying to be so nice and left him alone.

He pulled his collar away and smiled down at Ivy. She wasn't colicky like some of the babies from foster care. As long as he kept her fed and changed on schedule, she was an angel. It was almost as if she was as determined as he was to keep up this charade.

Sunlight winked in the dew as he rounded the final bend

in the road. As always, he ensured his shirt was draped and didn't cling to Ivy before climbing the church stairs.

The door was locked. He knocked. After shifting on the landing for a bit, he went around to the back door. Also locked. Now what?

"Yoo-hoo! Harvey!" Pearl waved him over from her front porch.

A weight slid from his shoulders and rested heavy in his chest. He muttered softly to Ivy. "All right, stay quiet and be still so she doesn't think I have an alien growing in my gut." He walked to Pearl.

"Pastor Thomas won't be coming in today and asked me to watch for you. He hated that you'd have to come all this way, but he didn't have your phone number."

"Oh. All right." He took a step back, ready to pivot on his heel.

"Wait, Harvey. He doesn't have a list for you, but the trash is supposed to run this afternoon. Would you be a dear and empty the trash cans into the dumpster around back before you go? He said he'd pay you for the full day." Her hand trembled as she held out the key.

He nodded and took it from her, trying to decipher the pinched expression on her face.

Thrilled with the prospect of spending the rest of the day with Ivy, worry-free, he turned toward the church.

"Harvey." His name came out so abruptly it was as though it had pressed against her lips and jumped out against her will.

He faced her, and his heart did an odd stutter step in his chest at the moisture glistening in her eyes.

Her bunny-slippered feet shifted on the porch. "I'll be

right back. I have something for you. I've been meaning to give it to you. But, well, wait right there." She disappeared into the house.

Pearl was always cheery and overly kind. But today she seemed on edge. He felt an odd sort of kinship with her evident anxiety. While he waited, he coached himself on a calm and polite response, no matter what she offered.

She emerged from the house holding a pair of new work boots in front of her chest. "I'd like you to have these, if they're the right size."

The soft quaver in her voice drew him forward. He held out his hands. A breath she must have been holding rushed out of her, and the creases around her eyes relaxed as she placed the boots in his hands.

"These are awful nice. Are you sure?"

She shrugged. "You'd be doing me a favor. They've been sitting at the back of a closet. Boots like these are supposed to be used."

"Uh . . ." He glanced down at the boots. They were just a pair of boots, but the sound of her voice made it seem as if they had a heart and soul of their own.

"Harvey, please?" Her voice a whisper.

He managed a nod. "Yes, ma'am. Thank you." He checked the boot size. Eleven. He swallowed. "They're my size."

Her smile trembled at the corners. "I've got things inside to tend to. Have a good day."

He paused, his equilibrium off-kilter. He was the one who was supposed to be trying to get away before he lost control.

Harvey unlocked the church and walked through the handful of classrooms, emptying and replacing the trash bags. The classrooms had that old elementary school smell.

No matter where he was placed over the years, the classrooms always smelled the same—books, glue, and something indefinable. He studied the crafts on the wall. Men in tunics and sandaled feet. One with a big boat and a lot of animals.

He continued on to Pastor Thomas's study. His desk was impeccable, a mirror of the man himself. There were only a handful of wadded papers in the bottom of the wastebasket. Harvey picked them out and placed them in the larger bag.

Ivy squirmed against his chest. He unbuttoned the large shirt and left it open. He scooted the piece of fabric aside and kissed her on the head. She blinked at him and smiled one of her sleep smiles, making whisper-soft snuffles and squeaks.

"Little Miss, we have free run of the place. Let's go visit the nursery for your feeding and changing instead of the gully this time."

In the nursery, he lifted her out of the stretchy cotton wrap and placed her in a colorful bouncer with a sea creature mobile so he could prepare her bottle. By always having her against him, he could anticipate her needs before she ever cried. Her slight squirms told him she'd be ready to eat in about ten minutes, and then about ten minutes after her meal, another bit of restlessness indicated she'd need a diaper change.

Attachment parenting, the baby book called it. It said this type of parenting created strong bonds and well-adjusted independent children by teaching them about secure attachment and quickly having their needs met. He shook his head, laughing to himself.

Was it possible for him, of all people, to teach her about secure attachment? When he was six, the state-appointed child psychologist had labeled Harvey to explain why foster parents had such a hard time with him. Reactive attach-ment disorder, or something like that. The doctor said the combination of trauma and unstable foster placements had rendered him incapable of forming normal relationships.

"Ivy Rose, I don't know if it's possible for me to teach you anything about connecting to the world, but one second with you did something for me no one else could."

Harvey picked her up and reclined in one of the gliders to feed her. They let out a simultaneous contented sigh. She blinked sleepily, enjoying her bottle.

Harvey leaned his head back into the plush glider. "I don't know about you, but I could get used to this. I don't remem-ber the last time I sat on something so soft." He let his eyes close, soothing himself with the gentle motion and the warm weight of Ivy in his arms.

Propping her on his shoulder, he patted her back. She felt so fragile under his hands. Ivy let out a man-sized burp.

He lifted her away from his shoulder, supporting her wob-bly head. She looked at him wide-eyed with her mouth in a pucker as though she were in the mood to pass out kisses. A dribble of formula ran down her chin. "Gosh, girl, you're not even two weeks old, and you're louder than a grown person."

Tucking her back into the wrap, he hummed a lullaby as he ensured all traces of their nursery visit were erased. He hoisted the trash bag over his shoulder Santa Claus style and then headed down to the basement to check the trash in there.

The can was mostly full. He tugged the stretched tight rim of the trash bag until it popped free. As he lifted the bag to pull the drawstring, the papers on top shifted. There was a gift box dented in on one side, tied with a green ribbon. Who would throw away an unopened gift?

• ● •

After the garbage was in the dumpster and the doors locked, Harvey returned the key to Pearl. She rocked in her porch swing, but it was like she wasn't even there.

He cleared his throat. "Mission accomplished."

She snapped her head around. "Oh. Hi, Harvey." Standing, she reached for the key he dangled from one finger.

"Thank you again for the boots. They fit perfect."

"I thought they might." Pearl offered a half-smile. "If you want to leave your phone number, I'll pass it along to Pastor Thomas. Next time he's going to be out, he can call you instead of you coming all this way." Her voice was flat and quiet.

He shook his head and his mouth went dry. "I . . . I don't have a phone."

She gave a small nod. "I hope you have a good rest of the day. I'll see you tomorrow."

Pearl seemed so sad, he nearly offered to stay, but then again she hadn't invited. He gave a small wave as he left.

• ● •

On the sidewalk, fifty feet from the bargain store, Harvey glanced around—no familiar faces. Pastor Thomas was sick or something. Pearl hadn't seemed in the mood to be out and about. He removed his oversized shirt and tucked it in his bag. He'd found the fitted T-shirt last night, the same color as Ivy's wrap.

Before entering the store, he checked his reflection in the storefront glass.

His hair was too long and his face scruffy. Sweet Ivy snuggled tight against him with only her fuzzy crown visible—his only endorsement that he was of worthy character.

He chose a cart and squeaked toward the baby section. People's heads turned as he passed. But maybe the screech wasn't what drew their attention. There was a softness about their glances.

He stopped at the shaving aisle and splurged on a pack of the least expensive razors for himself.

Voices drifted over from the previous aisle. "Did you see that man with his daughter?" The voice was elderly with a lazy southern drawl.

"Oh, I know it. Wasn't that the sweetest thing? This world would be a better place with more doting fathers like that one."

Harvey warmed.

The two voices chirped out a synchronized greeting. "Hi, Pearl."

The warmth vanished. Harvey abandoned the cart and edged away from the voices, fingers flying as he buttoned the shirt over Ivy. *What a stupid idea.* Risking being noticed with Ivy. Had Pearl followed him? That didn't make sense. He'd left fifteen minutes ago, and it'd only take her five minutes to zip over in her Oldsmobile.

"Hello, Margaret, Eva. How are y'all doing this afternoon?" Her voice had more of its usual spunk, but it sounded forced.

He edged farther around the corner, stole a peek at the group, then pressed against the end-of-aisle display as the women exchanged pleasantries. Pearl said something about sugar, and then he heard the retreating squeak of her orthopedic shoes on the vinyl floor.

He held his breath until she passed by his aisle.

Hushed voices from the two ladies drifted his way. "That woman is a pillar of strength, I tell ya. I don't know how she's still standing."

"I know it. Such tragedy, her son. Did you know she was the one who found him?"

Harvey, pulled by their words, strained his ears as they walked away.

The other voice gasped. "No. Oh my. I can't imagine."

"To have him survive a war zone, and then to lose him anyway."

"Two weeks before Christmas too."

A breath stuck in Harvey's lungs as he studied the boots on his feet. *Oh, Miss Pearl.* No wonder she'd been so undone today.

He walked mechanically to the baby aisle. All the bright colors blurred together. Why would she want someone like him wearing her son's boots?

EIGHTEEN

PRESENT DAY

An incessant pounding throbbed in the distance. Why was the maintenance man hammering in her neighbor's apartment at this hour? Ivy rolled over on what she thought was the queen-sized bed in her bedroom with a groan that turned into a yelp as she rolled off Grandma's sofa.

"Oomph." Ivy sat up and scrubbed her face as her disorientation faded. Her insomnia-induced classic film bingefest came back to her.

The pounding continued from the front door. Ivy checked the time on her phone.

9:15.

Reese.

How long had he been out there?

Ivy scrambled to her feet and staggered toward the door. She smoothed her sleep-tangled hair from her face and then yanked the door open. Reese stood on the doorstep with a cardboard cup in each hand, looking like he'd walked off a modeling shoot. Her gaze traveled from his neatly combed hair and hazel eyes to his fitted T-shirt. The morning sun turned his normally light brown hair to honey gold.

Reese's eyes widened. "Hey, sorry to wake you. I should have called first."

Ivy pulled her dry lips inside her mouth, swiped at the crusty spot on her cheek, and then shoved her hands into the pockets of her baggy sweatpants. "No, it's all good. I stayed up late and accidentally dozed off."

Laughter sparked in his eyes. "You're cute in the morning." The lines around his eyes deepened.

"Oh, hush." She nodded to the cups in his hands. "Please say one of those is for me. There's no coffee in this house."

He extended one cup to her. "One cream, two sugars. Just the way you like it."

Ivy held the steaming cup under her nose and inhaled the comforting scent of fresh-brewed goodness. "You're the best friend a girl could ask for."

Reese stepped inside, studying the white linoleum on the entryway floor as he ran his thumb over the smooth, close-trimmed edges of his fingernails. When he glanced up, something lived in his expression that connected with an ache in her own heart. He looked to the living room window where morning light streamed in. "I try to be. When you let me." His words were muttered under his breath.

Ivy winced. "Well, we'd better get going. Today we're delivering the porcelain Victorian ladies to Mrs. Thatcher. *She* was a volunteer in the hospital nursery for as long as I can remember. She would know something about a motherless child showing up." Without waiting for his reply, she headed for her room to get ready.

No matter how much he wanted to know why their relationship had changed—why *she* changed—she wasn't ready to hash out what had happened with Seth. With her job. Not then. Maybe not ever.

● ● ●

At noon, Ivy headed to Grandma's front porch with cups of sweet tea while Reese brought a bag of chicken fingers and french fries back from Carla's. They settled on the porch swing for a makeshift picnic lunch.

Ivy jumped up from her seat. "I just remembered." She went inside and returned with an unopened jar of caramel sauce she had spied in the near-empty pantry last night. She couldn't help but wonder if Grandma had left it just for her.

Reese wrinkled his nose. "Disgusting. I can't believe you still do that."

Ivy stuck out her tongue, then dunked the fry in caramel and ate it with flourish. "After two hours of chitchatting with Mrs. Thatcher and four other people on Grandma's list, I learned a big fat nothing."

"I thought it was pretty enlightening myself."

Ivy sighed. "It was sweet hearing Mrs. Thatcher talk about how my parents changed when I became a part of their life. How did she say it? That there was a new "aliveness" about them when they brought me home." She shrugged and dunked another fry. "Just sweet stories I already know. But I still don't know who took that journal and why."

"I think you're looking so hard that you're missing something right in front of you."

She jerked her head in his direction. "Do you know something you're not telling me?"

He picked at the breading on his chicken strip. "I don't know anything about your birth family. But what if this whole thing is really about finding your missing pieces?" He tapped his chest.

"Maybe I'll never really know who I am until I know where I came from. Who my birth parents are. What happened. Where they are now. I've tried my whole life to get away from that and I always circle back here in the end."

Reese stared out toward Grandma's old shed. "I know it must be hard expecting that journal to be there, and having the truth jerked away. But it's my deepest hope that my genes have absolutely no bearing on the man I become. It's the hope I hang my future on."

Ivy hadn't intended to poke his wounds. She still remembered that day in third grade when an older boy called Reese trailer trash and asked if all his brothers and sisters went by numbers instead of names since there were so many of them.

Reese had blackened the kid's eye, but after that day Ivy noticed a change in Reese. An increased drive to build a reputation he could be proud of. A reputation built on hard work, self-control, and dedication—a far cry from his father who gambled away his paychecks and had been in the middle of more than a few bar fights.

Reese dropped his Styrofoam container into the paper sack and brushed the crumbs from his hands as he stood. "I have an appointment with a new client I can't miss. Will you be okay to work on this on your own for a few hours?"

She smiled. "Of course. Is business going well? Mom said you decided to go out on your own, a remodeling venture?"

"It's definitely a learning experience. When I come back this afternoon, I'll bring stuff to cook if that works for you."

She nodded. "I think Uncle Vee is coming too."

After his truck disappeared down the drive, Ivy headed to the garage for her next task. She opened the side door. Light streamed in. There was a scrabble of movement. Ivy stifled a shriek as an animal with light-colored fur darted through a hole in the back of the garage.

She exited the building. A white dog ran for the woods, tail tucked between its legs. In the back of the garage she discovered a hole in the corner where a bit of the wood siding had broken away near the ground. Beside it was a little circle where autumn leaves and grass clippings that had blown in had become matted down. Poor thing. This was no place to make a home.

She'd bring it some dog food after her errands—let it know she was a friend.

Ivy continued exploring and found the plastic totes she had been searching for beside the dilapidated Oldsmobile. One by one, she dragged them into the sunlight.

Ivy whipped a hand towel from her back pocket and brushed off the fine layer of dust.

She pried the lid from the first bin and sorted through wall hangings that came straight from the 1950s—a picture of ladies sitting under giant hair dryers, vintage signs advertising perm creams and shampoos, a giant pair of scissors meant to hang on the wall.

Ivy rocked back on her heels and swiped at the sweat beads on her nose. Babette at the salon would adore the relics.

She peeled off the lid to the second box and stared at twenty different reflections of herself. A box of hand mirrors. Each ornate wood-framed mirror was different and painted with bright colors.

Ivy searched her reflection, touching her cheekbone. The mark Seth left had faded but the internal scar remained. Ivy trapped her lips between her teeth and grabbed the lid to cover the box, but a white 4x6 rectangle caught her attention. In Grandma's script were the words, *Ivy's Family.*

Her thoughts scurried as she unearthed it. A picture of her birth parents? Her birth mother?

Ivy pulled it free and flipped it over.

It was one of her favorite pictures but nothing extraordinary. In it, Ivy was about five, wearing a pink frilly dress, surrounded by her favorite people in the world. Mom, Dad, Grandma, and Uncle Vee. The five of them couldn't have looked happier. Ivy walked to the porch and tucked the photograph into her purse.

Then she lugged the bins to the back seat of her sedan.

She rolled her windows down on the way to the salon. The sticky breeze provided far more efficient cooling than her car's defunct air-conditioning. Her long brown strands were sucked out the window and whipped on the wind.

After a year of agonizing over her appearance, she'd ignored mirrors since leaving Seth. She'd wasted too much time trying to look the part of Seth's fiancée. All for a man who refused to be pleased.

Ivy might never come out of her baggy sweats and old college T-shirts. If they repelled male attention, all the better.

She pulled into the parking lot. Clipity-Do-Dah was sandwiched between a family-owned bookshop and a thrift store in a strip mall in need of a face-lift.

Arms loaded with the first box, Ivy nudged her way in the door. A cowbell clanked against the glass.

"Be right with ya, hon."

No matter who entered her door, male or female, young or old, everyone was "hon" to Babette.

Ivy hurried for the second box. As she set the bin in the vinyl chair, Babette rounded the corner. Her bleached hair was swept into a curled ponytail. The fine lines around her mouth made faint trails for her red lip stain to run beyond its borders. "My my, look what the cat dragged in."

Ivy smiled at her syrupy drawl. "Hi, Babette. Grandma wanted you to have these things. She said to keep what you wanted and take the rest over to the thrift store."

"Oh my, honey. Your grandma kept after me to come get these things. But every time I came over to do her hair in those last years, we'd get to talking, and I'd plumb forget. God rest her soul, she was a good woman. Gave me a chance when no one else in the town would—on account of the fact that I was a horrid hairdresser. Your grandma wouldn't give up on me even though I turned her hair blue on more than one occasion."

Ivy chuckled. "Are you serious? All I've ever heard was you're the best around."

"All thanks to your long-suffering grandmother, dear." Babette flicked a glance over Ivy. "While you're here, why don't you take a seat in my chair, and I'll freshen up your hair. Just a trim, or a shampoo and blow out?"

Ivy attempted to smooth the mess, and her fingers snagged

about halfway down. Her face flamed. "I don't know . . . I
. . ." Ivy took a step toward the door.

"Get in here and sit your fanny down. My afternoon appointment canceled. We can catch up."

At her words, Ivy nearly salivated like one of Pavlov's
dogs. If anyone knew anything in this town, they'd told it
to Babette at one time or another.

Ivy leaned back in the shampoo chair, her neck cradled
by the cool rim of the salon sink. Babette prattled on about
who had married who and how many babies they had. Warm
water sluiced over her strands and Babette's practiced hands
massaged Ivy's scalp. She sighed, the tension inside her dissolving.

"How's your folks?"

Ivy flinched. "Oh, they're good. Mom and Dad are doing
a lot of traveling this summer." She let the words trail from
her lips like a trickle from a faucet, searching for something
of substance to add.

Babette returned Ivy's chair to an upright position and
squeezed her hair with a towel.

Ivy wrinkled her nose at her reflection.

"Now what are we going to do today, hon?"

Ivy lifted her shoulders. "Maybe just a trim?"

"Maybe? Because you don't want to trouble me with what
you really want, or because you don't know what you want?"

"I . . ."

"How about I take the length to about here." Babette
placed her hands at the peak of each shoulder. "And then
add subtle layers to give it texture."

Ivy worried her lip. A change would be nice, even if it was
only a few inches. "Okay. Let's do it."

Ivy moved to the styling chair, and Babette snapped the black cape in place.

Now to get Babette's chatter focused in the right direction.

While she pinned hair on top of Ivy's head, Babette dipped her chin toward Ivy's bare left hand. "Would you believe it? Rumors were buzzing you had a ring on your finger."

A weight sank in Ivy's stomach. Of course she'd wait until Ivy was trapped in her chair. She tucked her bare hand under the cape.

Babette pursed her ruby-red lips. "Some fancy lawyer man, I heard it was."

This was the problem with consulting a skilled gossip— the investigator had a way of unwittingly tripping into the hot seat.

Ivy shrugged. "It just didn't work out."

Babette patted Ivy's shoulder. "At least you figured out you weren't good together before the wedding." Babette chattered on, quoting the perils of marriage. She had plenty to say, considering she'd been married four times.

Babette paused her snips and unending stream of conversation to take a sip of water.

It was now or never. If she wanted to mine Babette's knowledge of town history, Ivy had better speak up before she became completely lost in her incessant chatter.

"Babette, you know everything about Triune and everyone in it. I've been going through Grandma's place for the estate sale, and I'm starting to think she knew more about my birth than she let on. Do you know anyone else who may have known my birth mother? Or anything about the circumstances around my birth. Anyone who might not want me to know?"

Babette's wide-tooth comb paused in Ivy's hair. "What do you mean? You found something in the house?"

Ivy shrugged. "She said she left something for me, but it seems to be missing."

She tapped her comb against her hand. "I can't think of anything, honey. But if something jogs my memory, I'll be sure to tell you. I *can* tell you this—your grandma loved you. You came into her life at just the right time. She'd had so much heartache. She brightened right up after you'd been in Triune a few months. Went on and on about how you'd pulled them all together and made a family where there wasn't one before."

"But she never mentioned where I came from? Or who left me on their doorstep?"

Babette shook her head. "No, hon. There sure were rumors a-flyin' though. Lord, one of the zaniest was that your uncle was actually your real father but couldn't raise you for some reason. I forget. Is he on your momma's side or your daddy's?"

"He's one of Grandma's relatives, I think. A nephew by marriage, or something or other."

Babette studied Ivy's hair, combing through for any stray hairs she missed, lips pursed. "Huh. I was pretty sure she didn't have any living relatives."

It was an oddity to the general population, Ivy supposed. To have a family unit where no one gave a whit about biological links. They never chatted over dinner about aunt so-and-so having those blue eyes that skipped a generation, or who was whose second cousin twice removed. It was freeing in a way, to have a family built on love by choice and not relational obligation.

There were certain drawbacks though—like harboring a longing to recognize a bit of herself in someone else's features when she was insecure. Did her parents realize that all those times they scolded her staring habit, she'd just been searching for a glimpse of herself in a stranger's face?

NINETEEN

October 4, 1994

Pearl wiped away the raindrops from last night's downpour and sat in her porch swing.

Harvey's troubles were compounding.

Yesterday evening, Harvey took off again. After visiting with Pastor Thomas, she'd stumbled upon Harvey talking to himself while kneeling next to a purple blanket in the woods. She didn't know if he was doing some sort of New Age meditation practice or prayer. Maybe it was drugs after all.

He'd spun around grasping at his shirt collar, his expression like she'd walked in on him naked in the shower. And then he'd fled with his work half finished. Again.

Grass trimmings had clung to Pastor Thomas's suit pants and polished loafers as he coaxed the old mower Harvey had abandoned in the middle of the churchyard. Mild mannered as the pastor was, he kicked the blade guard when the motor stalled the fifth time and refused to crank. Miriam probably had kittens when he got home with scuffed shoes and green pant legs.

When Pastor Thomas arrived this morning, he exited his black sedan and stepped around the fallen limb in front of the steps, walking into the church with a resolute set to his shoulders. Did Harvey understand he was out of chances? Pearl took a sip of her sugared coffee and closed her eyes.

Lord, I know you see Harvey right where he's at. Help me to help him. Open the way so he'll let me in. Use me any way you see fit to serve this man—to show him your love and that there's more for him than this life he lives.

She lifted her head. The glow of the new sunrise spilled a pink filter over the landscape. Southbound geese honked as they passed over. The nip in the air bit the tip of her nose. The season was about to change.

Pearl left her cup sitting on the yellow table by her front door and shuffled to the church to get into place before Harvey arrived. Hopefully Thomas was already in his office or absorbed in his morning prayer.

She'd told Thomas she wasn't a nosy church lady and that she was there for him if he ever needed to talk. She knew what it was like to be the pastoral family. People who've lived their entire adult lives in a fishbowl know better than to throw stones.

This morning's reconnaissance mission would tarnish her pristine reputation, and she'd prefer Pastor Thomas not know. She kept her tread light on the creaky hardwood as she wound through the hallways to the church classrooms and down to the nursery.

The nursery provided the best view of Harvey's gully hideaway. She turned the worn glider toward the window and settled in with the crossword she had tucked into the oversized pocket of her husband's old fisherman cardigan.

Now all that was left was the wait.

● ● ●

Harvey groaned. Today was going to be a bad day. If Pearl had walked up on him a moment earlier yesterday . . .

He shook his head. And then he'd taken off like a moron instead of playing it cool.

Ever since he lost his parents, he'd taken up the habit of running whenever he found himself in a tight spot. His mother and father couldn't help the way they left him, but he learned the one who did the leaving had it easier than the one left behind. Harvey fled from foster parents, social workers, and other children before his escape from the system at sixteen—his pièce de résistance.

As he walked to the church, he kept his eyes focused on his boots. Pearl's son's boots. His stomach twisted. He owed her an explanation for his rudeness, but what could he say? Give up the fact that he harbored an undocumented child? It didn't matter that he was all Ivy knew. Unless there was a piece of paper proving she was his, she'd be ripped away. And he'd bleed out.

He hugged his arms around the bulk at his middle, his baby girl curled in sleep. Surely there was a way to get through the workday without seeing Pearl, to delay the confrontation as long as possible. He groaned. Work . . .

The image of the mower abandoned in the half-mowed grass flashed in his mind. This was definitely going to be a bad day. Pastor Thomas was a patient man, but just like love, patience was a limited resource.

The church steps loomed over him. He scrubbed his hands over his freshly shaven face, blew out a long breath, and went to face what he had coming.

Pastor Thomas was pacing in the foyer. The creak of the ancient hardwood stilled as Harvey closed the door behind him. "Harvey, we need to talk. In my office." He turned on his heel, not waiting for a response.

Harvey trailed behind, feeling like a puppy who'd peed on the rug. His first job had lasted twenty-four days. A miracle, all things considered.

"Come on in." The pastor motioned him through the door, his voice more heavy than harsh. "Have a seat."

Harvey cleared the tightness in his throat as he sat, willing Ivy to sleep soundly. He was usually only around the man long enough to say good morning and receive his daily tasks. In the tomb-silent office, even her sleepy sighs would echo off the walls. Hopefully Pastor Thomas would get to the point and fire him before he found out about her too.

"I'm sorry about the mow—"

Thomas held up a hand. "Listen. We have a problem. If it were up to me, I could give you time to adjust to this position, if that's what it took. But it isn't up to me."

Harvey picked at his ragged nails.

"You see . . . the thing is . . . you aren't officially on the payroll. I've been personally funding your salary. A board member noticed you around the church and started asking questions."

A knot twisted in Harvey's gut. They'd seen him with Ivy.

"And I don't know if you know much about church boards, but at this church they approve new hires, and I don't know how to put this delicately other than to say you don't exactly fit the bill of a job candidate."

Harvey let out a held breath. This was only because he was the odd shoe of the universe. He rose from the chair. "I'm sorry if I've caused a problem. I'll just—"

"Harvey, sit down. I'm not firing you. I need you to know that if you really want this job, you have to get more work done. You can't leave without notice. I need to be able to justify selecting you when I bring my decision before the board. I'm new around here—an outsider in this tight-knit world. I'll do what I can to make this happen, but you've got to meet me there in the effort department."

Harvey nodded, but his heart weighed heavy. He didn't want to let this man down. Especially not when he'd gone to such great lengths, far overpaying him out of his own pocket for his measly accomplishments. But there was nothing to be done. Ivy couldn't be convinced to hold out on her feedings.

Thomas slapped his thighs and stood. "Okay, great. I know we can make this work. So for today, I need you to get up on the roof and check the shingles and move the branches stuck up there. I'm sure you noticed the big limb in front of the church. It hit the roof and then slid off from the winds last night. After you check for damages, I'd like you to rake and clean up the churchyard, do your regular cleaning inside, and then meet up with me at the end of the day. We'll go over what you finished and strategies to increase your efficiency if you're struggling."

Harvey nodded and offered a tight smile, though his heart fell out of his chest. It must have been beating against the floor, because he was still alive.

He couldn't take Ivy on the roof. But what excuse could he give?

"I'll let you get to it." Thomas showed him out. "By the

way, I like the new look." He patted his own clean-shaven chin.

"Oh yeah, thanks." Harvey heaved a sigh and then went to the basement. How was he going to pull this off? No way Ivy was going on the roof with him. But losing this job wasn't an option.

Outside the church, he leaned the ladder against the building and then stared at where it rested against the church. He paced a circle and ran his hand over the cool aluminum rung as if a genie would pop out and grant his dearest wish and whisk him and Ivy away.

Around the side of the church next to the woods, he knelt by a cluster of bushes. They were visible from the roof but hidden from the casual passerby. Harvey placed a hand on the ground beneath the arc of branches. Dry.

This was wrong, hiding her unattended. Harvey rubbed his face. He could check her from above as he worked. If he hurried, he'd be up there no more than ten minutes. She should stay asleep for a good thirty minutes, as long as he didn't wake her when he lifted her out of the wrap.

He groaned. There was nothing else for it. He had to. Pulling aside the wrap, he slipped her out in a smooth movement, and laid her on the blanket in the bed of leaves. She squirmed a moment and then settled. Unless someone walked close, she was perfectly concealed.

Harvey returned to the ladder and eyed Pearl's house. It was uncharacteristically still. The garage was closed. She must have gone out on an errand.

He shinnied up the ladder. From above, he checked on Ivy. All was quiet. He threw down the stray branches on the side of the church opposite Ivy. So far the shingles appeared intact and undisturbed. The pastor would be pleased no repairs were in order.

A little more picking up, and he could cross this assignment off his list. Though the task was quick, tension built in his chest and tightened the longer he worked. Ivy's absent warmth was like a gaping hole in his person.

Scrambling over the high point of the roof, using his hands to keep himself balanced, he fumbled with his footing as he straddled the peak. Bracing against the pitch, he turned, eyes eager for the purple blanket.

His heart slammed in his chest. An invisible force squeezed the air from his lungs as his world went sideways. His nails scraped the shingles as he grasped for something to keep him steady. Though his body was fixed and stable, he experienced the sensation of falling.

This couldn't be happening.

• CHAPTER •

TWENTY

OCTOBER 4, 1994

Pearl held a bit of heaven wrapped in a purple blanket. She started at the scrabbling sound from above. *Good heavens.* She should have thought before she dashed out of the church and scooped the baby from beneath the bushes. She'd almost made Harvey fall off the roof.

So this was his secret. *A baby.* Now his odd build— scarecrow with plump middle—and the stiff way he always squatted with chest erect made sense. But why hide her? She stood and turned as he climbed over the ridge and scooted toward the ladder.

Harvey came toward her with his face devoid of color, eyes full of something that wrenched her heart. He froze five paces away.

"Harvey, is this your child?"

He started to nod, but then halfway through he jerked his head to the side. He closed his eyes and shook his head. His Adam's apple dipped and rose. He took another step forward, arms lifted toward the baby, but then he stopped and let them fall to his side.

"Where's her mother?"

He trembled from head to toe. "My sister's. She . . . uh . . . she wasn't able to take care of her."

Pastor Thomas wouldn't begrudge him for caring for a baby. Did he think he'd be fired for having her with him? Was that why he was so afraid?

"Go on back to work so you don't lose your job. I'm taking her home. When you're done, we can sit down and talk." She willed her voice to stay no-nonsense, but the tortured way the man looked at her made a lump rise in her throat.

He remained fixed to the spot.

"I'll take good care of her. I promise." She walked past him to her house.

"Miss Pearl." His voice was a mere breath of air.

She turned to face him. He held out his bag in front of him, his hands white-knuckled on the strap.

"She'll want a bottle in about ten minutes. Three ounces."

Pearl couldn't help but smile as she slipped her arm through the strap. "Of course."

He looked like an abandoned child. It took everything in her not to bring him back to her house to mother him too.

The baby's dark eyes were now open. Newborns had such an enchanting way about them. Perhaps it was their newness. Fresh from God's hands, blissfully unaware of the harsh realities of life.

Once inside the house, she marveled over the child. She smelled of baby shampoo and powder. It was obvious he took great pains to ensure she was well cared for. Precisely ten minutes after leaving Harvey, she started fussing to be fed.

Pearl glanced out the window at him. *Bless his heart.* She'd thought she'd seen him undone all the times he'd darted off. But it didn't compare to how he behaved now. Like a boat unmoored, listing after a storm.

Her ache for him pulsed in her chest. Why was he so upset? He was caring for his sister's child. Not some dark secret. No one would fault him for it. There had to be a way to build his trust so she could help the dear, fragile man, but how?

● ● ●

A tall cedar growing in the woods just off the highway bore twenty-six tally marks. Twenty-six marks for the twenty-six days that new life had beat in Harvey's heart. He had felt things. Had a reason for being. The accident when he was five ripped hope out of his life, but it was nothing compared to what he felt as Pearl took Ivy from him.

Pearl was a breath away from figuring everything out. She'd never see him as an adequate parent substitute, even if she continued to believe his lie. He wandered, picking up limbs on autopilot. Pearl told him to work so he wouldn't lose his job. But she didn't know that Ivy was the reason for this torture. If he lost her, he was unfettered from these awkward circumstances. But strangely, his old life now felt like shackles. Shackles he didn't want to wear anymore.

He stopped. His chest ached from his panting breaths. Oxygen. He needed oxygen. Harvey leaned over and propped his hands on his knees, hating the empty space on his front where Ivy belonged.

Somehow he finished his work, then consulted with Pastor Thomas. He must have made intelligible conversation while he held a full trash bag to disguise his suddenly flat middle.

Harvey shuffled down Pearl's long sidewalk feeling like he was volunteering for his own execution.

The path wasn't long enough for him to find a way to say goodbye to his daughter. Because even if he didn't have a piece of paper saying so, that was who she was. *His*.

He reached to press the doorbell, but the door popped open before his finger made contact.

Pearl motioned him inside. "Come in, Harvey. Let's talk."

Where was Ivy? Gone? This woman had figured out the truth and hadn't even let him say goodbye. His voice croaked out like a clamp was fastened onto his vocal cords. "Where is she? Tell me where she is. Where's Ivy?"

"Ivy? What a beautiful name."

He ground his teeth. "Where is she?"

"Calm down. She's sleeping in my room. She's safe." Her forehead creased. "Why don't you sit down before you collapse. Can I get you something? Water? A paper bag? Don't hyperventilate on me."

He sank into a chair, sucking shallow breaths. She was here. No one had taken her. Yet. "Can I . . . could I . . . I need . . . can I hold . . . ?"

Pearl stepped to him and placed a hand on his shoulder. "First you are going to breathe. Then we're going to talk. You're going to tell me why you've been hiding her, and where her mother is."

Harvey stood and paced. A stomping giant among all her old lady things. Doilies, trinkets, photo frames.

"Sit down, Harvey."

He sank into the chair. How to explain that he and Ivy were the same? Abandoned with no one to miss either of them. The world was the problem, trying to make them fit

148

in a box—follow rules that shouldn't apply to unwanted people.

He opened his mouth. His chin wobbled. No sound would come. He clamped his jaw tight.

Pearl pulled a footstool in front of him and sat, the toe of her raggedy slippers inches from his boots. She placed her wrinkled hands on his jittering knees. "Look at me."

He lifted his chin. Something raw and tender swam in her pale eyes.

"I want to help you. I sense you're a good man with a good heart and that you love Ivy. But I can't help unless I know how to. I can't know how unless you tell me the truth. *All* the details. Where's her mother?"

His eyes widened. Help? Did she mean she wanted to help him keep her?

Words spilled out of him, saying anything he could so that those twenty-six tallies could become twenty-seven.

"One night my sister showed up with a baby. Said her boyfriend left her and she was in trouble. She didn't have any money and her baby needed to eat. I'm not proud of this, but I really wasn't any better off than she was, so I broke into the Pantry to get what Ivy needed. That's when I met Pastor Thomas and he gave me the job.

"Then I woke up one morning a couple weeks ago, and my sister was gone. Left a note saying she'd be back and asked me to keep Ivy safe. So that's what I've been trying to do. Keep her safe."

She listened with a hand pressed to her mouth. When he concluded the story with today's events, she sat back, hands folded in her lap.

"You can't keep bringing Ivy to work."

A jolt went up his spine.

"You're going to bring her here before you're due for work every morning. I'll care for her during the day. You make sure you meet Pastor Thomas's requirements, so you can keep this job. And we'll go from there. What do you say?"

As if he had options. "Yes, Miss Pearl."

"Now, Ivy is resting. No need to rush off. How about I get you a drink and let your nerves settle." She quirked a half-grin. "You look like you might be of a mind for a stiff drink, but I only keep water and sweet tea around here."

His voice came soft. "I don't drink. Never have. I wouldn't turn down a coffee though."

She tilted her head like she was trying to read what emotion lay behind his words. Pearl went for his coffee and returned with his customary mug. He willed the warm brew to wash away the cold knot in his chest. He was getting pulled deeper, entwined in these peoples' lives, when all he wanted was to get away. Back to camp with Ivy, to a world that was safe.

TWENTY-ONE

PRESENT DAY

The wind ruffled Ivy's freshly cut hair as she cruised toward Grandma's house. A faint scent of honeysuckle whispered on the breeze.

Reese and her uncle should be there about the time she arrived. She stuffed down the thrill of coming home to a full house. She'd never been very good at being alone. So much so, that for most of Ivy's life she suspected her parents had named her for her childhood tendency to cling.

But according to Babette, Grandma had seen things in a different light. She saw her as one who pulled people together. Not out of desperation, trying to force nonexistent bonds. It was an inherent character trait.

Ivy trapped her lip between her teeth as she flicked her blinker and turned on Church Street. As she approached the steepled building, the pastor rounded his car and jogged toward the drive that ran along the church property and ended at Grandma's.

Ivy pasted on a smile and slowed to a stop. The pastor was a nice guy, though he tended to talk too much. A hazard of the profession, she supposed.

"Hi, Ivy!" The middle-aged man mopped at his forehead with his handkerchief. It was a hot one, pushing ninety. In moments like these Ivy almost missed the Mercedes.

"Hi, Pastor. How are you?"

"Good, good. And I hope you are too. I know it can't be easy going through Pearl's things. I won't keep you. I'm sure you've got places to be. But your grandma gave me something to give you before she passed."

Ivy's heart pounded in her ears. The journal? Had there been some last-minute switch to Grandma's plans, not reflected in the letters?

"A real treasure, this is. I'm not sure why she didn't give it to you herself, but, well, here you go."

He held out a weathered leather-bound book. Ivy froze, leaving the thick study Bible arching from the pastor's grip on the spine. Grandma's Bible was as much a part of her grandmother as her right arm. Ivy knew she should feel honored, but she couldn't shake the letdown that slumped her shoulders. She tucked the Bible into her bag. "Thank you. I'll try to hurry with the house and get out of your way."

"You're very welcome, and there's no rush. You're right where your grandmother wanted you."

Ivy's brow crimped. "Pardon?"

"I'd better go and let you get on with your evening plans."

Ivy's tires crunched on gravel as she rolled down the drive. A bead of sweat dripped down her spine.

Uncle Vee's red landscaping truck and trailer was parked next to Old Bessie. A wide smile cramped her cheeks.

Ivy scanned the porch, the yard, and the garden. Empty. Where had they gotten off to? Maybe they were around back. She pulled her keys from her purse, grabbed the small bag of dog food she'd picked up on the way home, and hurried down the walk.

She set the bag on the porch. As she reached to insert the key, the door popped inward. Ivy stifled a shriek. Reese's low chuckle filled her ears. "Your uncle let me in," he said as he pulled the door wide.

Reese had changed from his T-shirt and shorts from earlier into a button-down and jeans.

"Hey, nice haircut."

She swiped her fingers through her hair to tidy the wind-ruffled strands.

A dimple appeared in one of his cheeks. "Why do you always think I'm joking when I tell you I like the way you look?"

Heat flooded her cheeks. He was clearly oblivious to how vulnerable she was to him, especially now. Particularly his pure, unassuming kindness. Like holding out a drink to a person lost in the desert.

She edged around him, entering the house. The faint scent of his cologne, something sandalwood and cedar, teased her senses.

He shut the door behind her. "Come on, Rosie-girl. Let's eat."

She blinked, recovering from her momentary lapse in concentration.

When she entered the kitchen, her uncle dropped his ladle with a clatter on the stove and wrapped Ivy in a crushing hug. The tension in her chest released like an exhale of breath she'd been holding too long.

"It is so good to see you. Are you well?"

She tried to answer, but her words were muffled by his shirt front.

He released her and smiled down at her with his large palms resting on her shoulders. His expression tender.

"I've missed you." His expression grew watery, and he sniffled as he quickly turned back to the soup bubbling on the stove. The savory scent was so familiar.

"I was just telling your uncle here about your plot to break into the church after you locked yourself out of the house."

Ivy shot Reese a playful glare.

Uncle Vee let out a quiet laugh. "I didn't know you'd taken up burglarizing since I'd seen you last."

"I wasn't—"

"Yeah, she was creeping around the churchyard like a ninja, except she was wearing a white shirt. Stuck out like a sore thumb."

Ivy shook her head at their ribbing and walked to where her uncle stirred the soup. "Grandma's recipe?"

Uncle Vee nodded.

"The garden and yard are beautiful." She didn't want to embarrass him, but he needed to know how much it meant to her.

A slow smile curved his mouth, deepening the sun-weathered creases around his liquid-brown eyes. "Old habits die hard. Any time I was overseeing the church landscaping, I could hear her in my head. Fussing about the grass grown too long or the weevils taking over the garden. It bothered her to no end when she wasn't healthy enough to get out there to tend things herself." He shrugged. "I guess everybody mourns in their own way. Taking care of her place is mine."

Babette's words echoed in Ivy's head. The ridiculous bit about people gossiping that he was her biological father. As he worked in the kitchen, Ivy studied his profile, searching for a shadow of resemblance in the slope of his nose and the shape of his jawline.

They were a pair of opposites. He was tall and broad; she had always been the shortest in her class. While her facial features were curving and pixie-like, his were bold and angular. Their ordinary brown eyes their only commonality.

Ivy shook her head, interrupted by the sound of Reese chopping lettuce with more force than the job warranted.

"Is there anything I can do?"

Reese paused his chopping and cleared his throat. "No, I think we're about finished. So, how did things go today? Did you find anything new?"

"Nothing besides a stray dog who's taken up residence in the garage. Scrawny. Super skittish."

"You know, I thought I saw a dog the last time I came to mow, but he disappeared when I pulled up." Uncle Vee came to the table with a stack of bowls. "Is there anything in particular you're looking for?"

"Grandma wrote me a letter before she died. There was a journal she wanted me to have, but it seems to be missing."

"Oh?" He set the bowls on the table in slow motion. The air seemed to go from the room as her uncle eyed her. "Did she . . . did she say what the journal was about?"

She shrugged. "I think it has something to do with my early days. Before my adoption."

The creases between his brows deepened and his gaze shot to the floor. He went to the refrigerator and pushed around the paltry contents.

"Do you know the journal she was talking about? Or where it might be?"

He closed the refrigerator and turned. His every movement measured, like the second hand of time had slowed. He shook his head. "You should let the past go, Ivy. I'm not sure what it is she wanted you to know, but you can't live life looking backward. The past is just information. Your choices today make you who you are."

TWENTY-TWO

OCTOBER 5, 1994

The smell of bacon hung in the air in Pearl's tidy kitchen, but the savory scent turned Harvey's stomach. Or was it the way his arms were empty, while across from him, Pearl fawned over Ivy? The perfect picture of grandmother and child. He was just the homeless guy at the table trying not to have a panic attack. He ripped his gaze away from them and stared out the kitchen window, pretending he could feel the breeze on his face. Open air.

"Harvey?"

He jerked to attention. "Yes, ma'am?"

"Are you okay? I have a table and chairs around back. A nice little sitting area if you'd prefer to sit outside."

"That's okay." It was eerie, the way she seemed to read him.

Pearl grinned at Ivy. "Goodness, she is such a gem. I got her a few things while I was out last night." She shot him a sheepish look. "I never had a girl to shop for. I couldn't resist."

He gripped the chair to keep himself from taking Ivy from her arms. Ivy was his. He was the one who was supposed to take care of her. To buy her things.

"Oh, Harvey. I wasn't thinking. I should probably let you hold her if you'd like. I'll have her all day."

Harvey stood and reached. "Please . . ." He hated how desperate the barely managed whisper came off his lips.

As she leaned to transfer Ivy to him, she lifted her chin to meet his eyes. "It will be okay. I promise to take good care of her."

He leaned away, Ivy now securely cradled in his arms. She poked the tip of her tongue in and out of her rosebud lips as if discovering it for the first time. Harvey gained a solid breath.

Pearl shuffled back into the kitchen, weighed down by her purchases. "I got a few cute outfits and the same brand of diapers and formula you had for her in your bag yesterday. I thought it'd be easier for you if you didn't have to worry about packing her bag every morning."

Something hot and unkind twisted in his gut, but he managed to say the appropriate thing for once. "Thank you."

"Oh, and before you head out, I got her a bassinet to nap in. Would you mind putting it together?"

Harvey followed her into what must have been Pearl's room. Pieces of the bassinet littered the carpet in the tidy room.

Pearl reached for Ivy. "I tried to get it together, but I think Little Miss would be safer if you took a crack at it."

He knelt in front of the scattered pieces. The frilly place

where Ivy would sleep took shape while he worked. The hot thing in his middle twisted tighter until pinpricks stung the backs of his eyes. Pearl offered her clothes, piles of diapers, a pristine white bassinet, a real house.

What did he offer? Just enough formula and diapers to get through each day? He closed his eyes against the pain of reality. Was he selfish to insist on keeping her?

Pearl was a sweet old lady with a nice house, but she didn't need Ivy like she needed oxygen. To her, she was just another cute baby.

He had the few pieces together in less than ten minutes and positioned the bassinet by the east-facing window so the light spilled in through the filmy curtains.

Pearl rocked Ivy in her front room. Ivy's eyes drooped, almost asleep. "I don't know why I brought the bassinet home. As if I'm going to put her down once she falls asleep." Pearl beamed up at him. "Any last instructions, boss? It's obvious you know what you're doing with her."

An unfamiliar sensation swept through him, causing him to stand a bit straighter. But at the thought of walking out the door without Ivy against him, the feeling shrank into a twisted knot. "Don't leave her to cry. Ever. Don't ever, ever leave her wondering if anyone is coming, or if there is anyone there to hear her. I want her to always know someone will come for her if she needs them."

Pearl's pale blue eyes locked focus with his. She swallowed. "Of course. Of course, Harvey. I'm here. I'm not going anywhere."

He turned and his heart stretched the distance between them, longing to turn around and take Ivy out of there. This was only a season. He would work, save his money, and then he and Ivy could get away. Disappear. And then they'd never have to be separated. He reached for the doorknob and looked back.

Ivy was fast asleep in Pearl's arms. Peaceful. Her little trusting spirit at rest. If she was okay, he'd find a way to be okay too. "You'll get me if she needs me?"

Pearl nodded. "Absolutely. Now go on to work, dear. You're worse than a new mother on her first day off maternity leave."

"Yes, ma'am. Thank you, Miss Pearl." He dipped his chin.

"We'll see you this afternoon. Go on, now."

Harvey forced his feet to move and left his sweet girl in the care of another. He'd thought it impossible to trust someone to care for him. This was a million times worse.

• ● •

Harvey chipped at the peeling red paint of the church's front door with a scraper. If he worked at it, he could have one of the towering arched doors prepped for a fresh coat by the end of the day.

He had to admit, he'd gotten a lot more accomplished in the past three hours than he normally did in a day. It was easier maneuvering when he wasn't constantly worried about jostling Ivy.

A thread of tension tightened his spine. He tried to shake it, but it intensified with the passing moments. Something was wrong. Off.

He pulled his watch from his pocket. Rather, Pastor Thomas's watch. Ivy needed to eat. He left the scraper on the church steps and hurried to the parsonage. It was funny. She'd changed his internal clock, and he knew she needed him even without her squirms.

He strode across Pearl's porch, and as he reached to knock, a sound froze him. Singing.

> "The Lord has promised good to me,
> His word my hope secures.
> He will my shield and portion be,
> As long as life endures.
> Amazing grace! How sweet the sound . . ."

Harvey crept around to the window and peered through. Pearl was rocking the infant, bottle balanced in her hand as Ivy fed.

The tension dripped out of him as he sank to sit beneath the window. Ivy was fine. She was cared for. Which was good. But if it was good, why did it make him hurt so bad?

The front door creaked.

"Harvey James, get back to work and stop skulking on my porch. Ivy's fine." Her mock scold was softened by the kindness in her eyes.

He felt anything but fine.

"There you are, Harvey. Those doors are looking great."

Harvey's head jerked up and his breath hitched in his chest. Pastor Thomas was strolling down Pearl's sidewalk.

"Whose do you have there, Pearl? Whose baby?" He picked up his pace and went to her. He gasped. "My, my she is a beautiful little one. Now I know why my lunch companion was absent today."

Forgotten, Harvey slunk back to his peeling paint, willing his heart to stay inside his chest, but it felt like it scraped raw against the pavement with every step. Now two people knew he was taking care of Ivy full-time. How long could he go on without them figuring out the rest?

* * *

At the end of the workday, Harvey came down Pearl's walk as if pulled by a string. Weary yet eager, he reminded Pearl of a fish who'd been fighting the line all day and was now relieved to jump on the plate. He froze when he spotted her sitting on the swing.

"Where's Ivy?" His fists clenched at his sides.

"Hi, Harvey. How was your day? Mine was lovely also." Pearl smiled. "Ivy is napping in the bassinet. I checked her two minutes ago."

He began breathing again.

So many questions begged for answers. Where was Ivy's mother? Did Harvey think she was coming back? But he was so edgy, so distrustful. She'd never get a word out of him in this temper. "I've made supper. We could let her snooze a little longer. You don't have to, of course. If you'd rather not."

He shifted his feet. "Sure . . . that is . . . let me check on her first. And dinner outside? If it's not more trouble?" He motioned to the door. "May I?"

She walked over and patted his shoulder. "Of course, dear. You don't have to ask to go in my home. When you get back, pull the table and bench over and we'll enjoy this nice fall evening."

She followed him into the house and fixed their plates while he was with Ivy.

Her son had been that way after his first tour of duty.

Always preferring open spaces to being indoors. Though strangely enough, when he was lost in one of his panicked episodes, he'd head for the closet.

What *was* Harvey's story? He seemed to have sprung up from the earth like a loblolly pine, born of the sun and water and bent by the wind.

Today she'd made a call to her friend at the police department. There were no local missing persons reports. For a woman or a child. No one knew of a man named Harvey. They couldn't live far though. The man walked everywhere he went.

Harvey helped her carry their supper plates out, his rigid posture softening after setting eyes on Ivy. Pearl settled on the swing, and he sat opposite on the bench.

He took a bite of her buttermilk fried chicken. She swelled with delight as he closed his eyes with a sigh.

"You know what they say about feeding strays, don't you?"

She chuckled. "Is that a promise? Because I've started a collection, and I kind of enjoy it, to tell you the truth. Poor Pastor Thomas doesn't even know how to fetch his own lunch anymore."

"If you feed him like this, why would he want to?"

Pearl reached and patted his large, rough hand. "So how was your first day without Ivy?"

He ducked his head and slipped his hand away. "Hard. Being away from her. But I put it into my work. Hopefully, Pastor Thomas will approve."

She nodded.

"How was Ivy? Okay?"

"She's a dream, Harvey. I don't know if I've ever met a quieter newborn."

He beamed. The first real smile she'd ever seen from him. "She's something, isn't she?"

"Your sister. How long did you say she's been gone?"

Harvey swallowed the bite of chicken he'd just put in his mouth and winced as it went down. "Uh . . . right . . . uh . . . right after Ivy was born."

"Don't you think you should file a police report?"

Color drained from Harvey's face. "I don't want to get her in any sort of trouble."

Pearl leaned toward him. "Mothers don't usually leave behind their babies on a whim. She could be hurt or in danger."

Harvey stared at the floor, pain marring his features. His words came out like he had to wrestle them from his chest. "Trust me. She'll be fine. If I file a report, I'll ruin everything."

Ivy's cry broke through the silence, and Harvey jumped to his feet like a shot had been fired.

Pearl tipped her head toward the house. "Go on. Go get your little one." She nudged her toe against the porch, setting the swing into motion. Where would his sister have gone, and what would've forced her to leave her child behind?

Harvey returned and sat back on the bench while he fed Ivy her bottle. Little by little his tensed shoulders dropped.

"It's getting dark. I hope you don't have a long walk home. Where do you live again?"

Harvey, struck by a coughing fit, turned a few shades of red.

Pearl stood. "Let me get you more water."

When she returned, he seemed magically composed and was settling Ivy in the wrap.

"You're right, it is getting late. I'd better get on."

"All right, Harvey. Have a safe trip. If I had a car seat, I'd give you a ride. I'll check and see if anyone around town has an extra they don't use anymore. For next time."

Harvey gulped and he backed down the porch steps onto the walk. "No. No, ma'am. You're doing plenty for us. No need. I like to walk. See you tomorrow."

He turned and his long stride spilled distance between them before she could utter a reply—running away again. Did he think she didn't notice?

She puttered in the kitchen, washing dishes and making chamomile tea. The little house with trinkets and doilies had spent its life with Pearl's men stomping around, making the space feel small. She loved it, the way Harvey's tall, lanky maleness filled the void.

Sweet Ivy and lost Harvey. What a picture they made. The sorrow on his face was such a fixture she wondered if he'd ever known anything else. She weighed which drew her to him more—the way he cared for a helpless child or the way he seemed like one himself once you got beyond his exterior.

TWENTY-THREE

PRESENT DAY

Ivy sat cross-legged on the center of the bed with the sunflower comforter draped over her shoulders. She scrolled through her email on her phone, begging there to be at least one response on the applications she'd put out. Everything from dog grooming to waitressing to school counselor positions. Her heart twisted thinking about the kids she wouldn't see next year. Their sweet faces looking to her when they needed to be reassured. She'd give almost anything to have her old job back.

A notification flashed across the top of her screen.

Ivy groaned. *Seth*.

Hey, babe. Call me. Please? I've been doing a lot of thinking. I know I took things too far and I need to change. Just call me. I want to get help. For you. For us. I promise I'll make things right.

She'd heard those words before, words meant to ensnare

a lonely heart. He'd admit fault and commit to working on their relationship. She'd feel validated for all the feelings he'd shut down so many times and give in. Things would get better for a while. And she'd get sucked back into the cycle.

She turned her phone off and pulled Grandma's Bible from her purse. Ivy flipped to Psalm 139:14—the verse Grandma said in paraphrase over her like a benediction in Ivy's coming and going. *You are fearfully and wonderfully made, my child. And the works of the Lord are wonderful. Don't you forget it.*

She turned the onion skin pages, all in a colorful wash of faithful highlights and notes in the margin.

The verse she sought was underlined in purple ink. There was a heart drawn beside it with her name written in the center. Tucked in the pages was a slip of paper. She unfolded the sheet. The edges were ragged like it had been torn out. *From the journal?* It was written when Ivy would have been about six months old.

February 20, 1995

Seeing the joy on the faces of Ivy's parents makes me feel like a traitor of the worst kind. Even though I haven't found any clues about who birthed that tiny girl, I can't stop looking. Motherhood is such a beautiful gift. I waited so long for it to come into my life, and it was taken away. Twice. That pain is more than any person should bear. If there's even a chance the child's birth mother was robbed of this gift against her wishes, I would never be able to live with myself if I didn't continue this search.

Everyone else is satisfied with the results of the po-lice investigation into the child's origins, which expect-edly came up fruitless. And I don't blame them, not for a minute. It certainly is simpler to rest in knowing the Lord brought us that little girl and let the details fade to an unacknowledged buzz. But I can't get that child's mother out of my head. Whoever she may have been.

Oh, how I miss my boy. He'd laugh if he heard me call him a boy, but I couldn't help but see a childhood version of himself in his sad brown eyes. I hope he knows we aren't angry or disappointed in what he did, but that we understand. I hope he knows that love is waiting to welcome him home.

The journal page trembled in Ivy's fingers. Nothing about the words made sense.

Knocking from the front door brought her back to the present. A band tightened around Ivy's rib cage, and she took a strangled breath. Seth's unanswered text messages. He'd promised he could find her if he wanted to.

Ivy paced the bedroom. Triune was tiny. All it would take was him flashing his suave smile and any resident would helpfully point the man to his destination.

She walked into the living room and stood five feet from the door. The knocking became pounding. She could call the police. That would scare him off. Except for the fact that he'd probably make friends with them in an instant and convince them she wasn't in her right mind.

She could call Reese. But setting up a confrontation between her fiercely protective friend and her emotionally abusive ex-fiancé on her grandma's porch?

"Hey, Ivy? You there?"

Air rushed from her lungs and her knees wobbled beneath her as the tightness in her chest released. *Reese.*

She turned the knob; his hand was raised to knock.

"What are you doing here?"

At the sight of her, the flex in his jaw relaxed. "What are *you* doing? I tried to call before I came, but it went straight to voice mail. And then when you weren't answering the door, I started to worry."

The place between her shoulder blades tensed until it ached. Ivy lifted her arms, palms out, and then let them fall to her side. "I was right where you left me half an hour ago. I don't need a babysitter." She clamped her hand over her mouth and shook her head. "I didn't mean that. I just wasn't expecting anyone. You scared me." He didn't need to know the reason why.

Reese massaged his forehead. "No, you're right. I'm sorry. This seemed like such a great idea ten minutes ago." He picked up a box sitting on the weathered table on the porch. "I stopped at Murphy's on my way home, and I saw this box of pink donuts."

She cringed and crowned herself the world's biggest jerk.

"And I couldn't help but remember the way you used to complain how people always overlooked strawberry-iced donuts in favor of chocolate or powdered."

A corner of her mouth quirked against her will.

"I didn't want to barge over unannounced. But you didn't answer the phone, and I was already so close. Then you didn't answer your door . . ." As his words trailed off, he picked at a ragged spot on his fingernail. "This is going to sound so weird, but I'm going to say it anyway. When you didn't answer your door, I got this feeling. Like something was wrong. I've been getting that feeling on and off all year long. Obviously you're fine. More than fine. I . . ." He took a step, closing the distance between them. The box of donuts brushed the front of her loose fit T-shirt.

His gaze flicked to her lips and back to her eyes.

Pulled forward, like a kite on string, she shifted her weight onto her toes ever so slightly, catching the faint scent of his cologne or soap. Whatever it was, it smelled good.

"Ivy . . ." He said her name like a caress.

Her lowered eyelids flashed open wide. She stepped back into the doorway. A safer distance, one that didn't leave her heart skittering around in her chest like a hunted rabbit.

She needed distance. Like a closed door between them so she could become a rational human being again. One minute she was snapping at him, the next imagining what it'd be like to kiss him. "Uh. It's getting late. I'll see you tomorrow?" Ivy stared at the straw welcome mat.

Lines crinkled the corners of his eyes. "It's eight thirty."

"Were you expecting me to invite you in?"

He glanced over his shoulder toward the church. His lips parted and then closed.

Her face flamed. "I didn't mean anything by that. I meant, like, for donuts and a movie or something. You and me, we're friends. We do friend stuff. Right?" Somebody, shut her up. A lightning bolt from heaven would do nicely. Duct tape. Anything.

In the light of the porch the color of his face deepened as he rubbed the back of his neck. "Is there a reason for me to think you meant anything—" He grimaced. "You're right. It's late. I should go. I told myself I'd give you the space you obviously want. So sorry to have disturbed your evening."

He placed the box in her hands and was in his truck and gone before she could ask for an explanation.

TWENTY-FOUR

OCTOBER 5, 1994

Walking back to his camp, weariness sagged Harvey's shoulders. Being away from Ivy had been like a piece of his heart walked around outside his body.

But tonight he could curl up near her warm, solid form. Something real that anchored him and reminded him why he kept doing things that threatened his way of life.

The job, letting Pearl in his life, caring for a baby—all necessary struggles, but now the elderly lady wanted to give him rides home at the end of the day. An impossibility on two accounts. One, she couldn't know he stayed in a lean-to in the woods. Two, he didn't do cars. Hadn't been in one since the last foster home transport and would never get in another, if he had anything to say about it.

He tucked Ivy into bed and slipped to the creek for a quick wash-up.

As the cool water dripped down his face, the old memory played. The look of disdain when six-year-old Harvey landed on a stranger's doorstep with his black trash bag of unwashed clothes and a layer of grime covering his stick-figure frame. That hadn't been his choice. But those people hadn't known.

The scalding water. Those hard-lined eyes glaring down at him as they scoured his soft kid-skin raw. The hope that he'd found a soft place to land had swirled down the drain with the dingy bathwater. Harvey blinked away the memory.

At the cedar tree he carved another mark. Twenty-eight days he'd protected Ivy from that world.

Damp and shivering in the cool air, he curled up next to Ivy to grab a few winks before she woke. His mind swirled, searching for a way to get Pearl off the scent of a sister who didn't exist. Guilt pricked his conscience. She could be lying awake right now, worrying about the safety of a mere figment of his imagination. Weariness drooped his eyelids.

● ● ●

Harvey shot straight up, flung from his comatose state by the squeal of skidding tires and the impact of metal on metal. Panting, he strained his eyes in the black night. Ivy snuffled faintly beside him. He shook his head. It must have been the phantom of a dream that haunted him on occasion—vague and brief. The sound of squealing tires, then a slow-motion sensation of weightlessness, but never the impact.

He leaned over, head between his knees, and tried to recall the tactics the childhood counselor had attempted to teach him to stave off panic attacks. The vice around his chest choked the life out of him.

He staggered out of the lean-to. The light breeze swept away the heat rising in his flesh. He pressed his palms against his face. In the direction of the highway, two beams spilled light into the woods. The wrong angle for headlights on the highway.

The familiar nausea rose in his throat. It hadn't been a dream, but surely they didn't need him. Someone would happen by sooner or later. Harvey glanced back to where Ivy slept soundly, his tongue turned to sandpaper in his mouth.

He'd never rest unless he knew everyone in the car was safe. He'd made an oath a long time ago to help whenever the opportunity presented itself. After settling a drowsy Ivy in the wrap, he snatched the flashlight and his makeshift first aid kit and trudged off in the direction of the headlights.

The guardrail was wrapped around the crumpled front of a white sedan. A deer carcass lay a few feet away.

His pulse thrummed, discordant and wild. A car seat in the back. A small child.

Bile rose in his throat. His nostrils flared as he inhaled air his lungs wouldn't receive. Harvey staggered toward the rear passenger door. Locked. Child safety locks.

A boy not more than three wailed from inside. Blood dripped down his chin. "Mommy . . . Mama . . ."

Harvey's gaze darted to the driver. Slumped. The airbag had failed to deploy. Dread curled in his gut, and his peripheral vision clouded.

Bracing against the car to keep upright, he stumbled around to the driver. He couldn't do this, relive his past—watch a child lose a parent. Yet, he couldn't walk away and abandon the bleeding child in his moment of terror. Hand quaking, he opened the door and checked the woman's pulse.

His weak knees nearly gave out from under him in sheer relief at the strong, rhythmic thump beneath his fingertips.

He smoothed the sticky tendrils back from the goose egg on the woman's forehead. She groaned and blinked, her eyes unfocused.

"Carter . . ." The name slurred and mumbled.

He placed a hand on her shoulder. "Carter is safe. Help will be here in a few minutes."

He looked back at the boy. The whites of the child's eyes shone in the darkness. "It's going to be okay. I'm going to get help. Your mommy . . . is . . . sleeping. Yeah, a little nap, and then someone will be here to take care of her."

His gaze darted around. In the center console there was the soft green glow of a car phone keypad.

"911, what's your emergency?"

"There's been an accident with injuries on the 460 by-pass. Mother and child. Between mile markers forty-one and forty-two."

"Who am I speaking with?"

Harvey pressed the red button and put the phone back where he found it, then reached and activated the hazard lights and unlocked the rear doors.

He found a towel on the rear floorboard for the child's bleeding lip. "Here now, let me see your boo-boo." The child accepted his presence and care without question. "Is your name Carter?"

The boy nodded, puppy dog eyes wide.

Harvey curled his lanky frame into the seat next to the child, and Ivy squirmed in the wrap. "I came to sit with you until the nice police officers get here." He had to bend at the neck to keep the top of his head from brushing the ceiling.

"Where Teddy? I lost him in the boom-crash. He hurt too."

A well-loved teddy bear rested face up on the floorboard, its button eyes glinting in the moonlight. "Here he is. No worse for the wear. He just took a tumble." Harvey handed the bear to the boy, who squeezed it to his chest and shut his eyes.

Harvey dabbed at the small horizontal cut on the boy's lip, already starting to seal.

"I scared. I want my mommy wake up." The tremor in the child's voice rent Harvey's heart. He reached over and placed a hand on his knobby knee.

"I know, buddy. I know. She will soon enough, and then she'll scoop you into her arms and hold you tight."

"Pwomise?"

"Yes. You're both going to be fine. Now I need to know something very important. Do you hurt anywhere besides the boo-boo on your lip?"

The boy shook his head, and then arched his back against his car seat. "Get me out, pwease. I wanna see Mommy."

"I know. But I need to leave you in your car seat until the ambulance gets here. It should only be a few minutes. Then those nice people will take care of you. Don't be afraid. They only want to help."

The boy needed to know that. Harvey had hated those doctors and nurses in the hospital. They'd been the ones he'd pinned the blame on for disrupting his life for years until he was old enough to know better.

"There will be bright lights and loud sirens to tell you they're coming. They'll strap your mommy to a little bed, but it's just to keep her safe and secure while they drive her to the doctor. You'll go with her."

Big tears welled in his eyes. "I don't wanna shot."

Harvey stifled his chuckle and patted his knee. "There, there. Don't cry. I don't think you'll need a shot."

Distant red lights strobed over the eerily still highway.

"Carter, help is coming. I need to go now."

The boy squeezed his bear. "Okay. Bye, Tall Man."

And as he always did, Harvey left the scene like a ghost who'd never been there before anyone had the presence of mind to ask questions. An apparition. A placeholder until the real rescuers arrived.

TWENTY-FIVE

Present Day

Ivy rolled out of bed feeling like sandbags clung to her frame. Seth. The missing journal. The questions she was afraid to ask. The awkward dance around the donuts with Reese.

She hated this discordant rhythm to their friendship. Like one of them waltzed while the other did a frenetic cha-cha.

Ivy walked outside, attempting to clear her head and check on ghost-dog. She smiled at the empty bowl. She refilled it with kibble. "Hey, buddy. If you're in there, it's me, Ivy. Let's be friends, okay?"

She returned to the house and showered and got ready for the day. Still her mind felt like clogged pipes. She grabbed her phone and scrolled through her mood-booster playlist. Dance therapy was one of her students' favorite ways to decompress. Maybe it was worth a try. Besides, there was no one there to witness her looking like a fool. She grinned and bit her lip, thumb hovering over "Shake It Off," by Taylor

Swift. She shook her head, laughing at the memory attached to that song.

Sick to death of the old-time gospel radio Grandma had been playing all summer, Ivy had snuck and changed the station when she left the room. "Shake It Off" had just come on the radio when Grandma cleared her throat behind Ivy. She turned, ready for her disapproval when Grandma said, "Hmph. I like the sound of that girl. She's got *spunk*."

Ivy clicked play. "This one is for you, Grandma."

She bounced on her toes, finding the beat. Letting her arms hang loose at her sides, completely focused on releasing the tension in her shoulders. When the chorus swelled, she cut loose. Ad-libbed spins and side-to-side twists. Gyrations of her own creation. It wasn't pretty, but it felt so good. Free. A reprieve from the anxiety and pain she'd tried to keep tamped down.

Ivy grabbed her bottled water off the side table like it was a microphone and lip-synched the lyrics.

A tap sounded on the front window. Ivy dropped the water bottle and spun toward the window with a yelp.

Reese stood on the other side of the glass, arms crossed over his chest with a smirk on his face.

She buried her face in her hands with a groan and slunk out of view until the song ended. At least this would overshadow her weird behavior last night.

"Hey," his slightly muffled voice came through the door, "are you going to let me in?"

"Do I have to?"

"I've known you since you were five. This isn't the first time I've witnessed your . . . erm . . . stellar dance moves. Besides, I brought coffee."

She opened the door a crack. "Fine. But you aren't allowed to make fun of me."

"Agreed."

She opened the door to let him in, and he picked up two coffees from the little table by the door. He handed one to her. "Careful, Taylor, it's hot."

"Reese . . ."

"Okay, okay." He snickered. "I'm all business from here on out."

Taking separate rooms, they picked through the house, collecting the items Grandma had listed to go to Abiding Love Ranch, a women's shelter where women healed from abusive relationships.

Uncle Vee's landscaping team buzzed in the background while Ivy filled the boxes with the majority of Grandma's small kitchen appliances. Every now and then she'd catch the sound of Reese humming "Shake It Off" under his breath.

She really needed to get this job done and get out of Triune. It had gotten harder being around him over the years. Secretly longing for their relationship to be closer, more than it was.

Ivy rubbed her hands over her face, banishing her wayward thoughts. The dust particles on her hands sent her into a sneezing fit.

"Bless you."

Ivy started at his voice behind her. "Ha, thanks. Didn't know you were there."

"Yeah, you were pretty deep in thought."

Thank goodness the guy couldn't read minds.

Reese placed a waffle iron in the box. "I've been thinking about this whole 'Where did Ivy come from' mystery."

She lifted a brow as she placed the toaster next to the waffle iron. "Oh yeah?"

"You have to have been born in Tennessee."

Ivy froze. "What? Why? What did you find?"

His lips twitched. "Nothing, but you're the only ten *I* see."

She narrowed her eyes, wadded the dustrag hanging from her pocket, and chucked it at his head. He ducked.

"You really are awful."

He snorted and wrestled his expression into feigned penitence. "Sorry. Too far."

She smirked. "Please tell me you don't use that awful pickup line on the girls you date. I mean, do they *actually* go for stuff like that? Or is this nonsense reserved just to torment me?"

He flashed a full grin. "Just for you. You know I don't date."

"I've never understood why."

He wrapped the blender glass in newsprint. "I guess I got a little hung up on this one girl years ago. I tried seeing other people, but when I was with them, I was always thinking about her. Problem is, she doesn't see me like that."

A sputtering laugh burst from her lips. "Yeah, right. Like that's ever been an issue for you." Since fifth grade there had always been a girl or two making goo-goo eyes at him and passing him notes.

He inspected the wrapped blender glass and shrugged. "You'd be surprised, Rosie-girl."

Ivy propped her hands on her hips, ignoring the prick to her heart. "So who is this girl? Does she know? Do I know her?"

He leaned his hip into the kitchen counter, crossing his

arms over his chest. "Nope. She hasn't a clue. In fact, if I told her how I felt about her right now, I have a strong suspicion she'd laugh in my face."

"Why?"

"Whenever I try to tell her I like her, she won't take me seriously."

"Come on. Who is she?"

"I'll tell you what. You answer a question from me, and I'll answer a question from you." A dare glinted his hazel eyes.

Caught up in his mischief, she lifted her chin. "Fair enough."

"Why didn't you call me when you got engaged?"

Well, she'd cha-cha'd right into that one. "This box is full. You wanna take it to the truck, and I'll start on a new one?"

He paused, the corner of his mouth twitching as he lifted the box and passed her. "Sure thing, Rosie-girl."

● ● ●

After hours of sorting and filling boxes, Ivy had one left.

Reese returned from depositing the previous load in his truck.

She plopped a patchwork quilt into the box. "I think this is the last of it. I'm cleaning out this linen closet and then we can go."

"Can I ask you something?"

His last question remained unanswered and fresh on her mind. A ripple of caution skittered up her spine.

"Have I done something to upset you? Is there a reason you suddenly stopped taking my calls several months back?"

She picked at the hem of her shirt, searching for an answer.

She could take this conversation a couple of different directions, either one riddled with relational land mines.

"I had my phone off last night because . . ." She sawed her bottom lip between her teeth. He wasn't going to stop asking questions. She might as well give a little and hope it was enough to satisfy his curiosity. "Because my ex was texting me. Trying to get back together with me, and I can't deal with it right now. I can't let myself fall back into talking to him."

He took a deep breath and spoke through his exhale. "You're not over him?"

Ivy ran her tongue over her teeth as she stacked an unopened pack of sheets in the box. She might never get over the way Seth exploited all the cracks in her heart. "No, I'm not."

Reese hitched his thumb in his pocket and gave a single nod. "Gotcha." He paced the hallway while she worked. A slow amble. "So . . . you miss him and he wants to get back together. What's stopping you?"

Ivy sighed. "It's not that simple. That relationship . . . it wasn't good for me." Understatement of the year. She reached for the stack of towels on the top shelf of the linen closet. Rocking up on her toes, she was still a half-inch short.

"I have to admit, I never really got you and Seth as a couple."

Ivy turned and swallowed. She'd never confess why she went out with Seth that first time. She'd been waitressing at an upscale restaurant while Seth sat at a table of men and women, all dressed in power suits. The affluence dripped from them like honey. He'd flirted with the lonely wallflower struggling to land a school counselor position. She finally felt seen by someone. Someone important. She shrugged. "He's smart, successful, and knows all the right things to say." *And all the wrong things too.*

He gave her a tight smile. "I guess that's every girl's dream, right? Still, you never seemed happy with him, not really." He crossed his arms and leaned into the doorjamb of her uncle's old bedroom. "You've had sad eyes, Rosie-girl, and you deserve someone who makes your eyes spark."

Exposed by his simple phrase, heat rushed Ivy's face. She yanked her gaze to the carpet. "Sparky eyes, huh? I guess you have to know who you are and what you want to be happy. Somewhere along the way, I got a little lost."

At the muted sound of his steps drawing nearer, she lifted her chin, doing everything in her power to keep her expression neutral. He smiled. His full-on, carefree Reese smile. The kind that lit his face when they were a couple of sixteen-year-olds cruising down the back roads with the windows down. "Well, you're in luck."

She fidgeted with the fresh cut ends of her hair, and then turned back to her hopeless towel retrieval endeavor before he could detect the heat radiating from her cheeks. "Oh?"

"I'm here. And that's what lifelong friends are for. To remind you who you are when you lose your way."

Ivy ground her teeth. The effect he had on her wasn't fair. They were friends, just friends. Exactly as it should be. Whatever she thought she saw in his eyes last night was a figment of her lonely imagination.

She couldn't be in this house with him anymore. She needed air. To clear her head. Get the towels and get out. She stretched her petite frame as far as it would go. Almost there.

"Hey, let me get that, silly."

She stretched, balanced on one tiptoe. "No, I got it."

He edged close to her, reaching around her. His chest brushed against her back. Her spine stiffened as she sucked air through her nose.

"You're so hardheaded. Accepting help now and then wouldn't kill you."

She turned toward him. His face mere inches from hers. "I said, I got it. Back—"

The vulnerability in his eyes stole the words from her lips.

He raised his hands, palms out, and stepped back in surrender.

Ivy swallowed and turned, jumping to snag the corner of the bottom towel. The stack toppled, raining down towels on top of her head. A four by six paper rectangle wafted to the carpet.

TWENTY-SIX

October 6, 1994

Miriam sat in the corner booth, inhaling the yeasty scent of baking bread. The quirky soup and sandwich shop was a pleasant surprise stuck in the middle of a run-down strip mall.

She checked her watch. Thomas should be there any minute.

Miriam relaxed into the booth, reflecting on last night's gathering. She thought of how she had worked with Ashley and her friend to make meals to stock the girls' freezers. How they constantly asked Miriam for reassurance. Who would have thought spending an evening with those young mothers could have been so fulfilling?

Ashley's words still warmed her. *"I wish my mom would've done things like this with me. Taught me how to cook. Christmas cookies, or something. She wasn't ever really there for me and my little sister though. This is so nice, Miriam."*

At her words, something sweet and tender had unfolded in Miriam's chest. It should have amplified the opportunities she would never have with her own children or the recent loss of her mother, but the light in Ashley's eyes woke a world of redemption for missed opportunities. She was able to be a part of that because she had opened her home and . . . her heart.

"Miri, I'm so sorry."

Thomas stood in front of her with a tenderness in his expression that must have been there all along, but she hadn't been of a mind to notice until lately. Her insides warmed at the sight of him in his suit and his hair a bit ruffled by the wind.

"Oh, it's all right. I've been enjoying the ambiance of this place."

He slid in beside her on the circular booth. "I had to make a quick stop by the hospital before I came."

"Is someone sick?"

"No. Mary Grayson and Carter were in a car accident late last night."

Her heart clenched. "Was it serious?"

"They hit a deer on the highway. She had a concussion and was unconscious, so they kept her overnight for observation. She's being released now."

She loosened her grip on the edge of the table. "And little Carter is okay?"

Thomas gave her a crooked grin. "He was there with his dad. Kept going on and on about the Tall Man. In the words of a three-year-old, 'Tall Man rescued me and wiped my boo-boo.'"

"A paramedic?"

"Carter insisted the man came before the ambulance. Somebody called 911 from Mary's car phone, and it certainly wasn't Mary. No one was with them when the police and paramedics arrived, but the emergency flashers had been turned on."

"How strange."

"You know what they say . . . about entertaining angels unawares."

She glanced around and then lowered her voice. "Do you remember the guy who showed up out of nowhere when our tire blew out?"

Thomas shook his head. "Sort of. I mean I couldn't pick him out of a lineup. The rain was coming down in sheets, and we both had the hoods of our slickers pulled down tight over our ball caps. He didn't say more than a few mumbled words through the pounding rain and vanished before I had the chance to thank him."

"Could it have been the same guy?"

"I guess. But who could it be? There's nothing but abandoned farms in the area."

She shrugged and twisted her wedding band. That night she'd been hunched in the passenger seat, sulking as Thomas worked on the trailer tire.

Already missing her home in the bustling metropolis and exhausted from the trip, she had glared outside at the men hunched by the spare tire. The blowout had felt like one more sign Thomas was wrong about his plan to leave their old church behind.

Shame heated the back of her neck for the way she'd behaved. She should have been by his side out there helping him. Not that the perpetually chivalrous man would have let her. But she'd never offered, and that was indictment enough.

"I'll go up and order for us. Italian sub and a side salad?"

Miriam nodded and watched him approach the owner of the establishment. She smiled at the way he so easily connected with people. It didn't make sense that the church didn't respond in the same way. Unless . . . it was her fault.

Thomas returned to the table with their drinks. "Look at the bread this place makes." He pointed to the bakery racks behind the counter. "I hope Pearl won't be offended if I make this my new lunch spot. With you as my date, of course."

She grinned. "I hope this doesn't bruise your ego, but from what you've told me, she won't even notice."

"The baby has been so good for her."

"Pearl keeping Ivy gave me an idea. What if I organized other retired women in the community to assist with childcare and mentoring these young women? They're more receptive and ready to learn than I ever imagined."

A spark lit in his eye as he leaned forward and covered her folded hands with his own. "Oh, Miri. What a wonderful idea. You could bridge so many gaps in this community. Especially if you were the one to pitch it to the women in the congregation. Told them your experiences. I mean, if you feel up for it. I don't want to push you."

"It's made such a difference in my own heart getting to know them personally. To see their hearts and struggles. I was so judgmental toward them weeks ago because of my own life—and, well, you know . . ."

Thomas squeezed her hands and leaned close. His forehead brushed her cheek. "I know, sweetheart. I know. I felt awful, because I was sure my encouragement to be involved was making things worse instead of better. I'm happy about your idea, but so much more than that. It's the light I've seen growing in your eyes over the past week."

She gave him a wobbly smile and wriggled a hand free to push her wayward red curls back from her face. "Thom. It's been a good week. I just want you to know this thing I'm going through is a day-to-day thing. And—"

"I'm sorry. I know I'm getting overly excited. I'm in love with your plan and your heart behind it. Take your time and do whatever you're ready for. Seriously, Miri. I don't care what anyone says. It's not your job or my job to pull this community together. The Lord works on his time. On you, on me, on all of us."

"What anyone says? They've been complaining because I haven't been there, haven't they? They must think I don't care about you or the church or—"

Thomas held out his hand. "Miri. Stop. Be more involved when you're ready. I mean it. Appeasing the church people's preconceived notions is not your job. Your job is to heal and to make peace with things. And yes, when you feel able, I do love you being there. You bring something to a room I never could."

She cut her eyes toward him. "Brownnoser."

"I prefer the title 'Infatuated Husband.' Now our soups and sandwiches are headed this way, so let's put our focus into what really matters." He winked.

Miriam shook her head. Thomas was a rare man among men—rare among pastors, for that matter. He didn't see her as an ornament adding to his appeal. He saw her and gave her the space she needed to become the woman she was meant to be. Maybe someday she'd know who that was.

TWENTY-SEVEN

Present Day

Ivy slung the fallen towels aside and knelt to retrieve the piece of paper. Kodak's watermark covered the back. "It's a photograph."

She flipped it over and her eyes widened. It was a slightly out of focus picture. A tiny baby wrapped in a purple blanket. Some broad-shouldered figure held the child, but the person's head had been cut off by the photographer. Whoever it was, they wore the tackiest Hawaiian shirt she'd ever seen.

Emotions she didn't understand swelled inside her chest. The baby was her. It had to be. She had a blanket just like the one in the picture in the memory box her mom kept. Ivy stared at the only newborn picture she'd ever seen of herself. Who held her and who took the picture? Who were these people in the in-between, before her parents started fostering her as a three-month-old? And would she ever find her answers?

Her shaking hand tightened on the picture, creasing the edges.

Reese knelt beside her and tenderly worked it from her hand, laid it aside, and wrapped his arms around her shivering frame. Solid and safe.

Ivy tried to fill her lungs, but it was as if they'd been replaced by a sieve.

Reese cradled her against his chest with her head resting beneath his chin. He rubbed slow circles on her back. Ivy clamped her eyes tight against all the swirling thoughts. "What's going on in that head of yours?"

Ivy straightened and shifted away from him. "I can't make sense of this. Grandma had to have known my birth parents to have this newborn picture. Known me before I ended up on my parents' doorstep. The man holding me . . . could he be m-my dad? Why would she have kept me from knowing them?"

He brushed the hair back from her face, tucking it behind her ear. "But the story about the doorstep. I thought you didn't . . ." He left the words dangling.

There was always one fairy-tale version or another Ivy crafted around her birth story. When she was young, Ivy envisioned herself like Briar Rose from Sleeping Beauty, hidden to be protected from some evil being. And one day her mother would return to tell her the spell had been broken and they could all be together. Both sides of herself—adopted and biological together as one.

Secretly clinging to the doorstep story was her grown-up fairy tale. But if Grandma knew about her before her adoption, what was the real story of how she ended up with her adoptive parents? Whatever it was, it had to be so terrible that someone stole an elderly lady's journal to keep it a secret.

Ivy hiccupped, swallowing back a sob that was trying to break loose and wrestling emotions she didn't really understand.

He held his arms open, beckoning her back into his embrace. "Come here."

She pressed her eyelids, willing the tears to retreat before she lost all handle on them. There was just too much. Too much hurt. Too much confusion about her feelings for Reese. And too many scattered pieces to her life seeming to go to a dozen different jigsaw puzzles.

She took a breath that hitched in her ribs. "I'll be okay. Let's go."

His shoulders sagged as he looked away. "All right, Rosie-girl. If you say so." He stood and held out a hand, pulling her to her feet.

Ivy tossed the fallen towels in the box, hoisted it, and left Reese to trail behind.

● ● ●

They rolled down the long maple-lined drive of Abiding Love Ranch and stopped in front of a large lodge ringed by a half circle of smaller cabins. There was a hush about the place, a hovering peace usually found in quiet chapels. A sharp contrast to the stilted silence between Reese and Ivy on the thirty-minute drive.

As Ivy unhooked her seat belt, a woman with shoulder-length, salt-and-pepper hair strode toward them wearing faded jeans and western style boots. Ivy hopped from the truck and approached, hand extended. The woman gripped Ivy's hand with a firm, calloused handshake.

"You must be Pearl's granddaughter. I'm Raylene, the director here at Abiding Love Ranch."

"Yes, ma'am, it's good to meet you." Ivy motioned to Reese as he exited the truck. "This is my friend Reese. Grandma's things are in the back of his truck."

She nodded a greeting to Reese, then turned and took both of Ivy's hands. Her kind blue eyes pooled but held the tears from dripping down her sun-spotted cheeks. "We're so grateful to your grandmother for thinking of us. She's been such a staple to this place for the past twenty years. Even when her health wasn't good, she always found a way to send help in one form or another."

Ivy stilled. "Grandma volunteered here all these years? She never mentioned . . ."

"Oh, yes, She—"

"Miss Raylene, where would you like me to unload these?" Reese walked over, his arms loaded down with boxes.

"You can carry them to the side door of the main house. Margerie in the office will show you where to put them." Raylene moved to grab a box.

Reese shook his head. "Leave those to me. I'll let you two talk."

Ivy mouthed the word *thanks*.

He dipped his chin and continued on toward the house.

"I'd love to hear more about Grandma's work here, if you don't mind. She never talked about it. And it sounds like it was a big part of who she was in her later years."

Raylene motioned to a large pavilion on the edge of a pond. "Why don't we head over this way so you can see more of the grounds? Abiding Love Ranch provides temporary housing, job training, and counseling for up to thirty residents at a time. Most of the women who come here are from imminently dangerous situations, so as you can imagine, anonymity and privacy are of the utmost importance. But we do our best to make this place feel as normal as possible."

Ivy chewed the inside of her cheek as her pulse upticked and she kept pace with Raylene. "So, domestic violence?"

Raylene nodded. "Some are cases of domestic violence. We've also housed victims of human trafficking who are healing and starting a new life. Others haven't been in physically abusive relationships but come here to escape emotionally and verbally abusive partners."

Ivy swallowed and stared at the fine grit crunching under her feet. "Emotional abuse?" The way Raylene looked at her when she posed the question left Ivy naked. Exposed. As if Raylene could see all the shame and embarrassment Ivy carried.

"People normally ask me to explain that one. They don't think emotional abuse warrants coming to a place like this. But sometimes people need support while they heal from wounds people can't see."

They settled on a bench in the gazebo and gazed over the water. A blue heron stalked the water's edge, hunting lunch. On the other side of the pond, a group of three women rode on horseback. The acrid scent of campfire wafted on the gentle breeze. Ivy's eyes fluttered closed for a moment. Woodsmoke was one of her favorite smells.

Raylene pointed in the riders' direction. "Equine therapy makes a huge difference with a lot of the ladies." She shook her head. "I'm sorry. I've been rattling on. Is there anything in particular you'd like to know about your grandmother's work at the ranch?"

Ivy picked at the tassel on her peasant blouse. A thought wriggled its way to the front of her mind. Something that pushed the scattered jigsaw pieces of her history closer together. "Was there any certain woman my grandmother talked about? Or that she spent a lot of time with?"

"There were many your grandmother got close to over the years. She was so good with them. That gentle mothering way of hers had a way of crumbling the hardest of facades. I have something one of the volunteers put together after your grandmother passed. A tribute of sorts. I'd originally planned to keep it in the library, but you might like to have it. Follow me."

Ivy stood and wiped her sweaty palms on her jeans and followed Raylene's steps.

On the walk back, Ivy passed a young woman about her age. Her eyes were dark-circled and weary. She glanced at Ivy, and her gaze skittered away. She stepped off the path as she passed, giving Ivy and Raylene a wide berth.

Raylene tilted her chin, her expression tender. "One of our new residents. They go through a lot before they get here. So many people have been betrayed and hurt by the people closest to them. Some were even sold into sexual slavery by their own families. By abusive boyfriends, fathers . . . mothers. Being able to finally look another person in the eye is a monumental feat for some of them."

An ache throbbed in Ivy's heart for that girl. And for the way her expression and behavior reflected how Ivy felt on the inside. Edging away from anyone who tried to come close. But Ivy hadn't been through a fraction of what the girl had likely been through. Ivy ought to be stronger. She ought to be a lot of things.

Inside the office, Raylene placed a scrapbook in Ivy's hands. "There are a lot of pictures of your grandmother with past residents and other volunteers. First names only. At least the names we knew the women by. Some used aliases to protect their identities."

Ivy sank into a chair and thumbed through the book. She couldn't help but smile, no matter how much her heart ached when she saw her grandmother smiling back at her, posed with much younger women. There were even a couple with her grandma on horseback and camping. Things she never knew her grandmother took an interest in.

Reese met them in the office, dusting off his hands after depositing the last load in the corner closet. "All finished. Whatcha got there?" He sidled over, edging around chairs in the cramped office to come stand behind her shoulder.

Ivy turned the page. "A tribute to Grandma."

Reese let out a low whistle. "Who is that she's with? That woman is your spitting image, Ivy."

Ivy's jaw slackened. Grandma, a less bent and wrinkled version than Ivy remembered—stood next to . . . to whom? With shaking hands Ivy slipped the photo from the corner tabs holding it in place. On the back of the photo were words written in blue smudged ink.

Pearl Howard and Rose, 1998.

• CHAPTER •

TWENTY-EIGHT

DECEMBER 14, 1998

Laney shifted her backpack and eyed the diner's storefront from behind a stand of bushes. She watched the people coming and going. She shouldn't have stopped. It only teased the hollowed-out ache in her middle.

She fingered the damp edges of the five bucks she slipped from Vance's wallet. It wasn't stealing. Not when that money should have been hers.

He'd find her again. Just like always. But if she made him look long enough, hard enough. Sparked his anger high enough, maybe he really would kill her this time. Finish the job he threatened so many times. And then she'd finally be free.

The thought of freedom, of never having to look over her shoulder, propelled her toward the diner. Why be cautious? Might as well get a warm meal in her cold, cramped stomach. Enjoy whatever temporary pleasure was in front of her. Vance couldn't really hurt her. Not when he'd already destroyed everything that mattered.

She tucked her tangled, damp hair beneath her ball cap and tugged it low. Her wet jeans chafed her thighs and her raw feet seared as she walked toward the door. Maybe last night's rainstorm was enough to delay Vance's search a little longer. That and he'd been drunk out of his mind.

Laney slunk into a corner booth, back to the wall. Eyes on the door. She glanced at the menu, thankful this greasy spoon offered cheap food and heat. The warmth in the narrow diner seeped through her damp clothes. She shuffled up to the counter and ordered a cup of coffee and a biscuit with gravy.

Her stomach full for the first time in as long as she could remember, Laney relaxed a fraction. Until the front door clanked. She flinched and peered under her ball cap, knowing it was Vance, coming to drag her out the door. But no, it was a short little old lady. She tottered in and sat at the booth across the aisle, chatting up the cook like they were best friends.

Laney stood to pay. Better get on her way. Travel as far as the fuel in her belly would take her. The old woman passed her, heading toward the restroom. Keeping her eyes cast down, Laney paid the cashier and slipped one dollar into the tip jar. The other she pocketed. One whole dollar. Might as well stick that in the jar too for all the good it would do her.

She passed the lady's vacant booth. The car keys she'd left on the laminate table glinted from the overhead lighting. All alone in the wide open.

Laney's finger twitched. So easy. Her answer right in front

of her. Grab the keys and drive the car until the gas ran out, ditch it, and keep running.

Out the front window, she spied a brown Oldsmobile. Classic old lady car. She stepped to the booth. Might as well. It wasn't as though one more sin would paint her soul blacker than it already was.

She grabbed the keys, their teeth cutting into her palm. A hand gripped her forearm. Laney gasped, body frozen in place.

But it wasn't the crushing, scarred hands she'd expected. Instead, they were bony fingers with pink-painted fingernails.

"You got trouble over there, Pearl?" The grizzled line cook called out from behind the counter.

The lady whispered next to Laney's ear, her voice scratchy. "Do I?"

Laney dropped the keys on the table with a clank and shook her head.

"We're all right over here, Steve."

Still the woman didn't release her. Laney lifted her gaze, prepared for the scorn she'd see there. But the woman studied Laney's arms, not her face. The bruises and the track marks. Both put there by Vance to keep her under his power. Laney wrenched her arm away and backstepped.

"I can help you." The woman's voice was tender and light. "I know a place you can go. Hot meals. Roof over your head."

Like she hadn't heard those words before. Depending on the kindness of a stranger had ruined her life.

Laney edged away. "Where? County jail?"

"I know desperation when I see it. Just let me help you get somewhere safe."

Laney lifted her head to lock eyes with this woman who promised things no one could deliver.

The woman's eyes widened, and she sucked in a soft breath. The lines in her face deepened. Staring like she was a long-lost child.

"What?"

The lady shook her head as if to clear it. "Just let me help you. Please."

"No, I—" The front door clanked. A dark hulking figure appeared, shadowed by the morning light behind him.

Laney sank into the booth, tugging her hat lower. This was it. Ten lousy miles of freedom and one hot meal. Oh, how she'd pay for it.

"What's the matter, dear?"

"That man. At the door. He's here for me."

"He's the reason you were about to abscond with my car?" The woman turned toward the door. "Honey, there's nobody—"

"Shh!" Laney hissed.

"I can take you to a place he won't be able to get to you. But you have to come with me. Walk out the back door of this diner and don't look back."

Laney lifted her head a fraction. "We'll never make it."

The woman thumbed at the paunchy cook who hummed and wiped the countertops like he hadn't a care in the world. "You see Steve there? He's an old friend and he knows how to handle himself. Wouldn't believe it by looking at him now, but he used to be part of a motorcycle gang in another life. He'll make sure we get out of here without being bothered."

"He'll just follow us once we leave."

"I'm trying to tell you. I don't know what you thought you saw, but nobody's come through that door since I came back from the restroom. Whoever is after you isn't here. If we go now, I can get you somewhere safe. We won't have to worry about anyone following us."

The old lady was blind. Maybe crazy too. Laney shifted in her seat and leaned to steal a glance at the door. Like she'd said, no one was there. But he could be out in the parking lot, tucked around a corner, waiting to ambush her.

The woman sat and gripped her hand. Laney flinched and the old woman released her hold. "There's a better life for you out there than the one you're living. All you have to do is take hold of it. Follow me out that door."

"I don't have no money." Laney's heart pounded in her chest—hope rebelling against the doubt roiling inside her head. What if the lady was somehow in on it? A trick to lure her, and then the old bat would just drive her back to Vance. Then again, maybe, just maybe this was her ticket. Maybe the path to freedom didn't involve death at Vance's hands.

"You don't need money. Your way has already been paid in advance."

"All I got is the clothes on my back. I can't give you nothing." Laney crossed her arms over her chest. "No currency you'd be interested in anyway."

"I don't want your money. I just want to get you somewhere safe. Everybody deserves to be safe." She stood. "Come with me."

Laney stood, legs trembling. Eyes darting, searching for Vance's henchman—her keeper when Vance was too drunk or drugged up to do the job.

She followed the woman to her car and climbed into the passenger seat of the brown Oldsmobile. The car had to be ancient, but it had a shine like it was brand new.

Inside the car, her own damp, unwashed smell filled her nose, and her face heated. If this woman had met her five years ago, she wouldn't recognize her. "How do you know I'm not an ax murderer?"

Pearl cranked the car. The engine purred. "I know that look. You're not out to hurt. You need help."

Help. What did that word mean for her anymore? She was beyond help. Had been for a long time. She resisted the urge to press her hands over her ears in a futile effort to silence the phantom newborn cries that filled her ears without warning.

"I'm Pearl Howard, by the way."

Laney nodded.

"And you are?"

Laney's lips trembled. "Rose. Call me Rose." The name she'd used when she'd tried to run away before and failed.

She wished she really was her aunt Rose. Aunt Rose was strong and bold. Laney had always loved that she bore her aunt's name as her middle name. As if she somehow carried that same strength just by association. If Aunt Rose hadn't died months before Dad kicked her out of the house, none of the horrible broken things would have happened. Laney Rose would have a life. A beautiful life. With a high school diploma. A future.

But instead, she'd been forced to rely on a stranger. A stranger who broke her.

Maybe even though Aunt Rose was gone, taking on her name could be her shelter. Vance didn't know it. Let Laney disappear and Rose would live on in her place. And Rose would be strong. She would overcome. Not cower in that dark dank backwoods trailer like Laney had.

TWENTY-NINE

OCTOBER 17, 1994

Pearl worked in the kitchen, elbow-deep in suds, listening to Harvey's sweet tones as he babbled with Ivy. It was funny how a person's voice altered when they spoke to a baby. Awkward and abrupt Harvey chattered away like it was second nature.

He'd changed over the past few weeks. He met her eye when he spoke to her now. Instead of a staccato word spillage as anxiety twisted him into knots, Harvey became expressive, using actual sentences.

Warmth filled her at the idea—that he could be at home here. She balanced the bowls and spoons on the tray and nudged her way out to the front porch.

Harvey wasn't far behind, cradling Ivy as she drank her bottle. He lowered into one of the yellow rockers. "Don't wait on me. I'm going to enjoy this little one while she has her dinner."

"You're going to spoil her rotten."

"I plan on it. Everyone needs a little spoiling."

Like him. She hoped she was spoiling him rotten, because she got the feeling he'd never had that. How she craved the story behind the man who shied from human contact, skulking about as though he didn't deserve ground to stand upon. Yet, he nurtured a child with the tenderness and care of one who'd spent a lifetime receiving love.

He looked up at her. "Pastor Thomas said you used to be a hairdresser."

She nodded. "In my younger days."

"This weekend, he's sharing with the board about me working. He thought it might be good if I got a trim, and he thought you might . . . but you don't have to." He flicked a glance over her blue-gray bouffant.

She laughed. "I'd be happy to. And don't worry. I didn't do this to myself. I let this lady in beauty school do my hair even though she makes a mess of it every time. She needs the practice, and she's earned a bit of a reputation. I'm the only one brave enough or crazy enough to keep going back."

"I'd appreciate it. I want to look my best."

When Ivy finished her bottle, he placed her on the blanket. He scrounged in his pocket. "I have something for you. It's stupid, now that I think about it. But I found this and thought of you." He held out his hand with the shyness of a boy giving his teacher an apple. In the center of his palm was a black button.

He glanced at her feet. "Your left bunny is missing an eye."

She pressed her hands to her cheeks. "Did I ever tell you the story of my slippers?"

"No, ma'am. Just thought you were partial to 'em."

"They were an accidental gift from my son. He was on a

deployment and wasn't going to make it home for Christmas. He called Elliot to ask him to pick up a gift for me, but the satellite phone must have had a bad connection. When Marshall came home, I made sure to have them on. I was so confused when he teased me about them. When we finally figured out the mistake, we laughed until tears came from our eyes. It had been a long time since any of us had laughed like that.

"They're ratty as can be now, but I can't make myself replace them. Thank you, Harvey. For the button. It means a lot."

He shrugged and his face reddened. "It's nothing."

"What about you? What was your favorite gift?"

"Me? Oh, I don't know. I guess it would have to be that little girl." Ivy cooed and waved her arms as though excited by his sentiment.

"Oh, that's a given. I meant from when you were growing up."

Harvey fiddled with the zipper pull on his sweatshirt. "One time at the children's home, a boy won a bike in a drawing. Everyone was so excited."

A children's home? That explained some things. "Oh, that must have been nice for him. But I meant you. Have you ever been given a gift that meant a lot to you?"

"Uh . . . not when I was growing up." His face turned red. "But someone once gave me a pretty special pair of boots."

She ducked her chin. "My goodness. I forgot all about the chocolate chip cookies. I'll be right back."

Inside the house, her tears ran rivers down her wrinkled cheeks. The mothering place in her heart—that precious flame prematurely stamped out—surged in her chest.

• ● •

Harvey braved opening his eyes. Dread curled in his stomach. Thick piles of brown hair coated Pearl's checkered linoleum. Not that Pearl could do any worse to his hair than the ugly mop it had been, but there was an awful lot of it on the floor. He probably resembled a skinned cat about now.

"How's it going, Miss Pearl?" He raised his voice over the buzz of the electric trimmers.

"It seems there is a real boy underneath here, after all. A fine-looking one, at that." She switched off the clippers and scissor-cut the top.

It had been odd at first, being touched—someone standing so close. But the gentle way she worked over his hair—it had opened up a shut-away place. A place that remembered what it was to be comforted. To be loved. He wrinkled his nose when a few snipped strands fell beneath his nostrils.

"I like this look for you, Harvey. I left it longer on the top and tighter on the sides."

"I like my hair short but hadn't gotten around to getting a trim." A half-truth. He was full of those lately.

"All done. You ready to see Harvey James, church employee edition?"

A herd of jumping beans sprang loose in his stomach. He lifted the hand mirror Pearl had plopped in his lap and paused at half-mast.

She faced him with an expectant spark in her eyes. "Go on. Look already. A reflection can't bite." She clasped her hands and tucked them under her chin.

He grinned. Despite her mile-high hair and creased skin, she reminded him of a child on Christmas morning. He lifted the mirror. This man smiled back at him. The smile dropped. Harvey ran his hand across the close-cropped sides, and then down his jawline that had a square shape he hadn't noticed before. He turned his head to the left and the right. Pearl had swept the longer part on top slightly to the side with gel to hold it in place.

"How much you hate it?"

Harvey blinked and placed the mirror back in his lap, remembering the woman in front of him. "It's . . . I . . . don't hate it. Thank you."

She walked behind him and dusted the back of his neck with a barber brush.

"I . . . uh. I look like somebody."

"Like who?"

"No. I mean I look like somebody who belongs with . . . you know . . . regular people."

"You've always been somebody, but if this little ol' haircut was a part of you recognizing who you've always been, I'm glad to have helped. It does suit you."

Harvey managed a tight smile. "Pastor Thomas said it would be good if I wore something other than my usual. I have a gray T-shirt and a newer pair of hunting pants. Do you think it'd be okay? My only collared shirts have palm trees."

She unsnapped the cape from around his neck. Loose hair fluttered to the floor. "The T-shirt's okay. It'd be better tucked in with a nice pair of jeans or slacks."

There was no way he was wasting money on new clothes for himself to impress a bunch of church people who were probably going to turn him away. Saving up to get out of Triune was top priority. Pearl wouldn't let this game of playing house with Ivy go on forever.

She'd tried to get him talking so many times. *Have you heard from your sister? Don't you think it's time you made a report? Are you going to try to get custody of Ivy? There's a lawyer I know . . .*

He and Ivy had to get out of town. Soon.

"I know it would be better." He looked at his hands. "I just don't have a whole lot of options." Heat pulsed in the tips of his ears. He'd never been ashamed of his clothes. Liked them—no. Their level of appropriateness had never mattered, but now they left him feeling naked.

Pearl bustled about, sweeping hair into a pile. "I might have a few things. I don't know if they are your style. But I think they'd be good for your interview."

He smirked. "You have a spare kimono?"

She burst into laughter. "Harvey, I do declare you have a sense of humor under that stoic manner of yours. Although my old kimono would make a statement." She sobered. "I wasn't offering *my* clothes. They were my son's. He . . . he passed almost a year ago. He didn't wear them or anything. Some people are funny about things like that. They were supposed to be part of his Christmas. That he . . . uh . . . that he never had the chance to open."

There were still tears on her face, but he suspected the present ones were born of something heavier than laughter.

A chill sank in his stomach. He'd hurt her. He should leave jokes to comedians. "I'm sorry about your son."

"War is a terrible thing."

He nodded.

She swiped at her cheeks. "You hang tight. He was built a lot like you so I think it all should fit. I don't know where in the world he got his height. My husband, Elliot, was a shade over five foot eight. And Marshall turned out a lanky six foot two."

She shuffled away.

Inhaling the scent of the soup reheating on the stove, he peered out the kitchen window overlooking the churchyard—the one he'd caught Pearl spying on him out of time and time again. What had once seemed threatening had taken on an endearing quality. Maybe she hadn't been making sure he wasn't burning the church to the ground. Could it be she was instead concerned about . . . him?

He turned away and shook his head to clear the silly thought. Thought, or *longing*. Harvey swallowed. He needed air. The walls closed in—the cozy kitchen oppressive.

Pearl poked her head around the kitchen entryway. "Sit down on the stool and close your eyes."

Harvey jerked at her intrusion on his anxiety meltdown. "What?"

"Oops. Sorry to startle you. Now don't 'what' me. Do as you're told. Sit down, close your eyes, and pretend you like your gift."

"Why would I pretend—"

"Because that's what polite young men do when old ladies buy them ugly clothes for Christmas."

"It's October."

"For heaven's sakes, let me have my moment. Ivy is about to wake up, as you well know. And December's a hard month for me now anyways. I'd rather celebrate in October this year."

Harvey sat on the stool and closed his eyes, his knee bouncing. She shouldn't be making such a fuss over him—she wouldn't if she knew the truth. All the lies he'd told. He took a breath and forced himself to still. The least he could do was play along, be grateful even if he didn't deserve it.

A plastic shopping bag crinkled as it was plopped in his lap. "Open your eyes." She smiled, but there was something ragged in her expression.

He pulled out two pairs of blue jeans. One dark, the other medium blue. Next was a dark green collared shirt of thin material like Pastor Thomas wore. He sucked air between his lips. The last shirt in the bag was brushed flannel in navy-and-green plaid. The empty bag fell to the floor. Harvey stared at the clothes he'd piled on the table. All brand new with the tags still on.

"I know they probably aren't your style. But I thought . . . for the interview—"

In a flash, he was eight years old all over again, discarded in a children's home after three consecutive sets of foster parents found him "difficult." A blonde woman handed him a green-and-navy checked shirt, brand new with the tags still on. Her tender smile had whispered that everyone was wrong about him. That he could be loved.

Harvey had worn that shirt almost every day for two years until a house mother trashed it. Despite his tears, she'd deemed it unsuitable just because the cuffs rested halfway up his forearm, and three buttons had popped off the too-tight chest.

He pulled in oxygen and willed his voice to cooperate. "It's what I would've picked out if I had the choice. Thank . . ." He let out a puff of air. "Thank you."

He forced himself to meet her eye as his heart battered around inside his chest.

Her chin quivered when she opened her mouth.

Ivy let out a cry from the bedroom. Pearl put a hand to her cheek. "Oh, Little Miss doesn't want to be left out of the party."

Harvey half rose.

She patted his shoulder. "You go try on your clothes. I'll see to her." Pearl slipped from the room before he could argue.

He hoisted the stack and wandered down the hallway, looking for a place to change. He pulled a door to one of her spare bedrooms. He slipped on a pair of jeans and the plaid shirt. Everything seemed to fit. He turned in search of a mirror.

The chair in the corner with a ragged bear caught his attention instead. Then his gaze roamed over the photograph in a bronze frame. It was of a young man, probably five or six years his junior, trim and proper in his military uniform. A folded flag sat beside it.

Harvey swallowed. He wasn't supposed to be in here. In this room. In this house. It should be this young man, his wife, and Pearl's grandchild stopping in for a visit. But instead, she was left with society's reject and a baby who didn't belong to either of them.

He scooped up the clothes and slunk out of the room before Pearl realized where he'd stumbled—in a place he had no business being, wearing clothes he had no right to possess. He closed the door softly behind.

Pearl rounded the corner, babbling with Ivy. When Pearl caught him closing the door, the color drained from her face. He dropped the clothes and rushed forward to scoop Ivy into his arms.

She placed her arm against the wall to brace herself. "I

wasn't going to drop her, Harvey. I . . . you startled me, is all."

"That bad, huh?" He glanced down at his attire.

"No. You reminded me of my—you look really nice. The plaid shirt suits you. I had a feeling it would. I don't know why, but I've always thought you seemed like a plaid kind of person. Here, let's go out in the living room where I can take a gander at this new version of you." She shuffled over and retrieved the clothes he'd dropped.

He carried Ivy to the living room and laid her down on the play mat with pink butterflies and flowers dangling over her that Pearl had bought. Harvey straightened. "I had a shirt like this a long, long time ago."

A strange look crossed her face, but then she shook her head as though dismissing whatever notion passed through her head.

THIRTY

PRESENT DAY

Ivy rubbed her bleary eyes in front of the bathroom sink, desperate to rid herself of the images printed on the back side of her eyelids. Her sleep had been plagued by nightmares of her parents taking a crying child out of the arms of the haunted young woman from the scrapbook. But those were only dreams. Weren't they?

With shaking hands, Ivy picked up her phone and dialed.

Was it hereditary, winding up in abusive relationships? She'd been raised by what was quite possibly the strongest married couple on Planet Earth. It stood to reason Ivy would've learned something about choosing a mate from her adoptive parents. And yet, if the woman from the picture really was her birth mother, she'd ended up far more like a person she'd never even met.

"Hello, Ivy." Her dad's voice came through the line, rich and smooth.

"Dad, I need to ask you a question. And I need the truth. Who is Rose? Why is her name my middle name?"

"Ivy, slow down."

"My birth mother. Did you know her?"

"Ivy . . ."

"How did I get my name?" Ivy gripped the phone so tight her knuckles ached.

"From someone who loved you very much. We wanted to honor that love when we adopted you."

"Who?"

A heavy sigh came through the line. "I can't reveal that information. I wish I could say more but—"

"Not even for me? You're making some stranger's need for confidentiality more important than what I need? Why is keeping this from me such a big deal?" She winced, dreading the impact of her next words. "Did you and Mom take Grandma's journal?"

"I don't know anything about a journal, sweetheart." The seconds of silence throbbed in her ears. "As to why I won't reveal the secret of another, I'm allowing space for God to work."

"Space for God to work on what? I'm twenty-four years old. Isn't that time enough?"

Ivy ended the call and wrapped her arms around her middle.

Her parents and Grandma had been in league to protect somebody. But who? Why?

● ● ●

Ivy rocked in the porch swing, her mind flipping through memories. Through the bits and pieces she'd collected over her lifetime. But no matter how she twisted and turned the pieces, she couldn't make a cohesive picture.

Movement in her peripheral view snagged her attention. The ghost-dog stood outside the garage sniffing at the empty dish. She hurried inside for some deli meat.

He'd come a little closer to her yesterday evening. And he hadn't run at the sight of her.

She walked slowly toward him, crooning in low tones. "Hey there, buddy. It's your friend, Ivy. We're friends, right?"

The dog's tail dropped between his legs, and he cowered. But his nose wiggled at the meat she offered. It was the first time she'd gotten an up-close look at him. One blue eye, one brown. Floppy ears with black specks.

"You're pretty cute. You know that?"

She knelt, making herself smaller. Holding out the turkey, she clucked her tongue, inviting him forward. He crept closer. Ivy placed the meat on the ground in front of her. Hunger drove him, but it was obvious the pup waited for the worst. For the moment the hand that fed him would rise to strike him as well.

"What happened to you, huh? Did someone hurt you?"

He crept closer, belly almost to the ground. Ivy sat in the grass.

"That's it. You've almost made it." Gravel crunched in the driveway. The dog's head popped up high, and he scurried for the hole in the garage and disappeared. Ivy sighed and put the abandoned meat in the food bowl. "It's okay. We'll try again tomorrow."

Ivy turned toward the house.

Reese strolled up the sidewalk with his hands in his pockets. "Hey you, whatcha doin'?"

She lifted a corner of her mouth. "I'm supposed to be working on this house, but I got a little distracted."

He shielded his eyes against the afternoon sun. "Do you want to get out of here for a little bit? Go for a drive?"

She shrugged. "I wouldn't mind a change of scenery."

At the end of the drive, Reese stopped the truck before pulling onto the main road. He tapped out a staccato beat on the steering wheel even though the only sound coming from the radio was the rasp of static. He sawed one corner of his bottom lip. She leaned forward and clicked off the radio.

"What's up?" she asked.

He gave her a tight smile. "There's something I've been wanting to show you. One of my first big projects now that I'm out on my own. I'd like to know what you think."

"Sure thing, friend. Let's do it."

He gave a tight nod, his lips pressed in a line. "Friends. Is that the right word for us?"

She flinched.

Reese shook his head. "That didn't come out like I meant it. Sometimes I just wish you . . ." He released a breathy, humorless laugh. "Never mind."

Flooded by the need to explain why she'd distanced herself, words spilled from her. "I'm so sorry, Reese. I know I've been weird lately. It's complicated." She shook her head. "Actually, it's not. I just didn't want you to see the way I lost myself. I caged myself in a really terrible relationship and couldn't find my way out. I was about two steps from ending up at a place like Abiding Love. I never should've shut you out."

Reese grimaced. "I wasn't accusing you of being a bad

friend. I just—" His eyes narrowed. "Wait. What did you say?"

Ivy swallowed. That wasn't supposed to come out of her mouth, especially the bit about the ranch.

His knuckles whitened on the steering wheel. A muscle ticked in his jaw. "Are you trying to tell me . . . Did he . . . Did he *hurt* you?" His expression pinched as if he were the one who had experienced physical pain.

"Nothing like that." Even as she said the words, she could feel Seth's vice-like grip on her wrist.

Reese took his eyes from the road for an instant. He wore an expression laced with doubt. "You can tell me. We don't have to put up a pretty front for each other. You know that." He gave her a half-smile.

"I don't want to talk about Seth. I'm trying to heal from a messy relationship. Let's leave it at that."

He flicked a glance toward her, still gripping the steering wheel. "All right. If you change your mind, I'm listening."

She shrugged. "Enough about me. What is it you wanted to show me?"

Reese glanced her way. "Roll down your window and close your eyes."

Ivy narrowed her eyes. "Why—"

"Good grief. For once in your life could you do one thing I ask without arguing?" A smirk teased the corners of his mouth. "Humor me for five minutes. I want to see your first reaction so you can't pretend you like it to spare my feelings." He turned the crank to roll down his window.

She stole a glance at the sunlight reflected in his hazel eyes and the way the breeze ruffled his hair.

With her own window down, she closed her eyes and

propped her head in the crook of her arm, her elbow on the rim of the window. As they cruised down the country lane, she let the wind blow her hair wild. Everything wounded and roaming in her spirit stilled as the scent of honeysuckle tickled her nose, and she basked in the sweet southern sunshine.

She became so relaxed she forgot where she was or where she was going. When the bright sunlight shadowed, she opened her eyes without thinking and realized they'd entered into a more wooded area.

"Hey, you're supposed to have your eyes closed."

She sat up and turned toward Reese. There was something raw in his expression. Tender. Searching.

Ivy swallowed the lump in her throat. "One of us ought to watch the road."

He turned his face forward. "Both of us could drive this road blindfolded, and you know it." The husky quality to his voice jolted her middle. She snapped her eyes shut.

He cleared his throat. "You were so peaceful. At ease just being you. You want to know who Ivy Rose Lashley is? That's her. That's who you are."

She took a deep breath, absorbing his words. That's who she used to be.

After a few more minutes he took a turn, and a wide smile cramped her cheeks. "I know where we are."

"I thought you might. But you promised. Eyes stay closed."

It was like those childhood days of dozing off while returning from a long trip. She always had a way of waking up on the last turn. Like something inside her never forgot the path home no matter how far she'd strayed.

A moment later, he pulled to a stop. "Wait here. I'm coming around. Keep your eyes closed."

She unhooked her seat belt before he had a chance to get closer than necessary.

The door groaned as it opened. "Give me your hands."

Ivy gulped as his calloused hands engulfed hers. Warm. Solid.

She swayed a bit with her feet on the ground, and he led her forward before she was quite steady. A yelp squeaked out of her. "I'm going to fall. Can I open my eyes yet?"

His voice was soft and low. "I wouldn't let you fall, Rosie-girl. Just a little farther."

She walked a few more steps, swathed in the heady scent of magnolias. He took her by the shoulders and angled her slightly. "Okay. Open."

Ivy blinked in the sharp afternoon sunlight. She gasped. "It's beautiful." The last time she'd seen the historic farmhouse she grew up in, it was well on its way to being condemned. Complete with hip-high grass, chipped paint, and a sagging porch.

Today, it shone. Bright and white against the green of the close-shorn grass and ancient oak and sycamore trees. The wraparound porch, a new addition. The windows winked in the sunlight. "Wow. It looks new. And yet, not. The character and history are still there." She turned to face him. "You did this?"

He squeezed the hand she'd forgotten he still held. "You really like it?" Hope in his eyes warmed Ivy to her toes.

She nodded as she slid her hand away and took a step forward. "I do. Feels like coming home."

"Come on. Let me get your professional opinion on the

rehab on the inside. It's not all pretty like this yet, but it's getting there."

"I guess your client must be impressed with it."

Pride shone in his eyes. "Yeah, I think it's safe to say he's feeling pretty good about it so far."

THIRTY-ONE

OCTOBER 18, 1994

Early Tuesday afternoon, Miriam rapped on Pearl's front door. If anyone had advice on how to engage the retired ladies in the community for her cause with young single mothers, it would be Pearl.

"Coming," Pearl called sweetly from within.

In a few moments she appeared with a baby wrapped in a purple blanket in her arms.

Miriam swallowed and backstepped, as if the increased distance could spare her heart. How had she forgotten Pearl was babysitting?

"Miriam, what a surprise. I'm so glad you stopped by." She motioned her in. "Sit down, and I'll get tea started. Take Ivy for me, and I'll be back in a jiffy."

Pearl thrust the baby toward Miriam as the protest formed on her lips. Miriam blinked. The older woman vanished, leaving a warm bundle in Miriam's arms.

The vice around her battered heart squeezed tighter. The

baby in her arms was so tiny. One little fist wriggled free from the lilac blanket and waved erratically. The tip of her tongue barely visible between berry-red lips. She blinked, her dark curled eyelashes brushed her plump cheeks. An ache twisted in Miriam's chest. She was the most beautiful child she'd ever laid eyes on.

Even though the warning bell clanged inside her head, Miriam sank into the rocker and nuzzled the place beside the baby's perfect seashell ear, inhaling her delicate scent. Miriam squeezed her eyes tight against the pain throbbing in her heart. The things she ran from.

Whenever she went to the store, she averted her eyes from the cooing babies in shopping carts. She planned her route through the aisles to avoid the racks of tiny pastel clothes. Emblems of the life she longed for but could never have. And now, everything she wanted rested against her chest but didn't belong to her. *Where is Pearl with the tea?*

The rattle of cups against their saucers announced Pearl's reappearance. Miriam tore her gaze from the baby.

Pearl had a tender smile on her face as she set the tray on the coffee table. "She's a doll, isn't she?"

Miriam refocused on the reason she'd come, shaking off the heartrending bliss of holding the child. "Pearl, I—"

"Here, let me take her. It's about time for her nap. I'll lay her down and we can chat." Again Pearl swooped close, then was gone. Miriam's arms still felt the weight of the baby that was no longer there.

Pearl popped back into the room. She was a wonder, the spring in her step at her age a miracle. Pearl passed Miriam a saucer and teacup. "I noticed you've been able to be at the church more. Your health has improved?"

Miriam's grip faltered, the tea sloshing onto the saucer. Her mouth worked, but no words would come. What had Thom told her? All of it? The breakdowns? The depression? The infertility? Bile rose in her throat as she set her tea on the side table, waiting for some trite statement about God's will.

"I know it must be costly traveling back and forth to your doctors in California. I don't want to pry, but if you tell me the type of specialist you need, I could make a recommendation. Nashville's not too far, and they have top doctors there."

Her blood heated. "What made you think I've been traveling to and from California for health reasons?"

The elderly woman pressed her mouth in a thin line and glanced in the direction of the church and back. Her mouth opened and closed.

"I'm not sick." Not physically anyway. "I haven't been traveling for doctors."

"Oh, I'm sorry if I spoke out of turn. I—I don't know why he would have said as much if that wasn't—"

Miriam knew why. For all his words of support and patience, Thom was ashamed of her depression and her inability to overcome it. And he'd hidden behind something more readily acceptable to the church population. Her blood temperature rose to boiling. "If you'll excuse me . . ."

"Of course, dear. Tea another time, perhaps."

If she'd responded to Pearl, Miriam couldn't hear her own words over the pounding in her ears. After all the apathy she'd drowned in, it was freeing—embracing the adrenaline-fueled anger coursing through her veins.

She made her way across the parking lot and into the

church building. When Miriam reached Thom's office, she slapped her palm on the door. It swung wide, and Harvey and Thomas jumped to their feet.

"Miriam?" Thomas's forehead creased as he took a step toward her.

She turned to Harvey, attempting to hide her rage beneath a forced smile. "Excuse us, please. My husband and I have something we need to discuss."

Harvey stood, edging around the couple like they were a pair of vipers, and closed the door softly behind him.

Miriam faced her husband, clenching her fists to hide the trembling. "How dare you?"

He placed his hand on her arm. "Miriam, what happened?"

She stepped back, shrugging out of his touch. "Don't. Don't pretend like you care about anything besides yourself, your job, and your reputation."

"I'm a little lost here, sweetheart. Slow down."

She shook her head, the hot burst of anger short-lived like the burst of a firework. "I can't do this. I'm going home. The women will be arriving at the Pantry for their shopping day any minute. You can handle it. Lie about why I'm not there if you need to, since you're so good at it."

"Miriam." His face had gone slack like he'd been slapped. He gripped her upper arm.

"Let go of me." She wrenched her arm away. "I guess I understand being embarrassed of my depression. The church doesn't know how to handle things like that. But I feel lied to, Thomas. All the 'support' was just to help me 'get over it' so I could fill this role you've put me in."

The color draining from his face shouldn't have been so

satisfying. She spun on her heel, leaving him leaning against his desk to keep himself on his feet.

Her anger fizzled on the drive home. As she crossed the threshold of her front door, it dissolved completely. Miriam buried her face in the couch and let the pain behind the rage wash over her like a wave, pulling her back into darker places. Thomas—the rock she thought anchored her to the shore—was ashamed of her.

●　●　●

After Miriam sped off in her silver car, Pearl hurried over to Harvey, who was raking leaves under the oak tree. The parking lot beside the Pantry was filled with patrons.

"Harvey, can you go sit with Ivy? Pastor Thomas needs my help."

He froze, concern creasing his brow.

"It's all right. The pastor needs me over there more than he needs these leaves raked right this minute."

Harvey nodded and shifted his gaze to the place Miriam's car had been. "Did I . . . Did I do something wrong?"

She patted his shoulder. "Honestly, Harvey. Contrary to your belief, you're not responsible for every earthquake and disaster. I'm not exactly sure what happened. But it didn't have a thing in the world to do with you or Ivy. It seems I unwittingly poured gasoline on an already burning flame."

"Will they be okay?" His face reminded her of the boy in her Sunday school class who prayed every week for his divorced parents to reunite.

"Sometimes conflict needs to happen. Like a forest fire that is by all appearances destructive but gets rid of all the undergrowth. From everything I've seen, Pastor Thomas and

Miriam love each other very much. Well-meaning people who love each other make mistakes and hurt each other. Whatever this is, I have faith that after they clear out the brush in their relationship, the love will remain."

He nodded slowly. "Okay." A small smile tugged at his lips. "I'll make a sacrifice and go sit with Ivy."

"Don't you pick that baby up out of the bed to hold her while she sleeps." She wagged her finger. "You'll ruin her."

He laughed, eyes wide and innocent. "What makes you think I'd do that?"

She smirked as she walked to the church. Ivy had them both wrapped around her pinky finger.

Inside the Pantry, Thomas sat at the cashier counter, staring down at a blank sheet of paper as though it held an answer. She stepped through the doorway, then glanced back toward the young women chatting with each other in the parking lot.

"Pastor?"

He lifted his gaze, expression vacant. "Uh. Hello, Pearl." He ran a hand over his face, and then stood and straightened.

"Why don't you head up to your office and take a few minutes. I can handle this."

Thomas swallowed and ducked his chin. "I owe you an explanation." He shook his head. "No. An apology. I—"

She held up her hand. "Now isn't the time. I can handle the Pantry. Take a few minutes in your office to gather yourself, and then go home to your wife. Whatever things you haven't been saying to each other, it's time for you to clean out the wounds before things get worse."

He nodded and trudged up the stairs, the burden over him evident in his halting steps.

She eased into the metal chair. He had so little faith in her support, he thought it necessary to cloak where his wife had been and why. Judging by the way Miriam had cradled baby Ivy, paired with the lack of children of her own, Pearl had a pretty good guess.

Pearl released a sigh. She empathized far more than they could ever imagine.

The door swung open, and in walked a trio of young women from the parking lot, their arms full of squirming babies. Pearl smiled and let the troubles fade. It was a special thing, seeing these young women carry such joy on their faces. Miriam had done a good job with them, nurturing the confidence that they really could build strong, stable lives for their children. She hated that Miriam wasn't there to enjoy the fruits of her labor.

"Hello, ladies. How are you this afternoon? Check out the clothing racks. I helped them sort the new stock the other day, and there are some really darling items in there. Miriam couldn't be here this afternoon, so I'm her stand-in."

Pearl brought out the coffee and cookie tray and placed the items in the center of the room. This was more than a shopping day that gave financial relief; it was a time to connect and remind these young women they were loved and valued. Respected members of this community.

A few hours later, Pearl closed up shop. On her way back home she caught a glimpse of Thomas's black car glistening under the front parking lot lighting. As much as she wanted to prop up her aching feet and enjoy a cup of tea, she couldn't let him get away with hiding up there. Not tonight. His wife was hurting, and it was time he went home.

Pearl reentered through the basement and hobbled up the stairwell. She tapped lightly on Thomas's office door.

"Come in." His voice was gravelly.

His hair stood on end and his tie was loosened and off-kilter. He scrubbed a handkerchief over his swollen eyes.

Pearl closed the distance between them and pulled him into her arms. He flinched at first, but then sank into the hug like a child in need of comfort. After a long moment, she stepped back and sat in a vacant chair. "Thomas, why are you still here?"

He averted his eyes and sank into his desk chair. "She's so angry. She has every right to be." He tipped his head forward into his palms. "But I didn't intentionally deceive you."

"Are you sure?"

"No . . . I . . . well, I don't think . . . I mean, I was thinking of her, not myself. But I should have clarified when you drew your own conclusions about her absence when I hinted she was unwell. She does have a therapist in California she occasionally calls. We moved because I thought Triune would give her a respite from high-pressure expectations of leading a large congregation, but then she couldn't even bring herself to come to services. Things got worse instead of better, and I didn't want to expose her."

"Or the fact that things weren't perfect in the pastor's own home?"

"I—it's not the thought that's been in my head. But the Lord knows my own motives better than myself. I'll ask God to reveal it to me if it's there." He gave her a tight smile. "I wish you would have known her before. She was luminous. Fiery like the hair on her head. Joyful."

"Thomas, the Lord will restore. Now go home to your wife and let her know how much you love her."

His smile broke as the corners of his mouth pulled downward. "She won't listen. She won't believe me. Not after I didn't correct your assumption."

She patted his shoulder. "I've seen the way you look at her. No matter how hurt and angry she is right now, deep in her heart, she knows you love her. Prove it by opening up the vulnerable places to make room for the Lord to handle what you've both been hanging on to."

He lifted his chin to meet her eyes. "You make a good counselor, Pearl."

She shrugged. "Occupational hazard. Now, scoot. I'll leave to let you lock up." On her way out, she turned. "I'm praying. For you both."

●　●　●

Harvey stretched out on the living room floor, both he and the baby on their stomachs. He grinned up at her, boyish joy softening his features.

"You've had a good afternoon," Pearl said as she came in.

He laughed. Her heart warmed at the sound.

"Yes, ma'am." He sobered and stood. "But won't Pastor Thomas be upset? You know what he said about getting things done and being able to show the board I'm worth hiring—"

"Harvey, I'm so proud of how you've cared for the church. It shines from top to bottom. Inside and out. Don't worry about one workday. Take my word for it, Pastor is dealing with enough. Your task list isn't his first concern right now."

"She left him, didn't she?"

"Miriam went home. People who love each other fight sometimes. It's the strength of their love and commitment that helps them work their way through it. Coming through this will only make them stronger."

His brow furrowed like a man working out the mysteries of the universe. "But how do you know love is strong, that it won't fall apart?"

"Because you build it bit by bit, day by day. But there comes a point when you have to step out and believe it will hold through the storm."

THIRTY-TWO

PRESENT DAY

Tennessee humidity poured over Ivy as Reese showed her out of the house. Thick as hot, sticky molasses.

"So you really like it?"

"It's amazing. I know you're not finished yet, but wow." She pressed her hand to her chest. "I've really missed this house. So many good memories."

He smiled. "Always was one of my favorite places." He rubbed the back of his neck. "I know you and your parents have your issues, but . . ." He released a heavy sigh. "They're good people. The best. And you were really blessed to have them to raise you."

She studied the porch's wood grain. "I know." Her voice a weak whisper. She shrugged. "I need to make things right. Find a way to apologize for being distant and work through this weirdness about my adoption. I'm just trying to find the words . . ."

He brushed the hair off her shoulder. "'I love you' is always a good place to start."

The tips of her ears burned, and she swallowed, looking across the yard at the sheltering limbs of the magnolia tree she once used as a childhood hideaway. "Yeah." *I love you, Reese Wright. I've spent my life trying not to love you too much, but I'm not any good at it.* She scrubbed her hands on her face to rub out the rogue thought.

Standing on the porch of the house that used to be hers, in the town they grew up in—it was bittersweet. After Reese and Ivy became friends, Ivy's house became his favorite escape from his chaotic household. She smiled, remembering the skinny boy who used to sit at her family's dinner table, always shoveling down her mother's home cooking like it was his last meal. He had almost been more upset than she was when they moved away after their ninth-grade year.

"You want to try the swing out back?"

"Uh . . ." She envisioned rotted boards hanging lopsided from frayed ropes in the old sycamore.

"Don't worry, it's new. Come on, Rosie-girl. You gotta see the view." He wrapped his hand around her forearm and tugged her forward.

Adrenaline surged through her and she yanked her arm back.

He froze, fingers splayed. "I'm so sorry. I wasn't thinking."

Her heart battered around in her chest. This was Reese. Not Seth. *Reese.*

He stepped toward her and lifted his hands like he wanted to comfort her, but then he seemed to think better of it and let them fall to his sides.

Ivy's knees trembled. "Not your fault. *I'm* sorry." She

closed her eyes, trying to shut off the emotions rising and crashing inside of her.

His voice came out not more than a whisper. "It's not your fault either. Please know that."

How she wished it was true. If he'd seen how she had cowed to Seth time and time again, he wouldn't feel the same.

Reese took two steps backward. "Will you come with me to the backyard? Please?"

She nodded and swallowed, taking slow breaths to calm her racing nerves. This was ridiculous. She was as bad as that stray dog of hers.

They strolled side by side over the fresh-cut grass around the side of the farmhouse. The swing hung from a high branch in the old sycamore. Light filtered through the leaves, illuminating the wooden seat like a storybook picture.

"Give it a spin for old times' sake. You sit, and I'll help you fly."

A soft laugh whispered between her lips. "I can't. I don't have my cape and aviator goggles anymore." She smiled up at him. The memory of standing on that swing, pretending to fly, was as real as the panic that swallowed her moments before.

"You were a regular Amelia Earhart."

"I was a weird little kid." Ivy sat in the swing and nudged her toe against the ground, softly swaying.

"Normal is overrated. I really liked that girl." From behind he took hold of the ropes, pulled the swing back, and let her go. "Hang on."

A manic giggle escaped from her chest. "If this thing gives and I end up in a heap on the ground, I'll warn the whole town about your fix-it skills."

"Ivy?"

Her shoulders tensed at his serious tone.

"I want to ask your forgiveness. The other day, at Carla's, when I picked you up and put you over my shoulder—I'm sorry if I scared you. Or made you feel out of control. Or unsafe. I was just playing around. I didn't know . . ."

She stopped the swing and looked over her shoulder. He blinked glassy eyes and swallowed. Ivy bit down on her lip to keep her emotions at bay. Seth never apologized. Not really. If he did, he had this way of turning the apology around to leave her holding the guilt. And here was Reese, who hadn't done a thing wrong, asking for her forgiveness.

She gripped the ropes to keep herself rooted to the spot. Her arms ached to hold him. Whether to comfort him or herself she wasn't sure.

When she trusted her voice not to crack, she spoke. "You didn't do anything wrong. I was laughing. You were laughing." She shrugged. "I'm not scared when I'm with you." Not entirely true. But the only person she was afraid of in his presence was herself.

He released a heavy breath. "Promise me, if I do anything that makes you uncomfortable, you'll tell me."

She turned her head away and nodded. She couldn't witness raw emotion on his face and keep it together. He was so impossibly good. When contrasted with the way she'd been treated the past year, it was too much. Like summer rain on parched soil. The ground couldn't soak it up fast enough. She needed the subject to change. To get him to talk about anything besides her and her relationship history.

He gave the swing a gentle push, setting her back in motion.

"Was it hard leaving your old boss to start your own company?"

"It was definitely a leap of faith. But the guy I worked for was doing things that weren't exactly illegal, but they weren't right either. The constant tension between what he expected and my convictions was too much. Leaving the security of a steady paycheck wasn't easy, but in the end, it was exactly what I needed."

"I'm glad you're happy, Reese." She didn't mean to sound so sad when she said it.

"If I could do anything to make you happy, whatever it was, I would do it. I hope you know that."

She stared at the ground as she glided in the swing. Back and forth. Back and forth. She clamped her eyes shut. "I know you would. But I think I have to find happiness for myself."

"I know." His voice held a faint rasp normally absent from his soothing voice.

He pushed her in the swing for a while, and then he leaned against the trunk of the sycamore tree. Ivy kept on swinging.

The two of them relived childhood memories until the fireflies came out to play.

THIRTY-THREE

OCTOBER 18, 1994

The headlights of Thomas's car pulling into the drive sent flickering light through the house. Miriam's flight instinct jerked to attention, but having spent all her energy, she curled back in place on the sofa. Even if the farmhouse had offered a place to hide, Thomas wasn't the type to leave her be. He always insisted on talking things out before unspoken things could fester.

She gripped her blanket. Except he never mentioned he was hiding the reason she missed church so often. Pretending she was afflicted with a physical ailment, something more socially and church accepted. If the congregation couldn't deal with the fact that their pastor's wife was crippled by depression, then it was the wrong place for them.

Simple as that.

But it wasn't. Thomas had left behind his dream position and the massive congregation who loved him, because he thought being out of the spotlight would help. His struggle now—her fault. Because she couldn't find a way to be content with what she had. Because she couldn't shake the twisting ache in her heart when the blessings she had should've been enough.

Keys jangled and the front door creaked. She stiffened like a mannequin in a store display.

Halting footsteps echoed in the foyer. The sound approached, then paused. Steps that either brought an apology or a defense. Ready to respond to neither, she held her breath and refused to turn. The footsteps retreated up the stairs until they were muffled by the carpet on the landing.

Cold dread sank in her middle. This was how marriages ended. The one strong person in the relationship cracked.

She stared out the window, her eyes raw from spent tears. A picture of their wedding day on the side table snagged her attention. One of her favorites. It was a candid shot captured by one of her friends. Her head was thrown back in laughter, an insubordinate curl had slipped out of her updo and framed her face, and her veil was tangled. But it wasn't her image she adored. It was Thomas, standing beside her and looking at her like she was the only woman in the world.

She closed her eyes. The thing was, he still looked at her that way. It was she who had changed.

Thom had given everything he could to try and make her happy, even when it hadn't been in their best interest.

She pressed her palms to her eyes, against the pressure of the tears building. Through it all Thomas had been steady and loving while she fell apart. And even that had riled her anger. But after tonight she didn't know what to think. He practically *lied* to people about her problems to avoid judgment.

Miriam padded up the stairs. As she turned the doorknob, she heard the sound of soft snoring. She sighed. It was just like a man to fall asleep in the middle of a fight. He lay with his back to her, fully clothed. Lamp on.

She walked over and flipped the switch, relieved. Truth was, she was too exhausted to deal with it tonight. After climbing onto her side of the bed, she stared at the ceiling for three hours before her mind finally wound itself in so many circles she drifted off.

• • •

In the early morning after Harvey had left for work, Pearl swayed with Ivy in her arms, humming the tune the mobile over the bassinet played. The breakfast dishes were piled in the sink, but they could wait. She glanced out the kitchen window to the church swathed in the reddish light of sunrise.

"Uh-oh. You know what they say, Ivy, love. Red in the morning, sailor's warning." She flicked on the television to see if the weatherman concurred with her assessment. Sure enough, evening thunderstorms were in the forecast.

"If big bad Harvey thinks he's going to walk you home in a thunderstorm, he's got another think coming." She brushed the curl off Ivy's forehead and gazed into her dark eyes. "So tell me, little one. Where do you live?"

Ivy stuck out her tongue and blew a raspberry. Laughter tickled Pearl's chest. "Learned a new trick, did we? Harvey teach you to answer like that?" She lifted the baby up on her shoulder, kissed her on the cheek, and inhaled her scent—a mixture of baby soap, pine, and another faint woodsy scent she couldn't name. Almost like . . . campfire.

240

Surely not. But it did connect. The fact that he wouldn't let her see where he lived. Because his home didn't have walls?

She carried Ivy to the living room and sank into the upholstered rocker. Letting him be the temporary custodian for his sister's baby for a couple weeks was one thing. But letting him keep a baby at a campsite as a permanent arrangement?

Pearl massaged her temples. What had she been thinking? She'd gotten so caught up in their routine over the past few weeks. She'd been so filled with happiness where there once had been emptiness that the fact that this arrangement wasn't permanent had faded to a quiet buzz in the back of her mind. Ivy had a mother out there who had either willingly abandoned her daughter or had done so against her will. Something had to be done.

The doorbell jarred her from her circling thoughts.

Miriam stood on her doorstep, dressed in a pretty maroon wrap dress and high heels, her pocketbook clutched in her hands. "I wanted to, no, needed to talk to you. To explain about yesterday. May I come in?"

Pearl stepped aside. "Of course. Come in, dear. Coffee? Tea? What can I get you?"

Miriam leaned near the baby as she entered. Her voice soft and breathy. "Oh, she's asleep."

Pearl glanced down. So she was. All of Pearl's frantic rocking had sent Ivy straight on to sleep whether her distracted caregiver noticed or not.

Miriam smiled. "There's nothing more precious than a sleeping baby."

The tenderness in her eyes tore Pearl's heart. "She's an absolute angel, this one. I should put her to bed. What can I bring you on the way back?"

"Coffee, if you're sure it's no trouble."

"Don't be silly. No trouble at all. Make yourself at home there in the living room, and I'll be back before you can say boo."

Pearl padded back to her bedroom with Ivy. She hoped Thomas hadn't pressed Miriam to come. After all, if anyone owed her an explanation, it was Thomas, not his wife. Miriam had never tried to be anyone she wasn't.

● ● ●

At the sound of footsteps, Miriam jumped to her feet and placed the picture frame back on the side table where she'd picked it up from moments ago. Pearl tottered into the living room with a plate of sliced cream cake and two cups of coffee.

"Oh goodness, Pearl. Let me get that for you."

She let her take the tray and motioned to the coffee table. "You didn't have to get up, honey. I'm stronger than I look, even if my hands do get a bit shaky every now and then."

Pearl inclined her head toward the picture frame. "That's Elliot and my son, Marshall, on their last fishing trip. It's one of my favorites."

Miriam righted the photograph, and carefully turned it in the precise angle it had been before. "I can't imagine how difficult this past year has been."

Pearl's response was halting, as though she weighed each word before it passed between her lips. "It's been trying. But I find things greatly improved over the past few weeks with my new charge."

"I can imagine. With a sweet baby around, it would be hard to feel anything but joy." She took a sip of the perfectly brewed coffee and savored the rich flavor and warmth.

"Yes. The baby is a joy. But, dear, I was talking about Harvey."

Miriam sputtered, nearly spitting coffee across Pearl's living room. *Harvey?* The thirty-year-old man who could barely string three coherent words together without darting off? Who behaved as though it set his eyes on fire to make eye contact? That was who left Pearl filled with joy?

"You mean he helps around the house with the manual labor?" Her incredulity did funny things to the cadence of her voice.

"He does lend a helping hand, but that's not what I meant. Having him around here is like . . . it's like a new chance at motherhood. You see, my son was about Harvey's age when he passed. Did Thomas tell you I was forty-one when Marshall was born? I had given up on having children years ago. I had wanted to adopt at one time, but my husband was never comfortable with the idea. It was more of a hush-hush thing back then. He knew a friend that was adopted and didn't know until he was fifteen. He said his friend was never the same after he found out. So time went on and we found a way to be contented, the two of us."

Something hot stabbed Miriam's chest. That was her problem. Not knowing how to be content with her lot in life.

"My dear, there are all kinds of ways to be a mother. I used the mothering love God placed in my heart to love many a child in my Sunday school classes, or even to comfort a child I passed on the street who'd fallen and scraped their knee. Love is love. Nurturing is nurturing. It doesn't take a blood relative. We're all adopted into God's family through Jesus. And I decided long ago that if it was good enough for God, it was good enough for me. So I set in my heart that I would love and mother anyone who crossed my path who needed that kind of love."

Miriam worried her lip between her teeth, blinking away the moisture gathering in her eyes before Pearl noticed.

"What about you, my sweet Miriam? Why did you come here today? Surely not to hear an old lady ramble."

Miriam choked on a sob. "I don't know. Maybe it's because I need a mother too." The last of it came out as an embarrassing wail, but Pearl closed the distance between them and wrapped her in her arms. Miriam buried her face in Pearl's shoulder. There was surprising strength found in those ropy arms.

When shuddering sobs and hiccups subsided, Miriam leaned back from the embrace and took the tissue Pearl held out. "Thomas is avoiding me."

Pearl tilted her head. "I was under the impression he was going home to talk things out with you."

Miriam shook her head. "It's not like him at all. You know the verse about not letting the sun go down on your anger? It's like it's his life verse. And now he's hiding instead of talking. Maybe I've pushed him further than he can handle. He's only human, after all."

"You've got one thing right. He's human. I think he's ashamed and knows there isn't anything he can say to excuse himself."

"All this time, he seemed so loving and supportive, but he was actually embarrassed of me."

"I have my own theories, but it's none of my business."

"I don't know what to do. To say."

"Tell him you love him. No matter the mess between the two of you, you love him, and he loves you. And you both love the Lord. Start there and work onward. With those things in clear view, no mess is quite as complicated as it seems at the outset."

The baby cried out from the bedroom down the hallway. Miriam fought the urge to jump from her seat to go to her. She released a soft sigh as Pearl left the room. Her mothering instinct wouldn't quit, even though she had no baby to hurry to. *Why am I the one with empty arms, Lord?*

THIRTY-FOUR

OCTOBER 19, 1994

A gust of warm air swept the churchyard, scattering piled leaves back across the lawn. Harvey propped his rake against the tree in surrender. The clouds looked like dark, pregnant rain barrels aching to burst. Distant thunder rumbled and Harvey hurried to stow his tools, weighing his options.

There was a state park not too far away with cinder-block bathrooms where he occasionally took hot showers during the cold months. It had been his shelter the last time a tornado threatened.

His lean-to was fairly sturdy. He'd deemed it good enough for himself and had weathered many a storm under its shelter. But the thought of Ivy under the grove of stringy pines as the wind bent them to and fro? Not an option.

State park it was. Although the thought of squatting there overnight made him feel . . . well, like he was homeless. Strangely it was something he hadn't experienced in some time.

He marched up the back stairwell to Thomas's office. If they had any chance to make it to the park before the skies unleashed the building fury, he needed to take an early leave.

The door was open, and the pastor sat with his back turned, staring out the window. Harvey cleared his throat. The chair squeaked as it made its slow turn.

"Yes, Harvey?" The pastor's voice had a quality that reminded him of a raindrop in an empty bucket. Hollow.

"Sir, with the storm coming, I wanted your permission to leave early. Seeing as I have to walk . . . home." He winced. With a statement like that, he was going to end up with another person offering him rides he couldn't take.

A shadow of a smile passed across Thomas's face. "Of course. Thank you for asking, but yes, of course, go. Do you think you have time to stay ahead of it?"

"Yes, sir."

"Take care. I'll see you tomorrow."

"Yes, sir." A weight settled in his middle. The problem between Thomas and his wife felt like his fault somehow. A curse seemed to follow him. A wake of disruption. As a child he'd watched it a hundred times. He was thrust into a family, lingered for a while, but when he caused too many problems, the solution was always for him to go.

Thunder rumbled, low and ominous. He picked up his pace. When he turned the basement door handle, the door flung out of his grasp and crashed against the wood siding. And then the air stilled, almost as if he was in a vacuum.

He jogged across the grass, leaves swirling at his feet. There was an odd color in the sky, a yellowish gray. Like dirty dishwater.

In the next gust he was hit with a smattering of rain that stopped as suddenly as it had started, almost as though the rain traveled in the wind itself.

He swiped the droplets from his face when he arrived on Pearl's porch. The door swung wide when he reached to knock.

"Come in. Come in. No, don't stop to wipe your feet. The floor'll mop."

Harvey cringed as his muddy shoes squeaked and skated on the white linoleum of Pearl's entryway. He tried to shuffle as little as possible as he slipped off his boots.

She'd already disappeared farther into the house, muttering all the way—something about toothpaste.

He picked up his bag and stuffed in Ivy's purple blanket that had been draped over the chair. He tried to follow Pearl's chatter, but she bounced from room to room like a frantic rabbit.

After a moment he gave up the chase and went back to where Ivy slept in her bassinet. Whatever bee buzzed in Pearl's bonnet, he didn't have time for it. He reached to scoop Ivy up in a practiced movement that wouldn't wake her.

"What on earth are you doing?" Pearl hissed from the doorway. "Let that baby sleep."

He backed out of the room. "Miss Pearl, I don't have time to stay for dinner tonight. The storm is coming, and we've got to go."

She grabbed his hand and pulled him down the hallway toward the kitchen. "Good heavens. Have you not been listening to a word I've said?"

"I tried, but—"

"There's no use arguing. I've already told you, Ivy and I

went to the store and picked up a few things for Marshall's room—I mean, the guest bedroom."

Harvey felt the blood drain from his face. "You took her in the car?"

"Yes, and we lived. I don't know what the fuss is all about. Henry Ford and his moving assembly line made them commonplace in 1913. Well before either of our times, yet you act like they're UFOs."

He tried to form a response through the tightness in his throat.

"There is a toothbrush for you in the bathroom. Extra clothes and things are in the bedroom you changed in the other day. I've removed all the things dear to me and packed them away. Anything else in there you want or could use is yours."

Pearl's words kept coming at him, ricocheting off one throbbing thought. Ivy riding down the road. There could have been an accident.

Suddenly, he was no longer standing in Pearl's kitchen. He was the one in the car, headlights pointed in the wrong direction, coming straight for him. He opened his mouth to cry out but—

"Harvey. Harvey?"

He jolted and blinked. Pearl braced him at the elbow. It was an absurd scenario—her trying to steady him, tall as he was. She led him to a kitchen chair, where he slumped down to sit and stared at the black-and-white-checked linoleum.

Pearl softened her voice. "I didn't mean to upset you. I know I should have asked, but I knew you'd say no. To the store trip, to staying here, everything. But I can't let the two of you go out in this. Tell me the truth. Do you have a safe place to stay tonight?"

"No." The admission slipped through his battered defenses. He squeezed his hands into fists until his shorn fingernails bit into his skin. "But we can't accept. We can't stay here."

Pearl straightened and jutted out her chin. Thunder pealed, long and low, like the groaning skies conspired to strengthen her point. "I'm afraid I'm going to have to insist. I've gone along with this for the past few weeks because you've taken exceptional care of this child. But I won't let you endanger her."

Harvey worked at swallowing the lump in his throat. His pulse was doing all sorts of things. It seemed to race as if he were being shoved down a path he didn't want to travel, and then there were moments it seemed to slow, like the earth's rotation had suspended.

"I can't stay here."

"I swear on my life if you walk out the door with that child, I'll file a report myself."

The impulse to bolt from her house and never look back yanked him out of his seat. With liquid knees he attempted to stand. Lightning flashed and a moment later thunder rattled Pearl's windows in their panes.

From down the hallway came Ivy's startled cry, and instead of running for the door, he went to her. No matter how wrong this scenario felt, choosing Ivy was the only thing that ever made sense.

He scooped the baby into his arms, patting and shushing her, but the child was the one anchoring him.

Pearl stepped up behind him. "Dear, you're shaking. Bring

Ivy into the living room and sit down. We'll turn on the news and keep an eye on the weather warnings."

He followed Pearl on autopilot, concentrating on the weight and warmth of Ivy. Trying to remember how to breathe. Harvey might not belong on the abandoned land he squatted on, but it was proof he was self-sustaining. He certainly didn't belong in this woman's home.

He was getting too comfortable here in this new world. In the end, not even haircuts and nice shirts could change what was at the core of a person. People like him didn't get to keep babies or start over. That was the problem though. Once you let a little soft place in your heart, it craved more. More of the things that weren't his to have.

She'd redone her house, her son's room, so a vagrant could stay over. A weight settled in his stomach. This was all wrong. Burdening an elderly woman like this.

The TV image of the weatherman and his maps where he drew X's and O's buzzed in the background, festering his anxiety.

"Harvey," Pearl whispered.

He froze. He rocked in the chair like a madman trying to soothe inner demons—not like a parent comforting a baby. Harvey softened his hold on Ivy.

"Don't you think it's time you told me more about yourself, about what's got you so undone? After all, if I trust you enough to let you stay in my house, don't you think you can trust me with your story? I've been told I'm a good listener by a few people. Give me a chance."

He shook his head, his throat too tight for speech. The lights flickered and went out.

Harvey suffocated in the inky darkness as the heavens

split and hail pounded the roof. Nights like these brought forward those murky flashbacks of that night—

"Harvey, there's a flashlight on the table beside you." Pearl's voice reached for him through the racket, and he dragged himself out of the memory pit.

He took a steadying breath.

"Everything's okay. You're safe. It's only a power outage. There's a flashlight to your right." She raised her voice to be heard above the onslaught.

Ivy squirmed in his arms. He was clutching, not cradling. He propped her in one arm and patted the table until he found the cool metal shaft of the flashlight.

He depressed the rubbery button, the light beam slicing through black. Pearl was crouched on the floor on her hands and knees.

"Miss Pearl! What happened?"

She sat back on her heels, blinking and blocking the harsh light with her hand. "I'm fine. You wouldn't answer me. I didn't know if the power going off had . . . affected you, and I was coming to you. You're all right?"

He blinked and nodded. Not even the social workers and the foster parents who were privy to his history understood him like this woman.

The hail ceased as abruptly as it had begun, leaving only the mournful howling of the wind.

Pearl straightened and returned to her seat on the couch. "My son had problems. Things like sudden movement, sounds, changes in the environment would cause him to . . . I don't really know what you'd call it, but it was like he was back on the battlefield."

Harvey swallowed and nodded. Her helpless expression

highlighted in the shadowy light made him long to erase her pain.

"What about you, dear? My son went back to the battle-field. Where do you go when your world is falling apart?"

He stiffened. "I don't know what you mean."

"Yes you do." She huffed. "I'm going to the kitchen to get Ivy her bottle. She'll be wanting it soon."

Harvey handed her the light and watched the beam bounce against the walls as Pearl shuffled on. Blips of the photo-graphs illuminated—snapshots of Pearl's life he'd taken little time to consider. How had a straitlaced, old-fashioned pas-tor's wife seen him as a person worthy to care for a child? Much less, trustworthy enough to stay in her home when he wouldn't reveal a thing about himself.

Pearl returned a moment later, carrying a tray with two steaming cups, Ivy's bottle, and the flashlight. "Who knows when the power will come back on. We don't want to waste the hot chocolate." She set the tray on the coffee table.

Pearl reached for Ivy. "Let me hold her a minute. My kero-sene lamp is over there on the piano, and there's a box of matches too. Do you know how to light one?"

He passed Ivy and walked to the lantern. "You've already fueled the lamp?"

"Yes, the mantles are beside it."

In moments he had the fuel primed, the mantles tied, and the lamp lit. A warm glow suffused the room.

Pearl smiled at him. "You've had practice. It takes me for-ever to get that thing going, but I pulled it out of storage when I heard the forecast this morning. This area is bad about outages."

He took a sip from his mug. "I like to camp. It's comfortable in the woods."

"Did you camp a lot as a child?"

"Once. It's one good memory I always hold on to."

Pearl's glance flicked in his direction. "Tell me about it?"

He let out a ragged sigh and sank back down, his eyes on Ivy. "It's nothing really."

"It's not nothing. I've never once heard you admit to being happy. I'm virtually on the edge of my seat."

He rubbed his hands over his face as if the action could conjure the memory from the depths. "I had just turned five. My mother and father took me on our first family camping trip. It was an absolute disaster. My mom hated camping and bugs. Our tent leaked, and it rained the whole time. The tent was on a slight incline, so all the moisture collected on one end of the tent. So my dad, my mom, and I squished in the dried patch. I had my mom in front of me, and my dad behind me. I remember feeling like a human peanut butter sandwich. I squirmed, driving them crazy. So my mom sang to me until I fell asleep. It was the song I heard you singing to Ivy the other day. Something about grace?

"But yeah, that moment right there is the one time I can remember feeling like I had a place. I was the peanut butter that held the sandwich together."

Pearl's gaze bored through him, a laser homing in on what she imagined lived beneath his words. "Where was your sister?"

He inwardly groaned. *Idiot.* She had tricked him into talking about himself again, and he'd about blown everything. "She was too young to camp."

She nodded, seeming deep in thought. "And that's why you're fond of camping? That trip?"

"It was the last clear memory I have of feeling safe." Harvey pressed his lips tight against the unintended admission.

Pearl leaned in. "What happened to you, Harvey?"

He turned his head away, fighting for control. His voice, not more than a breath, slipped out under the growing weight on his chest. "What happened is why I don't do cars. And I especially don't do cars in the rain."

THIRTY-FIVE

Present Day

Ivy filled ghost-dog's food bowl, backed away, and sat in the grass. A little later, a snout appeared in the hole, sniffing the air. He wriggled through and Ivy remained as still as she could, watching him out of the corner of her eye. He went to the food bowl, keeping his gaze on her.

"That's a good boy. Such a good, brave boy."

His lowered tail raised a fraction and gave the barest of wags. A grin spread across her face.

After he finished his food, he walked closer to Ivy and curled in the sunshine. He wasn't close enough to touch, but his tail thumped the ground. His tongue flicked out and he whined.

She patted the ground. "Come on. You can do it." He wiggled closer.

"I think you need a name. You aren't a ghost." She eyed the black specks on his ears. "How about Pepper? You could be a Pepper."

He lifted his head and his floppy ears perked.

Ivy laughed. "Is that your name? Pepper?" The dog tilted his head.

"All right then, Pepper it is." Ivy stretched out on her back and stared up through the tree limbs. "This is my safe place too, you know. Where I'd come when I thought my parents weren't being fair or I'd had a bad day. My grandma and my uncle would always cheer me up, help shift my perspective. And when I was in those weird high school years, this was where I came to remind myself who I was. Now Grandma's gone. The house isn't hers anymore. I hoped being back here might get my head back on straight, but I don't know."

She rolled her head toward the dog. His chin rested on the ground. His doggy eyebrows shifted as she spoke like he was processing everything she said.

"It does a number on you when the person you trusted to love you hurts you instead, doesn't it, Pep?"

Ivy stood slowly and walked to the porch. "I'd better get to work. That house won't sort itself." She peeked over her shoulder. Pepper followed at a distance. A smile stretched over Ivy's face.

She sat on the porch swing, and Pepper approached her. Tail low and wiggling. Slowly Ivy reached out and stroked his back. "Look at you, you brave boy." She crooned in a silly baby voice. He looked at her with soulful eyes. "You just want to be loved, don't you? No matter how scary it is."

Her uncle's landscaping truck pulled into view. Pepper tensed. "It's okay. He won't hurt you."

Pepper edged away.

"All right. I'll see you later, buddy." The dog disappeared around the corner of the house.

• ● •

After the sound of the mower faded, Ivy filled two glasses with water and went in search of her uncle. She found him securing his mower to his trailer. She passed him a glass of water. "Your landscaping crew was doing the lawn just the other day. I was surprised when they left Grandma's house untouched."

He shrugged. "I like doing it myself." He surveyed the land around them. "Although it's probably time I give that up. It won't be her place much longer."

"How long did you live here?"

Uncle Vee gave her a half-smile. "It is the only home I've ever known." He laughed, soft and breathy. "In the last few months of her life she pestered me to death to buy my own place. I'd have felt put out if I didn't know what she was really up to."

Ivy arched her brows.

"I bought a house, but I stayed with her until she passed. There was no way I was going to let her be alone in her final days. I tried so hard to take care of her, but her focus was always on taking care of me. She wanted to prepare me in the only way she knew how." He swallowed hard.

Ivy averted her eyes and blinked. She lifted her water glass toward the woods. "Wanna take a walk?"

He nodded. She placed their empty glasses on the porch rail, and they headed toward the woods.

While the house had always been Grandma's domain, those woods were hers and Uncle Vee's. Whenever she became impatient while her parents worked at the church, he took her exploring at the old creek out on the farthest bounds of the church property. In that trickle of a stream, she waded, and he helped her find crawdads and salamanders.

"It's been a long time, huh?" She nudged him with her elbow.

They crunched over decaying leaves and pine needles. The shade offered a slight reprieve from the summer heat.

He nodded. "Too long. I know it won't be the same with your grandma gone, but don't be a stranger, okay? I have an extra bedroom anytime you want to stay." The lines around his eyes creased, and he stared at the ground as they walked.

"I'll take you up on that." She'd do better about visiting. Be there for him.

The corner of his mouth twitched. "And you can call off your watchdog. I know it was you asking Reese to check up on me after you went back home. I miss her, Ivy. More than words can say. But I'm okay. Promise."

Heat filled her cheeks.

He placed a hand on her shoulder. "What about you? Are you holding up all right? Do you need help with anything at the house?"

"You're crazy busy with your landscaping company. I have Reese. We've got it covered."

"But if you need anything, you know I'm there for you, right?"

Anything? Words pressed against her lips, questions begging to be asked. She glanced at him. A carefree expression on his face. This quiet walk with him so perfect. Overdue. Could she take the chance of spoiling it?

"Can I ask you a question?"

"Of course."

She swallowed hard. Maybe her mom and dad evaded

giving her clear answers, but surely her uncle, the man she could always depend on, would shoot straight with her. "Did you know a woman named Rose?"

Uncle Vee's face paled as he froze. "You're still looking—don't, Ivy. Leave it alone. I don't know what your grandma was thinking bringing up that ancient history, but nothing good can come of this. Nothing. I mean it. Leave the past where it belongs."

THIRTY-SIX

FEBRUARY 16, 1999

Rose scrubbed the long laminate tables in the ranch's mess hall. Not a bad gig, but she preferred the stable duty that had been her assignment last week.

Pearl stood across the room talking to the lady who ran the place. As she cleaned, Rose moved down the table. Closer and closer to Pearl. Pulled against her will. Wanting her to look up. To see her. Like she recognized Rose in some way. It was stupid, craving Pearl's attention like that. But Pearl was one of the few people that had ever kept their word to her.

Questions bombarded Rose's mind. Haunting her waking hours, louder now that every moment wasn't spent just trying to survive. She needed these answers no matter how they hurt. And Pearl would tell the truth.

When the last woman trickled out, she swiped at the tables, worrying her lip between her teeth. What would happen if she let these memories loose? Would it be her salvation or her undoing?

Pearl approached. "You're looking well, Rose."

Rose dipped her head. "Well" was a relative word, she guessed. Detoxing from the stuff Vance kept pumped into her system had been no picnic. She'd never have survived without Pearl helping her reach Abiding Love.

"You wanted to ask me something?" Pearl looked at her.

How did she know?

Words she thought would be so hard to form slipped out of her like an exhale. "You remember when you asked me about a month back if I had any children, and I said no?"

Pearl stilled.

"I lied. I . . . I . . . Do you think babies born in sin go to heaven if they die?" She scrubbed at an imaginary blemish on the clean surface.

Pearl sucked in a breath.

"My daddy told me when he kicked me out of the house at sixteen that me and my baby would burn in hellfire."

Pearl placed a hand on her shoulder. Her expression searching, desperate.

Rose gripped the soiled rag to stop the trembling. "He was born too early. Probably my fault, not getting to the doctor regular."

"He?" Pearl's expression flickered. Almost as if she were disappointed, but then, the expression softened. "Oh, honey. All children are precious in the Lord's sight. They don't choose how they come to be. Sometimes losses happen, and there's nothing you can do to stop it. Jesus loves your baby boy."

Rose stared at the fake wood grain of the laminate table. The weight she'd borne on her shoulders for the past five years lifted by a degree. More buried words found the surface. Stories she'd sworn she'd never speak. But the way Pearl looked at her, touched her shoulder with more gentleness than she'd known in her lifetime, it was more than she could bear.

"I didn't think what he said sounded right." She went back to her scrubbing. Trying to hold control, gripping the rough fabric of the soggy rag. She refused to give in to the things her counselor said weren't real—that lurked just below the surface waiting for her to become weak. The phantom baby cries. Seeing Vance's hulking figure around every corner. The counselor told her a hundred times she was safe. Maybe she should try to believe it. Say out loud what haunted her day and night.

"I didn't have nobody when I lost my baby boy. Daddy wouldn't let me come back home. My boyfriend wouldn't have nothin' to do with me. I got real sick, and this older guy, Vance, took me in. He seemed so nice." She swallowed. Heat roiled in her middle. "He wasn't."

Pearl sank onto one of the long wooden benches. Sorrow widened her eyes. But all Rose could feel was rage. There was no room for the grief she witnessed on the woman's face.

"He had a real love for alcohol. Drugs too. More important than the light bill. But anytime he ran short on cash, he'd call up one of his buddies. Money would exchange hands, and I'd be dragged to the back bedroom of that tin-can trailer." She glanced out the window of the dining hall, steeling herself. "If I didn't go willingly or if I embarrassed him, as he so put it, he'd make me pay later. I tried to get away once, and he found me. I was a stupid, scared kid."

"Oh, Rose."

She shrugged off the compassion, determined not to

crumble. If she let it all loose out into the world, maybe it'd stop rotting her life from the inside out. "I got pregnant again. Don't know who the daddy was. Baby wasn't made in love like last time, but with pain and rage in my heart. When I went into labor, Vance told me he'd take me to the hospital later on but then he drank himself stupid.

"I left. There was someone I thought might help me. I met him out by the highway the last time I tried to get away. Said he lived nearby. Such a dumb plan, but it was all I had."

She shook her head. "Baby was coming too fast. One of Vance's friends found me and convinced me to get into the back of his musty old Cadillac Seville. Wasn't nothin' else I could do. I don't remember much but blood and pain. And that baby's first cry. I hear it every night in my ears when I'm trying to fall asleep.

"I passed out, and when I woke back at that old trailer, Vance told me my baby died. That it was too weak. But he did something to it. That cry I heard before I blacked out was full of strength. That baby was a fighter. Not like me." Her voice came flat and detached, even to her own ears. Like someone else told her story.

"How . . . how long ago did you lose your second child?"

"It'll be five years in September." The date was tattooed on the inside of her. A part of her.

Pearl's wrinkled cheeks were drenched with an emotion Rose had long ago forgotten. So many things flickered in the woman's expression as she'd spilled her story. Concern. Sorrow. Confusion. And something Rose couldn't understand for the life of her.

Light and . . . hope.

• ● •

Confessing her story to Pearl was supposed to make things better. Release her from her chains. But as the week passed, the bonds only seemed to tighten. Rose wandered through the stable, horses nickering as she passed.

Pearl had been so strange since that day. Quieter. As though her mind was filled with things. Too many things. It wasn't judgment in her eyes though. It was worry. For what, Rose didn't know.

She approached the stall of a dapple-gray pony and hooked her elbows over the stall door. The pony snuffed and shifted in the stall.

A dark figure sat in the corner. Rose flinched and gripped the stall door. Never had he been so close. All the times she'd seen him before it had been across a field. Or lurking at the edge of the woods.

She squeezed her eyes tight and pressed her hands over her ears. He wasn't real. He wasn't real. No one could see that phantom figure but her. But no matter how much she chanted the words inside her head or how tight she pressed her hands over her ears, it wouldn't banish the stale scent of his hot breath on her face or his cold, cruel whisper.

"Come with me, Laney."

She quaked, knees turning to gelatin as she curled against the stall door. "No."

"I'll hurt the old woman. I know she helped you escape. I followed her home. I know where she lives."

"No," Rose moaned. "You're not real. You're not."

"I'm as real as the air you breathe. You'll never get free of me."

Rose stood on shaking legs and raced from the stable, refusing to look back. From inside her cabin, she peered between the crack in the curtains.

Vance stood at the edge of the woods, looking her way. But there was nothing fuzzy about his form this time. All hard angles and strength. Solid. Real.

Her only choice was to run.

THIRTY-SEVEN

OCTOBER 20, 1994

"What on earth are you doing out here?"

Harvey startled awake at the sound of Pearl's voice. He sat up from where he'd slouched, asleep in the porch swing. She didn't look angry. More sad than anything.

"I . . . I just needed some air." He slunk away from Pearl and ducked into the house. She wasn't supposed to catch him sleeping on the porch. The truth was, he couldn't get comfortable in the borrowed bed. The borrowed room. The borrowed clothes. The borrowed *everything*.

The outdoors was different. It was more his than anything else. Maybe because the outside air couldn't be owned. No one could negate his right to walk down the side of the road. He shucked off his dew-damp clothes and turned on the shower as hot as it would go.

As the steaming water poured over him, he replayed the night before. Did Pearl realize he'd offered her the only story, the singular memory he had of his life before the accident?

He'd never told anyone that one precious piece of his life. Not the social workers, or the counselors, or any of his foster parents.

Of course, she'd wanted to know what happened next. But it was too much. The similar weather. The flashbacks. He might have lost it, and she already thought he was half out of his mind. No reason to thoroughly convince her.

He dried off and changed into borrowed clothes from the borrowed room. When he looked in the mirror, a stranger stared back. This man could be anyone. A teacher. A businessman. A father. He slipped the watch Thomas gave him onto his wrist.

He made some coffee and filled their customary mugs.

When he entered the living room, Pearl was patting Ivy's back, the empty bottle on the side table. She smiled sweetly. "I could get used to this. A handsome young man bringing me coffee, and a sweet baby girl in my arms. I don't know what I've done to deserve this blessing."

He placed her mug on the table and sat beside her. He lifted a corner of his mouth. "You'll make us blush. Me and Ivy both."

Pearl leaned down and laid Ivy on a blanket and settled back with her hands cupped around her steaming mug. "While I was feeding Ivy, I was thinking—"

Uh-oh. A Pearl plan.

"I have two extra rooms here. You'd be right by work . . ."

He put down the mug. The hot liquid crept back up his throat, setting fire to his insides. He shook his head. "No, ma'am. We couldn't—"

Pearl's telephone clanged, jarring the conversation. She held up her hand. "Before you turn me down, we need to talk this out. Sit tight."

She shuffled to the kitchen phone. He didn't mean to eavesdrop, but her voice sliced through the thickness in the air.

"Well, hello, Miriam . . . No I wasn't asleep. An accident! For heaven's sake. Is he okay? Oh, mercy."

Air became trapped in Harvey's lungs. He bent at the waist with his head between his knees—a buzzing in his ears distorting sound.

"Bless his heart . . . Oh, Harvey is here, actually. He stayed through the storm. Okay, I'll tell him. I'll be praying."

Harvey gripped his knees. This was why you didn't let people close. Because they drove cars, and bad things happened, like accidents in the rain.

He could control his solitary life in the woods. But these people twined together, and he couldn't stop the pain from wriggling in. People died. Attachment equaled loss.

A steady hand landed on his shoulder. "Harvey, are you feeling okay? What's wrong?"

He propped his elbows on his knees and lifted his head.

"For goodness' sakes, you look like you've seen a ghost. What hap—" Pearl pressed a hand to her cheek. "You overheard . . ."

She knelt beside him, and laid her wrinkled hand on his knee and peered into his eyes.

"Pastor Thomas had an accident. He's banged up pretty badly, but he's okay. You are okay. Everybody's safe."

Ivy wriggled and cooed on her blanket, oblivious to the way the earth shattered with such ease. He turned the watch around his wrist. These people. He cared too much. He needed to escape, but he couldn't. They'd wrapped their way around him just like Ivy had.

He lifted a hand, wavered for a moment, and placed it on Pearl's bony shoulder. "Thank you." His words, a gravelly whisper from the tightness in his throat.

* * *

"Miriam?" Thomas's voice, thick from sleep, roused her.

She sat straight with a groan. She'd slept on the floor, half-upright against the couch where Thomas had slept all night. She must have dozed off again after calling Pearl. She arched her back, stretching out the kink. "I'm here. Are you in pain? What can I get you?"

She stood and brushed the hair on his forehead to the side. He was pale under the bruising on his face.

"You slept there all night? On the floor? You should have gone to bed." He glanced to the clock on the wall. "I better get up and get to work. Harvey will be waiting."

"I already called Pearl and told her you were taking the day off."

"I'll be all right. A few bumps can't keep a man down." He struggled to sit up, wincing. Even more color drained from his face.

She helped him shift upright, and he sank back into the overstuffed couch's armrest. "Okay. You win. Maybe a day off wouldn't hurt."

"You know, you scared me last night, Thom. I can't believe you wouldn't let the hospital call." His police officer friend had given him a ride home.

"You would have come out in the storm."

"We're kind of in this whole life thing together. At least we're supposed to be." She paused for a second. "Maybe you need to stop trying to protect me. That's why you weren't

270

straightforward with why I haven't been in church, isn't it? To protect me?"

He rubbed his hands over his knees and swallowed. "Maybe. Maybe to try and protect us both. I don't want to think I'm that selfish. But what if I am?"

She sat beside him and pressed a kiss to his temple. "If you are, it makes you human."

His eyes brimmed and he blinked. "I should have handled explaining your depression better. Forgive me? Although I know I don't deserve it."

She placed a hand on his knee. "*Pastor Thomas*, I think I've heard a sermon or two from you about undeserved forgiveness. Besides, you're not the only one who needs forgiveness. I've been so wrapped up in my own pain I couldn't see beyond my disappointments and unmet expectations."

He probed the dark purple bruise under his eye and winced. "I hope you know I never expected you to just snap out of it. Please know that. But I've prayed for your suffering to lift every day."

"I wish I had done a better job of dealing with things. I just couldn't seem to see through the fog. But I'm starting to."

His eyes closed. "That's the thing I'm learning—that we don't have to have it all figured out. That it's okay to stumble. Even to lose sight of where we're going at times. God isn't looking for pretty, he's looking for real."

She picked up a folder from the coffee table and placed it in his hands.

Thom opened it and scanned the paperwork. "Miri?"

"I . . . I think I might be ready to foster. I filled the papers out last week and was planning to surprise you with them, but with everything that happened . . ."

"You mean it?" He took a breath, expression sobering. "I don't want us to rush into this."

She nodded. "The whole process will take time. We can go at our own pace. But I think I want to explore it."

"My body feels like I've been beat by twenty grown men, but my heart feels like heaven right now. Good things are ahead, Miri. I feel it."

Miriam smiled, embracing the peace in the air. "On that note, how about a glass of water? And I have your pain medication from the emergency room if you think you need it."

"Ugh. No more of that stuff. I was out of my head last night. I barely remember it, but I know I couldn't walk a straight line when Officer Michaels helped me inside last night." He smiled a half-smile. "Hopefully he won't share those stories with the congregation. There's no telling what I said." He shifted on the couch with a groan. "But maybe I will take an ibuprofen."

While she was in the kitchen getting his water, painkillers, and toast, Miriam laughed under her breath as she remembered how her husband had staggered through the door. He mumbled unintelligible apologies to her, while the officer, who had happened upon the wrecked car, explained what had happened.

The doorbell rang.

When she answered it, Harvey stood on the porch, wide-eyed and breathing hard. "Mrs. Lashley?"

Miriam tilted her head. "Harvey? Pearl said she'd tell you Thomas wasn't coming in today."

He shifted from side to side, picking at the cuff of his plaid shirt. "Is . . . is Pastor Thomas really all right?"

Miriam glanced out behind him. The only car in the drive was her own. "Did you walk the whole way here?"

He shrugged. "I don't like cars much, ma'am. And I know Pearl said he was doing okay. I needed . . . I wanted to check and see if he needed anything."

"Oh, uh sure . . . Come in."

He wrung his hands. "I'm sorry. Is this a bad time? I should have called, I guess. I didn't think about it."

"Now's fine. I'm getting him breakfast. He's around the corner in the living room."

He didn't think about calling, but walking five miles was a natural inclination? By the high color on his face, and his heavy breaths, it seemed more likely the athletically built man ran instead of walked.

He looked so different with short hair and clothes that fit his frame. His posture was straight and square, no longer stooping and slouched like the phantom person who tried to disappear before he was called upon to speak.

Thomas called from the living room. "Who is it? Is it about the car?"

She pointed Harvey toward the living room. "Go on in."

Harvey nodded and shifted a watch around his wrist as he passed. *Thomas's gold watch.* She shook her head. *That man.*

Their muffled conversation drifted through to the kitchen as she toasted the bread and spread the strawberry jam. But when she walked into the living room, Thomas was alone.

She raised an eyebrow. "He's gone?"

Thomas laughed, but then winced and sobered. "That's Harvey for you."

"He walked the whole way from the church, and then left after less than five minutes?"

Thomas lifted a shoulder. "I think he needed to see for himself that I was okay. And once he did, he got embarrassed and didn't know what to do next, so he left."

"I don't know if that's insane or sweet."

"I think there's a broken person who has a lot of love to give hidden underneath all the . . . oddness."

"How can you tell? He hardly says more than five words strung together."

"How many men do you know who would rearrange their life to help their sister raise a baby?" Thomas propped his feet up on the couch and leaned back into the pillow. He flinched, and Miriam remembered the ibuprofen in her hand.

"He has sad eyes." She placed the toast on the coffee table and handed him the water glass and tablets.

"I don't think we have even an inkling of what that man has been through." Thomas knocked back the ibuprofen with a long swig of water. He fumbled with the blanket until she came over and pulled it back down where it had inched up his leg.

"Thank you. I'm sorer than I realized."

"Are you sure you don't want something stronger for your pain?"

"No. It's just aches and bruised ribs."

She sat on the opposite end of the couch and settled into the crook of the sofa arm. She wedged her toes underneath his thigh. "I barely recognize Harvey. He's changed a lot."

"That he has. He's a different person from the man who broke into the Pantry a month ago."

She sucked in air. "He what?"

"Oh, that . . . I didn't tell you, did I?"

She crossed her arms over her chest. "No."

He made puppy dog eyes at her. "Any chance you'll let an invalid off the hook out of pity? I'm in pain and giving up all my secrets."

"Yeah, like the fact that you gave Harvey your watch."

He gave her an apologetic smile. "He didn't have one."

"So you gave him the best watch you own?"

He gave her the mock puppy eyes again, but then sobered. "Wait, did you say he was wearing it?"

"Yeah."

"I've never seen him wear it. At first I thought he'd sold it, but then one day I saw him pull it out of his pocket to check the time. Maybe he's starting to accept that people really do want good things for him."

• CHAPTER •

THIRTY-EIGHT

PRESENT DAY

Ivy sat cross-legged on the bedroom floor. The box of linens she'd been packing for donations to the local homeless mission sat deserted. She spread out the photo of Rose and the one of her as a newborn in an unidentifiable man's arms. Next to it, she placed the journal entry from Grandma's Bible. "What was all this about, Grandma?"

Ivy released a shuddering breath and leaned her head back against the dresser. Her phone chimed. Probably Reese texting from the garage, wondering what was taking her so long to pack a single box.

But it was Seth. Again.

> Listen, I know I screwed up what we had. But think about it, how many times did we actually argue in our relationship? Once? Twice? We were good together. That last argument went way too far. I know that. Give me a chance to

fix this. Let's not throw away the past year and
a half. Okay?

The phone trembled in Ivy's hand. What was this hold he
had on her? It made no sense. Her thumb hovered over the
call button. Maybe just one conversation would make it clear
that there was no hope of them working out. But then her
gaze found the picture of Grandma and Rose. She dropped
her phone in her lap and pulled her knees to her chest.

She was just like Rose.

"Ivy?" Reese's voice sounded through the house.

Ivy jumped to her feet, swiping at her face.

Reese entered the bedroom and gave her a once-over, his
focus pausing on the pictures scattered on the floor.

"Hey, you okay?" He stood in front of her, resting his
hands on her shoulders.

Her chin quivered as she turned her face away. "All this
time I was the one who had it wrong. I've spent so much time
being angry at Mom and Dad, but maybe they were right
by not being forthcoming. Nothing good can come from me
knowing this mess about my past."

"Ivy—"

"It might make a difference if the little fairy tale they
wrote was true. That I was left on their doorstep because I
was loved. But . . . but I could be a product of human trafficking. Abuse. I see what you mean now. It's better if the
past doesn't make a difference in who we become or where
we go in life."

He gently squeezed her shoulders. "Why this sudden
change of heart? There's still a lot more to discover. How
did you end up with your parents? And did your grandma

ever find out for sure if Rose was your birth mother? Is Rose still out there somewhere? Does she know about you?"

Ivy shook her head. "I can't do this anymore. I'm done with this. With this house. With the search. The church can deal with the estate sale. There's nothing else I need to know."

He tugged her into a hug. "Sorry, friend. That's not how this story ends."

"I mean it, Reese. My name is Ivy Rose Lashley. Child of Miriam and Thomas Lashley. It's enough for me." She swallowed. "That's all I can handle."

"Oh, Ivy. You've got to hang on a little longer."

"I . . ." She lifted her chin to look into his hazel eyes. Eyes full of compassion. Gentleness. Strength. Patience. Steadiness. The knot in her middle loosened a fraction.

"I've got the truck loaded for the homeless mission if you're ready. Or if you'd rather, I can just take it?"

She stepped back and picked the photos off the floor, setting them on the table nearby. "No, no. I want to go. I need to get out of here."

Ivy locked the door behind them as they headed outside. When she opened the door of Reese's truck, a package wrapped in rumpled brown paper and topped with a lopsided bow rested in the passenger seat.

"What's this?"

Reese snatched the package. "Oh, uh . . . well, it was meant to be a joke. Not a joke. But something funny. It's not the right time. I'll just . . . forget about this, okay? I'll give it to you later."

Ivy sighed, trying to slough the weight off her shoulders. "I could use a little comic relief."

Though her flat tone couldn't have been convincing, Reese handed over the package.

She pulled off the bow and unfolded the paper. Her fingertips landed on satiny smooth fabric. Ivy yanked the paper open. Her old aviator goggles rested atop the pink superhero cape Mom made for her back in her swing-soaring days.

Ivy stared. "Where did—how did—Reese?"

His low laugh filled her ears. "It was in a box of things your grandma gave me before she passed. I'd forgotten about it until we were over at the house last night with you in that swing. I think she wanted me to tell you to not be afraid. That no matter how life knocks you down, don't outgrow the belief you can fly."

Ivy swallowed the lump in her throat and squeezed the bridge of her nose. "I thought you said this was supposed to make me laugh."

Mischief played across his expression. He reached across her and cranked down her window. As he cruised down Grandma's drive, he wriggled an eyebrow. "Put the goggles on, Rosie-girl."

She dangled the goggles from her fingers. "No way. No how."

"You'll do it, or I'll spend the rest of the day talking in pig latin."

Ivy mock groaned. "That's too far." Back in fifth grade, Reese had spent an entire week only speaking in pig latin for the sole purpose of annoying her.

"Just do it. Put on the goggles. Hang your head out the window like Mr. Johnson's old hound dog, and I guarantee you'll be laughing in five seconds flat."

"And how do you plan to compensate me if your guarantee falls through?"

He grinned, a slow lazy grin. "I dunno. How would you like me to compensate you?"

For some reason him leaning in for a kiss played in her mind. Her cheeks flamed. "You're impossible." She tugged the goggles over her eyes and leaned out the window before Reese could catch a glimpse.

At that exact moment old Mr. Coulter stepped out onto his front porch as they zipped past. The poor man about broke his neck spinning around to get another look at her.

Reese hooted with laughter and gunned the engine.

Ivy bit the insides of her cheeks to keep from giving in too quickly to the silliness bubbling up in her chest, but she completely lost it when he cranked up his stereo to full volume with R. Kelly singing "I Believe I Can Fly."

She plopped back down into her seat and pulled off the goggles, gasping and gripping her sides. "Stop it. Turn it off. I can't—" But she was laughing too hard to get words out. Tears streamed down her face.

He snorted as his shoulders shook. "Told ya I could get you to laugh in five seconds flat."

● ● ●

At the homeless mission, groups of men and a few women sat at picnic tables conversing and eating lunch. Reese nudged Ivy with his elbow and jerked his head sideways.

Uncle Vee was sitting next to Leah, the director of the homeless mission. She laughed at whatever he had just said and placed her hand on his forearm.

"What's going on over there?" Reese asked.

Ivy shrugged. They sure looked cozy, angled toward each other. Her uncle wasn't the touchy type, but he didn't seem bothered by Leah invading his personal space.

Her uncle frequently came to the homeless shelter to interview employees for his landscaping crew. Some came and worked with him for a few months to get back on their feet; others stayed for years. The community had once been put off by the people he employed, but after seeing the crew's exemplary work, they overlooked their less-than-traditional backgrounds. Although, it looked like Uncle Vee was here for personal reasons today.

Ivy grinned. "I think my uncle has a girlfriend."

As they approached, Uncle Vee jumped up from his seat and walked toward them. "Hey, you two. What's going on?"

Ivy gave him a quick side hug. "I think the bigger question is what's going on with you . . . and Leah?"

He scrubbed his jaw with this hand. "Just lunch. She had questions about how my new hires are working out." He coughed to clear the gravel in his throat.

How cute. He was embarrassed.

Reese hitched his thumbs in his pockets. "You two seemed pretty cozy over there."

Uncle Vee sputtered. "Oh . . . uh . . . yeah, no. We're friends. Good friends."

Ivy bit the inside of her cheek to check her smile. "Didn't look like *just* friends to me."

Her uncle glanced from Ivy to Reese and back. A corner of his mouth twitched. "Uh-huh. As if the two of you know the difference between friends and more than friends."

Reese coughed as he headed for his truck. "Uh. I need to . . . the boxes . . . unloaded. I gotta go unload the boxes."

THIRTY-NINE

NOVEMBER 6, 1994

Pearl leaned against the doorframe, her hands hugged around her teacup brimming with chamomile, watching Harvey in his favorite location—stretched out on the floor with Ivy. He was at his best in moments like these. The little places around his eyes relaxed, and the perpetual crimp in his forehead smoothed. His movements were languid instead of rushed.

Too bad she hadn't convinced him to come to church that morning. Although right now she'd be happy to simply convince Harvey to sleep inside. Every morning for the past three weeks, she'd found him in the predawn hours curled up on the porch swing again. He had to have been freezing last night. It was fifty degrees, and he hadn't brought out a blanket or jacket.

He made the same excuse. Blaming restlessness. Did he honestly think a bed in a home was more than he deserved?

She set her tea on the side table. Despite her stiff joints, she sat on the floor next to Harvey and the baby.

He smiled up from where he lay. "We're an odd bunch. All sitting on the floor, surrounded by furniture."

Pearl let out a chuckle. Maybe if she put herself on the same physical level with them, he'd let her move him up from whatever lowly cubbyhole Harvey had placed himself in. If only he'd trust her to show him just how much goodness he deserved.

She pursed her lips against the sour-tasting words about to come from her mouth. It was probably the wrong way to handle this, but she couldn't have him spend another night shivering on her porch swing.

"Harvey, you know I wish you'd sleep in the bedroom. Everything in that room is yours. But I also want you to get a good night's sleep. If you would be more comfortable, there's a camping cot and a zero-degree sleeping bag in the garage. You could put them on the porch and sleep there instead of wadded up on the swing."

His brow took on its normal furrow. "I'm sorry if I hurt you because I did that."

"You haven't offended me. Sometimes when a gift is offered, we aren't quite ready to receive it. But if I were you, I would make sure you're up and the cot stored before Pastor gets here in the morning. He would surely have an abundance of questions if he discovered you slept on my porch every night. Least of your worries, why I was so cruel as to not invite you inside."

"Yes, ma'am."

"Now you listen here. I'll allow this until cold weather comes, and then you *will* sleep inside. Do you understand me, young man?"

"A reasonable request, Miss Pearl." He wiggled a rattle

in front of Ivy, who made sputtering gurgles in response. The baby lifted her pudgy arms and waved them wildly, too uncoordinated to reach her goal.

A six foot two man with work-roughened hands, lying on the floor with a plush pink rattle between his fingers. He and Ivy were a pair of antonyms. Shadowed and bright. Big and small. Anxious and peaceful. Rough and soft. The harmonic existence between them was the most beautiful thing she'd witnessed in this life. She couldn't bear that she'd have to be the voice of reason and put a stop to their little fantasy world. Someone needed to do something about the child's abandonment. Sooner, not later. What would happen if Ivy had an emergency and there was no way to contact her mother?

"You're so good with her. Your devotion takes my breath away."

The silly expression he made at Ivy melted from his face, and he sat up.

"I couldn't let her grow up like I did. No child should."

Pearl tilted her head and willed every aspect of her expression to convey openness. Acceptance. "And how did you grow up, Harvey? Children's homes, you said?"

He lowered his eyes, and a muscle jumped in his jaw. "Those people in children's services, they try to do a good job. But it's not the same as being loved by a mom and dad. It's not love when you can be given back when it gets tough."

Oh, Harvey. The man was ripping her heart out of her chest and didn't even know it. The lanky man with calloused hands and weather-roughened cheeks had disappeared. To her he was . . . so much like that little boy with doe eyes she'd given a plaid shirt to all those years ago, whose face had never left her. "No, that's not love. Love endures through all things." She struggled to stand, and Harvey reached over to steady her. Pearl went to the piano, where her worn Bible sat.

Sitting on the piano bench, she flipped through tissue-thin pages by memory to 1 Corinthians 13. "Love is patient and kind. Love is not jealous or boastful or proud or rude. It does not demand its own way. It is not irritable, and it keeps no record of being wronged. It does not rejoice about injustice but rejoices whenever the truth wins out. Love never gives up, never loses faith, is always hopeful, and endures through every circumstance."

Harvey picked Ivy up and sat on the couch. "Those are pretty words, but nobody loves like that. No one's love can endure all things."

She set the Bible aside. "You love Ivy that way."

He rested his cheek softly against the top of Ivy's head and closed his eyes. "I can't be what I want to be to her. This world won't let that happen. Everybody leaves. My parents left me. I'll never be able to prove I'm the best parent for Ivy, and I'll have to leave her too. It's just the way it works."

Pearl snapped her head toward him. "Your parents left you? I thought—"

"There is more than one way to leave a person. They couldn't help it. It wasn't their fault. If it was anybody's fault, it was mine. But, whether left in death or life, I was still left behind."

Throat too tight to speak, she nodded, his words having exposed the raw wound. She'd been left by her son by his choice, and her husband was taken by cancer. The pain throbbing the deepest was the feeling of being left behind. But there was a difference between her and Harvey. Pearl had never felt alone in her suffering.

He was across the room but on another planet. She cleared the tightness in her throat. "Would it bother you if I sat by you?"

He gave a thin smile and glanced to the empty space beside him. "No. Plenty of room over here."

She crossed the room and then tentatively sat, wanting to hug him, but knowing it was asking too much.

He let out a heavy breath and scooted, closing the space between them. He shifted Ivy to his other arm and held his arm closest to Pearl suspended over her shoulder for a long moment. Something akin to fear in his eyes.

Then he draped his arm around her and pulled her in an awkward half hug. He laid his head on top of hers, crunching her gray curls flat against her head.

A faint tremor went through his body like a man trying to hold a heavier weight than he was able, and her heart wrenched thinking of how much the simple expression cost him.

In a whisper she said, "That verse I read wasn't really about human love. You're right. It is above what we're able to give. But we try. This is the way God loves us. He never leaves nor forsakes us no matter what happens or who leaves us. Knowing that is the only way I've survived this past year myself."

Harvey's reply came raw and ragged. "It sounds nice, Miss Pearl. The pretty words you say."

Pearl swallowed the pain in his words. "Harvey, what do you feel for Ivy?"

He lifted his head. His chest rose and fell with heavy breaths. "I feel like I would give my life, give up anything to make sure she was safe."

Pearl leaned away so she could see his eyes. "That's how God feels about you, and so much more. And even though bad things have happened to you, he's always been there, loving you all along the way.

"Everything I've lost was part of bringing me to this moment. Your hug was one of the most precious things I've ever received. Sharing my home with you is a gift I could never have imagined. He has such good things in store for you too. I believe that with all my heart."

Harvey glanced down to the baby in his arms. He let out a slow sigh. "When . . . if they take Ivy away from me, do you think they'd let you keep her?"

Pearl swallowed back the rising emotion. He trusted her far more than she'd imagined.

Not wanting to give him false hope, she searched for a way to convey her heart without breaking his. "Oh, Harvey. I don't think they'd see an old woman like me as the best fit to raise her. But, if they would, you better believe I'd shower all the love I had in my heart on that child. I don't think anyone could love her quite like you do, but I'd give it my all."

He ducked his chin and nodded. "Thank you."

"For what?"

"For letting me find my own way."

"I know a lawyer. If you could get in touch with your sister, he could help you sign forms for temporary custody. That would give you time to get things in order. Find out what your sister's intentions are. If she's amenable, you wouldn't even have to involve child services until it was time to make permanent arrangements for Ivy. Have you heard from her at all?"

Not even a glimmer of hope touched his features. "I appreciate what you're trying to do, but I can't contact my sister about this." He passed the baby to her and went to the garage for the cot and sleeping bag.

That night, Pearl slept with a lost boy on her porch and an abandoned baby in her bedroom. Both loved more than she had words to express. She had the feeling she was about to lose them both.

· CHAPTER ·

FORTY

NOVEMBER 14, 1994

After a month of living with Pearl, Harvey adjusted to the fact that his evenings consisted of sitting around chatting with an elderly lady instead of scavenging along the side of the road and cooking fish over a campfire. And mornings were now filled with a hot breakfast and a hot shower instead of a quick dip in an icy stream.

As he crossed the yard to the church, his boots crunched on the hint of frost on the ground. He shook his head; *adjusted* was a relative term. He had days, maybe a week, before he had to make an exit plan. Pearl kept going on and on about ways for him to get legal custody of Ivy. What she didn't know—no matter how hard they worked to prove he was a good father to Ivy—was that he had no real claim to her.

He entered the sanctuary. Once a looming mystery, now, after polishing it from top to bottom, felt like an old acquaintance. He ran two fingers over the worn spot on the edge of the back pew, another person paying homage to a place of rest.

In the office, Pastor Thomas stood with a book propped on his arm. As he thumbed through the pages, he hummed under his breath.

Harvey paused a moment, puzzled over the change that had come over him. When they first met, the pastor seemed weary and alone, and then bereft after whatever conflict had risen between him and his wife.

The stability of the people in Thomas's little circle should have imploded. Instead, if anything, the accident had lifted them.

His wife was around more too. Something about her used to hurt his heart when he looked in her eyes. And though there was still a lingering sadness, it was different. Softer.

Harvey cleared his throat. "Good morning."

"Hi, Harvey. How are you?"

"Doing okay, sir. Do you have a list for me this week?"

"I do. But before we get to that, why don't we sit a minute. Did you have a nice weekend?"

Harvey flashed back to taking Ivy for a walk in the wrap while Pearl was at church. It was like old times as he tramped through the woods and over to the rolling hills of an abandoned farm. Fall had come in earnest and a chilly breeze chased the warmth of the sun. "It was a nice weekend. I went for a hike."

Thomas nodded. "Good few days for it. Hey, I've been meaning to ask if you might want to join us for church service? No pressure. It's not a job requirement. I just wanted you to know we'd enjoy it if you came."

Harvey shrugged. "Thanks for the invite. I . . . I'll think about it." He hated to lie, but he didn't want to hurt Thomas's feelings. It wasn't personal, but church was the last place he belonged.

"All right. Thanks again for all you do around here. The whole church can't stop talking about it. You polished light back into this place. You took the old and made it new."

The familiar cramp between his eyebrows pinched, and he opened his mouth to protest.

One corner of Thomas's mouth twitched up toward his ear. "Go on. Here's your list. I'm not going to listen to you downplay your success."

Harvey glanced at the paper before stuffing it in his pocket. It wasn't as though he did anything noteworthy. He merely tried to work off the nerves that rose from being away from Ivy and the uncertainty of how much longer he could maintain this way of life.

"Oh, and don't worry about tracking me down at the end of the day. Miriam and I have a class every Monday afternoon, so I'll be leaving early."

Harvey left Thomas and made his first stop at the Pantry. He paused for a moment to appreciate the new light fixtures that covered the once-naked bulbs. The bright coat of paint on the walls. The repurposed shelving and peg boards he had painted and cleaned.

Maybe it had become more than a job, working and serving these people.

After lunch with Pearl, he went out to rake. The windy night had left a new coat of leaves on the browning grass. His thoughts wandered as he worked.

Thomas appeared from the basement door, rake in hand. "Need help? Maybe your landscaping skills will rub off on me."

Harvey nodded, and they worked in silence for several minutes. Harvey puzzled over the pastor emerging from his office. All these weeks the man had kept to that spot. He wasn't an outdoorsy type. He worked hard in other ways.

"Uh. Are you okay, Harvey?"

Harvey stood still next to his pile of leaves. He darted his eyes sideways and cleared his throat. "Oh, yeah. Just lost in thought."

"About?"

Harvey busied himself with raking and spoke with his back to Thomas. "I was thinking you're a different sort of person. I mean . . . well . . . you've always been kind to me and given me chances no other person would. You saw past bad first impressions." He turned to face Thomas, who had ceased raking. "I've never thanked you for that. I'm not good with words. I don't know what to say. Thank you."

Thomas ducked his chin and ran his hand through his hair. "You aren't saying goodbye to me, are you? Because that felt like a goodbye. You're scaring me a little."

"No, sir. Not saying goodbye. I'm sorry. I don't express myself well." Harvey spun around and went back to raking.

Pastor Thomas was having a hard time clearing his throat behind him. When he spoke there was a thickness to his voice. "Don't be sorry, and don't sell yourself short. Your words are fine. More than fine."

Harvey gripped the rake handle.

Thomas raked beside him. "My dad left my mother and me when I was a kid. For years I thought I did something wrong. That if I had been better, he would have stayed—that love had to be earned. But when I was sixteen, at a summer camp, I learned about the unfailing love of our heavenly

Father. For the first time in my life I realized Dad leaving wasn't my fault. He was the one broken on the inside. God, my true Father, loved me no matter what.

"That's where ministry began for me. I never wanted anyone to believe they have to look a certain way or play a role to receive love."

Palms slick on the rake handle, Harvey gave him a quick nod and went back to his task.

Harvey worked his way around the yard. He knew Thomas was still working with him by the steady scratch-swish rhythm of the rake on the leaves behind him. But he was afraid to look at him. Afraid more awkward words would pass between them.

After another half hour, Thomas called out. "Hey, Harvey, I've got to run, but would you like to grab coffee or let me buy you lunch this week? I'd like to get to know you better."

Harvey swallowed and turned to face Thomas, who had a fine sheen of sweat across the bridge of his nose, his dress shirt damp in some places. Not at all ready for that class he was about to go to.

Harvey nodded. "Okay." Hopefully it was an empty invite. Because he couldn't tell him or anyone else more about himself without accidentally exposing more holes in his story.

* ● •

Pearl scooped up Ivy, who was working up a fuss on her play mat. "It's just you and me this afternoon, little girl."

The doorbell sounded. "Well, I guess not."

Pearl opened the door to Miriam. Her fiery curls were tamed into a high bun, and a modest skirt and blouse accentuated her tall, curvy frame. But it was the tranquility in her blue-green eyes that made her beauty shine.

"Hi, Pearl. I'm meeting Thomas in a few minutes. It's been a few weeks since we've been able to chat, so I thought I'd stop by before I headed over to the church."

Pearl nodded. "It's been good seeing more of you around here. We appreciate the female company, don't we, Ivy?"

Miriam moved closer and gazed at the baby with a hint of a smile. She stretched out her hands. "May I?"

"Oh, of course. Here, snuggle this little bug while I get her bottle ready."

When Pearl returned, Miriam had Ivy propped against her shoulder as she flipped through a scrapbook on the coffee table.

Miriam smiled. "Is this you in this photograph?"

Pearl handed Miriam the bottle and picked up her reading glasses from beside the album. She ran her fingertip over the washed-out pictures. "Yes. I was sporting the blonde bombshell look back in those days." Pearl winked. "I traded it for this lovely blue-gray fiasco compliments of Babette. Bless her heart. She'll get the hang of color one of these days." She chuckled. "I hope. For her sake, and mine."

Miriam smiled. "And that's your husband in the picture?"

"Yes. After homecoming service. The year before I got pregnant with Marshall. A real miracle, that was."

Pearl snuck a glance at Miriam. She hadn't meant to poke at Miriam's wounds. But the young woman was looking at Ivy. Pearl wasn't sure if Miriam heard a word she'd said.

Miriam looked up suddenly. "I have a secret, Pearl. I'm dying to tell somebody, but Thomas wants to keep things quiet until we're further into it. I hear you're a good secret keeper . . ."

Pearl mimed zipping her lips.

Miriam bit her bottom lip. "Thomas and I are applying to become foster parents. We're almost finished with classes, and our home visit is tomorrow."

Pearl sucked a breath in through her nose as her gaze flicked from Miriam, down to Ivy, and back. She walked over to her couch and sank into its comfort. "That's wonderful, Miriam."

Miriam grinned. "We thought we would start out by working with kids who need temporary shelters or respite care. You know, with parents dealing with legal issues or health problems. Or long-term foster parents who need a weekend break to regroup. Then we'll see if we think we'd be up for more permanent placements."

"You and Thomas will be wonderful. I always wanted to foster and eventually adopt, but my husband never warmed up to the idea. I did what I could, and I visited children's homes around Nashville every Thanksgiving."

"I never thought I would find fostering or adopting fulfilling, but after opening my home and heart to those young mothers and"—Miriam let out a soft chuckle—"oddly enough, watching how you've loved Harvey, and how he's come out of his shell from your love."

"Oh, that's the Lord's doing. I've been stumbling along."

Miriam smirked. "If you say so." The lines around her playful smile softened into something wistful. "It's funny. I'm starting to see that when I let go of my grip on my pain, I make space for new things. Things that bless me in a way I never would've imagined. I'm getting there little by little—

learning how to release my disappointments and embrace the gifts I have."

"I, for one, am thankful for God's patience with his children." Pearl patted Miriam's knee.

"So you had Marshall when you were forty? That must have been a shock."

"That's an understatement. My husband and I were under the impression we weren't able to conceive. When I scheduled a doctor's visit, I thought I was ill. Turns out I had severe morning sickness. Baby Marshall and I about sent my poor doctor to an early grave with all his worries about my age. But they were needless. Both the baby and I were as healthy as could be."

Miriam traced a finger over the bridge of Ivy's nose. The baby's eyelids drooped with sleep. "What a blessing it must have been, after having waited so long."

"Oh, yes. He was this energetic, sociable, ray of sunshine. I wondered how I had been so fortunate to raise such a joyful child. And I promised the Lord I wouldn't take a moment for granted with him. But even still, I didn't have him in my life nearly long enough. It about ripped my heart in two when he went off to war."

"I can't imagine. And he . . . he didn't make it back?"

A lump swelled in Pearl's throat. When Marshall came up in casual conversation, she normally implied she lost him as a casualty of war and let people draw their own conclusions. It was simpler that way. It allowed people to see him for the patriotic hero he was. She took a slow breath. The church members knew the full story. It would be better if Miriam heard it from her instead of the rumor mill.

After Pearl recounted how his tours of duty changed him and the ways she tried to help him but failed to see the things festering beneath the nightmares and extreme mood swings, Miriam pressed her hand to her heart. Her voice came out soft and tender. "I cannot begin to imagine. I think of how I've struggled with my own pain, and it suddenly seems rather trivial."

Pearl shook her head. "It's not about my pain versus your pain. It's about sharing in the human experience and knowing what it is to hurt. It takes courage—stepping forward and healing when it's so tempting, so safe, to stay and worship the altars we've built to our pain. Harvey has been a big part of my healing over the past few months. I guess helping him feels like a second chance."

* * *

That evening, Harvey carefully supported Ivy on his knees, singing her a rhyme about a horse.

"What a cute song. Where did you learn it?"

Harvey's open expression clouded. "Not sure. Must have been from the foster homes. One of the foster moms had a baby."

Pearl straightened, ears perked for details. "Oh, I didn't know you had foster parents."

Harvey poked his tongue in his cheek and turned his head away. "Fourteen sets of 'em." The words came out a weighted sigh, likely with fourteen separate sets of emotions to match.

"That many?"

He pulled Ivy close. "The ones with the new baby, they tried a lot longer than I expected. Eventually they wearied of the dark shadow following their bright little family around. Just like everyone else."

The sheer number of times he'd been uprooted left her

breathless. No wonder he didn't trust anyone. And he was so matter-of-fact, as if such treatment was expected. "You said children's homes the other day."

"Children's homes when they couldn't find anyone to take me. Most people are wary of taking on a kid who has a panic attack every time he gets in a car. Puts a damper on the errand running."

"Fourteen foster homes, and children's homes on top of that." Pearl closed her eyes and saw not the handsome young man before her but a fractured child carrying the unimaginable ache of belonging nowhere, of being too much trouble to be loved.

"Foster parents are the people who want to help but aren't brave enough to commit."

She pictured Thomas and Miriam and their heart to love those who needed it. "Do you really think that's fair?"

"I don't know, Miss Pearl. If you were me, would you say it's an accurate assessment or not?"

She tipped her head in acknowledgment. "Then what? You never had a permanent placement? You aged out of the system when you were eighteen?"

He lifted his shoulders and his mouth stretched in a line. An expression probably intended to convey nonchalance but didn't quite make it. "Something like that."

"You and your sister, were you able to be together?"

His mouth dropped open and then closed, and he offered a shrug.

She cupped the side of her face, trying to imagine a child who never knew security being turned out into the world to fend for himself. "What did you do? How did you ever manage?"

He bowed his head until his chin rested on the top of Ivy's head. "I found my own version of safety. And this little stinker messed it all up. I'm probably as lost as I've ever been."

After his proclamation, Harvey became tight-lipped and sullen.

Growing dread weighed on Pearl's chest, reminding her of her last days with Marshall. Something was brewing. But she didn't know what it was or how to stop it.

FORTY-ONE

PRESENT DAY

Reese pulled out of the homeless mission's parking lot. "You want to take a break from the house and go fishing for old times' sake? It's a good day for it."

Ivy stared out the windshield, watching the scenery slip past. "Actually, that sounds perfect."

"I've got a couple fishing poles in the back of the truck. Let's stop at the bait shop, and we can head over to the pond near the church."

He parked in front of the old cinder-block building with chipping white paint. In a few minutes he returned with a can of night crawlers and two Cokes with condensation beading on the chilled glass. After he passed her a Coke, he held up a bag of peanuts. "Want some?"

She wrinkled her nose as he poured several into his opened Coke. "No thanks."

"Aw, you just don't know what's good." He put the truck in gear after passing her a bottle opener.

The top released with a hiss. She took a long draught, and the fizz burned her nose. It had been a long time since she'd had a bottled Coke. It took her back to walking to the bait shop on hot summer days with her uncle. Relishing the feel of the cold glass in her hands, a reprieve from the summer heat, and lifting a hand to wave to the people driving past while they sat on the wide front steps. She relaxed into the truck's seat back. It was good to be in Triune, where life was slower, and the childhood memories were laced with the sweetness of magnolia blossoms.

Her phone chimed out a sing-song tone. She glanced at the screen. The peace dissolved.

"Who is it?"

She groaned. "I need to block his number."

Reese's grip tightened on the steering wheel. "I'll talk to him. I promise you won't have to bother with getting his number blocked."

A corner of her mouth lifted as she tucked the phone away. "I appreciate the offer. But I can't spend my life expecting other people to fight my battles for me."

"I guess not. But there's nothing wrong with inviting someone to fight the battle alongside you."

She shrugged. The line between having someone fight her battle for her or beside her was too blurred.

He parked on a gravel pull-off. They grabbed the tackle box and fishing poles and took a five-minute hike to the pond.

The bullfrogs croaked and, in quick succession, plopped into the water at their approach. A turtle basked on a half-submerged stump. Below the steep bank, mud ringed the pond where the water level was lower than normal.

Reese handed her a pole and set the bait between two logs that were the perfect size for sitting. Ivy baited her hook and cast with a whiz and plop. She took up the slack in her line and sat as she studied the ripples undulating from the fluorescent bobber.

"You want to know who you are? You're the kind of girl who isn't afraid to bait her own hook. Who's brave enough to do things her own way, and not have a care in the world if she's different from everyone else. With this amazing ability to see past the surface to the heart of the matter. To really grasp what's going on with a person behind the mask they hold up."

She jerked her head in his direction. "I wasn't brave back then and I'm certainly not now." And she definitely didn't have the abilities Reese claimed she possessed. If she had, she'd never have messed up her life with Seth.

He shook his head. "You are braver than you know. And more loved than you realize."

She stared at him, taking in the softness in his gaze. Her heart clenched. What was she supposed to say to a declaration like that? She settled for a quick smile.

"Rosie-girl, you've got one on the line. If you don't set your hook, he's gonna get away."

She blinked. "Huh?"

"A fish. You've got a bite, silly."

"Oh!" The bobber was out of sight. She yanked her fishing pole, stood, and reeled. The satisfying resistance in the line kicked up her pulse. "I think it's a big one." Her sandals squished in the muck as she edged closer to the steep bank.

"Better watch yourself. The fish is supposed to come to you, not the other way around."

Ivy reeled until the fish came free from the water. On the end of her line was the tiniest bream she'd ever seen.

Reese wrapped his arms around his middle as he howled with laughter. "Yep, it's a big one, all right. Hold him up, I gotta get a picture of this giant pond monster of yours."

She turned her back to the pond and held the tiny iridescent fish near her cheek, cutting Reese a playful glare as he snapped the picture.

Ivy eyed the fish dangling from her line. "All right, little buddy, time to go back home. You're too small to fry."

"Hand him here, I'll throw him back for you."

She shook her head, edging backward toward the drop-off. "Uh-uh. You know the rule. Whoever catches it has to be the one to get the hook out."

She poked her tongue in the corner of her mouth as she slid her hand down the line and over the fish, smoothing back the spines on its dorsal fin.

As the hook slipped free, the fish must have decided it was time for his last stand. It wriggled from her grasp and a shriek squeaked out of Ivy's throat. She stumbled backward, snatching the fish from the air. Her flip-flops skated backward down the slick bank and popped off her feet. Her rear end landed with a plop in the mud. The fish slipped from her hand and sailed over her head. A splash sounded behind her.

Reese half slid, half hopped down the slope, eyes round. "You okay?"

She released a dry laugh and swiped at the specks of mud freckling her arm. "Nothing wounded but my pride. That scrawny fish sure took me down a peg or two."

He smiled as he reached to help her up, but a crease appeared between his brows. "You're bleeding."

"No, I don't think—" But then she saw the smudged streak of red on her arm.

She held up her muddy hand that trembled when blood welled from a two-inch cut in the middle of her palm. Funny how the pain only registered when she saw the wound.

Reese nodded to a ragged piece of green glass protruding from the mud. "Watch yourself, there's a couple more pieces to your left." He steadied her as she stood with mud squishing between her toes. "Let's get you to the tackle box and I'll clean it up for you."

Reese eyed the slick bank and then Ivy, who was cradling her injured hand. "I'm going to carry you up." He plucked her sandals from the muck and tossed them to the landing and then moved to her side.

She stepped away. "Uh. No, I can make it just fine on my own."

With his eyes wide and innocent, he said, "Do you really want to risk getting even more pond scum in that cut?"

"Why do I get the feeling you're making a far bigger deal out of this than it is?"

He shrugged, an impish grin quickly replacing the innocence.

Her stomach dropped like she'd taken a plunge on a roller coaster.

"So will you allow me to be gallant and sweep you off your feet?"

Ivy's face flamed. "Reese . . ."

"Come on, put your arm around me. The bank really is slick, and I don't want you to have to put that hand down for balance. I guess I could boost you from behind."

"No!"

Mischief danced in his eyes. "Okay. Then put your arm around me. Stop acting like I'm a copperhead about to strike."

She swallowed and put one arm around his neck and held her bleeding hand away from him.

He scooped his arm under her knees, lifting her like she didn't weigh more than a loaf of bread. She inhaled the fresh scent of soap lingering on his skin, and she fought the urge to lay her head on his shoulder. It was solid and certain.

He took the first step on the slope and his foot slid back three inches. Ivy yelped. "If you drop me—"

He cut his gaze toward her. "I won't."

He took another sliding step. "Slow isn't going to work. Hang on."

When he took the first running step, she clenched her eyes shut and swallowed back the squeak trying to break from her lips. In two jarring strides they were back on flat ground.

Reese paused a moment before releasing her. "Uh. Yep. Tackle box."

He set her down, his manner suddenly abrupt. She held her injured hand in front of her, trailing behind, and then sat by him in the grass.

He flicked a glance at her hand. "When did you have your last tetanus shot?"

"No worries. I got everything up-to-date at the beginning of the school year."

He cradled her hand in his, dabbing away the blood with gauze. "It's not too deep. Does it hurt?"

"I'll live." She'd never admit her stomach was a tad queasy.

"I have a bottle of water in my backpack. Hang on."

When he went to the bag, she dug through the memories of all the fishing trips before. The summers of cruising down old country lanes. The hikes. The long phone conversations. Had it been there all along? The hazy way he looked at her moments before?

She shook her head. Was her slight blood loss sufficient to claim as a reason for depleted mental faculties?

Reese knelt beside her with the water bottle and twisted his mouth. "It'll probably sting. But you're a pretty tough nut." He winked.

She felt that wink all the way to her toes.

He cupped her hand and poured a slow stream of water, gently massaging away the thin layer of dirt and blood on the uninjured parts of her hand.

His grip tightened a fraction as the stream of water covered her open wound.

She sucked air through her teeth at the sting.

He wrinkled his nose. "Sorry. I'd feel better if I had running water to flush it out better. I do have rubbing alcohol. It'll hurt though."

"No peroxide? No iodine? No sting-free antiseptic? Your first aid kit needs an upgrade."

Before she could argue further, he gripped her fingers and poured a splash of rubbing alcohol onto her palm. She gritted her teeth and squeezed her eyes closed against the involuntary tears welling at the sting.

"I don't think it'll need stitches." He slowly wrapped the middle of her palm with a layer of gauze and a self-adhesive wrap. "Keep an eye on it. Don't let it get infected."

"There's no way any germs survived that scouring."

He rubbed his calloused thumb back and forth over her

open fingers, lingering even though he had finished bandaging her hand. "Still, be careful."

Her eyes searched his.

Afternoon sunlight slipped from behind a cloud, filtering through the tall grasses. He swiped at a streak of mud on her cheek with his thumb.

She could blame what she did next on stress, or perhaps blood loss. But when she leaned up and let her lips brush his for the barest of seconds, she could only blame her heart.

Her eyes flew open wide as the reality of what she'd done coursed through her. She scrambled to stand, gasping for air.

Reese closed his eyes with a grimace.

Her pulse roared in her ears. "I'm so sorry. I shouldn't have . . . I don't know why . . ."

He let out a slow breath. "Ivy, say anything you want. But, please, please don't apologize."

• CHAPTER •

FORTY-TWO

NOVEMBER 18, 1994

Pearl crossed the churchyard with her heavy sweater pulled tight against the chill. Maybe Thomas had a feel for what was going on with Harvey.

The pastor was on the sanctuary platform, putting cornucopias and fall-colored flowers on the accent tables.

"Getting ready for the Thanksgiving services, Pastor?"

He turned around with a smile on his face. "Yes, indeed."

The church service after Thomas's accident had somehow changed everything for the man. She wasn't sure, but the fact that he'd shown up with a black eye and sore body seemed to have earned him a measure of respect.

By the next week, there was a marked difference in the way they treated him. Not that she'd ever witnessed outright disrespect. But they'd previously addressed him in a manner that hinted at his youth and inexperience. After he'd shown up and preached in obvious discomfort, his dedication had altered their stance.

Pearl walked up and sat on one of the platform chairs. "Where's Harvey?"

"Working down in the basement organizing things and throwing out what we don't need. Although, with him, not much is deemed unusable. If it won't work in its original purpose, he takes whatever it is apart, and makes something new out of it."

"Sounds like Harvey. Speaking of which, how do you feel like he's doing? Overall? I mean, I know he's outwardly changed, and he makes eye contact more. But you're a perceptive man. What's your take?"

Thomas stopped arranging and sat in the adjacent chair. "You're worried about him."

"I am."

He reached over and took her hand between his two. "I don't want to say anything out of turn or insensitive."

"Go on. I'm a tough-skinned old bird."

He swallowed, compassion creasing his face. "With you coming up on the anniversary of . . . of losing your son and your husband, do you think those feelings are transferring to Harvey? The worry, and the feeling something's wrong? Because, Pearl, of course something isn't right. When we are grieving, we're painfully aware things are not right, or as they should be, or as we had hoped they'd turn out."

Pearl pinned her bottom lip between her teeth. *Maybe.*

"You can trust God to take care of Harvey."

Trust. She'd been so worried about Harvey's trust. But had she trusted God to take care of him? No. She'd taken the responsibility on her own shoulders. She tore her gaze away and stared at the jewel-toned glass.

She had trusted God with Marshall and her husband.

Somewhere along the way, she began to believe that she could somehow control things. Do the right things to get the outcomes she thought best. "I understand what you're saying, but I can't help but feel like he is about to make a choice."

"What choice?"

"That's what I don't know."

"If it makes you feel any better, I've been trying to spend more time with him. Like I should have a long time ago, but I was so consumed with my own problems. He's opening up to me little by little." Thomas tilted his head. "Where's the baby today? With her mother?"

So Harvey hadn't told Thomas the full story about his sister's abandonment. "Miriam stopped by. She said she had things to pick up from the Pantry, but I have a sneaking suspicion she wanted an excuse to see Ivy. I thought I'd leave them in peace for a few minutes. It's been a while since I've come to disrupt your day."

"It was no disruption, and you know it. You probably kept me sane all those months."

"You did the same for me, Pastor."

"Funny how things have changed so much in such a short period of time."

"Yes . . . funny. Hey, do you want to come over while Miriam is there? I could make a fresh pot of coffee, and I made a strudel cake."

"Sounds perfect."

● ● ●

Pearl took a sip of coffee, enjoying the sight of Miriam and Thomas cooing over Ivy, who was making big eyes at them and poking out her tongue. It could be a scene from a holiday commercial.

"She smiled!" Miriam pressed a hand to her cheek.

Thomas made a silly face at Ivy, who responded with a giggly coo.

"She's a doll." Miriam was giddier by the moment at the baby's every squeak and squeal.

She angled toward her husband. "Thom, what did the church board ever say about Harvey?"

Pearl bit her lip, leaning into their conversation.

He broke off his nursery rhyme recitation midline. "Actually, nothing. The meeting was overlooked in the excitement over my car accident. Then I asked the head elder about rescheduling, and he said if I approved the man, then they were fine with the hire."

"Are you serious?"

Thomas grinned from ear to ear and nodded.

"After the hard time they've given you about any little thing you wanted to change?"

"Yes, but the church has transformed with all of Harvey's elbow grease. It was run-down and sad when we got there, but with all his work, it's been renewed."

The front door swung open, and Harvey's heavy trod sounded on the linoleum entryway. "Hi, Miss Pearl. I just stopped by to grab a coffee refill if there's any left from this morn—"

Harvey froze at the entrance to the living room. His focus flicked from her to Thomas and Miriam and then locked in on the baby in Thomas's arms. Harvey's face blanched, and he took two steps back. "Excuse me. I didn't mean to . . . interrupt company. I need to get back to work."

"Harvey, wait. You're not—" But he was already gone. Miriam and Thomas were frozen in place.

"I need to go check on him. Excuse me." Pearl put on her slippers and headed out the door.

She padded across the lawn toward Harvey's retreating form. "Harvey, stop. You didn't need to leave. That's your home. You belong there as much as I do."

He spun around with a wildness in his eyes, unrestrained emotion bursting forth. "No, Pearl, it's not my home. I don't belong. Just write the weird guy out of the story, and then you'd have a perfect picture of a family. That's what's happening, isn't it?"

"You're being irrational."

"No, I'm not. I'm like this pesky spare part left over after the toy is put together, and nobody knows where it goes."

He was rather articulate when he was riled. "Are you . . . jealous?"

"Jealous? Why would I be jealous? Just because if the Lashleys had found Ivy, the state wouldn't think for a minute they were unfit to raise her? I love her. And it should be enough. More than I ever had."

"I don't know what to say. I've tried telling you over and over again how much you mean to me. How much I want to help. Why can't I get through to you?"

"I wouldn't worry about it. No one can. I'm impossible." His voice was flat and matter-of-fact.

"With God all things are possible."

"Okay, sure." He rolled his eyes and strode toward the church.

"Harvey—"

He disappeared into the basement without a backward glance.

Something niggled in Pearl's mind. Why had Harvey said if the Lashleys had *found* Ivy?

· ● ·

Harvey banged around in the storage closet, chucking items into haphazard piles that were neat stacks when he'd started. Pearl was supposed to be on his side. But he'd stumbled upon a covert operation he wasn't a part of. Thomas and Miriam sized up Ivy to fit her for a new family, and Pearl sat there pleased as punch with the whole scene. He didn't need them deciding Ivy's future any more than he needed government intervention. It was all the same with these people.

It would be fine. He'd almost saved enough, and then he and Ivy could cut out of there—find an old codger-type he could rent from who wouldn't give a hoot about references or credit as long as the rent got paid. It would work. There were people all over this country who had no legal paperwork.

That's it. He could get forged paperwork for Ivy in case anyone asked. Then he'd have proof she was his.

He might have felt a little twinge of guilt for planning to write Pearl out of his life when she'd done so much, but it was easy enough to discard, considering her betrayal.

· ● ·

That evening, Pearl pounced the minute he came in the door—like a matador waving a red scarf in front of his face. "Harvey, Miriam and Thomas overheard our argument. What we said was vague enough they don't know the depth of the situation, but they know something is up with your sister."

"That's your fault. You let them close to Ivy. Of course they have questions now." The edges to his voice were razor sharp, but he was in no temper to censor himself. So what if she kicked him out.

Harvey tightened his fists, his nails biting into his palm. "What'd you chat about? A couple from the church who would be better parents for her than me?"

Pearl perched her hands on her hips and drew herself tall. "Sit down. Take a breath and stop talking to me like that."

"I trusted you."

Pearl cringed and turned away. "I know. And I'm trying to protect her. To protect you. We've both known we can't keep going this way, and we've carried on like this is best for everyone. For heaven's sake, the child needs a legal guardian. Something needs to be done." Her voice softened. "You need to take the risk and see if the state will let you take custody."

Harvey sank into the rocker. He sat on his hands to still the shaking, but tremors shook the core of him. "You don't understand. They'll never let me raise her. They'll take her from me. If I lose her, I lose me. She's all I've got."

Pearl walked back over to him. "She's not all you've got. You have me. I love you. You know that. And if you truly love Ivy, you have to think about what's best for her in the long run."

He shook his head. "I can't do what you're asking."

Her shoulders slumped. "I'm tired, and we're not getting anywhere here. I'll talk to you in the morning. I'll ask around if you want. Make sure you have everything in place to meet the state requirements before you do anything."

On the front porch, he slid into his sleeping bag, pulling it high on his shoulders against the chill. He'd felt circumstantial rage, but he had never been angry at a person before. The realization slapped him across his cheek. You had to care to be angry.

He stared out at the world beyond the spindles of the porch rail. It might not be the same as his connection to Ivy, but Pearl's feelings and opinions meant something to him too.

Harvey had to formulate an exit plan. He was a ghost, and so was Ivy. There was no way this could work out in either of their favors.

FORTY-THREE

Present Day

She'd kissed Reese. *Reese.* What had she done?

She took a shaky breath, staring at the ground where he stood, only a couple paces away. "I'm sorry. I shouldn't have k-kissed you. I'm not thinking straight. And—"

He shook his head as he took a step toward her. "Don't."

She edged back.

He swallowed, raking his hand through his hair and gripping the back of his scalp. "If you think that was a kiss . . ." He released his hair and swallowed. Stared over the water and shook his head.

Her face flamed. Was he making fun of her? Of the way the brush of a kiss affected her? She ground her teeth into the inside of her cheek, fighting for control. "I gotta go."

She turned on her heel, her feet slipping on the muddy soles. Her pulse throbbed in her ears. Tears welled, blurring the path in front of her. Air refused to fill her lungs no matter how she gulped for it.

At the sound of crunching leaves behind her, tension zinged up her spine.

A heavy hand landed on her shoulder. "Ivy . . ."

All the pain. All the times she wanted to be strong but failed crashed over her all at once. Mixed in the wave were imagined images of the woman named Rose, abused and broken, unable to speak up for herself. Out of the midst of it all surged a force that shook her. She spun. "I said, back off, Seth!"

Reese released her shoulder and backstepped, his palms raised in surrender. Sorrow or pain, something of that variety, swam in his eyes. "I'm not him, Ivy. I could never be him."

A knife sliced through her middle as her senseless panic cleared. "I know."

He scrubbed his hand over his face. "When you kissed me I thought you'd started to see that . . . that I—" He pinched his lips in a line and looked away. "Forget it. Just . . . you don't have anything to be sorry about on my account."

His words faded into an indecipherable buzz. Ivy wrapped her arms around herself as hot tears spilled down her face. "I can't do this right now."

"I know." His voice was thick. "Let's grab the gear and go back to the truck. I'll drive you home."

She shook her head and walked toward the road. Getting away was the only way out of this mess.

"Ivy, please . . ." There was a hunger, a pleading that stole her breath. Pure and vulnerable, a polar opposite of Seth's emotional manipulation. But she couldn't face Reese's pity. Ivy heard two steps behind her and then a pause. She refused to look back.

The entire hike home she waited for the engine of his truck pulling up beside her on the road, him telling her to get in his truck. And then once she was home, she waited for the phone call. The knock at the door demanding she face him.

She didn't know if she was disappointed he hadn't come for her or relieved he respected her enough to give her the space she needed to sort out this mess she'd made.

● ● ●

Ivy trudged into the house and peeled off her muddy clothes. She fumbled through a scalding shower with her injured hand hanging outside the shower curtain.

Her stomach clenched. Her friendship with Reese had always been perfect. So free from drama. All her years of hard work to maintain that were out the window. She wrapped herself in a plush white towel and padded down the hallway. There was a double knock on the door. Ivy stiffened. She couldn't see him. Wouldn't.

An engine cranked and tires crunched on the gravel driveway. She headed down the hallway and put on her trusty sweatpants. The black ones with moth-eaten holes and pink bleach spots.

She made herself a cup of tea in her wildflower mug—the one Grandma picked out for her at a craft fair when she was twelve—and went out to the swing. She longed to call her mom and ask her what to say to Reese so that her stupid kiss didn't change anything. Resting on the swing was an envelope. Her name was written in large letters.

She recognized Reese's angular print as she pulled out the single green sheet from a steno pad.

Ivy Rose Lashley,
The thought of my touch striking fear in your heart causes me more pain than words can say. Knowing

someone used love as a weapon makes me angry enough to overturn every rock in the country to find the lowlife who hurt you. But I know it's not what you need.

Even though I want so much to see you, to talk this out, I won't push where I'm not wanted. But know that I'm not running from you. I'm right where I've always been. If you need me. If you want me. I'm just a phone call away.

Reese

P.S. I don't regret that almost kiss.

She swiped at her eyes, put the single sheet of paper back in its envelope, and sipped her chamomile tea while she sat on the swing. She nudged her toe against the porch, sending the swing into gentle motion. What now? Should she call him? Apologize again? Beg him to forget it happened?

Pepper appeared around the corner of the house. He looked at her with his sad eyes and whined, then he lay at her feet.

"You're not afraid of me anymore, are you?"

When her teacup was empty, she rose from the swing and called Pepper, smiling when he followed her inside like a shadow.

The old house had grown barer by the day. She only had a few more errands. Some books for the used bookstore and a box of her old baby things in the garage was meant for the single mothers' pantry at the church. After that, it was time to tag the remaining items for the estate sale. And then what?

She curled into a chair, drowning in imagined flashes of

her birth mother's life. Of what happened in the span of Ivy's birth and her parents ending up with her. And now, this complicated mess with Reese.

● ● ●

A knock sounded on the front door a few hours later. Pepper jumped to his feet and let out a low growl. Hackles raised.

"It's okay, buddy. I'm not letting anyone in here."

Reese had given her time, and now he wanted to talk. Fine. She'd brave answering the door, but she'd leave him to do the talking before she made a fool of herself again. She'd let him speak his mind and be done with it.

She pulled open the front door, and the man on the porch turned. Ivy swallowed and tried to push the door closed, but Seth shot forward and stuck his foot in between the door and the frame.

"Ivy Lashley, I've been worried sick about you. Why haven't you been answering my calls? I've got high-powered clients breathing down my neck, and I'm traipsing around this grease spot on the map to make sure you're okay." He flicked a glance over her sloppy ponytail, hole-riddled sweatpants, and bandaged hand. "And clearly you aren't doing well."

Ivy glanced behind her to where her phone rested on the side table. Seven feet away. Too far for her to reach while still holding the door closed on his foot. Although, if he really wanted to, he was strong enough to push his way in. Like so many times before.

Reese, now would be a fine time for that Ivy's-in-danger radar to kick in. She took a deep breath and stood as tall as her slight frame could manage. "No, Seth. Not because of me. Because of you. You took off work and came all this way for no reason. We're over. I've made that abundantly clear. There's nothing left to talk about. You need to go."

His face softened. "Now, Ivy. I've given you time and space. Couples fight. It's a normal part of every growing relationship. If you'd have just stayed and talked instead of trying to storm off like a lunatic, our last argument would've never gone that far. I'm working on my anger management. Meet me halfway and, you know, toughen up a bit. Don't be so sensitive."

His tactics might have been more effective a couple days ago. She wouldn't have caved completely, but she would have replayed scenes of their last fight, looking for ways she might've handled things better. But Reese and Triune and Rose and Grandma's mission to help Ivy Rose Lashley remember who she was bolstered her.

"Seth, get your foot out of my door. Get back in your fancy little car, and if I ever see your face in this town again, if you so much as knock on my door, I'll have a restraining order put on you. Don't call. Don't text. Don't harass me anymore."

Seth tilted his head, turning his eyes down in pity and pinching his lips in a line. "Harass? Ivy, you've always had a flair for the dramatic, but come on. I figured after a few weeks on your own, you would have seen all I added to your life, but—"

"Leave."

"Honey—"

"She asked you to leave."

Ivy's heart went to her throat. In the dusky night the shadowed form of her uncle was like sighting a rescue plane while stranded on a sinking raft in the middle of shark-infested waters. Her uncle stepped onto the porch. His broad, six-foot-two frame was drawn to its full height.

Seth glanced over his shoulder, his smile oozing condescension. "This is between Ivy and me. Just a friendly conversation."

"She made it quite clear the conversation's over. And if you're not man enough to respect what she said, then I'll help you out." He methodically rolled the cuffs of his plaid shirt without taking his eyes off Seth as he stepped closer, until he stood catty-corner to where Ivy still held the door closed against Seth's foot.

Maybe this was what Reese had been talking about, having someone fight beside you.

Seth turned back to Ivy. "You don't really want me to—"

"Go, Seth."

"If I leave after coming all this way, don't expect me to listen when you finally come to your senses and—"

"I am more sensible now than I've been in a long time. Go."

He slid his Italian-leather shoe from the space in the door. Rage colored his face. "I'm done wasting my time on you. You're not worth it." He stalked to his sports car, slammed the door, and slung a spray of gravel as he sped out of sight.

Uncle Vee released a long breath. "You okay, Ivy Rose?" For as imposing as her uncle appeared with the flint in his eyes and his height and breadth of shoulder, he was one of the gentlest people she knew.

Knees turned to jelly, Ivy crossed the porch and sank to sit in the swing. "I am now."

Pepper appeared in the open doorway, tail tucked, eyeing

Uncle Vee. He skirted away from her uncle and sat on the porch next to her.

Uncle Vee leaned against the house and gestured to the dog. "New sidekick?"

"This is Pepper. The stray I told you about."

"You invited a stray pup into your grandmother's house?" He laughed, low and quiet, shaking his head.

"Think she'd have been mad?"

"Nah. She . . . she'd probably think he fit right in."

She tilted her head. "Any reason you stopped by?"

"Reese asked me to. Said he was worried about you and you'd had a rough day. Was it about that guy?"

She shrugged. "I don't know what I would have done if you hadn't shown up when you did."

With fatherly pride softening his features, he said, "Ivy Rose, you're stronger than you think."

FORTY-FOUR

November 24, 1994

"Miss Pearl, don't you think all this food was a bit much for two of us? I thought the whole church was coming for Thanksgiving." Harvey cleared away his and Pearl's plates. A sea of slow cookers covered the counter, and the sink was piled high with empty pots and pans.

She gave him a sheepish smile. "I suppose I got a little out of hand. I started cooking and couldn't seem to stop. Just needed something to keep my hands busy."

Harvey thought about how hard it must be for her, the first Thanksgiving without her husband and son. "Hope it freezes well. I wouldn't want it to go to waste. I thought Thomas and Miriam might be coming."

She lifted her shoulder. "They were hosting Thanksgiving at their house for the single mothers and their children. They invited us too. But I didn't think you'd be up for it."

He cringed. It had been a week since their argument, but things had stayed oddly quiet while he'd expected everything to blow up in his face. He wanted to be on the road, on to a new life for him and Ivy, but he hadn't been able to bring himself to leave Pearl. Not before Thanksgiving. And now Christmas was close on his heels. They had to leave though, no matter how much it would hurt her. "If it makes you feel any better, it was the best Thanksgiving I've ever had."

She smiled the first unguarded smile he'd seen in the past few days. "I'm so glad. I wanted it to be special for you."

His insides felt like he'd swallowed a bucket of night crawlers. He wasn't without conscience. Every day he stayed, he lived a lie. He walked over to the sink. "All right. Where do we start with all this?"

Ivy cried from her bed, the sound plaintive and hoarse. Pearl spun around. "I'll get her. If you want to start putting food away, I'd appreciate it."

He flipped open the cabinet that stored carefully stacked plastic containers. He navigated her kitchen with the same ease as his camp stockpile. Harvey scooped the cornbread dressing into a bowl.

"Harvey, something's wrong."

The rich meal filling his stomach turned to stone. Pearl cradled Ivy and pressed the back of her wrinkled hand to her cheeks. Ivy arched and fussed in her arms, the feeble cry followed by a dry cough.

He swooped over, pulling Ivy into his arms. With the corner of her blanket he dabbed at her runny nose. "Oh, baby girl. What's wrong?" He stroked her forehead. "She's hot. Why is she hot? She's not sick. She couldn't be. She hasn't been around anyone who's sick. Maybe she's allergic to something. Did you change the laundry detergent? The formula? New diapers?"

"Whoa. Slow down. You sound like the index from your baby book. Babies are prone to sniffles and colds. I'm sure it's nothing. She probably needs snuggles and Tylenol." Pearl put a hand on his shoulder. "Breathe. You two go sit in the rocking chair and see if you can get her to settle. I'll bring a thermometer."

But Ivy's fussing and squirming made the thermometer slip from under her arm over and over again. Harvey called to Pearl, who was banging around in the kitchen. "Her temperature is 100.5. What do we do? How do I fix this? What do you think it is—whooping cough, the croup, RSV, pneumonia, influenza type A?"

Pearl shuffled closer, her slippers making a scuffing noise against the linoleum. "It's a low-grade fever. We'll make her comfortable, and maybe she'll sleep off the bug and be right as rain by tomorrow."

"What if she's not? What if she's worse?"

"Your worry won't make her any better. Sit and rock her. I'll take care of the kitchen. If you're upset, she's going to sense it."

He took a few calming breaths. The pulse pounding in his ears slowed. Pearl was right. But Ivy had never been sick. And he couldn't exactly pop over to the pediatrician with her.

Guilt barbed him. She was two months old, almost three, and hadn't had a checkup. Sure, she was better off than if he'd never found her. But he should have found a way to get her looked at. Was this his fault?

Pearl came in with a teacup of steaming yellowish liquid. "It's chamomile. It's calming."

"For Ivy? I don't think hot tea—"

"No, for you. You're white as a sheet."

"I don't understand how she got sick. She's only around you and me."

"These things happen. Germs travel . . ." Pearl raised her hands to her face. "Oh no! It's me. It's my fault."

"You're not sick."

She looked away. "No, but a boy in Sunday school sniffled and coughed all over the place. He started feeling worse, so he climbed in my lap and sat there all through church. I meant to shower off and change clothes when I got home, but I must have forgotten. I'm so sorry."

Another reason being close to people caused problems. They carried germs. He huffed. "Don't be sorry. You didn't do it on purpose." Ivy coughed again and let out a soft whine, rending his heart in pieces.

Harvey rocked her until she dropped off to sleep. Her temperature lowered after the medicine had kicked in. She would be fine. They'd get through this, and then they'd find a way to extricate themselves from this mess he'd created.

● ● ●

"Harvey, wake up."

He jerked awake. Pearl hovered over him, whispering. Ivy was fast asleep with her head tipped back. Her mouth was open, her breath slightly gravelly in her chest.

"Don't sleep in here. Hand me Ivy. I put the bassinet in your room so she can be close to you."

She picked up Ivy out of his sleep-limp arms.

"Wait. How is she? Her fever. I'm so warm with her on me I can't tell." His tongue was thick in his mouth.

"Up you go, on into the bedroom. I don't want to wake

her to check her temperature. She's resting and seems about the same."

He shuffled behind her, rubbing at his eyes.

"I didn't mean to fall asleep. I should stay up. Keep watch over her."

"She's fine for now. You aren't going to do her any good by wearing yourself out."

He sat on the edge of the bed while Pearl laid Ivy down.

"Go on. The bed doesn't bite."

He leaned sideways and rested his head on the pillow.

"You're allowed to get under the covers."

"I'm fine, really."

Pearl slid the blanket at the foot of the bed out from under his feet. She spread it over the top of him, then walked over and flipped the light switch off. "Good night, Harvey."

He closed his eyes and was asleep in a minute. The first time he'd slept in a bed in fourteen years.

FORTY-FIVE

PRESENT DAY

Ivy balanced the box of baby things on her forearms as she walked to the church. She climbed the tall stack of stairs and entered the foyer.

Most people were accustomed to walking into a church bustling with people. But this, the quiet empty space, was the memory of her childhood. This building had been her playground where she wandered while her father studied for sermons, set up for special events, and counseled in his office. The smells, the echo of her shoes on the hardwood in the stillness, the color of the light spilling through the stained glass—they were as much a part of her as the heart beating in her chest.

At the back of the sanctuary, she placed the box on the ground and rubbed her thumb over a little place on the last pew where the finish had worn over the years. Like it was the place people stood deciding if they wanted to stay.

In the quiet chapel she laid down the pain she carried. From the shame. From trying to hold everything inside. *I want to do better. Help me lean into you and not away when I fall short.*

She left the box with the pastor and told him she'd be finished with the house by next week.

On the way back to the house, she paused by the towering oak. The place she and Reese used to hide their eyes while they counted for hide-and-seek. She walked a ring around the oak tree, letting the rough bark scrape against her un-injured palm.

What was she supposed to do about this thing with Reese? Was there any way to come through it without damaging their friendship more than she already had?

A white sedan crunched down the driveway toward Grand-ma's house. Ivy followed in its wake.

She stopped and stared as the car door opened. A woman with burnished red hair and a delicate silver streak in her bangs emerged from the car with an overnight bag. Ivy's heart throbbed in her chest. "Mom?"

The woman turned slowly and took a hesitant step in her direction. Her hands clutched her bag. "Ivy."

Ivy rushed forward and wrapped her arms around her mom, who half bent to set down her bag.

All the emotions of the past week coursed through her as Ivy sank into her mom's gentle embrace. Her mother was tall and beautiful, seeming to catch the attention of everyone who passed. Ivy had always felt dull and small in her shining presence. But, in this moment, she was sheltered by it.

Ivy's voice came out a whisper, remembering Reese's advice. "I love you, Mom. I'm so sorry for the way I—"

Mom ran her fingers over Ivy's hair, "Shh . . . let's not do this right now. Let's just hold on to one another for a minute."

On the porch swing, Ivy and her mom leaned into each other.

"I thought you and Daddy were traveling."

"Reese called and asked if I happened to be free. Said you needed me. Insisted you wouldn't mind. Stuff you were learning about the past. Your dad can handle the conference responsibilities without me for a few days. This is where I belong."

Again Reese was proving how different he was. While Seth pulled her away from all the people dear to her, creating a scenario in which she relied upon him completely, Reese gathered an army of people to stand beside her. Even after she'd pushed him away. Especially then.

Ivy straightened and lifted her chin to meet her mother's eye. "Can we talk? Really talk about where I came from?"

"I'm sorry we caused you pain by not talking about things enough. It's just . . . whenever we did talk about it, you became so tense. Edgy."

Hearing the words from her mother's lips, she knew it was true. As curious as Ivy had been then and even now, a part of her didn't want to lose the fairy-tale ending. It was like she asked questions with her hands over her ears to shut out the answers.

"We thought we were causing you pain by talking about it. Your adoption was . . . different. And the best thing for everyone was to provide a simplified version of what happened. As time went on, we let the story fade to the background, and people finally stopped being so curious."

Ivy swallowed against the nausea churning her stomach. "I overheard some ladies talking after church when I was about eight. Talking about how I'd been left on your doorstep. It wasn't true, right? Where did you find me? How did I get to you?"

A corner of her mother's mouth lifted as tears filled her eyes. "You really did drop into my life, seemingly out of nowhere."

"And I was what? In a basket? On the ground? In my birth mother's arms? I don't understand. None of this fits."

Mom tilted her head. "None of what?"

"Grandma left a letter about a journal that's missing. She said it was all about where I came from. I found this picture of an abused young woman named Rose, and she looks just like me. If you know what Grandma was talking about please, please just tell me. Don't protect me from the truth anymore. Did someone take me from my birth mother? Did you take the journal?"

Her mother shook her head. "I never knew anything about a journal or a young woman named Rose, and I had no idea your grandma kept looking for your birth parents. I always had a feeling your uncle knew more about where you came from than he let on, but I can't fathom the idea he'd do anything to hurt you. He loves you so much, sweetheart. With a love so tender and sacrificial I can't explain it with words."

"How did you and Dad get me?"

"Your grandmother . . ."

"Grandma?"

She nodded.

"Why did Grandma have me? What happened before?"

"Please, don't be angry when I tell you this, Ivy. I know little more than what I told you. Truly. But you really need to talk to your uncle. I think it's past time for you to know the truth of who he is to you. I just hope he's ready to tell it."

FORTY-SIX

November 26, 1994

"Miss Pearl. Are you awake?"

Pearl bolted upright at the distress in Harvey's voice and glanced over to the large digital clock. Two a.m. Her voice came out craggy. "I'll be right there." She fumbled in the dark for her glasses and robe. Poor Harvey sounded beside himself. With good reason, of course. No parent could stand to see their child uncomfortable. He was worn ragged watching Ivy battle the cold for the past two days. And with her uncertain guardianship situation, everything was more complicated.

Pearl walked down the hall, pausing at Harvey's door. Ivy's cry was raspy and punctuated by a chesty cough. Harvey murmured, "It's okay. You're going to be fine."

Pearl opened the door. "She's not doing good, is she?"

He edged around her into the hallway, Ivy held close, as though guarding the baby from her. He stepped toward the bathroom. "I think she needs another round of steam."

"Wait—" She grabbed his arm. "She doesn't need steam.

She needs a doctor. Do you hear how she's breathing? She's having to work at it a bit. It's not too bad yet, but we can't wait for her to get to that point. She needs medical attention." Pearl pressed her hand to the baby's cheek. "And she's hot. Really hot."

Harvey clamped his lips and shook his head. "No. The steam will help her breathe. You said."

"She needs to go to the hospital. Go pack a bag. I'll change, and we'll go." She kept her voice low and soothing. Calm even though she was dying inside for him.

"I can't take her to a hospital."

"She needs to be seen, Harvey. Now, not later."

He looked up, emotions warring on his face. "Hospitals are where kids go only to wake up and find out they don't have parents anymore. And all that's left are people paid to care." His words tumbled on top of each other like rocks in a landslide.

"You need to calm down. You're not making any sense."

"Riding home with my parents one dark, rainy night, I distracted my dad when I dropped a toy on the floor, and he didn't see that deer jump into the road. I woke up in a sterile white place with people who wouldn't quite meet my eye. No one wanted to be the one to explain what it meant to be an orphan to a five-year-old. If I take Ivy there, she'll never see me again."

Pearl, stricken by his story and the urgency of the moment, clenched and unclenched her hands. "No one is going to take her away from you. I'm sure they'll have questions that need sorting out, but you're Ivy's family."

He panted for breath, eyes wide. "I don't have a sister, Pearl."

Pearl froze. "Harvey?"

He squeezed his eyes tight. "I-I found Ivy one night in the woods, all alone. I lied to protect her from being thrown into the system."

Ivy fussed, and the hoarse sound broke Pearl's heart. Her mind raced, trying to piece together the truth and search for a solution all at the same time. "Miriam and Thomas are certified foster parents now. If they bring her to the hospital, there's a chance Ivy will be able to stay in their care while she gets medical attention, and while they work out the legal aspects of her case. And then they could—"

Harvey's face twisted. "Foster parents? That's code for keeping a child until it gets too hard or too complicated."

"You aren't being fair. You know Miriam and Thomas better than that. Especially Thomas. You've worked with him for months, and he never once gave up on you. Ivy must get help. Period. If you love her, there comes a point in which you have to sacrifice your needs for what's best for her. You said you kept the truth about her a secret to protect her, but you were really protecting yourself."

He shook his head, eyes full of anger. "You don't understand. No one took your son away from you. No one ever questioned if he belonged to you. You didn't have to make the choice to never see him again."

"You know what, Harvey? You've had a hard life, but you aren't the only one who's had to make hard decisions. When my son stood on the sidewalk in uniform waiting to leave for deployment, do you think anyone asked if I was okay with that? And nobody asked if I was okay with them sending him back even though I knew something was wrong when I looked in his eyes."

Harvey paced the length of the hall, bouncing Ivy, who fidgeted in discomfort. "That's different. He was a grown man."

"How little you know about being a parent. No matter his age, I could remember the weight of him in my arms the day I brought him home from the hospital. My precious baby boy. The child the doctors told me I'd never be able to have. My miracle. And when he came back, not once, but twice, I thought I was in the clear. But then my beautiful child took his life into his own hands."

Harvey narrowed his eyes and shook his head. "He made his own choices. Ivy has no choice. I have no choice."

Pearl lifted her hands in a gesture of surrender and let them fall. "Go ahead. Tell me I don't know what I'm talking about to make yourself feel better. I'll overlook it because I know you're in pain."

Ivy's hoarse cry filled the air between them.

"When I found my boy, his heart was still beating, faintly, but he was still alive. I had so much hope. He was on life support for days. His brain activity was feeble, until it wasn't at all. My beautiful son, who laid there with his eyelashes resting against his cheeks, looked like the baby boy who used to fall asleep on my lap instead of a military man who had seen things I couldn't comprehend. I had to choose to say goodbye, to take him off life support, because that's what was best for him. So yes, I think I know a thing or two about making hard choices. Of losing people I love because of those choices. You're being selfish. Especially when you're standing in the way of her care."

Harvey handed Ivy to her. "Take her. I need to get a few things."

He stepped past Pearl into the bedroom and started open-ing and closing dresser drawers in rapid fire. Pearl bounced the inconsolable child.

He dropped a packed bag at Pearl's feet and laid Ivy's favorite lilac blanket on top. He slipped a yellow knitted cap on the baby's head and matching booties on her feet.

"The blanket. Can you ask for it to stay with her? It was the first thing I ever bought her. No matter what happens, she'll have a piece of where she came from. Someday, maybe you could find a way to tell her that there once was a man who loved her like a father, but he had to let her go. That there was no other way."

He leaned over and kissed Ivy on the forehead. And then he kissed Pearl's cheek, a touch as faint as a butterfly wing. "Thank you for everything you've done for me, Miss Pearl. Please tell Pastor Thomas thank you for me also. You're the only two people who never gave up on me."

"Harvey, tell him yourself."

But he had already walked out the door.

● ● ●

"Thomas? Someone's at the door."

"Huh?" Thomas rolled over in bed and swiped at his eyes, his voice scratchy from sleep. "You heard something, Miri?"

"Someone's knocking. Remember, the doorbell quit work-ing."

"It's nearly three a.m."

The knock sounded again. "You're the pastor. The hour doesn't matter in an emergency."

He groaned as he sat up, bleary-eyed. "Yeah . . . yes . . . of course. You're right." He stumbled around getting dressed, then padded down the steps. "Although, a call to warn me wouldn't hurt," he muttered on his way down.

Miriam listened from the bedroom doorway as he answered the door.

"Pearl! What's wrong? Why do you have the baby?"

Miriam hurriedly dressed and took the steps two at a time.

Pearl stood in their entryway trembling. "He's gone. Ivy's sick. You've got to take her to the hospital."

"Why us? Where's his sister?"

Pearl took a shuddering breath. "There's no sister. Never was. He found this child in the woods and has been trying to take care of her for nearly three months. But now she's sick, and he got scared and disappeared. I came because y'all are certified foster parents, and I'm not. I thought they might let her stay in your care—at least while everything is sorted out."

Miriam leaned close to peek at Ivy, who was swaddled in a purple blanket. The world in front of her swayed. She listed toward Thomas, who gripped under her elbow. The yellow hat. She could still remember the feel of the butter-soft yarn against her cheek. The things belonging to her baby. The dream she put in the trash can. This child in possession of them.

"Miriam, are you okay?" Thomas's face was creased with worry.

"Oh, I think I jumped out of bed too fast. I still have sea legs." Miriam's heart tore at the sound of Ivy's cough. "Poor little one. Let's go. Let's get her the attention she needs."

Pearl lifted the baby into Miriam's arms. "I'm going to find Harvey. If I can. Perhaps the simplest explanation is Ivy was left on your doorstep?"

Thomas nodded, wide-eyed.

"Thomas, come get the car seat out of my car, and y'all can be on your way."

He blinked. "You've known all this time she was an abandoned child?"

Pearl shook her head. "Not until about ten minutes ago." She shrugged, helpless. "Get Little Miss to the hospital. I'd wager she's going to be fine after a breathing treatment and a round of antibiotics."

Miriam tried to compute the facts as she rode beside the flush-cheeked baby. Little Ivy. An abandoned child. The little girl she'd been drawn to, even when she'd sworn off babies forever. In her car. Wearing the hat and booties. Harvey must have found them, and of course he couldn't have thrown them away. A new warmth spread in her chest at the thought of him caring for her when he seemed to have so little.

And poor Pearl. He'd left her. Just like she'd feared.

*   *   *

Pearl scanned the edges of the road along the route Harvey walked. She knew his path as far as Nolensville Pike, but after that she hadn't a clue.

He was on foot. She should have been able to find him, but after driving around for two hours, she surrendered.

He'd come back. Wouldn't he?

The phone was ringing when she walked in her front door. "Hello?"

Thomas's haggard voice came through the line. "Hi, Pearl. Any sign of Harvey?"

"No."

"It's just as well. There would have been a lot of questions. As of now, the authorities are looking into missing persons reports and records at surrounding hospitals of women coming in with postpartum issues but no baby around the time Ivy would have been born.

"Ivy's doing all right. She's getting fluids, breathing treatments, and a round of strong antibiotics. They're keeping her overnight, but she should be free to go home tomorrow morning as long as she's still improving."

"Home? Home where?"

"With Miriam and me. They asked us if we were open to being her temporary placement, and of course we were."

Pearl let her head fall back and a small smile tugged at her lips. "Thank you, Lord. I'm so happy. For the two of you and for her. And Harvey, if I ever find him again."

"You will. The prodigal will return."

Harvey had become a son to her, but maybe a thirty-something man wasn't in want of a mother. "You're more confident than I."

"Pearl, you've wormed your way into his life. He's changed. He thinks he can go back to life before, but this time he'll be painfully aware of everything missing. I'm telling you, he'll be back."

"I hope you're right." But she couldn't help remembering his words from their argument last week. That Ivy was the only one he had in this world. Did he really believe that?

Pearl hung up the phone. She slumped in her chair, the silence in the house deafening. Normally at this time, Harvey would be bouncing Ivy in his room, singing a lullaby painfully off-key.

She shuffled toward her bedroom, but the cracked door to Harvey's room drew her in. There was a pile of money on the bed, a gold watch, and a note.

She sat on the bed and picked up the paper covered in big scrawled letters.

For Ivy. I'll always remember you both. Thank you.

She stacked the cash on the dresser, then collapsed in his bed. The place both her sons had slept. Both miracles. Both gone.

FORTY-SEVEN

PRESENT DAY

Ivy and her mother spent the next day tagging items in the living room. While they were working, Mom turned toward her. "So, when are you going to tell me what's going on with you and Reese?"

Ivy pasted on a smile. "Nothing's going on."

"Ivy . . ." Mom always could see straight through her.

Ivy groaned. "I kissed him, Mom. Well, sort of. I kissed my best friend, and I ran away. And now I don't know what to do." Ivy sank into the wingback chair.

A wide grin broke across her mom's face. "About time."

Ivy's hands dropped to her lap. "Reese is the worst possible person for me to let myself fall for."

"And why in the world would you say that?"

"I lean on him when I shouldn't. I have to learn how to stand on my own two feet. And with the whole Seth thing, I've forgotten how."

"Ivy, honey, back before you were in our lives, your dad

tried so hard to get me to lean on him. My depression had taken on a life of its own. There were days I couldn't get out of bed. He was so patient, and I pushed him away over and over again. His strength was evidence I couldn't measure up to what I thought I ought to.

"There came a point when it was like a knife had cut through the fog. Marriage, relationships, they were made for leaning. Not as an excuse not to grow, mind you. But we all need a place to rest and be reassured. God puts people in our lives to have and to hold. To give this existence richer meaning. I don't think we were ever meant to fight life's battles alone."

A small smile tugged at the neutral expression Ivy tried to maintain. "Reese said something similar the other day."

"If you don't have feelings for Reese, that's a whole different matter. No need to make the relationship into something it's not. But if you love him, don't let your fear keep you from such a good man."

Ivy stood and paced the living room. "We've been best friends all our lives. That's all we are supposed to be."

"So you keep saying. Who are you trying to convince—him, you, or me? I've been expecting this day for *years*."

"What are you talking about? You and Dad didn't bat an eye when we ran all around the countryside together. And you both were so overprotective when it came to dating."

A musical laugh floated from her mother's lips. "Oh, honey, we knew the boy was smitten. You were the reason we weren't worried."

"Me?"

"The boundaries you put on the relationship were so clear they were almost tangible. Your words, your body language, the way you looked at him. It was clear you wouldn't allow it to be anything more. Your dad and I always expected that to change eventually. But it never did. Though every girl in Triune was half in love with him, you seemed immune."

Ivy swallowed. "I wasn't immune, just scared. Still am. If it doesn't work out, I'll lose my best friend."

"Relationships change with time. You and Reese will change one way or another, whether you like it or not. You can't hang on to what once was forever."

Ivy buried her face in her hands.

"Reese is over at our old house. He called this morning and told me to tell you he'd be there all day."

Ivy peeked through her fingers. "I . . . I should stay. You . . . you've come all this way."

"No, hon, I think you should go. Go to him and sort this out. You and I both know it's what you want." Her mother smiled and winked. "Besides, we'll still have all morning tomorrow for you to fill me in on the details before I have to fly out."

● ● ●

Ivy cruised down the drive, relishing the blast of frigid air-conditioning from her mom's rental car. At least this one time she could show up in front of Reese not looking like she'd been through a wind tunnel.

Her car stayed the speed limit, but her heart raced fast enough to make it three times around the world and back on the ten-minute drive. No matter how Ivy weighed and tested her conversation with her mother against her memories with Reese, she couldn't recall a single time he put distance in their relationship. Not once in the eighteen years she'd known him. He was the one who consistently urged, "Come here, Ivy." Because she was always the one edging away.

She made the final turns, the curves of those roads burned into her memory. One by one she wiped her sweaty palms on her jeans.

As her car tires crunched on the gravel drive, Reese stood from the porch, squinting against the light of the sun as it made its slow descent over the ridge.

She parked the car and paused a moment, with the intent of saying a quick prayer, but found she lacked the wisdom for the right words.

Reese sauntered over with his chin ducked and thumbs hooked in his belt loops.

She took a long breath, drinking in oxygen before getting out of the car. As he approached, she moistened her lips and stood. Her voice came out raspy, and she coughed to clear her throat. "Hey . . . hey, Reese."

He lifted his chin, a shy smile playing at the corners of his mouth as he scuffed his work boot against the gravel. "New car?"

A breathy laugh escaped her. "Mom's rental. Thank you for that, by the way."

"Sure thing, Rosie-girl. Glad you got to enjoy a little air-conditioning." A muscle in his cheek twitched.

Ivy shook her head. "You know what I mean. For my uncle coming, and Mom. For making sure I was okay."

His gaze traveled away from her, out over the yard. His Adam's apple rose and fell. "I heard about Seth."

"It turned out all right. I have a deep appreciation for my uncle's impeccable timing."

Relief softened his features. "He does always have a way

of being at the right place at the right time." He brushed his foot over the grassy edge of the driveway as if searching for something in the shorn green spikes.

"Reese, we need to—"

"Ivy, I—"

Both of them laughed like a couple of nervous middle schoolers at their first dance.

Reese looked up at her. "Go ahead."

"Can we talk? Really talk."

He gestured to the porch where he'd been sitting before. "We could go sit. I've got lemonade if you're thirsty. The sun's on its way down. It's a beautiful view right there."

Her insides squirmed at the thought of sitting beside him, gazing up into his eyes. "I'm kinda in the mood to walk, if it's okay."

They strolled the perimeter of the property, their shoulders bumping as they went. Ivy rolled words around in her head, hunting for an opening to the conversation.

Reese Dylan Wright, I've loved you my whole life. I've tried to ignore it, but I can't any longer. A little too much.

Hey buddy, I didn't hate kissing you as much as I acted like I did. Nope. Not that one either.

"Did you find out anything new?" Reese studied her as they continued to walk.

She took a steadying breath, willing her voice not to break over the words she knew she needed to say. "After I got so off track, so broken down, I thought I needed to know more about my past to know who I am, what I want. But I was wrong." Her chin trembled and her pulse throbbed in her ears.

Reese stopped and she followed suit. Under the branches

of the sycamore tree, he angled toward her, like they were two ends of a cracked-open book. She turned her face away from the depth of his gaze and swallowed.

"And what is it you want, Ivy?"

Her mouth went drier than drought-parched earth when she braved looking into his eyes. She prayed there would be no pity turning down his features when she spoke the words that had been burning in her heart as long as she could remember.

"You, Reese. I want you." A tear quivered in the corner of her eye. Her heart filled with hope and fear in equal measure.

He blinked and swallowed. His eyes searched hers. The corners of his mouth twitched.

He reached forward and ran one finger from her wrist down to the tip of her pinky. She drew a sharp breath as every nerve in her body woke.

His eyes floated closed, lashes thicker and darker than any man's had a right to be. The rasp in his tone made his words swirl through her core. "Right now it's taking everything in me not to pull you into my arms and kiss you like there's never going to be another chance. But the last thing I want to do is make you feel afraid in my arms. So, I'm askin', Ivy. Please . . . once and for all, come here to me."

That single step crossed a chasm.

He reached to brush away the wayward strand of hair that had slipped across her face, the slightest tremor in his fingertips.

Ivy leaned into his solid chest, wrapping her arms around his trim middle. She rested her cheek against his shirt front and listened as his pulse thrummed wildly, matching her own. She savored the strength in his arms when he returned the embrace. He rested his chin on top of her head. Like experiencing the safety and comfort of coming home and being shot to the moon all at the same time.

After a moment he released his hold. With the crook of his finger, he lifted her chin, a question in his eyes. His expression was so vulnerable and sweet all her reservations dissolved. She rocked forward on her toes, melting into a kiss far too long in coming. All the questions bouncing inside her head stopped and ceased to matter.

He brushed his fingers over her cheek and tangled them in her hair. An involuntary sigh rose in her throat as they broke apart and he pressed his forehead against hers. He'd been right. That thing that happened at the pond was not a kiss. Nor were any of the others in her lifetime.

A little while later Ivy sat in the sycamore swing, and Reese pulled back on the rope and let the swing carry her. Her brain tried and failed to catch up with her heart.

The crickets chirped and the fireflies danced in the dusky light. The fearless girl she'd once been didn't seem so far off as she once had. Maybe it was a silly notion, or the rush of the kiss talking, but suddenly it seemed it wasn't too late to believe she could fly after all.

FORTY-EIGHT

April 1, 1995

Over the past five months, not a minute went by that wasn't plagued with thoughts of Ivy. Where she was. If people knew she liked to be burped halfway through her bottle, and that light purple brought out the flecks of green in her brown eyes. Was she loved?

And for the past five months the tally tree tormented him. Forty-one marks for the forty-one days his sole focus had been protecting Ivy. What bothered him, though, was the empty space below the notches—the missing marks after he'd moved in with Pearl. After he'd stopped counting days.

Tangled in the lives around him, his life had become something beyond keeping Ivy safe. It had been about Pearl. And Thomas and Miriam. And—finding a place where he belonged.

He needed to face that those things were gone. He needed to forget.

Harvey grabbed his hatchet and approached the cedar.

Over and over again he hacked into that empty space below the marks he'd made. The dull blade biting into the bark— Harvey cried out from his gut with every blow.

"Harvey Ethan James." Her soft, aged voice cut him to the quick. He was hearing things now? A new low. He turned. The hatchet fell from his hand.

Pearl stood at the edge of his ring of pines, hands on her hips, something fierce blazing in her eyes.

His mouth gaped, and then he spoke the only intelligible word he could muster. "Ethan?"

"Well, I don't know your middle name, and Ethan slipped out. You deserve a middle-naming. It's a . . . a mom thing. Young man, do you realize I've been driving up and down this five-mile strip of highway every day for five months?"

He sighed, shoulders falling. "You shouldn't have."

She shuffled closer until she had to tilt her chin skyward to see his face. "You think you can drift off like you were never a part of my life?"

Tightening his fists to give his tension a place to go, he glanced toward the creek. "That was the general idea."

"It doesn't work that way."

"It's worked every other time in my life."

"This isn't that. You matter to me. And I . . . I think I matter to you. Come home with me. Move back into your room. Be my . . ." She heaved a shaky breath. "Be my son."

He stood taller, shoulders raised, heart slamming in his chest. "Miss Pearl, I'm a thirty-year-old man. I can't come home and be your son."

She shook her head, her breaking heart reflected in her eyes. "You think a mother stops being a mother when her son turns thirty? Age doesn't have a thing in the world to do with it. You need a mother, and I need . . . you, Harvey. Please come back." She stepped forward and reached up to place her hands on his upper arms—a ferocity and longing in her grip surprising for her age and stature.

He darted his focus around, anywhere but on those teary blue eyes of hers, lined by years of hard choices and loss. "I left. I already left. It's finished."

She tilted her head. "You walked away. But did you really leave? Tell me you're the same old Harvey—never lonely and only wanting his own company, and I promise I'll walk away and won't bother you again."

"I'm not the sort of person people need, that people love."

"What a stupid lie. You know it is. You're the man who won't throw anything away. You find a use for everything. Yet you discard yourself at every opportunity."

He shrugged out of her touch. "It's better for me to be alone, where I can't get things wrong. With Ivy—" Questions jumped in his mind. Things he needed answers for—to know what had happened to Ivy after he left. But he didn't deserve to know. Not anymore. Not after he abandoned her too.

"You loved Ivy when no one else did. She's alive because you found her. And letting her go saved her life. Maybe you can't be a father to her like you wanted, but that doesn't mean you can't love her."

He swallowed and the dammed questions spilled over. "You still get to see Ivy? How is she? Is she sitting up yet? Rolling over both ways?"

"Come with me and see for yourself. My car is on the side of the highway waiting. Let's go, Harvey."

He stepped back and crossed his arms over his chest. "You know I can't get in your car."

She shrugged. "I know, but . . . I'll walk. I'll walk back with you, and Thomas can come back and get the car."

"It's an awful long walk. I can't ask you to do that."

"You could ask me to do anything, and I'd try."

A corner of his mouth lifted against his will. "I know you would."

"Do you? Do you really understand how much I love you?"

He turned in a slow circle, taking in the sound of the road noise. Of cars speeding down the highway, connecting people from one end of the country to another. The sound he could always depend on to be his constant, connecting him to the shred of his past, a distant memory of knowing love. Then this woman offered him the chance for a different future. Not because of a baby in need but just for him. But could the hope she offered stand the test of time like that boxed-away memory? "I can't. Maybe . . . maybe someday."

Her voice came out solid and comforting. "All right, Harvey. I'll be waiting. Don't make me wait too long. I'm old." A spark flickered in her expression. "If you won't come back to stay, would you consider coming for a quick visit? Tomorrow. Sunday morning breakfast. Eight o'clock."

His insides squirmed. He'd made a clean break and here she was trying to lure him back, little by little. "Maybe. Punctuality isn't my strong suit, you know. Without Ivy as my timekeeper I lose—"

"Here. Take it." She held Thomas's gold watch out in her shaking hand. "He meant for you to have it. I had fresh batteries put in. Come for breakfast."

He stuffed the watch into the pocket of his camouflage pants. He shrugged. "Maybe."

She reached out and squeezed his hand. "Okay." Her expression laced with doubt. "I'll see you around."

She walked away, but at the edge of the clearing she paused and turned with a crooked smile on her face. "For the record, what is your middle name? You know . . . for future reference."

He lifted a shoulder. "I don't know. People weren't in the habit of using it when I was growing up."

"Then it's Ethan now. A good strong name, Harvey Ethan James. It was . . . it was my son's middle name."

He gave her a tight-lipped smile to keep his chin from wobbling. What could he say to that?

"Come home soon. All right?"

"Okay, Miss Pearl. I'll try."

• ● •

Pearl was up before the sun puttering around the kitchen fixing biscuits and gravy, eggs, sausage, and fresh-squeezed orange juice. A spread. Enough for six.

She cooked for him even though chances were he wouldn't come. Because of that new thing swimming in his expression that hadn't been there when she first met him. He'd always looked like a lost boy, but now he looked both lost and lonely.

In her bedroom, she slipped into her Sunday best. Even if Harvey didn't come, it would be an unforgettable day.

The tinny doorbell rang out. She checked the digital display on her bedside table. Eight sharp. Harvey. Taking a fortifying breath, she hurried to the front door before he could retreat. Enthusiasm in check, she pulled the knob in a slow, fluid motion.

He stood on the doorstep, clean-shaven, in his plaid shirt and jeans. The clothes he'd left in. He held a bouquet of three daffodils. "Hi."

"You came."

"These are for you." He held out the flowers. "My nerves had me ready to head for the hills about the time I reached Church Street, but the scent of sausage frying wafting in the air lured me on."

She smiled. "I love daffodils."

"I remember."

Pearl blinked. "Oh, I'm sorry. Come on in. I've left you standing on the stoop. Head for the kitchen. The sausage awaits."

She brought out his customary mug, the one he'd given her. The one she'd sipped coffee out of every day since the night he left. She filled it and sat it in front of him. "The winter was mild."

"I was thankful for that. And spring came early."

She sat across from him once she'd filled both their plates. "You look well. I'm glad you at least kept the one shirt. It suits you."

"I've always liked shirts like this."

She nodded. "When you were a little boy, a blonde woman visiting the children's home gave you a plaid shirt exactly like that one."

He froze with his fork halfway to his mouth and lowered it. "How . . . How did you know about that?"

Moisture gathered in her eyes. "Because I was the woman. You were the boy. You looked so lost and untethered, sitting alone. The entwined pattern seemed right."

His forehead creased. "That can't be. There's plenty of

lost kids in children's homes. It must have been a different boy. Different shirt. Not me."

"It was you. You had the same downturned chocolate eyes. I was even more sure after I cut your hair short, more like you wore it back then."

He sat back. Beneath the disbelief there was a glimmer of something—a longing to believe. "I wore that shirt every day for two years. Then this woman threw it out because it was ragged and too small. I never forgave her."

Pearl propped her chin in her hand. "I'm glad I got to give you a new shirt, Harvey."

She swallowed the lump in her throat. "And the plaid mug you broke. I bought it the day I left the children's home, because I couldn't get you out of my mind. I prayed for you every time I used it. And now, here you are in my kitchen all these years later."

He ran his hand over the side of his hair, now longer, but he'd parted it and combed it neatly back. He went still, as though his body was there, but his mind was traveling through time, piecing bits together. "Here I am."

Yes, hope was in his eyes that, despite all the hardships, and being cast out, there was someone connected to him all this time, pulling for him, and praying for his good. At least that was her interpretation. Because it was true. And she yearned for the chance to show him it wasn't by her orchestration but the Lord's.

Pearl continued eating. Harvey picked at his food. "Your food is great. I just—I'm just trying to take in what you said." He shook his head like he was trying to clear it. "I'd better go. You have church. I don't want to make you late."

"You won't make me late. You're coming with me."

He jumped to his feet and fumbled with his nearly over-turned chair. "I don't think—"

She walked around and pulled him by the hand. "Trust me. You need to come."

Harvey groaned but conceded, and followed as she cajoled him down her walk, across the churchyard, and up the front steps. She refused to turn loose his hand even as she pulled him to the front of the church into the row marked RESERVED.

"Here. Sit. I'll be beside you the whole time. No one is going to bite you. No lightning bolts from heaven."

She sat, still holding his hand—trying to steady him. She knew he would have preferred to slip into the back row, but this was where he belonged.

The beginning chords of "Rock of Ages" spilled over the sanctuary. People filed in and sat in all their customary seats. Several odd looks came their direction, intrigued by the pair of them. She nodded and smiled and introduced those curious enough to come over. Harvey handled himself well outwardly, even if she could sense the tension coursing through him.

Pastor Thomas walked out on the platform and shuffled through his notes at the pulpit. He raised his head. When he saw Harvey, he froze for a beat, blinked, and then smiled so big his ears rose an inch.

The chattering in the church ceased, and everyone took their seats.

"Good morning. I want to start today's service with a special bit of news. Long awaited."

Thomas turned and motioned. "Join me, Miriam."

Miriam walked out, holding Ivy in a frilly white dress. The baby clutched at the front of Miriam's blouse and swiveled her head from side to side, taking in the congregation. Ivy spied Harvey, smiled, and let out a delighted squeal. Pearl followed the child's gaze.

The rise and fall of Harvey's chest stopped.

"Church family, we are pleased to announce that as of this week, all the papers have been signed and approved. Miriam and I have formally adopted Ivy."

While he spoke about the dedication of children, Thomas shot Pearl a questioning look. With his hand down by the pulpit, he discreetly motioned for her to join them. She glanced over at Harvey, who had all manner of emotions playing over him, so full of tension she had no doubt he could blast off for outer space if the right fuse was lit. She gave Thomas a faint shake of her head.

"The elders are going to come up, and we are going to dedicate Ivy Rose Lashley to the Lord. Our baby girl. As they come, I want to introduce you all to her godparents. Mrs. Pearl Howard is, of course, well known to us all." He glanced to his wife, who nodded and beamed with tear-filled eyes. "And her uncle, Harvey James, whose love for this baby girl is matchless."

The elders gathered around the little family.

A choking noise came from the man beside Pearl. She slid her arm around his upper back and whispered in his ear. "I didn't mean to upset you. I thought you should see what a wonderful thing you have done for Ivy and the Lashleys. I know she'll always be your little girl . . ."

He shook his head and squeezed out words between gasps for air. "No. This is . . . more than . . . perfect. Did he call me her godparent? Her uncle? That means I'm . . . That we're . . ." His whisper was ragged and thick.

"Family, Harvey. We're family. All five of us."

Miriam and Thomas wiped the tears from their eyes at the conclusion of the prayer. "Thank you. Now let's open our hymnals . . ."

Miriam walked down the steps and stood in front of Harvey. She lifted the baby away from her with a question in her eyes.

He reached.

Ivy kicked her pudgy legs out from the frilly white dress and stretched her arms toward him. The baby laid her head on his shoulder, then reached up to tug at the hair resting on the top of his collar.

Miriam settled on the other side of Harvey, sandwiching him and Ivy between her and Pearl. The older woman couldn't help but smile. Harvey and Ivy, a bit of peanut butter sticking them all together.

As Thomas spoke, Pearl could hear the tears building in his throat every time he glanced their direction as he continued his discourse on being grafted into the family of God. Of how they were all sons and daughters.

FORTY-NINE

PRESENT DAY

Over the next week, Ivy and Reese finished tagging the final items for the estate sale.

Reese wrapped his arms around Ivy after they finished the final room. "Now what? How do we find this missing journal of yours?"

She pulled back from the embrace. "Part of me says to let it go, that it wasn't meant to be."

"And the other part?" Reese brushed a stray hair off her forehead.

She released a heavy sigh. "The other part of me knows my uncle is the one who took it. I just don't know why."

"What if you invite him over for one last meal in the house now that it's finished? If it feels right, ask him for the truth. Maybe he'll finally be ready to give it."

Later that evening, her uncle's truck pulled into the drive. Her stomach flipped.

Reese pulled her into a half hug. "You sure you don't want me to stay?"

"I'm sure."

Uncle Vee walked toward them. Ivy kissed Reese's cheek in parting, then met her uncle on the sidewalk. She mentally whispered a brief prayer for strength. For both of them.

Once she and her uncle had settled around the patio table and finished their takeout from Carla's, Ivy held out the photograph from the scrapbook. "Do you know this woman?"

His eyes shot wide open as he took the photograph. He swallowed convulsively and shook his head. "Where did you—" His eyes darted around the yard like he was searching out an escape route.

She peered up at him, waiting. Sawing her fingernails into her palm, she forced herself to give him time.

His eyes squeezed closed like he experienced physical pain. "I met her once. Shivering, walking down the side of the road. I gave her my coat, but she needed something I didn't know how to give. She asked if I had a place she could go. To hide. I never, ever let people see where I lived, so I hesitated. And in that hesitation, a man pulled up in an old Cadillac. Instead of standing there and protecting her, I backed into the woods like the shadow of a tree. She was in trouble, and I was too afraid to help. I should have found a way to help her."

Ivy took a shuddering breath. "You couldn't have called the police?"

"I didn't have a phone."

"She . . . she was my birth mother."

His gaze darted from the concrete porch to the garage

door. His voice was so soft she almost didn't catch it. "I know."

"You knew? How? Please, just tell me. Let me finally hear the truth from you, no matter how harsh it is." Trembling rattled her spine.

He shook his head. "I didn't realize it for years. No way to have known where you came from. She wasn't pregnant that night I spoke to her, that I know of. But, as you grew and became a young woman, there was no doubt in my mind. Her face was burned into my memory. I didn't know how or why you came to be abandoned by that highway, but I knew you had to have been hers."

"Highway? What are you talking about?"

He clenched his eyes tight and swallowed like a bitter pill refused to go down without a fight. "I promise I'll answer all your questions, but can I please show you something first?"

She followed her uncle to the truck. Those four words on repeat in her mind. Abandoned by that highway. What could he mean?

Her uncle drove with a vice grip on the steering wheel. A few minutes later, he pulled onto the shoulder. He climbed out of his truck and motioned for her to follow.

They trekked ten feet into the woods and he stopped and knelt, placing his hand on the pine needle carpet. "Twenty-four years ago, I found a newborn baby girl laying right here. All alone. No one to claim her. That little baby was you." His eyes watered. He cleared his throat and stood, motioning for her to follow him.

Ivy clamped her lips tight to keep back her flood of questions, afraid he might clam up for another twenty-four years if she let them loose.

They walked along the edge of the highway for half a mile, then entered the woods, stopping in a circle of pines.

He gave her a wobbly smile. "And this is where we lived."

Ivy turned in a slow circle. There was nothing there. "W-what are you talking about?"

"I squatted on public land, doing everything I could to avoid human contact. And your sweet, innocent presence ripped my life to pieces and made it whole."

Ivy's jaw went slack as he told her about the early days. This version of him felt so foreign. She tried to imagine being raised by a homeless man who gave up every shred of his comfort to make sure she was loved.

"And Mom and Dad? How did I end up with them?"

He walked to a tall cedar. The side of the trunk was covered with tally marks. "When we lived here, I made a mark for every day that I was able to keep you safe. There are thirty-eight more days not on here, after we moved in with your grandma."

Ivy walked to the tree and touched old, deep hack marks below the tallies. "And this?"

He offered her a wry smile. "That is the work of a man with a broken heart. Except this time, I'd been the one to do the breaking. This is regret. Hurt. Loneliness.

"You got sick, and instead of staying, I ran when you needed me most. After I left you with your grandma I tried to go back to my old life. But I couldn't. I wasn't that man anymore." He placed his hand next to hers on the scarred bark. "This is proof of that."

"Why didn't anyone tell me what you did for me?"

He shook his head. "I didn't want to hurt you. I spent my whole life unwanted, so I tried to erase abandonment from *your* story. Even if it meant erasing me. I begged them not to tell you."

She wrapped her arms around him, squeezing tight. Rivers flowing down her face, she looked up at him. "I love you, Uncle Vee."

He swallowed hard, chin quivering. "I love you too." He pulled her close, tucking her against his chest. "Before you were in my life, I never would have imagined how such a tiny person could change everything. Your little existence pushed me to your dad and your grandma. And as a thirty-year-old man I gained a mother. A whole family. Because of you, I finally learned how to love and be loved."

Trying to process all he'd said, Ivy walked around the perimeter of trees. Her first home. Across from the cedar there was another tree with tally marks in the trunk. Twenty-four.

"What are these marks for?"

He smiled. "Every year on your birthday, I come out here. I sit and thank God for your life and for allowing me to be a part of it. Then I add a mark to the tree. This time I'm counting blessings instead of things that were never in my control in the first place."

Ivy bit the corner of her lip to stop it from trembling. "Do you think I could come with you next time?"

He squeezed his eyes tight and nodded. "I think . . . I think I'd really enjoy that."

Back in the truck he placed a leather journal on her lap. "I took this the other day. You should have it. I didn't know until I was over for dinner that your grandma had left it for you, but when she passed I knew you'd find it. I panicked and took it the night before her funeral. I don't know why

I thought it would be so hard for you to know. I guess the longer you hold a secret, the harder it is to let it go."

After Uncle Vee dropped her off, she pulled the family photo she'd found out of her purse. There was so much light and joy in everyone's eyes. Finally holding all the aching and broken pieces, Ivy opened the journal and began to read.

FIFTY

Present Day

Ivy curled into the porch swing, a blanket draped around her shoulders. She scrubbed her grainy eyes, closed the journal, and watched the sun rise through the limbs of the old oak tree. All through the night she'd soaked in the stories. Her stories. Of being found and being raised by her uncle. Of Grandma's quest to help him. Of her parents' struggles. Now she reached the final pages. Pages that began to talk about Rose.

Ivy lifted her head and watched Reese approach with two cups of coffee in hand. She swiped her hair back from her face. She probably looked like a mad woman with bloodshot eyes, but she wouldn't know it by the way Reese looked at her.

He smiled and set the coffee on the side table. "Good morning. I guess last night turned out okay?" He nodded at the journal in her hands.

Sitting beside her, he swept a stray hair from her shoulder.

He paused a moment, looking for confirmation his touch was okay, then he leaned in slow, as if trying not to spook a wounded creature, brushing a soft kiss to her forehead.

It hit her then, how slow and measured he was in every movement, for her benefit. Making sure love didn't feel like a weapon but a comfort.

Ivy glanced down at the journal. "He told me everything he knew. Everything I've read in these pages so far. The last I read, Grandma had decided to ask Rose specifics about the birth of her child to try and match Uncle Vee's story to hers. But when she got to Abiding Love, Rose had disappeared. I . . . I don't have a good feeling about how this ends. I'm glad you're with me."

Reese tucked her beneath his arm, and she began to read the final entry dated September 8, 1999. As she read her grandmother's words, the moment played in Ivy's mind like a scene on a movie screen.

The shrill ring jarred me out of a dead sleep. She'd called. Five months since the last time I saw her face.

Her voice was slurred and speech broken. The throb of music in the background deafening. It took several long moments to believe it was her voice on the other line.

"It's five years today since they took my baby away. Nothing gets those newborn wails out of my head. Nothing. I tried to drink them away tonight. And I . . . I'm scared."

"Please, tell me where you are." Her descriptions were confusing and broken. Revealing no hints to what city or state or what back alley place she'd found herself

in . . . A club? A house party where she'd snuck off to a back room? I had nothing to go on. No one to call. The only thing I knew to do was to keep her talking and pray.

A whimpering cry started on the other end of the line, and I offered all I had. "God forgives you, Rose. For whatever guilt you carry."

The whimper turned to drunken sobs as she denied the possibility God could love her. I wished with all my heart I could crawl through the phone lines and wrap my arms around her. "He does. He loves you. He wants to hold you right now. Heal the pain. Do you want to let Jesus in, Rose?"

"Not here. Not in this filthy place."

"Yes, in that filthy place. Especially in that filthy place. Where are you?"

She mumbled confused strings of words with vague descriptions that didn't make an ounce of sense to me. Something was wrong, something beyond simple intoxication. I did the only thing I could. I told her about Jesus's love and prayed with her.

There was the sound of retching. I pleaded, "Are you still there? You need to get help."

"I can't."

"You have to. Listen to me, I think your baby lived. I really do, and I want you to meet her, but you have to get up and get help."

Her voice came thinner with each response, harder to hear over the pounding music. "My babies are in heaven. I'm going there now. Thank you for showing me how to get there."

"No, Rose, you're not going today. You're going to get help, and I'm going to come find you."

"My feet don't work."

"Make sure you're sitting up."

"Can't. Too . . . t-too cold."

I could hear her breath against the receiver slow and shallow. I had to keep her talking. "The night you were in labor. Where were you going?"

She sighed, her words like thin vapors. "Man who lived in the woods. Only man ever kind to me. Ugly shirt, kind heart. But I didn't make it. They found me. They took my baby."

To anyone else it would have been drunken ramblings, but to my ears it was evidence of divine grace in the midst of human suffering. The words spilled out, desperate to give her hope, to help her hang on. "He found her, Rose. The man in the ugly shirt. You did it. You made it far enough. He found your baby and took care of her. She's okay. Today she had a cake with pink frosting and five glittering candles. She's safe and loved. And she loves puppy dogs and butterflies."

A whispering dreamy sound came through the line. "She's okay."

"Yes. She's strong and she's beautiful. She's funny and kind. She's brought joy to places of sorrow. She's pulled together fractured people and given them a family. She's a miracle, this daughter of yours."

"I want to see her." At least that's what it sounded like she said. Then the line went silent. No matter how I yelled and begged into the phone, I couldn't get another response.

It was my fault. The desperate running she's been doing. If only I'd acted faster. Revealed more. Please Lord, forgive me.

Ivy swiped at the tears dripping down her face. She passed the journal to Reese. "Read the last part. Please. I can't."

He released a resigned sigh, and when the paper crinkled, she closed her eyes and rested her head against Reese's chest. Warm and comforted if only for a moment. His baritone voice was like a balm, but she had a feeling it wouldn't protect her heart from shattering. Not this time.

Dear Ivy,

I failed you. I'm so sorry for all the things I should have said. For the missed opportunities. Please know you've always been surrounded by love. By your birth mother. By your Uncle Vee. Your parents. The last time you visited I wanted to tell you, but the timing didn't seem right. I was probably wrong about that too.

Back in 1999, the police called me because they found Rose with a crumpled slip of paper in her hand. My phone number. I had given it to her months before in case she ever needed to talk.

I went alone to the morgue to identify her body. For this dear sweet woman, hardly more than twenty years old, there had never been a missing persons report. Not a soul looking for her besides me. A seventy-four-year-old woman who ought to have had more wisdom to know how to handle things.

There's a plot in the same cemetery I'm to be buried

in. If you go to the magnolia tree, there's a small marker with the only name I knew her by, Rose. They say a magnolia tree represents dignity. Maybe at least in her death I provided her that. I didn't know the day she was born or even her last name, but I wanted anyone walking by to know someone saw her and loved her even if I didn't know how to save her.

There really are people that are alone in the world. People who have no one to look for them. Like Rose. Like Harvey. If the story of my life could say one thing, I'd hope it would show the importance of venturing into the highways and the hedges to let invisible people know they're seen and loved. To invite them in.

I wish I could have saved Rose. To this day, I believe she was your birth mother. Maybe it was selfish, never telling Harvey or your parents about her. I couldn't stand the thought of her story being dissected for facts. Before I left this earth, I wanted you to know. I wanted another heart to hold her.

I love you, Ivy Rose Lashley. I hope you can find it in your heart to forgive me.

Grandma Pearl

Ivy turned to Reese, who through many starts and stops made it through the letter. "Ivy . . ."

She buried her face in his chest. There were no words. Only tears. Pieces connecting in her mind.

He held her until her eyes ran dry.

"Thank you." Reese whispered the words.

Ivy sat up. "For . . . for what?"

"I just needed to say it out loud. To Pearl. To Harvey. To Rose."

She sniffled and smiled, the corners of her mouth trembling. "Why?"

"For you, Ivy. I am who I am today because of the way you pulled me into your life back when we were kindergarteners. You gave me your family when mine couldn't be bothered with me.

"And it wasn't just that. You remember that summer we were sixteen, when we ran all over the countryside? It had been a tough year. I'd already made a few bad choices, and I was headed for more. But you showed up, Rosie-girl. And you, in all your sweet goodness, reminded me who I was and who I wanted to be."

Ivy shook her head and a new lightness bubbled in her chest. At her first cry, her birth mother deemed her a fighter. To Uncle Vee, the abandoned infant was called worthy of love. Grandma saw a little vine who pulled them all together. To her parents, a long-awaited treasure. Above all, Christ called her his and was gracious enough to give her people to remind her if she lost her way.

Could this version of herself be the truth Ivy had searched for all along? And now, despite the missteps and wrong turns—the things she couldn't erase—she knew what she wanted to do next. For Rose. For herself. For all of them.

EPILOGUE

As Ivy walked along the church's property, a weight lifted from her shoulders. Today's memorial, a tribute to Rose that raised community awareness for the ministry of Abiding Love, had gone just as she'd envisioned it.

Even though Grandma might not have known how to save Rose's physical body all those years ago, Ivy had the hope of embracing her in eternity. All because of Grandma's pursuit of the truth about Ivy's birth mother.

Ivy leaned against the oak tree in the churchyard. Everyone else had already gone their separate ways, but she wanted a moment alone with Grandma's old house before heading home to get ready for work the next morning.

Working as a counselor at Abiding Love wasn't the same as working with children, but for this season, it was just what she needed—connecting with pieces of her past. In a way, it was bringing her closer to Grandma and Rose.

Her uncle had readily let her move into his bungalow after the estate sale. There was something especially sweet about spending this time with him, now knowing how their relationship had begun.

Her phone chirped.

> Do me a favor, would ya? Meet me over at your
> old place.

A smile tugged at her mouth at Reese's text. They'd been together only hours before. What was he up to now?

When she arrived at the old farmhouse, every window glowed with light. Reese's silhouetted form strode across the porch and jogged toward her. When she stood from the car, he planted a kiss on her lips, long and sweet. Hand in hand, they crossed the yard to the porch.

He pushed the front door wide and motioned her to enter first. She drank in the sight of the impeccably restored entryway and living room. "Is it finally finished? I think your client is going to be more than happy with it. It's stunning. But . . . is that Grandma's wingback chair? And her piano?"

He stepped in front of her and took her hands. "It is. And if you want to check for authenticity, your Polly Pockets are still in the piano bench." A grin quirked the corners of his mouth.

"Your client bought up a bunch of her stuff?"

Reese took a breath, and the grin dissolved. "I . . . uh . . . a couple of the bigger pieces. Uh . . . okay, here's the thing. Don't be mad, but I have a teensy tiny confession." He rubbed the back of his head, averting his eyes. "I'm the client. I bought the house."

Ivy stared. "You bought my old run-down house and made it beautiful?"

He nodded, his gaze tender as he looked into her eyes.

Realization crashed over her, stealing the air from her lungs. "You . . . you did all this for me? Because of me?"

He shrugged. "I . . . not . . . *exactly*. I'd never put that on you. I bought this place because it's where my happiest memories happened. Around the kitchen table with your family. With you. I couldn't let the place rot away." He tugged her closer. "But I'd be lying if I didn't confess I held this unfounded hope that you and I could make more memories here someday. You were engaged to someone else when I bought it, so fixing this house was just me trying to hold on to a little bit of you and me."

"I don't know what to say."

"Say that even if you don't like the idea of living in Triune, you'll accept my gift of the wingback chair. I can't count how many times I found you curled up in that uncomfortable chair watching TV or reading. I'd say you could take the piano, but that thing is never getting moved again. But, of course, the Polly Pockets you can h—"

"The house is lovely. But I'm a little confused. I feel like you're asking me something, only I don't know what the question is. Are you asking me if I want to buy the house?"

He released her hands and ran a hand through his hair. "I'm so bad at this. I didn't think I'd be so awful." A breathy laugh escaped him.

She smiled, a helpless effort to fill the void.

He paced a step and then turned back to her and took her hands again. His were suddenly ice cold.

"Ivy, I promised myself I wouldn't rush things. But if you

look at it from my point of view, I've been taking my time with this, near about eighteen years. Although I guess I did ask you one time in third grade, but you told me no, so here's hoping this goes better."

"Reese?" He was rambling, not making a lick of sense. And Reese always made sense.

"Here goes nothing." He knelt, still holding her hands.

Her lips parted. "What are you—" And then her heart took off like a thoroughbred out of a starting gate.

He pulled a ring box from his pocket.

She clamped her lips closed as her mouth went dry.

"Ivy Rose Lashley, I've only ever loved one woman in my entire life. I loved you when you were a scrawny kid chasing bugs in your grandma's backyard, and while you were swinging in the swing "out yonder" in those goofy aviator glasses. I loved you when you were in that gangly in-between phase we all go through. And I loved you on the other side of that, when you showed up the next summer, lovely as a cool summer breeze. The most beautiful thing I'd ever laid eyes on. I loved you bold and confident. I loved you when you were searching and uncertain. Every version of you I've had the privilege of knowing, I have loved. I just have one request, Rosie-girl. There are versions of you that you haven't become yet. The ones ahead of you. Be my wife, and let me love them all."

"You . . . you said we'd . . . we'd take things slow . . ." Her voice cracked over the words.

"If that's what you want. It's just every minute you're not my wife, feels like it drags on a century. I'm sorry. I probably shouldn't have . . . actually, *I know* I shouldn't have—"

"Yes."

He rose from his knees, staring at the ground. "Let's agree to forget what an idiot—"

She stifled her laughter. "Yes, Reese. My answer is yes. I want to marry you."

He froze, eyes searching her face. "I didn't mean to pressure you . . . I—"

"You didn't."

"I didn't?"

She shook her head. "I love you, Reese Dylan Wright. Always have."

He pulled her into his arms and kissed her, lifting her from the floor. He brought her back to earth and slipped the ring on her finger.

"If you don't like it, we can shop for a new one. This one is kind of an antique."

Her jaw dropped as she stared at the oval diamond surrounded by a ring of tiny sapphires. "This was Grandma's."

He nodded.

"How did you . . ."

"You remember the box of stuff I told you she left for me? It was in there. She knew how I've always felt about you. So when I saw this in there, I tried to give it back in case her giving it to me was a mistake. It's not like I could give that ring to anyone else and you were engaged. But she wouldn't take it. I figured that if she thought you could love me back, there was still hope."

● ● ●

Harvey rocked in his recliner. Pepper curled on the rug next to him, twitching and chasing rabbits in his dreams. It was just a house when Harvey bought it. Ivy and her stray pup had made it home in a whole new way.

Maybe the three of them would only share this home a little while, but it was enough.

Ivy came through the door just after midnight, cheeks pinked and eyes sparkling. She held out her hand and gave him a small smile. Pearl's ring winked back at him. "I said yes," she whispered.

Harvey stood and pulled her into a hug. "Congratulations, sweetie."

She bit a corner of her bottom lip. "What do you think?"

He smiled and blinked back the moisture pooling in his eyes. Funny how the memory of her weight in his arms—just a tiny babe wrapped in a man's flannel shirt—was still so fresh after all this time. "I think . . . I still can't believe I get to watch this beautiful life of yours unfold."

Then the master said to the servant, "Go out into the highways and hedges, and compel them to come in, that my house may be filled."

Luke 14:23 NKJV

ACKNOWLEDGMENTS

Wow. It's been a winding journey bringing this book into the world. And I'm so thankful for the people who helped make it possible. There are far more to thank than I have space to name here.

To my parents, thank you for financing my childhood book addiction. Thanks for reading to me when I was too little to do it on my own, and for believing in my stories from the start. *Goodie the Wonder Horse* will never be on anybody's bestseller chart, but between us, we know it was the best story ever written.

To my husband, you see the things ahead and the things to come, while I always have to keep my eyes on that one next step. The first thing you did when I told you I wanted to write a book was to run out to the store with me to purchase the laptop I am typing on right now. I name everything. I can't believe that in seven years I haven't named my laptop yet. Maybe I should call him Harvey. And to Caleb, Ellie, and Levi, you three inspire me always—reminding me to hold tight to that spark of inspiration and dream God-sized dreams because even grown-ups can be creative.

To Leann, my BFF, my sister of the heart, thanks for being you. You've been cheering on my writing journey from the sidelines for years, listening to all my random ramblings. As iron sharpens iron, my friend. I would never want to do life without you!

To my Story Spinner girls, Patti, Angela, Lucy, Crystal, KyLee, and Kelly, thank you for all your support and advice. Thanks for telling me not to give up on this story too soon. It was your encouragement that nudged me to step out and put this story out there one more time.

To Kelsey Bowen, my editor, thanks for taking a chance on Harvey and Ivy. It means more than I know how to say. Partnering with Revell to bring this story into the world is a dream come true.

And to Jesus, thank you for planting this passion to put words on paper inside of me. In the fun times when words flowed and felt like dreams coming alive and in the times I kept writing even when I wanted to set my laptop on fire—I did it all with you. Writing with you by my side is what I was made for. Looking forward to the next story we get to write together, whether in life or on paper.

Loved this book?

Read on for a *sneak peek* of another captivating story *by* Amanda Cox!

COMING FALL 2021

ONE

PRESENT DAY

Sarah nudged aside last night's puddle of clothes with her bare foot, eyeing the exposed designer label on her black dress and all it stood for. At the dresser in her childhood bedroom, she tugged open the drawer that, without a doubt, was just like she'd left it when she moved out from under her parents' roof twelve years ago. The scent of lavender filled her nose.

The familiar sight of all her favorite T-shirts and the sachets Mom tucked into every drawer soothed the throbbing ache in Sarah's chest. Pain that had driven her from her mausoleum of a house in Connecticut yesterday, fleeing ghosts of the not-so-distant past until she'd landed, bleary-eyed, on her mother's front porch in Brighton, Tennessee.

She grabbed a T-shirt and a pair of cutoff shorts from the drawer and slipped them on in place of the borrowed nightshirt she'd been wearing, relieved that the shorts still zipped and snapped without too much effort. Sarah stood in front of the full-length mirror in the corner and inspected her reflection. The faded Old Depot Grocery T-shirt was a little tighter than she'd prefer, but it looked all right. Her gaze traveled downward to the large square bandages her mother had affixed to her knees. Cuts that she hadn't even registered until Mom pointed out the dried blood last night.

The whole effect of the reflection in front of her was something of a time warp—this skinned-knee version of herself. If she could forget that the minor injuries to her knees weren't from a failed roller skating attempt.

The aroma of Mom's famous biscuits and gravy drifted under the bedroom door, luring her from the room. Her high school throwbacks might fit now, but not for long if Mom kept feeding her like this.

Sarah left the bedroom and padded down the hallway's worn beige carpet and entered the bathroom. She splashed cool water on her face. When she lifted her eyes, seeking the basket of hand towels Mom always kept on the shelf beside the sink, Sarah spotted the large triton seashell from Aaron's and her honeymoon three years ago. A gift she'd sent back home to her parents.

Sarah held the shell to her ear, listening for the sound of waves. She remembered walking the beach, hand in hand with her husband, feeling as though they had an ocean of possibilities in front of them. She placed the shell back on the shelf and grabbed the towel.

Pressing her face into the terry cloth, she attempted to scrub away the memory and the warring emotions that went along with it. Was it possible to go back and get a redo on life? Pretend there'd never been a reality beyond this rural town and a little girl's dream to play shopkeeper for the rest of her life.

Following her nose, Sarah walked to the kitchen. Her mother stood facing the stove with a gingham apron tied around her waist, piling fluffy biscuits onto a platter. Overhead Mom's hen collection adorned her cabinet tops, lined up in all shapes and sizes like they marched in a perpetual parade. Sarah smiled.

"Morning, Mom. Breakfast smells amazing. You shouldn't have gone to all that trouble though."

Her mother turned and flicked a glance over her, but her expression remained placid. Inscrutable. "It's not every day my only daughter shows up for an impromptu visit."

Sarah tried and failed to detect the emotion motivating that statement. Whether it was sadness or wariness, Sarah wasn't sure.

Though Mom had been roused from a deep sleep when Sarah arrived at two in the morning, you wouldn't have been able to tell from the way she'd ushered Sarah inside, cleaned her wounds, and served her a cup of herbal tea before leading Sarah to her old bedroom. Ever a hostess, even when the guest was completely unexpected.

Or maybe Mom had expected Sarah to come these past two weeks, and the fact that it had taken her this long to seek her mother's comfort was the greater surprise.

Sarah sat and her mother poured her a cup of coffee. Once the cream and sugar were stirred in, Sarah took a sip, but the brew she normally found so comforting turned her stomach instead. She set the mug down on the pinewood table with a clank.

"Something wrong with the coffee?"

Sarah swallowed back the nausea welling in her throat. She shook her head, afraid to open her mouth.

Mom placed a plate of biscuits and gravy in front of each of them. She never took her eyes off of her daughter, as if the constant eye contact could pull the answers to unspoken questions from Sarah's lips. "Are your knees feeling okay this morning? Do you think we got out all the bits of glass?"

Crystal. It was Baccarat crystal. "Yeah. They feel fine. Thanks."

Sarah had felt strangely numb while she sat on the fuzzy toilet lid cover as Mom had inspected for grit embedded in Sarah's skin.

An accident, she'd said when Mom asked her what happened. But that shatter of delicate crystal on those mahogany floors before she fled the house yesterday had been the most cathartic thing she'd experienced in quite some time. The destruction had been intentional, cutting herself on the mess she'd made, not so much.

"So . . ." Mom took a long drink of her coffee.

Sarah picked at the edge of her biscuit, bracing herself for the question that would follow that long pause.

Mom set her coffee down and dabbed her lips with a napkin. "How long do you think you'll stay?"

She said the words with a gentle smile curving her lips, but Mom wasn't asking how many days she should expect Sarah's visit to last. What Mom really wanted to know was what Sarah planned to do now that her beautiful life had shattered. And to give an understood warning against thinking for one second that hiding out here was a long-term solution.

"When will Dad be back?"

Mom glanced at the wall calendar as though she didn't have her trucker husband's schedule memorized. "He'll be on leave in a week. He's supposed to get his usual seven-day break."

"Oh good. I'm looking forward to some quality father-daughter time." Hopefully that would be enough information to keep her mother from digging any deeper into Sarah's plans. And maybe two weeks would be long enough to ease Mom into the idea of turning the mother and daughter team that ran Old Depot Grocery, the store that had been in their family for decades, into a mother and daughter *and* granddaughter trio.

Sarah never should have left in the first place. It was time to embrace her heritage like she should have all along.

"When are you headed to the store?" she asked.

Mom massaged her hands. "Not until closer to noon. I have a doctor's appointment."

"Is something wrong?"

"Just a routine checkup."

Sarah pushed back from the table and dusted the crumbs from her hands. "I'm going to head to Old Depot to spend some time with Nan. Help out if she needs it."

"The only help she needs is in seeing reason." Mom muttered the words behind her mug as Sarah grabbed a Tupperware from the cabinet.

"What did you say?"

"Is that all you're going to eat? You're practically a toothpick as it is."

"Sorry. I'm feeling a little rocky this morning is all." Sarah placed her nibbled biscuit in the plastic container for later. Wasting food around her mother's house was not an option.

If her mother only knew how many casseroles Sarah had been given that were now untouched and molding in her refrigerator back home, she would have an apoplectic fit.

"Maybe you should stay in bed and get some rest."

The last thing Sarah needed was more time alone with her thoughts. "No. I think a day at Old Depot is just what the doctor ordered." Sarah set her plate in the sink.

"Sarah . . ."

"Bye. I'll see you later." Sarah smiled through her forced chipper tone and then grabbed her purse and keys from the hall tree by the front door. She slid her feet into Mom's spare flip-flops.

Her mother called out from the kitchen. "We need to talk. The store—"

Sarah cut off the words by shutting the door behind her. Mom never seemed to understand how much the store meant to her. Nan would understand. Nan would support Sarah's need to come back home.

She inhaled the late spring air, relishing just how fresh and floral it was before ducking into her car. On the drive, Sarah soaked in the sight of her little town. It had this old-fashioned air about it, like it was tucked into this little corner of the world, hidden from the effects of passing time. People sitting on their front porch lifted their hands and waved as she passed. Others were already hard at work in their flower beds. Sarah slowed her car for a tractor that was turning off the main road.

A few minutes later, she parked in front of the old store, having her choice of spots in the almost empty lot. She took in the familiar sight of the twin-gabled storefront. Between the gables the red-painted sign read OLD DEPOT GROCERY.

Sarah let out a long breath that cleansed her, heart and soul. This was coming home.

Sarah stood from the car and stepped over the dandelions that were sprouting from cracks in the sidewalk. Dandelions weren't pretty things, but they sure were resilient. They beat roses every time on that front. She'd wasted so much time trying to be a rose when she'd sprouted up from dandelion roots.

The front door burst open, interrupting her musing. Out stumbled a harried man in a suit with a strange little hop in his step. He was followed by Nan, who was scowling and jabbing the broom at the fellow who had already dived into his car and had it cranked and backing out of the lot in no time.

Sarah stifled a laugh at the terror her petite grandmother had incited in the large man fleeing from her store.

Nan jabbed the broom toward the retreating car once more for good measure and said, "And stay out, you . . . you miscreant! Old Depot Grocery has never, and will never, be for sale."

· CHAPTER ·

TWO

June 1965

Glory Ann trudged down the stairs, the morning light filtering through the east facing windows and wrapping her in a soft warm glow—the light it lent discordant with reality. It was a perfect day for the June wedding that would never be.

The weight of the world slumped Glory Ann's shoulders and the beginnings of new life turned her middle into a storm-tossed sea.

Her mother stood at the bottom of the stairs, massaging her temple. "Darling, please go change. It's a lovely summer day. That black dress washes all the color out of your face."

The time she'd spent hugging the porcelain commode was the more likely culprit. But Glory Ann would bear any burden for the privilege of carrying Jimmy's child.

"I'm in mourning." Who cared if no one wore mourning clothes anymore? It was her way to make sure no one forgot how much he had meant to her.

Her mother released a sigh that stooped her shoulders.

AMANDA COX

"I know you thought you loved him—" And there it was—the real reason she didn't like the way Glory Ann had been skulking about for a month in that same dress.

"Mother." Glory Ann hoped her tone was enough of a warning. She couldn't have this conversation again. Not after the fallout around the dinner table when she'd finally confessed to her parents the secret she'd kept for weeks. That at nineteen she, the minister's daughter, was pregnant.

Out of wedlock—the words Momma said would follow her all the days of her life.

She shook her head. The first words out of her father's mouth had been, "What are we going to do now? You can't have a shotgun wedding with a dead man, Glory Ann."

Her father appeared at her mother's side with the newspaper in his hand and his reading glasses perched atop his head. His face was lined and gray. The glory of the morning hadn't lightened the burden her father carried any more than it had Glory Ann's.

Her mother pinched the slim bridge of her nose. "Go change into that nice yellow dress you have. The one with the little white flowers sewn into it. Please."

It seemed her parents not only wanted her along on their visit with old friends today but they expected her to play the part of the little ray of sunshine too.

They both looked so weary that she complied. Glory Ann almost always complied. That's why it had been such a shock to her parents—that she and Jimmy, the poster children for good Christian raising, had taken things too far. Just that one time she'd sworn, but she could tell they doubted.

But it *had* been just one time. One moment of tears and fear, sorrow and hopes. His name had been called and despite his bravado, the death tolls in the newspapers were enough to keep desperation close to the surface.

Jimmy hadn't made it five minutes over there. She'd known he wouldn't. Those soulful blue eyes of his were made to behold long rows of thriving crops under a southern sun, not the horrors of Vietnam.

In front of the oval mirror, Glory Ann stripped off the black A-line dress and studied the Irish cream figure that was her reflection. Her hand found the tiny swell at her lower belly. The place where a little bit of her and a little bit of Jimmy was growing. A seed of love. Perhaps it shouldn't have been planted, but despite the shame she and her family would suffer, she couldn't bring herself to regret it. Not now.

After she changed into the cheery dress her mother had requested, Glory Ann tidied her rogue onyx curls and pinched color into her cheeks. She tucked the letter she never sent into her pocket.

If she'd dared to send it, maybe by some postal miracle Jimmy would've received it in time and known he was going to be a father before he died. Maybe it would have made a difference. Somehow.

When she walked out to the car, her father placed a small valise in the trunk. Mother must be bringing some quilting supplies to the lady of the house.

"I'm ready."

At the sound of her voice he lifted his head, his expression startled. "You look lovely."

She fixed the pretty smile that he expected on her face. There had been enough strain and strife lately. It would be best to make this beautiful early summer day a nice time together. She couldn't undo her choices, but she could make today pleasant. She opened the back door of the tan Cadillac.

"Ride up front with me, why don't you?"

"But Momma—"

"Your mother went to bed with a headache. It'll just be me and you today." He glanced away.

Despite her attempts to stir conversation throughout the drive, her father remained stiff in his seat behind the wheel, offering only quiet one-word replies.

Glory Ann gave up and stared out the windows at the verdant farmland. It sure hadn't been easy confessing what she and Jimmy had done. It was a secret she'd wanted to take to her grave. But some secrets demanded to be revealed. Some secrets grew with time and had a life and a heartbeat of their own.

What did Daddy think of her now? Did he love her still, or was he more concerned with how their tiny community would react when they realized the minister couldn't even keep his own family on the straight and narrow? He'd counted on her to be evidence of his good parenting skills outside of her brother's life choices, and she'd let him down.

An hour later they pulled into a one-stoplight Tennessee town named Brighton. The minister stopped at what looked to have once been a train depot. The weed-infested tracks were long abandoned by railcars. The sign over the door read OLD DEPOT GROCERY.

Her father killed the ignition and leaned his forehead against the steering wheel.

"Daddy?"

He straightened and offered her a tight-lipped smile. "You ready?"

For what? She'd thought they were going out visiting, not shopping at a small grocery two towns away.

"Clarence Clearwater is a very nice man. His parents were old family friends of mine. This is his store."

"Okay." She tilted her head. Why should she give a fig about Clarence Clearwater and Old Depot Grocery?

He hesitated, his mouth working as if he intended to say more. "Let's go in and I'll introduce you."

Glory Ann exited the car and watched the people coming and going on the sidewalk. The curious looks she garnered made it clear that new faces were always noticed in a town like this. Some were shabby farmers in threadbare overalls. Others nicely clothed in store-bought dresses in a similar style to her own. Yet all these people seemed to belong together. Like fabric stitched together on a patchwork quilt.

She trailed behind her father. What kind of looks would she receive when her pregnancy became obvious? How would her own little town treat her? Always the little darling everyone admired with her songbird voice, delicate figure, and demure manner. Now a fallen woman.

She released a breath and squared her shoulders. She'd just have to grow thicker skin, keep her chin up, and dare anyone to say a word with the fire in her eyes. Her days as a bashful minister's daughter were over. The sooner she faced it the better.

Once inside, her father approached a man in a green apron. He was probably about ten years her senior. He had narrow, stooped shoulders and a crooked nose that looked like he'd been punched once or twice and never had it set right. His too-close brown eyes were gentle and kind. He had that much going for him, but that was about it.

Her father inclined his head toward the man and they shared a quick, whispered conversation. "Come here, Glory Ann. I'd like to introduce you. This is Clarence Clearwater."

Glory Ann offered her hand. The stranger took it and gave it a soft squeeze. A question in his eyes.

He gave a decisive nod and his gaze locked with her father's. "Sir, I'd be honored to marry your daughter."

The room became stifling and close. Glory Ann's vision blurred and the room seemed to tip. Strong arms enveloped her, and her world went as black as the dress she'd donned earlier that morning.

Before becoming a stay-at-home parent, **Amanda Cox** spent her time counseling children, families, and individuals through life's challenging moments. Now she uses those same skills to develop layered characters and stories, bringing them on a journey of hope and healing. A journey she hopes her readers experience in their own lives as they read.

Amanda is a lover of words. A poet at heart. A seeker of still, quiet moments in which God speaks. A few of her favorite things are the sanctuary of the great outdoors, the feeling of pen on paper, the sound of her children's laughter, and soaking up the ambiance of new places. She lives in the hills of east Tennessee with her husband and three children. Visit Amanda online at www.amandacoxwrites.com.

MEET AMANDA

FOLLOW ALONG AT
AmandaCoxWrites.com
and sign up for Amanda's newsletter—*From the Sparrow's Nest*—to stay up to date on exclusive news, upcoming releases, and more!

🅕 🅞 🅨 AmandaCoxWrites